DEVIL'S ISLAND

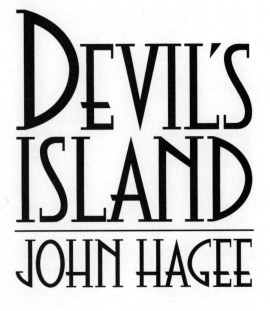

DEVIL'S ISLAND

JOHN HAGEE

THOMAS NELSON PUBLISHERS®
Nashville

A Division of Thomas Nelson, Inc.
www.ThomasNelson.com

Published in Nashville, Tennessee, by Thomas Nelson, Inc.

Library of Congress Cataloging-in-Publication Data

Hagee, John.
    Devil's Island : a novel / John Hagee.
        p. cm. — (The apocalypse diaries ; bk. 1)
    ISBN 0-7852-6787-5 (hc)
    ISBN 0-7852-6401-9 (sc)
    1. Church history—Primitive and early church, ca. 30–600—Fiction. 2. John, the
Apostle, Saint—Fiction. 3. Patmos Island (Greece)—Fiction. 4. Persecution—Fiction.
I. Title.
    PS3608.A35 D48 2001
    813'.54—dc21   2001044233
                                                                                                CIP

Printed in the United States of America

02 03 04 05 06 07 PHX 6 5 4 3 2 1

1

Ephesus, October A.D. 95

THE TWO SHIPS HAD NOT BEEN THERE when he'd left the wharf yesterday, Abraham was sure of it. The pair was docked at the curve of the horseshoe-shaped inlet, about two hundred yards from Abraham's warehouse-office, and even at a distance the ships instilled a vague sense of foreboding in him.

He lengthened his powerful stride and kept his eyes focused on the water ahead as he walked down the broad, straight avenue that led to the harbor. Pink-orange tendrils of daylight had just begun to streak the sky, but the commercial hub of the city was already buzzing with activity.

In a few moments, when Abraham arrived at the wharf and was able to get a closer look at the two new arrivals, he quickly identified the source of his apprehension: they were Roman warships.

Impossible, was his first thought. The Empire was not at war. And yet there was the Roman eagle, proudly ornamenting the prow, and there were the bronze-helmeted soldiers, forming ranks on deck. It appeared the troops were preparing to disembark.

"Quintus!" he bellowed.

Instantly his lanky assistant appeared on the wharf beside him. "Yes, sir."

Noting the direction of his employer's gaze and anticipating the question, Quintus continued without pause. "They arrived at dusk yesterday," he said. "I made a few discreet inquiries and learned the ships are carrying the First Cohort of the Tenth Legion."

"And their purpose in Ephesus?"

"I don't know. Several of the centurions came ashore last evening for a meal and a bit of carousing, but the tavernkeeper I spoke to said they remained tight-lipped about their orders."

The knowledge that it was the Tenth Legion on board the two warships struck Abraham like a punch to the solar plexus. The arrival of any cohort of Roman soldiers would have surprised and worried him, but the memories of his encounter with the Tenth Legion had not faded, not even after all these years.

"Only one cohort?" he asked Quintus.

"Unless other ships arrive later. I imagine five hundred men is roughly the number of troops these two ships could transport."

"Certainly not enough manpower for a military engagement," Abraham noted, "but enough to make an impressive show of force for the local citizenry." His stomach burned at the thought.

At just over six feet, Quintus was one of the few men who could look Abraham directly in the eye. But where Abraham was broad and stocky, Quintus was lean with a hungry look—though it was common knowledge he had an enormous appetite, with a particular fondness for honey-roasted mutton.

Quintus looked at his employer now, obviously perplexed. "In my entire life I've never seen Roman troops posted here. We are a senatorial province, not an imperial province—"

"I'm well aware of our political status," Abraham said abruptly. Asia's local government was accountable to the Senate in Rome, in contrast to imperial provinces, recently subjugated areas where a strong military presence was required. "But it is quite unusual," he added in a more conciliatory tone, "and worrisome."

"Shall I have someone follow them, to find out where they will make camp?" Quintus asked.

"No, but keep your ears open. Rumors are bound to be flying around the harbor."

Abraham removed his light woolen cloak and prepared to step

into his office. "I'm sure we'll learn the reason for their presence soon enough." His businesslike tone belied the undercurrent of fear that had made his pulse race since first catching sight of the warships.

Throughout the morning he kept an eye on the two ships, periodically thinking of an excuse to leave the warehouse and go outside to observe the noisy departure of the troops. The sound of their heavy hobnailed boots striking the wooden deck echoed loudly over the water, and the sun glinted off their spears. Abraham easily picked out the centurions by their distinctive red-plumed helmets.

The First Cohort was marching northward, toward the outskirts of the city, he noted. Abraham recalled his argument that morning with his son Jacob, and could not help wondering if the soldiers' arrival had anything to do with Jacob's recent preaching. Abraham agreed with his son's bold stand against emperor worship, but he had begged Jacob to temper his righteous zeal with a healthy dose of discretion; such visibility could have serious consequences.

If the authorities had wanted to arrest Jacob, they would have done so by now, Abraham reasoned, and it certainly would not require an entire cohort of Roman force. Yet he could not completely shake off an ominous feeling.

By late morning Abraham had rearranged the shipping manifests. The *Aurelia*, the oldest and largest of his cargo ships, had still not made port, and with the shipping season ending in a few weeks, and with his warehouse still holding a surplus of goods, he was redirecting some of the merchandise designated for the *Aurelia* to other ships.

He gave orders to load the *Valeria*, then went out to the dock and watched as the muscular stevedores braced a sturdy plank against the ship and began rolling heavy barrels of Cappadocian wine up the steep incline. After a few minutes, Abraham retired to his office.

So much work to be done, and Jacob wants to leave on a ministry trip with the Apostle rather than take care of business—the business he'll inherit one day, he complained silently.

At age fifty, Abraham had begun to think about the future of his shipping empire. He was in excellent health, a huge bear of a man, and intended to stay active as long as God gave him breath, but he knew there would come a day when diminishing strength would require him to relinquish control.

Who would take the helm then? Abraham had always assumed one of his sons would be his successor. But he doubted now that either of his twin boys—young men, actually; they were almost nineteen—would ever take control of his enterprises. Peter, quite simply, did not have the aptitude and Jacob, who did, lacked the inclination.

The only one of his four children who had shown both an interest in and aptitude for running the shipping business was Abraham's oldest child, twenty-four-year-old Naomi. But that was out of the question. Women did not run worldwide enterprises, they ran households.

Had Crispin lived, I would gladly have turned over the business to him, Abraham mused. His late son-in-law had been a great help to him, and Abraham still missed him. He also missed Crispin's ability to keep Naomi's spitfire under control. Her quick temper and iron determination tended to run rampant over lesser mortals—which, in her mind, comprised the rest of the world. Abraham had been trying to find a second husband for his daughter, but she had rejected every prospect he had presented—they were all too old, too poor, too stupid, too weak.

Reflecting on Naomi's stubborn opposition reminded Abraham that he had promised his wife, Elizabeth, to speak to the young suitor of his other daughter, Rebecca. *My baby,* he thought. *Still so young and vulnerable.* Yet at seventeen, she had reached the age when most girls were married.

Abraham sighed. The few minutes he had spent worrying about his family were more mentally exhausting than the hours of inventorying merchandise and recalculating cargo space. Marriage partners for two daughters. Career plans for two sons. And Roman troops arriving for God only knew what purpose.

God knows why they're here, he suddenly realized. Abraham chided himself for taking so long to think about God in the situation. He propped his forehead on the palms of his hands, his elbows resting on the tall writing desk where he stood, closed his eyes, and began to pray silently.

"I see you are deep in thought, old friend."

The booming voice startled Abraham out of his meditation. "Publius, forgive me. I did not hear you enter." Abraham turned and the two men clasped hands.

"I did not intend to surprise you, but the noise of your commerce has drowned out my plodding footsteps—a considerable accomplishment." Publius waved in the direction of the loading dock as he smiled broadly, his heavy jowls jiggling with the movement of his face. At least as heavy as Abraham, Publius did not enjoy his friend's height, and over the years his waistline had expanded until his belt had disappeared into his tunic.

"No need to ask you how business is going," Publius said. "It appears to be thriving."

"I've been very fortunate to have another profitable year."

"The gods have blessed you, my friend. Especially Fortuna. And perhaps Neptune, the god of the sea."

Abraham smiled at the lighthearted challenge. "Ordinarily I would debate the divine source of my good fortune with you, Publius, but I doubt that is why you have paid me the honor of a visit."

The two men had often engaged in a good-natured argument over the Roman pantheon of gods and goddesses. Abraham knew that Publius believed in none of them; however, Publius appreciated the stability the old religious beliefs brought to Rome and paid lip service to the ancient gods to benefit his political career. Abraham had made no secret of his belief in the One True God, but he had long ago given up trying to convert Publius. They had managed to forge a friendship in spite of their disagreement on spiritual matters.

"What brings you to the harbor?" Abraham asked. Seeing the smile on Publius's face vanish, he added, "Is this an official visit?"

Publius shook his head, setting his heavy cheeks in motion again. "No, merely a courtesy call on an old and cherished friend to, uh . . ." He paused and sighed, looking decidedly uncomfortable.

"To deliver a warning, perhaps?" It occurred to Abraham that the arrival of the Roman warships and the unexpected visit from his prominent political friend could be related.

"I delivered the warning months ago, Abraham, after the incident at the temple. I told you then that the *concilium* was very upset at the threat to public order. The council members voted to include the political disturbance in its annual report to Rome—"

"*Political* disturbance? Some kids threw a few stones at an old preacher. It hardly qualifies as a riot."

Abraham had heard about the incident from Jacob, who had been with John when they had encountered a group of worshipers leaving the Temple of Domitian. The Apostle had stood at the base of the majestic stone stairway and started preaching. Most of the crowd had ignored the elderly man with the fire of the gospel still in his bones, but a few young rowdies had started throwing stones and yelling curses. Jacob had gotten angry and chased them off.

"And that's what I tried to argue before the *concilium*—that it was strictly a local matter, a bit of religious fervor that subsided quickly. But my argument fell on deaf ears, Abraham. You know how important the Temple of Domitian is to our economy and to our standing in the Empire." Publius gestured broadly, warming up to his topic.

"If your Apostle had insulted one of the traditional gods, it might have been easily dismissed. But this could not be over-looked—and even today he continues to speak against the emperor."

"Only against the worship of the emperor. John has no political quarrel with Rome."

"In the current climate, Abraham, *everything* is political. The refusal to acknowledge the emperor's divinity is not just an offense to religious sensibilities anymore. It's a crime."

Publius looked around the room to make sure no one else had entered, then he leaned forward and lowered his voice. "Did you know that Caesar has executed his cousin, Flavius Clemens? And Clemens's wife—the emperor's own niece—was exiled to some island."

"For what crime?"

"*Impietas*—atheism. They do not acknowledge the gods of Rome. Most important, they refused to sacrifice to the emperor."

Abraham sat in stunned silence. He had heard from friends in Rome that several members of the royal family had become followers of Christ. While Domitian had a reputation for eccentric behavior and occasional cruelty, it had been directed primarily toward eliminating political opponents—he had not been known to persecute Christians. At least, not until now.

"Perhaps Caesar saw Clemens as a political rival," Abraham suggested, wanting desperately to believe there had been a different, less disturbing motivation for the murder.

"I wish that were so. But Clemens and his wife were not the only ones to meet such a fate. Several other wealthy Romans were executed at the same time, and others sent into exile."

"That is Roman politics, Publius. Surely you don't mean to imply that could happen here."

"I mean exactly that. You must wake up and realize the danger, Abraham. You are an enemy of Rome if you will not pay homage to the emperor."

"But I'm Jewish. Our faith has the status of a legal religion under Roman law, so—"

"Just how Jewish are you? You haven't set foot inside a synagogue for years, have you?"

"You know that is not by choice."

"No, it's because you worship Christ—and not only worship

Him, you are a leader of the Christians; they meet in your home. Therefore the Jews won't own you as one of theirs."

Abraham fell silent again, at a loss to counter the argument. Long before he had arrived in the city, the Jewish leaders had opposed the followers of Christ, no matter how impeccable their Jewish credentials. To this day, Abraham missed observing the Sabbath at the synagogue, even though many of the customs—Scripture reading, prayers, sermons—had been maintained by the Christians who worshiped in his home on the Lord's Day.

"And Rome no longer accepts the idea that Christianity is merely a sect within Judaism . . ."

As Publius continued speaking, Abraham reflected on the fact that the number of Gentile believers now outnumbered the Jewish believers. He could not recall exactly when that had happened, but he realized that the essential character of the church had been altered gradually, although the tenets of faith had remained unchanged.

". . . Therefore, being Jewish offers you no protection if you incur the wrath of the emperor."

The phrase "wrath of the emperor" broke into his reverie. "Not since the days of Nero," Abraham said, "have there been reports of citizens being killed merely because they were Christians. I was a young man then, and I never thought I would live to see that again in my lifetime."

"It grieves me as well to think that's what is happening, but I fear for your safety now. I've never understood your strange beliefs, yet I have valued our friendship. And I've done what I could to shield you and your family from repercussions, but it's out of my hands now." Publius extended his palms upward and shrugged, his posture denoting his helplessness.

"I know, and I appreciate everything you've done. It was politically risky to take the position you did."

"Well, I was a decided minority of one, but what were the other council members going to do—toss me out?" Publius patted his ample sides and smiled wryly.

The image of his hefty friend being bodily ejected from the *concilium* brought a fleeting moment of relief to Abraham's mind, but his worries quickly shoved the humorous image aside. He guessed that Publius had still not disclosed the full purpose of his visit.

"Why are you so fearful for my safety now, Publius? Have I personally come to the emperor's attention?"

"I don't know—but your friend John certainly has." Publius cleared his throat. "You undoubtedly noticed the two military ships that arrived late yesterday . . ."

Abraham nodded, encouraging him to continue.

"The commanding officer paid a visit to the *concilium* this morning. It seems our report to Rome, or at least the section dealing with John and his preaching at the Temple of Domitian, got Caesar's personal attention. Domitian took the unusual action of sending a cohort of soldiers to investigate—and to enforce a mandatory sacrifice to the emperor."

"So the Apostle has been targeted for this mandatory sacrifice, and if he refuses to offer it, he will meet the same fate as Flavius Clemens?"

"Execution or exile. That is the punishment."

The two friends stared blankly into space for a moment. Publius appeared quite pained as he continued. "If John is a target, it stands to reason that your son will also come to the commander's attention. Jacob accompanies the old preacher everywhere he goes."

Abraham's heart sank. *Jacob, oh Jacob,* he thought. *Why do you have to be so outspoken? Whatever made you want to be a preacher like John?*

"So if Jacob is singled out," Publius continued, "you're bound to be targeted as well. You know they can confiscate the property of anyone convicted of such a crime, and you're the wealthiest man in Asia. Actually, you wouldn't even have to be convicted of a crime, not in the sense of a trial. Damian has special orders from the emperor that override the local governing auth—"

"Who?" Abraham bolted forward as he snapped out the question.

"The commander," Publius replied, his eyebrows arching on his malleable face. "Lucius Mallus Damianus . . ."

Abraham did not hear another word Publius said. *Damian!* How could he bear to tell Elizabeth that Damian had returned, and that Jacob was his prey?

2

THE *TRICLINIUM*, WITH ITS THREE SLOPING SOFAS arranged around the large square table, was the most important room in the house, and dinner with her family was the highlight of Elizabeth's day. She slipped off her sandals and left them at the foot of the couch, then stretched out on the plush mattress covered in a rich, crimson-striped brocade.

Although each sofa accommodated three people, the family reclined in pairs when dining alone. Elizabeth and Abraham shared the center couch, the position of honor. Jacob and Peter occupied the couch to their left, and Naomi and Rebecca were to their right. The fourth side of the table was left open for service. While one servant poured wine and another placed dishes of boiled eggs in sauce, salad greens, and oysters on the table to begin the meal, Elizabeth leaned on her elbow and surveyed her family.

Peter appeared to be in pain, although he hadn't complained. In the last few years he seemed to have given in to it more; some days he never left his room. Elizabeth had often thought that if it had been Jacob whose ankle had been badly twisted at birth, he would have tangled with the devil himself rather than give up and spend the day in bed.

Her husband seemed to be distracted. Abraham had not touched his cup of *mulsum*, the warm, honey-sweetened wine he loved. *Probably brooding over a business problem,* she guessed. If it were something she needed to know, he would tell her later; they had no secrets.

Rebecca exhibited her usual sunny disposition. She was sweet and even-tempered, and remarkably unspoiled. *Unlike her older sister,* Elizabeth thought with a maternal pang. Naomi had always been self-centered, but lately she seemed to be gripped by cynicism. Naomi's attention was wandering now, and she drummed her fingers on the large napkin spread protectively over the curved head of the couch.

The twins presented a contrast, as always. Peter was typically quiet and merely picked at his food, while Jacob ate heartily and conversed with the others. He did seem a bit subdued, however, and Rebecca was quick to pinpoint the cause.

"When are you and the apostle John leaving?" she said to Jacob.

"We're not. At least not right away." Disappointment was etched in the set of Jacob's square jaw. "It's difficult for him to ride long distances anymore because of his advanced age—"

"Advanced? He's older than Methuselah." Naomi nibbled at one of the boiled eggs and grimaced. "Too much vinegar in the pine-kernel sauce," she commented. "Surely we could afford a better cook."

"I'm surprised you even know who Methuselah is," Jacob said dryly.

"I know much more than you'd ever give a woman credit for."

Elizabeth shot Jacob a warning look that stopped him from offering a quick retort.

He contented himself with a frown at his older sister and continued. "Anyway, John was chilled to the bone when I arrived this morning, and too stiff to mount a horse. He said he would write Polycarp and ask him to come to Ephesus, but I suggested we hire a carriage. I think John could make the trip that way."

"Who is this Polycarp, dear?" Elizabeth did not recall hearing the name.

"He's a disciple of John, someone he wants me to meet—a leader of the church in Smyrna, even though he's only a few years older than I am."

Two servants began bringing the main course to the table: mackerel smothered in herbs and coarse pepper, pieces of roast duck rolled in honey and poppy seeds, and several vegetable dishes. All of the household servants were Christians, and Jacob spoke freely in their presence.

"John said I could preach in some of the churches," he said eagerly, "and he feels an urgent need to visit them—'one last time,' he said—because he feels that something cataclysmic is about to happen."

For the first time during the meal, Abraham's attention was piqued. "What do you mean, 'cataclysmic'?"

Jacob shrugged. "I don't know—I don't think John knows, either. Perhaps it's simply that he's nearing the end of his life and knows he may never have another opportunity to minister to the other churches. Or maybe he senses in his spirit that something . . ." Jacob paused to take a sip of wine while he groped for the right words. "Something unusually significant, or disastrous, is about to happen."

Abraham stared so intently at Jacob that Elizabeth wondered if father and son were about to renew the argument they'd had this morning. *Dear God, no,* she prayed silently. *Let there be peace.*

"If you ask me," Jacob continued, "it obviously has something to do with Emperor Domitian's declaring himself Lord and God—"

"Oh, please. Spare us another sermon about the perils of emperor worship." Naomi spoke over her brother while rolling her eyes dramatically.

"—And receiving sacrifices at the grandiose temple our city fathers so thoughtfully built in his honor." Jacob glared across the table at his sister as he finished speaking.

"Hush, Naomi! As for you, Jacob—" Abraham's stern voice dropped a notch as Elizabeth placed her arm on his sleeve. "Son, your righteous indignation is appropriate, but you have a tendency to express it without thinking. You *must* be careful about speaking so openly in public, as I've warned you."

"But Father, how will people know the truth unless we preach it? They are lost and dying without God, worshiping idols of gold and silver, and now worshiping a man who dares to call himself Lord and God."

"And how will the people hear the truth if the preacher gets himself thrown in jail—or killed?"

Elizabeth gasped involuntarily at Abraham's words. She had not heard her husband talk like this before, and it troubled her. His opposition to Jacob's calling to be a preacher had stemmed from his disappointment that his son would not follow him into the business world—or so she had thought. Perhaps Abraham had been more worried for their son's safety than he had let on.

"We have enjoyed a great deal of toleration," Abraham continued more calmly, "but the political climate is changing. Drastically." He picked up the cup of *mulsum* and sipped slowly, his glance saying to Elizabeth, *I'll tell you about it later.*

"All I'm saying is, don't go looking for trouble, son; it will find you easily enough. Preach the truth, but be judicious about it."

Abraham turned and looked at his son for so long that Jacob finally asked, "Do *you* think something terrible is about to happen, Father? Something 'cataclysmic'?"

"My prophetic ability is limited to business forecasts." Abraham smiled wanly. "I'll leave spiritual prophecy to the Apostle."

Everyone fell silent; the mood had turned somber. "You should have told me John was sick," Elizabeth said after a long moment. "I would have sent food, and someone to look after him."

"He's not sick, Mother. Just old and stiff. Still as feisty as ever, but getting rather feeble." Jacob turned to face Abraham. "I will heed your advice, Father," he said deliberately. "I cannot promise to stop preaching, but I will promise to be more careful."

Abraham nodded. "Good enough." His voice had become husky with emotion and he cleared his throat. "You mentioned something about hiring a carriage so John could go on this trip."

Jacob's rugged features became instantly animated. "I figured all your wagons would be in service now, making deliveries. But I thought perhaps we could use your personal coach, or maybe you could arrange to hire a carriage for us."

"I can do better than that. Take the *Mercury* and sail for Smyrna or Pergamum, then hire a carriage to take John wherever he wants to go."

Jacob sat straight up and gave a jubilant whoop. Naomi's mouth flew open. "The *Mercury*?" She stared at her father for a moment, then turned to her brother. "How long will you be gone?" she asked, her voice frigid.

"What does it matter to you?" Jacob replied.

"I realize sending Jacob in my private cutter spoils your scheme of wheedling me into a trip to Rome," Abraham said to Naomi. "We'll talk about that later. For now"—he pointed at Jacob—"I want you to leave and tell John as soon as we finish dinner. I'll alert the captain and crew. Make whatever preparations you need, but be at the harbor ready to cast off by daybreak. I'll meet you there to see you off."

"Daybreak? Why the urgency?" Elizabeth swallowed hard. She was satisfied with Abraham's change of heart toward Jacob's ministry but wary of its suddenness. Now she had a premonition of disaster.

"John himself expressed the urgency," Abraham said, "and the *Mercury* is stocked and ready to sail. There's no need for delay." His tone of voice left no room for argument.

∽⚬∾

After dinner Naomi strolled along the colonnade of the large open peristyle adjoining their villa. Peeved that her father was sending Jacob on some fool's errand to Smyrna when she'd had plans to use their private ship, Naomi thought a walk would be soothing. She loved the peristyle with its spacious, meticulously tended garden and fountains. That is, she liked it now, when it was quiet and dignified; Naomi hated it on Sundays, when as many as a hundred people congregated on the tiled walkways surrounding the garden.

Actually, she did not mind large crowds of people—as long as they were the right people. But the people who gathered in their home on "the Lord's Day," as they called it, were not the right people; they were an odd mixture of young and old, rich and poor, well-bred and uncouth, and most of them either pitied her or scorned her. Naomi, in turn, pitied their dependence on a childish faith and privately scorned their sermons and hymns to Christ.

Naomi's mood did not improve when she found her sister sitting on a stone bench by the central fountain.

"I like your new dress," Rebecca said pleasantly. "I've never seen a blue that brilliant before."

Naomi did not value her sister's opinions on fashion, but at least Rebecca hadn't tried to insult her. Jacob had had the nerve to tell her she looked like a peacock.

"It's quite flattering, don't you think?" Naomi extended her slender arms and made a graceful pirouette, careful not to dislodge the numerous pins and combs that held her dark auburn hair piled high atop her head. She was quite proud of her abundant hair and its rich color, an exotic blend of her mother's fiery red locks and the glossy jet of her father's.

"And I like to wear vivid colors," Naomi added. "It lifts my spirits."

"The new dress, the new hairdo . . . are you expecting a visitor?"

"No, I'm just trying out some of the latest styles before I go to Rome."

"Father said at dinner you wanted to go to Rome, but it's too late in the year for him to take us now."

"I didn't say anything about the family going." Naomi's smile faded at the thought of her entire, boringly religious clan accompanying her; she hadn't suggested it to her father. He kept a small villa in the hills of Rome and sometimes took the family with him on business trips, but Naomi had a different purpose in mind for her trip, and she wouldn't be returning anytime soon.

"I think Rome would be a good place to find a husband," she announced to her sister.

"You make finding a husband sound like a shopping trip."

"That's exactly what it is. And Rome has a much better selection of merchandise." Naomi threw back her head and laughed.

"But Ephesus is a huge city," Rebecca said, "one of the wealthiest cities in the Empire. Surely you can find a husband here."

"Rome is the center of the world, and that's where I belong. Perhaps married to a senator—yes, I like that idea."

For a moment Naomi let her imagination take her all the way to the emperor's palace, seeing herself surrounded by the highest echelon of Roman society. A rich, powerful husband would be her ticket, and she would not even mind if he were old or ugly—or both—as long as he was stupendously wealthy and influential.

"I'm content to stay here and let Father take care of arranging a marriage," Rebecca said. "And how can you even think about going to Rome when Jacob could be in trouble?"

"He wouldn't be in trouble if he would learn to keep his mouth shut. And you're content only because you assume you'll marry your beloved Galen. What if Father has already struck a bargain with someone else? Perhaps a wealthy acquaintance who can inject fresh capital into the shipping business."

"We don't need that kind of money, and Father would never do that to me. Never." Rebecca's large eyes widened, and the contrast of her dark eyes and deep-nut-brown hair against her delicate fair skin gave her the appearance of a startled doe.

"Don't be too sure. Money begets money, dear heart, and money drives the world."

Rebecca folded her hands in her lap and composed herself. "Father is going to speak to Galen soon. Mother said so."

"I don't know what you see in him. I suppose Galen is handsome enough, but he's not forceful. And he's poor—a silversmith. If it weren't for his scruples, Galen could make a lucrative business selling charms and amulets and temple souvenirs. He wouldn't have any clients at all if Father hadn't introduced him to some wealthy merchants who can afford silver plates and goblets rather than stoneware."

"Galen is a very talented artisan, and also a Christian—something you seem to care nothing about in a husband but that is very important to me."

Naomi resented her younger sister's holier-than-thou attitude, and she couldn't resist goading Rebecca. "Perhaps Galen does not love you as much as you imagine, and that's why he has not asked Father's permission to marry you."

"That's not true! He does love me. He even wanted to—"

Rebecca suddenly stopped speaking, and Naomi knew she had been about to reveal something. From the crimson flame of Rebecca's cheeks, Naomi guessed what Galen had wanted to do. "He wanted to kiss you," she said knowingly.

"He is too much of a gentleman to kiss me before we're married." Rebecca's hands fidgeted nervously in her lap and her voice dropped to a dreamy whisper. "But he did hold my hand."

"Answer me one question," Naomi snapped. "Did Galen want to kiss you because of love—or was it lust?"

"Why do you have to talk like that?" Rebecca bolted from the garden bench and ran to the shelter of the colonnade.

The sound of Naomi's laughter echoed off the flagstones. *Poor lovestruck child,* she mused, almost regretting having provoked her sister, then deciding it was to Rebecca's advantage to have her illusions shattered. *She'll soon learn that love is never what you expect it to be. And it never lasts.*

❧

Abraham's heart was as heavy as his footsteps when he climbed the stairs to the upper level of the villa, where the bedrooms were located—all except Peter's. Elizabeth had converted a small room off the library on the ground floor into a bedroom for him.

Jacob had rushed out shortly after dinner, Elizabeth reminding him to take a torch because it would be dark by the time he reached John's house. Abraham paused at the door of Jacob's bedroom now, wondering if he was doing the right thing by sending Jacob away. But what else could he do? The Tenth Legion was here, with orders from the emperor, and with Damian in command.

He searched the recesses of his mind, trying to recall the monster's face. He'd seen it only twice, and as memorable as his encounters with Damian had been, Abraham wondered why the face was not permanently etched in his memory. But he remembered only bits and pieces of Damian's physical appearance, disjointed elements that he could not quite put together to make a composite. Dark hair, that was easy; he was a Roman. Bony knees—an odd thing to remember; but then Abraham had seen them at close range, looking up at them from the ground. And such cruel eyes. If nothing else, he would recognize Damian again from the hatred in his eyes.

It's been twenty-five years, Abraham thought. *Maybe he's bald and paunchy and toothless now.* No matter if he were. Damian had an entire cohort of soldiers to carry out his orders. Somewhere between four hundred and six hundred men, and they were here to root out Christians.

When Abraham entered their bedroom, Elizabeth was sitting on the side of the bed, her shoulders slumped. "I thought you had to go to the harbor," she said, "to make sure the captain is prepared to sail in the morning."

Abraham set the clay lamp he had carried upstairs on the table by the bed. Several lamps were already burning, and a charcoal brazier had been lit to take the chill off the room. "Kaeso is ready. I spoke to him before I left the harbor this afternoon."

"I don't understand. You mean you already knew you were going to send Jacob and John to Smyrna on the *Mercury?*"

"All I could think of was that I had to get Jacob away from here quickly . . ." He knew that was the wrong place to start, so he let his thought trail off, wondering how much to tell Elizabeth, wishing he could protect her from the truth, and knowing he couldn't.

Her fair skin shimmered in the flickering light, and her green eyes were flecked with gold. Abraham cupped her chin in his massive hand and tilted her face up to his. She looked both puzzled and afraid. He wanted to tell her how much he loved her and that he could never live without her, but he couldn't form the words. Instead, he leaned down and kissed the top of her head.

She wrapped her arms around his waist. "I'm worried about him, Abraham. I'm worried because you're worried, and I don't know *why* you're worried. Please, tell me whatever it is you're keeping from me."

"Let's talk in bed," he said. "You're shivering."

Abraham began extinguishing the lamps while Elizabeth removed her outer tunic and crawled beneath the covers. The wooden bed with a carved headboard and footboard was the first piece of furniture they had ever bought. As they had prospered beyond their dreams and built the villa, Elizabeth had purchased beautiful, costly furnishings for every room. But neither one of them could bear to part with their marriage bed. It had a new wool-stuffed mattress and a luxurious spread now, but it was the same sturdy bed they had loved and argued in, laughed and cried in, for twenty-five years.

Nestled in the shelter of their bed, Abraham began to tell Elizabeth about the arrival of the Roman warships and about his meeting with Publius. She shuddered when he told her about the order requiring a sacrifice to Domitian and how much danger Jacob was in. He held his wife close and told her not to worry, told her that everything would be all right, that he would protect her, and that God would protect Jacob because he was doing the Lord's work. But his words held a confidence he did not feel, and the one thing he could not bring himself to tell her was that Damian was the one in charge of carrying out the emperor's orders. It was just too much at once, he decided.

They lay curled together like spoons, Elizabeth's back pressed against his broad chest, the top of her head resting under his chin. Finally she began to breathe steadily and deeply, falling asleep in his arms.

Sleep eluded Abraham, however, as he alternately relived the day and tried to think of what to do on the morrow. Could the *Mercury* sail before the soldiers discovered the Apostle was aboard? If John knew they were here to arrest him, would he even leave? Or would the Son of Thunder gladly face the might of Rome, whatever the consequences?

John was elderly, and it was one thing for him to play the martyr. But Jacob was young and had his whole life ahead of him. And what if they did make it to Smyrna, or Pergamum, or any other city in Asia? Would Damian try to track them down when he learned they had left? How long would he search for John and Jacob?

Abraham's mind was flooded with questions. And so he stayed awake, groping for answers. *I'll figure out what to do,* he told himself. *There has to be a solution.* Abraham was the kind who wrestled a situation until he conquered it.

"I'll fix this too, Elizabeth," he whispered into the night. "I promise you. Somehow, I'll fix this."

3

EARLY THE NEXT MORNING, in the predawn stillness, Abraham listened to the screeching of seagulls and the soft rhythmic slapping of the water against the pier, the familiar sounds lulling his heightened senses. A light fog hovered over the water, and in the faint moonlight he could barely make out the shape of the two warships, still docked at the bend of the harbor. Although the troops had departed, the crews were probably still on board, and he wanted the *Mercury* to sail before too many sailors were stirring on deck. The fewer people who took note of its departure, the better.

His son's room had been empty when he left the villa, which meant Jacob had already gone to get the Apostle. *Hurry,* he urged them silently.

Abraham slipped between the buildings and walked back to the street side of the warehouse. He stood at the entrance, feet planted firmly apart and hands clasped behind his back, watching in the direction of Harbor Street. In spite of the darkness, he could see the broad avenue quite well. It was one of only three illuminated streets in the Empire—a boast Publius frequently delighted in making.

After a few minutes Abraham spotted two figures making their way down the street; one tall and straight, the other stooped. Abraham was glad for the lamps lining the colonnade, yet uneasy that the pair would be so easy to spot. He wondered if Damian was already on the lookout for John, and perhaps even Jacob.

I always knew I'd have to do something about you, Damian. Knew you'd make good on your threats someday, Abraham thought.

He was relieved when Jacob and John finally reached the harbor.

"Abraham." John greeted him in a voice that was still strong and authoritative in spite of his increasing frailty. "Thank you for the courtesy of your personal ship. These old bones appreciate yet another one of your kindnesses."

As they clasped hands, Abraham felt the bony elbow and the dry, leathery skin of the Apostle. He wondered for a moment how old the man was. Well into his eighties now, he calculated. John had not been a young man when they had met, and that was half a lifetime ago for Abraham. "I'm happy to make the *Mercury* available, John. You should have let me know sooner that you needed it."

"It never occurred to me to travel by sea; most of the places I intend to visit are inland. And had I thought of it, I would not have wanted to impose. This is a busy time for your business."

As Jacob walked up the loading ramp to deposit their gear on deck, Abraham explained to John that the *Mercury* almost never carried cargo and had been built primarily for speed and passenger use. "Watch your step," he said, taking John by the arm and helping him up the incline. A sailor carrying two small wire crates followed them. The contents could not be seen in the darkness, but the soft cooing of pigeons disclosed what was inside. No ship in Abraham's fleet, including his personal cutter, ever sailed without several pairs of the tiny messengers.

The captain welcomed his passengers aboard. "We're ready to cast off, sir."

Abraham nodded. "You'll be in capable hands," he said to John. "Oppius Marius Kaeso is the most seasoned captain in my employ." *Seasoned* was a good word for his trusted skipper, Abraham thought. An unruly head of salt-and-pepper hair framed Kaeso's weather-beaten face.

Abraham turned and embraced his son. "God be with you," he said roughly. "Be prudent."

"I will." Jacob touched the leather wallet fastened to his belt. "Thank you, Father."

"If you should need more money, Kaeso can arrange for it."

A sailor on the dock below grunted as he untied one of the heavy ropes mooring the ship and heaved it aboard.

"Take good care of him, John." Abraham squeezed the old man's shoulder.

"You have it backward. I'm bringing Jacob along to take good care of me."

Abraham ignored the hint of merriment in the raspy voice. "You know what I mean. Watch out for him. Try to keep him safe." A lump the size of a plum rose in his throat as he looked at his son.

"You worry too much, friend," John said.

"There is much to worry about these days. Much to worry about."

"Life is full of concerns." John glanced in the direction of the Roman warships, almost ghostlike in their faint visibility.

Did he look at them deliberately? Abraham wondered. *Does the Apostle know the emperor is after him?*

"But is the God we serve not bigger than all of your worries?" John asked.

Abraham gripped the Apostle's arm silently, then turned and walked quickly down the ramp. A crewman immediately moved the plank, and the captain gave the order to push away from the dock. The sleek ship began to move quietly out of the harbor as dawn arrived to burn away the mist.

Abraham watched the *Mercury* depart, softly quoting words from a favorite psalm:

> *Those who go down to the sea in ships,*
> *Who do business on great waters,*

They see the works of the Lord,
And His wonders in the deep.

ᘿᕲ

Rebecca waited in the atrium for her mother, whom she often accompanied on calls to the sick or needy members of the congregation. Sunlight filtered into the open portion of the main entry to the villa, warming the colorful mosaic floor tiles.

Standing in front of a niche in the wall, Rebecca studied the scroll displayed there. When her father built the villa, so the story went, he had been furious at the architect for designing the elaborate alcove as a focal point in the wall—"a perfect place for the *lararium*," the man had said. Every Roman home had its altar where the *lares,* the household gods, were displayed and daily prayers and offerings made. Abraham had been so angry at the unrequested innovation that he had almost made the architect tear the wall out and start over. Instead, he had left it intact and placed a beautifully copied scroll in the niche. The scroll contained the book of Joshua, and it had been opened to the passage that read, "As for me and my house, we will serve the Lord."

The front door opened and Rebecca turned as footsteps sounded on the tile. "Father!"

"Is your mother up?" he asked.

"Of course. She's filling a basket with food for our visit to Africanus's widow." Rebecca was quite surprised by her father's unexpected appearance. He never returned from the harbor before midafternoon, and it was still early in the morning.

"Get her for me, please."

Rebecca started to leave, then decided to ask the question that had been burning in her heart. She so seldom saw her father alone that she could not pass up the opportunity. "Father, have you spoken to Galen about me—about marriage, I mean?"

"This is not the time to get into that," he said curtly. "I have far more important things on my mind."

She was wounded by his tone but did not think she could live without an answer, so she persisted. "But you haven't promised me to anyone else . . . have you, Father?"

"What—? No."

Rebecca exhaled slowly, relief washing over her. She had been fairly certain that Naomi was only teasing, but she was never quite sure how to take her sister.

"I'll speak to Galen soon," Abraham said, his voice softening. "Now go find your mother."

She ran swiftly toward the kitchen and returned in a moment with her mother.

Her parents went upstairs to talk, and when Rebecca grew tired of waiting, she went up to her bedroom. She could hear voices coming from the bedroom next door but could not make out what they were saying. It must have something to do with Jacob and the Apostle, she surmised, since her father had returned immediately after seeing them off.

After a few minutes her mother began to sob. Rebecca grew more frightened with every minute that passed. Elizabeth was tender-hearted and cried easily, but Rebecca had never heard such plaintive weeping. She wanted to go and comfort her mother, who was obviously in great distress, but she sat on her bed, listening uneasily, until the sobs subsided and her father finally left the room.

Abraham came looking for her. "Your mother is too upset to leave the house," he told Rebecca. "Take the food and make the visit she had planned."

Her father's face sagged with sorrow, and his eyes were red from weeping. Rebecca wanted desperately to ask what was wrong, but he turned on his heel and walked briskly out. She went downstairs and retrieved the basket her mother had prepared, then left to call on the family of Africanus, a former slave originally from Carthage, who had recently died. His wife and children were now dependent on the charity of fellow believers to survive.

Later that day the atmosphere at the family dinner was strained. Her mother did not come downstairs, and that worried Rebecca; she could scarcely remember an occasion when her mother had been too ill to dine with the family. Her father was brooding and silent, and she could tell he was simply going through the motions. He ate little, and his repeated glances at Jacob's empty place made Rebecca suspect that the crisis in their home had something to do with her brother.

Naomi chattered about trivial matters, and even Peter seemed to talk more than usual, or perhaps it was just that for once he was not overshadowed by his more charismatic twin.

With obvious relish, Naomi disclosed the latest gossip she'd heard. "I wouldn't mention this if Jacob were here because we'd have to listen to another one of his sermons, but I learned today that the city is planning a big festival for the twenty-fourth of this month because it's Emperor Domitian's birthday. There will be games in his honor at the stadium, and of course a celebration at his temple. I know *our* family won't go to that because people will be 'sacrificing,' although it's really just paying respect to the emperor because of the greatness of the Empire."

"Jacob never draws the fine line," Peter said, "that the state religion calls for worship of the *genius*—the guardian spirit of the *gens,* or family clan—of the emperor."

Offended at her siblings' flirtation with Roman religion, Rebecca said, "I for one would never sacrifice to the *genius* of the emperor. It's pagan—and blasphemous."

"Jacob preaches against it," Peter said, "but I personally don't see what is so different between that and our faith's frequent references to the patriarchs, such as Abraham, Isaac, and Jacob, or Moses."

"But we don't worship the patriarchs," Rebecca countered, believing she should champion Jacob's cause although she felt completely inadequate to argue theology.

"We honor them, don't we? What's the difference between worship and honor or respect?" Peter asked.

"Well, we don't sacrifice to them," Rebecca said. "We sacrifice only to God." She paused, trying to formulate her thoughts. "Except we don't actually make sacrifices anymore. I mean, not like animal sacrifices or incense . . ." She looked to her father, silently appealing for support.

"We do not worship idols, and we do not worship any man, including the patriarchs," Abraham said, finally joining the conversation. "And you're wrong, Peter. It's no longer a question of sacrificing to the *genius* of the emperor. Domitian has declared *himself* to be divine. And the sacrifice is no longer an optional way of paying respect. 'Lord' Domitian, as he demands to be called, has made the sacrifice mandatory. Anyone who does not perform it is guilty of a crime."

"Mandatory!" Rebecca suddenly understood why her father had wanted to hasten Jacob's departure, and why her mother was so distraught. It also might explain why she had seen several Roman soldiers in the *agora* earlier. They had not appeared threatening and seemed merely to be haggling with vendors, but she hadn't known what to make of their presence and she'd found it unsettling.

"But you're right about one thing, Naomi," Abraham continued. "This family definitely will *not* attend the celebration on Domitian's birthday."

"And what if I decide to attend with Julia and her husband?" Naomi added a fierce look to her verbal challenge.

Abraham paused a long time before answering—a sign, Rebecca realized, that he was making a great effort to curb an outburst of anger. "You will not defy my decisions or defile my faith," he said softly but sternly. "Is that understood?"

Naomi sat up on the sofa she shared with Rebecca and glared at her father. "You don't care one iota about me. You don't even know anything about me or what I want out of life. I'm just another asset for you to manage." Like a kettle boiling over, Naomi's words gathered steam and spewed out, scalding hot in their fury.

"And you don't care about this family, either, or you would not refuse to participate in any cultural activities. You won't attend the baths or the games. You won't set foot in a 'pagan' temple even if it's just to attend a dinner party. I know, I know, 'We don't eat meat sacrificed to idols.' So don't eat the meat! But at least put in an appearance now and then so we don't become complete outcasts."

"That's enough, Naomi." Abraham was on his feet instantly, and he made no effort to restrain his temper this time. "Go to your room—now!" he yelled, pointing to the door.

Naomi stood and carefully folded her napkin, placing it on the table before turning to leave. Her back was straight and her head high as she walked slowly out of the room.

Abraham drained his wine goblet in a single long swallow and then left the room without saying another word.

"I think I've lost my appetite." Rebecca was on the verge of tears. "You'll have to excuse me, Peter."

"It's all right," he said when Rebecca stood to leave. "I'm quite accustomed to spending time by myself."

There was a sad note to her brother's voice, Rebecca thought, but his face was inscrutable.

How can you live with people all your life, she wondered as she walked upstairs, *and not understand them?* She didn't know why Peter was sometimes so withdrawn and aloof. And she certainly couldn't fathom the source of Naomi's increasing contempt for her family, particularly her father.

Naomi was growing more rebellious by the day, Peter was increasingly frail and forlorn, Jacob was in grave danger, her mother was terribly sad, her father was worried sick—Rebecca had an overwhelming feeling that everything in her life was dramatically changing. It was as if some unseen, unknowable watershed had been crossed, and nothing—no one—would ever be the same again.

4

IN THE THREE WEEKS JACOB HAD BEEN GONE, Elizabeth had aged visibly. Abraham's heart was grieved to the core to see her beautiful face looking lined and haggard.

As soon as he had returned from the harbor the day the *Mercury* had sailed, Abraham told Elizabeth about Damian. She had been devastated, as he expected. Devastated and terrified.

"Damian vowed he would kill you someday." Elizabeth's voice shook, and she placed an unsteady hand over her mouth.

"We don't know that that's why he's here," Abraham had said, grasping for a way to soften the news. "This is not necessarily a personal vendetta. Damian is here on the emperor's behalf."

"Because the emperor wants to persecute Christians—and you don't think Damian will use that to his own advantage? Don't try to placate me, Abraham. You know he'll seek revenge. He's come back to kill you, and when he finds out Jacob is your son, he'll kill him too."

Abraham could not argue with that—Elizabeth was merely giving voice to his own thoughts—so he had repeated what John had said to him, that God was bigger than all their worries.

"My head knows that's true," she said, "but try telling it to my heart." Then she broke down and sobbed until Abraham thought she would be ill. His wife would not let him hold her while she cried—"I cannot be consoled," she'd said as she brushed his hand away—so he stood at the foot of the bed and watched helplessly as she poured out her anguish. He tried to pray, but no words would come. All he could think was, *I've served You faithfully all these years, Lord. Surely You will not let this monster destroy my family.*

After that Abraham had started carrying a dagger, until Elizabeth had spied it under his cloak when he returned from the harbor one day. The discovery had triggered another outburst.

"What are you going to do—try to kill Damian before he kills you?" Her face was ashen, and her eyes quickly filled with tears and terror.

"No," he protested. "It's—"

"Don't bring that calamity on my head as well, Abraham. I did not marry a murderer."

"I'm not going to murder anyone," he objected. "I would use it only for self-defense."

"And can you defend yourself against an entire cohort of Roman soldiers with this dagger?"

Abraham touched the faint scar that ran down his jawline. He had faced three soldiers from the Tenth Legion armed with only a dagger once, and he had survived.

Nevertheless, he quit wearing the weapon, for his wife's sake. But he had kept it at his office. *Just in case,* he told himself.

Sitting at his desk now, Abraham opened the drawer and was studying the dagger when Quintus interrupted him.

"This message just arrived." Quintus handed Abraham a tiny scroll that had been tightly rolled and tied with a string of leather. "It's from one of our ships. The *Mercury*, I imagine."

Abraham unrolled the scroll and read the short message that had been flown in by one of his numerous pigeons:

> Sailing home empty. Cargo confiscated by authorities.
> Will explain upon arrival.
> — Op. Marius Kaeso, 23 Oct., Miletus

"Noooooo!"

Abraham's roar startled his usually unflappable assistant. Quintus reached out a hand to steady Abraham, who had started to rise and then fallen back in his chair. The scroll fell to the floor, and

Quintus retrieved it, glancing at the message as he placed it on the desk.

"I'm very sorry, Abraham." The expression on Quintus's gaunt face was grim. "Would you like me to send for your friend Publius? Perhaps there is something he can do."

"Yes . . . No, don't. He can't help me now." Abraham had seen Publius in the *agora* recently and had started to cross over and speak to him. Publius had avoided him, turning away and hurriedly entering one of the shops. Abraham had been certain Publius had seen him, though; their eyes had met briefly and Publius had been on the verge of speaking. But several soldiers were in the marketplace, and Abraham deduced that Publius had thought it unwise to be seen with him.

The First Cohort had been making its presence known throughout the city. Soldiers appeared in the shops frequently, asking questions. So far no one had questioned Abraham or his family directly, but he knew they had been the subject of inquiry. Several church members had been questioned about the Apostle and his whereabouts; the interrogators had also wanted to know where the Christians met and who their leaders were. Abraham's name was bound to have surfaced by now.

"That will be all, Quintus. Send Kaeso to me the minute the *Mercury* docks."

Quintus simply nodded and left his employer alone to fret over the disturbing message. Enough time had passed since the arrival of the First Cohort that Abraham had begun to think perhaps his family would escape the crisis. But it had been a false hope, and deep down he'd known that all along.

He was familiar with the tactics the Roman government used against their targets. The soldiers who had been freely questioning the populace were trying to recruit paid informers, who stood to gain a portion of the estate of a person accused of a crime. The temptation of Abraham's vast wealth would eventually prove to be overwhelming for someone of humble circumstance, perhaps a disgruntled employee or even one of his fellow believers.

Many people in Ephesus knew the Christians met in Abraham's home. They didn't advertise the fact, and since the arrival of the First Cohort the church had split into smaller groups for worship so as not to attract undue attention. But others outside their circle had inevitably become aware of their meeting place. And Abraham's son had even preached publicly alongside the Apostle.

Now the soldiers had arrested Jacob and John—"confiscated the cargo," as Kaeso had discreetly worded his message.

Abraham picked up the scroll and reread it. Kaeso had sent it from Miletus, not Smyrna. He must have dropped his passengers off in Smyrna, where they would have hired a carriage and traveled inland, and from Smyrna Kaeso had probably sailed south to wait for them at Miletus. Abraham mentally calculated the distance from Miletus to Ephesus: a homing pigeon could cover the distance in under two hours; the *Mercury*, although built for speed and not heavy cargo, would take four to five times that long, depending on the prevailing winds.

Even so, if Kaeso had sailed at dawn, he should arrive by late afternoon. Abraham decided to wait at the harbor for the *Mercury*'s arrival. He did not want to go home and tell Elizabeth what had happened until he'd had a chance to find out what Kaeso knew.

Later, as twilight deepened the shadows over the sheltered harbor, Abraham was still waiting anxiously. Although the official workday ended at noon, Quintus often worked until midafternoon with Abraham, and he came out to the dock now. Abraham had remained there all afternoon, searching the horizon for any sign of the ship.

"Kaeso should have been here by now," he said.

"He's probably sailing into a headwind," Quintus said. "That could delay him several hours."

Abraham appreciated the fact that his assistant had stayed so late.

He knew it was simply to keep him company; Quintus had finished his work hours ago. "You should go home now," Abraham told him. "I'll wait a while longer."

"If you need anything else—"

"No, I'm fine," Abraham said. "Just light a few torches for me before you leave."

Quintus spent several minutes lighting torches and placing them in iron brackets mounted to the outside wall of the warehouse. The black smoke from the burning oil irritated his eyes, and he was blinking rapidly when he returned to bid Abraham good night.

"If you want me to stay . . . ," he offered.

Abraham shook his head no.

"I wish there were something I could do," Quintus said.

"If there were, I'd ask it of you." Abraham extended his hand. "Thanks, my friend."

Abraham feared there was nothing anyone could do. For days he had racked his brain trying to think how to end this nightmare. Elizabeth was right: he couldn't fight his way out of this, not against an entire cohort of Roman military might. He'd considered bribery but didn't know whom to approach. Damian was out for revenge, so attempting to bribe him would be futile. And no one except the emperor had the authority to overrule Damian's orders. Abraham's carefully cultivated contacts with the influential powers of Ephesus were now useless, and he smiled ruefully at the irony: the richest man in Asia had no one to offer the fruits of his fortune in return for a political favor.

Darkness fell as Abraham maintained his solitary watch. When he could no longer see into the distant sea, he knew it was time to end his vigil. The family would have already had their dinner without him, and Elizabeth would be worried.

He had turned toward the warehouse to remove one of the torches for his walk home when he heard heavy footsteps on the pier. Abraham froze. Only one type of shoe made such a ponderous sound: the hobnailed boot of a soldier.

There were five of them marching swiftly toward him, all wearing segmented leather armor that hung in cumbersome pleats over their knee-length red tunics. One of them wore the plumed helmet of a centurion.

"Abraham of Ephesus," the centurion announced officiously, "you are commanded to appear before Captain Lucius Mallus Damianus to answer charges for the crime of treason."

∽✕∾

Elizabeth was frantic. She alternated between pacing and kneeling on the cold marble floor. Over the last three weeks she had spent so much time in prayer, she had worn her knees raw. Tonight she couldn't manage to concentrate long enough to pray for more than a minute or two, so she quickly resumed pacing. When that seemed futile, she knelt to pray again.

She had been worried when Abraham did not come home for dinner. It was so unlike him—he never stayed at the harbor after dark without sending a message. When several hours had passed, she knew something was terribly wrong, and now she was plain frightened.

"No word from Father yet?" Rebecca asked, yawning as she entered the *triclinium*.

Elizabeth shook her head.

The remains of dinner were still on the table, waiting for Abraham. Rebecca poured wine from a beautiful silver pitcher—Galen's handiwork—into a cup and handed it to her mother. "Drink some of this. Perhaps you can relax enough to sleep. According to Father's water clock, it's almost midnight."

Elizabeth took one sip of the wine and immediately started pacing again. Nothing would ease her mind enough to sleep, she thought. Only Abraham's return.

Rebecca walked over to the brazier and stoked the few embers still burning. "It's too chilly in here. I'll ask Servius to—"

"He's not here," Elizabeth said. "I sent him to the harbor to look for your father."

"Then I'll get one of the other servants to tend the fire. You're shivering."

"No, don't wake them. Just fetch my cloak."

Elizabeth circled the room restlessly as Rebecca ran upstairs and quickly returned with the cloak. She draped it around her mother's shoulders and then hugged her tightly.

"I'm scared," Rebecca confessed. "Do you suppose something horrible has happened to Father?"

Elizabeth held her daughter and stroked her hair. She longed to comfort Rebecca, to tell her that everything would be all right, but that would be a lie. Everything was not all right, and it might never be right again.

They both jumped when they heard the massive front door open, and they ran toward the atrium. *Servius must be back,* Elizabeth thought. *And perhaps Abraham is with him.*

Servius was alone. "I couldn't find him, ma'am." He picked up a clay lamp and shepherded the women out of the frigid open-air center of the atrium into the main part of the house.

"Servius, please—" Elizabeth implored as they entered the fading warmth of the dining room.

The old man held up a hand and motioned her silent. "Give me a moment to catch my breath and I'll tell you all about it." Had it been any other servant, Elizabeth would have scolded him for impertinence. But he had been with her family since she was a child. Her father, Rufus, had given Servius his freedom decades ago, but he had stayed to serve the family. And when Rufus had died a few years after Elizabeth had married Abraham, Servius became an important part of their household.

He sat down on the edge of the couch closest to the brazier.

"When I got to the warehouse, no one was there. Torches were lit along the dock, but I could find no sign of Abraham—or anyone else. On my way back, I stopped at the house of Quintus. I had to pound on the door to rouse him from sleep."

Servius paused and drew his cloak around him. "I need to rekindle the fire," he said, looking at the brazier. He started to rise but stopped when Elizabeth put a hand on his shoulder in an unspoken request to continue.

"Quintus didn't know where Abraham was," Servius said. "He told me he lit the torches for Abraham and then left him out on the pier. He was waiting for the *Mercury*."

"The *Mercury*?" Elizabeth exclaimed. "He was expecting Jacob!" She had a momentary glimmer of hope, which faded when Servius picked up her hand and looked at her compassionately.

"The *Mercury* was returning home without passengers," Servius said. "That's all I found out. Quintus would not have told me that much if he hadn't still been half-asleep; you know how tight-lipped he is about Abraham's business . . . Anyway, he didn't know Jacob's whereabouts either, ma'am. I asked him that too. Quintus told me to return home and said he would go looking for Abraham himself."

Elizabeth swallowed her disappointment. "Thank you, Servius. You did what you could."

"I'm going to do something about heating this room now," Servius said as he stood. "Then I'm going to wake the others and gather them here for prayer. I don't think any of us will be getting much sleep tonight."

5

ELIZABETH HELD REBECCA'S HAND while the members of the household staff who had assembled in the dining room prayed and sang hymns with them. Peter had stayed in his room, saying he was not feeling well. Naomi had come downstairs briefly, asking, "How am I supposed to sleep with all this racket? What on earth is going on?" When she discovered it was a prayer meeting, she had retreated hastily to her room, muttering that if God didn't hear their pitiful pleas, the neighbors undoubtedly would.

Her heart aching for her wayward daughter, Elizabeth asked the group to pray for Naomi as well as for the safety of Abraham, Jacob, and John. They prayed for divine protection, and they prayed for strength and courage. Throughout the long night they travailed in prayer, sometimes groaning, sometimes singing in the Spirit. Toward dawn a sweet peace settled over the dozen saints who had petitioned heaven so earnestly.

Elizabeth was still concerned about her missing husband and son, but she felt as if a heavy stone had been lifted from her heart. "I don't know why," she said, "but I keep thinking of a passage of Scripture. One we sometimes sing as a hymn. It's from the book of Job, I believe." She began to sing softly, and the others joined her:

> *I know that my Redeemer lives,*
> *And He shall stand at last on the earth;*
> *And after my skin is destroyed, this I know,*
> *That in my flesh I shall see God.*

"That is the source of our strength," Servius said when the last note of the song had echoed off the marble walls. "Our living Redeemer."

"Amen," said several of the worshipers.

"I was also thinking of a Scripture passage." Servius's face lit up. "One that makes me smile."

"Which one is that?" Elizabeth reached over and squeezed his hand fondly.

"The one in Luke's second book, where an angel led Peter out of prison. He went to the house where his fellow disciples were praying, and when he knocked on the door, the maid—"

"Rhoda!" Rebecca said. "I remember her name."

"Yes, Rhoda. She was so excited to learn that it was Peter at the door, she ran to tell everyone about his miraculous escape—and forgot to let Peter inside." Servius chuckled briefly and then became sober. "Perhaps we will hear a knock on the door even at this hour, and it will be our master, or young Jacob and the Apostle."

Moisture brightened Elizabeth's eyes. "Let it be so," she murmured. "Let it be so."

Elizabeth watched her daughter's head drop almost to her chest, then pop back up. "It must be almost daylight by now," Elizabeth said as she stood up from the sofa where she'd sat next to Rebecca for most of the night.

One of the women rose stiffly from the floor. "Ma'am, would you like me to prepare a light meal?" she asked.

"Yes, but just bread and oil with some fruit or cheese. And serve everyone here. We'll make room at the table."

One of the kitchen helpers left with the cook, and a moment later Elizabeth heard a knock at the door. But it was not the knock they had hoped for. It was a thunderous pounding, accompanied by shouts of "Open up!"

One of the servants, a young girl, shrieked in terror and someone clamped a hand over her mouth.

The dining room opened onto the atrium, directly across the

courtyard from the main door of the villa. The shouting was so loud that every word could be heard clearly by those inside.

"In the name of Lord Domitian, Emperor of Rome, open this door or we will break it down!"

No one moved. Rebecca clung to her mother, and several of the servants began to pray out loud. The pounding stopped suddenly but was followed by a mighty cracking sound as the solid wooden door splintered and crashed to the ground.

Elizabeth stepped from the dining room into the atrium, Rebecca and Servius close behind her. "We're in here," she said firmly. "And I will thank you not to trample my house the way you've just ruined that door."

Her calm dignity momentarily halted the soldiers streaming through the broken entry. A centurion came to the front of the marauders.

"You are holding illegal meetings here," he said to Elizabeth. "We have orders to remove everyone from the house and take you before the authorities to answer charges."

Several soldiers had already routed the others out of the dining room, using their long spears to prod the terrified group into the atrium. "Search the rest of the house," the centurion ordered his troops. A half-dozen soldiers went up the staircase and another group scattered through the main floor of the villa.

Elizabeth prayed silently and tried not to let her rising fear show on her face. *I know that my Redeemer lives,* she thought over and over as she listened to the heavy thud of boots moving from room to room.

In a few minutes, Naomi's voice drifted down the stairs. "Get your filthy hands off me. I am perfectly capable of walking unassisted." She maintained an imperious tone as she strode into the atrium, clad only in her sleeveless tunic, her long hair cascading down her back. Quickly discerning who was in charge, Naomi walked over to the centurion. "There's been some mistake," she said. "I am not one of *them!*"

The centurion circled Naomi slowly, eyeing her from head to toe. He lifted her thick mane of hair and held it on top of her head for a moment before letting it fall. "I believe I saw this little vixen at the baths yesterday," he said.

"So you did." Naomi smiled seductively. "I told you I was not one of them," she repeated. She appeared serenely poised, but her hands were balled into tight fists.

The soldiers who had searched the downstairs returned with the cook and her helper in tow. "We found these two in the kitchen," one of them reported to their commander. "The rest of the house is empty."

They didn't find Peter! Elizabeth realized with a burst of gratitude that at least one of her family members might be spared the coming ordeal. *He must have hidden in the library,* she thought.

"Let's go," the centurion ordered. "Commander Damian will be waiting at the temple."

Elizabeth stepped carefully over the shattered door of her home, a Roman spear at her back. The centurion had said his orders were to take them to "the authorities." Now he had clarified that he was taking them to Damian.

The calm she had felt earlier evaporated, and Elizabeth's cheeks went numb with fear. *Abraham, where are you?* she wondered desperately. *What's going to happen to us?*

෩

After his night in a cold dark prison cell, Abraham savored the sunshine, but his gratitude for its warmth was tempered by the cruelty of his captors. The centurion and four legionnaires who had arrested him returned early that morning. Now they marched him up the steep Marble Street, repeatedly shoving and poking him with the shafts of their spears. His back and ribs were bruised and burning by the time they reached the Temple of Domitian.

A crowd of spectators, both soldiers and civilians, surrounded the immense stone altar. Abraham looked up at the statue of Domitian with loathing. The monstrosity was more than twenty feet tall, a sculptor's testament to the emperor's enormous ego.

The noise of the crowd increased, and Abraham's attention was riveted on several dozen soldiers propelling a group of people toward him. *Elizabeth!* He spied his wife at the front of the prisoners, and cringed to see the spears pointed at her. Anxiously searching the throng, he found Rebecca and Servius and what appeared to be most of his household staff. And Naomi, looking as furious as she did fearful.

The sound of hoofbeats tore Abraham's gaze away from his family. A white stallion whinnied and reared on its hind legs as the rider reined it in beside the statue. The officer dismounted in a fluid motion and stood with his hands on his hips as the carriage that had accompanied his dramatic entrance stopped and disgorged its passengers.

Abraham's heart stopped as a soldier yanked the apostle John out of the carriage, followed by Jacob. His son's right eye was black and his face had been scratched as if he had fallen on the gravel. He had not surrendered without a fight, Abraham guessed.

The officer who had ridden in on the white horse turned and strode toward Abraham. The scrawny legs and bony knees would have been laughable, Abraham thought, if they had not belonged to the most menacing face he had ever seen. He instantly recognized the sinister, hate-filled eyes of Damian. A surge of anger rose up in Abraham, and he clenched his fists.

"I'm sure you'd like to have a little family reunion," Damian said sarcastically, "but we have official business to conduct, Abraham. It's time to find out just how committed you are to this contemptible faith you profess." His piercing black eyes never left Abraham's as he extended a hand toward the centurion standing nearby and snapped his fingers.

"Bring the incense," Damian growled.

With a start Abraham realized that *he* was about to be required to make the mandatory sacrifice to the emperor. He had worried so long about the consequences of his son being forced to sacrifice, knowing Jacob would refuse, had been so concerned about Elizabeth's well-being and his family's safety, that he had spent little time thinking of his own response. Now the moment of reckoning had been thrust upon him, and Abraham knew that his actions in the next few moments would determine the course of his life.

No matter what he did, his life would change irrevocably. If he offered the sacrifice, he would deny the God he loved and served, and face the eternal implication of his betrayal. If he held fast to his Christian beliefs and refused to worship Caesar, Rome would strip him of all his possessions and either execute him or send him into exile. Knowing Damian's deep animosity toward him, Abraham guessed that his refusal to sacrifice could result only in a death sentence.

He listened to the shouted commands of the legionnaires, the indistinct murmuring of the crowd, and the sound of feminine weeping. The scene was eerily familiar: armies using weapons to force political and religious beliefs on people who wanted only to live in peace, not be compelled to take sides.

For an instant Abraham let his gaze wander from Damian's. He had heard Rebecca crying and now saw Elizabeth cradling Rebecca's head against her shoulder. His wife's eyes were clear, and it occurred to Abraham that over the last few weeks she had emptied her reservoir of tears in anticipation of this moment. Now Elizabeth stood straight, facing her ordeal dry-eyed, and Abraham was proud of her resolve.

The requested bowl of incense in his hand, Damian took a step toward Abraham. "Perhaps you recognize the design," he said, holding the gold container aloft in admiration. "A souvenir from the miserable time I was stationed in Jerusalem."

Abraham looked at the small bowl, beautifully engraved with a pattern of figs, a motif synonymous with the nation of Israel. *How like Damian,* he thought, *to have kept plundered treasure for his personal benefit, and to savor its use for this sacrilege.*

A scene of looting flashed across Abraham's mind—Roman soldiers scrambling over the bodies of revolutionaries to gather the spoils of war while noncombatants, like himself, fled for their lives. But it was a simple response of nature, caused by not eating for more than twenty-four hours, that sent Abraham on a brief but intensely powerful emotional journey. When his stomach rumbled, it all came back to him . . .

6

ABRAHAM HAD ARRIVED IN JERUSALEM in the spring of his twenty-fifth year. His father had suggested the trip as a way of distracting Abraham from his newfound spirituality. "You should rediscover your Jewish roots," his father had said. "Walk where Abraham, Isaac, and Jacob walked. Celebrate the Passover at the temple of Solomon."

Disenchanted with the practice of law, Abraham had embraced the idea enthusiastically. He had always wanted to make the pilgrimage to Jerusalem, but his motives now were vastly different from his father's: Abraham wanted to walk where Jesus of Nazareth had walked and to worship in the birthplace of Christianity.

In the last few years he had defended several Christians in civil lawsuits brought by vindictive Romans. The Christians had become easy prey after Nero's spate of persecution following the burning of Rome. The emperor had made the "atheists" his scapegoat for the catastrophe—which, it was rumored, he had instigated in order to initiate a grand scheme to rebuild his palace and the heart of the city. Many followers of Christ were burned alive, some as torches to light Nero's estate; others faced martyrdom in the arena with wild animals. The savage persecution gradually dwindled, and four years after the fire, Nero committed suicide in the face of rebellion and public condemnation. The stigma against the Christians, however, survived, and they remained targets of harassment.

Abraham had found the Christian believers—most of whom were Jewish, as he was—to be peaceful, gracious, and kind. In short, they were upstanding citizens who had been unfairly maligned.

Over the months he had engaged many of them in lengthy spiritual discussions, eventually recognizing for himself that Jesus of Nazareth was, indeed, the Christ, the Son of God and Savior of mankind.

So Abraham traveled to his ancestral homeland, the origin of so much Jewish and Christian history, arriving just before Passover, and just about the time General Titus and four legions of battle-tested Roman soldiers encamped around the city.

Before his trip Abraham had been aware of the ongoing conflict in the area. Jewish nationalists had rebelled against Rome four years earlier and Rome had been trying to smash the revolt ever since. But when Nero had died two years after the outbreak of hostilities, Rome was forced to turn its attention to the ensuing civil war at home. Once Vespasian, who had commanded the forces in Palestine, successfully claimed the throne, he sent his son Titus back to Jerusalem to put an end to the rebellion once and for all. Rome knew how to be brutal.

When Abraham arrived the greater threat, at least initially, was inside the city walls: the rebel groups were deeply divided and battling for control of the Temple Mount. Ordinary citizens were often caught in the cross fire of the opposing factions.

Six weeks after his arrival, Abraham came face-to-face with not only the brutality of war but the dehumanizing despair of deprivation. For the first time in his life, he knew what it was to be truly hungry.

෨ᢞᠥ

"We have no food again. Nothing." In the early morning light Rivka's face appeared more haggard than usual, and she looked worriedly at the young child balanced on her hip. "I've been very careful with our supplies, Tobias . . ." Rivka's words dwindled to a frightened whisper.

"I know you have. It's not your fault." Tobias touched her arm reassuringly and Abraham's heart went out to the couple. He'd grown very fond of them in the few weeks he had stayed in their beautiful home in the Upper City.

Tobias was the son of a distant relative, one his father had encouraged him to look up when he arrived in Jerusalem. Of course, his father had not known that Abner was no longer alive or that Abner's son had become a Christian. Abraham relished the irony of finding that his father, who had intended for Abraham to renew his Jewish faith, had instead placed him in the home of a kinsman who shared his new faith in Christ.

"We should have left with the others," Rivka lamented. "But the baby . . . I was scared."

"You must stop blaming yourself," Tobias said. "Staying here, in our home, was the right thing for us."

Tobias had already told Abraham how most of the Christians in Jerusalem had relocated to Pella, a city in the province of Perea, east of the Jordan River. They had believed the anticipated Roman siege was the beginning of the troubles prophesied by Jesus, and that the city of Jerusalem would be destroyed. But when their friends departed, Rivka had been pregnant, and having a difficult time, so she and Tobias had stayed. And after the birth of their son, Joel, they had still been hesitant to travel because the child was sickly.

"Besides," Tobias added, "if we had left with the others, we would not have been here to welcome Abraham. Just think what we would have missed then."

"I'm glad we didn't miss that," Rivka said, smiling at last. "You've been a dear friend and brother to us."

What they would have missed, Abraham thought, *is another mouth to feed.* A burden no one in Jerusalem, overcrowded by the influx of pilgrims for Passover—pilgrims who were now stranded in the city—had needed. But his cousins, as he referred to them, had not seemed to mind at all. In fact, they had been bolstered by his arrival, and the bond of fellowship with them had become quite close-knit in a matter of days.

"Abraham, it's time for another adventure," Tobias announced, trying to keep a light tone. "Let's go shopping for food."

"We're getting quite good at this, you know," Abraham told Rivka, striving to match Tobias's feigned optimism. It was a charade both men adopted for her sake; they couldn't bear to tell her the truth about the increasingly desperate conditions in the city.

"Abraham's a born trader. You should see him drive a bargain." Tobias smiled and clapped Abraham on the shoulder as they told Rivka good-bye. "Stay inside," he warned his wife unnecessarily. "We'll be back as soon as we can."

The instant the two men stepped outside, the smiles faded. Tobias placed the palm of his hand against the closed door. "Keep them safe, Lord," he said softly.

"And grant us the favor of Your provision," Abraham added.

They left the spacious homes of the wealthy in the Upper City and made their way through the labyrinth of cobblestone streets and crowded houses of the Lower City. Several days earlier the Roman troops had breached the outer walls of Jerusalem and occupied the northern suburbs, shutting off access to most of the commercial area. Shops in the older part of the city had closed as well, their supplies confiscated by the revolutionary forces brutalizing the city from within.

Acquiring a few morsels of food had become a dangerous enterprise. Recently, when their pantry had been completely exhausted, Tobias and Abraham had purchased grain from their neighbors, paying exorbitant prices for a loaf of bread or a measure of grain. After a few days it had become impossible to find anyone with food to sell.

"Should we head for the old aqueduct?" Abraham asked. "It could be very risky, trying to sneak outside the city."

"Yes, but I think it's time to try it. We're not going to find anything here," Tobias said, studying the surroundings carefully as they walked. "And it's every bit as dangerous inside the walls."

"The stench is worse today too." Abraham wrinkled his nose and frowned. The smell of death permeated the air even more than usual.

"I would gladly risk danger for a few deep breaths of fresh air outside these walls—"

Abraham tripped and stumbled, and Tobias reached out a hand to steady him. When he looked down at the street to see what had impeded his progress, Abraham nearly retched at the sight. He had lost his footing on the body of an old man. Strands of gray hair flowed over the bloated face, streaked with blood and crusted with flies. Far worse than the frightened stare of his lifeless eyes, however, were the tangled remains of the lower half of his body: the man had been disemboweled. Abraham had not believed the rumors that the revolutionaries committed such atrocities on those they suspected of swallowing gold or jewels to preserve their riches from theft as they tried to flee the city. But now he knew it was true. The cutthroat armies of the Jewish revolution robbed, killed, or tortured their own people for food or valuables and left the bodies in the streets as a warning.

Shaken by the discovery, the two men walked silently toward the edge of the city. Abraham tried to pay close attention to their route so he could find his way home in the event they got separated. Tobias had spent a lifetime navigating the twisting streets and alleys, but Abraham found the layout confusing.

On one of their recent outings, Abraham and Tobias had come across a portion of an ancient aqueduct no longer in use. They had carefully explored it, discovering that it led under the city wall a short distance at the city's eastern edge, opening to a spot just south of where the Tenth Legion was camped on the Mount of Olives. An overgrowth of brush disguised the opening, and if they were careful, they could slip in and out without notice. They had discussed using it as a tunnel to get outside the city walls, where they could gather herbs or grasses on the hillside.

Today, they decided, it was time to implement their plan. "Perhaps we should split up," Tobias said as they approached the entrance. "I'll go through the aqueduct and see what I can find outside. You stay here and look."

"No, if we part company, I should be the one to go." Abraham picked his way over the rubble and followed Tobias underground. He had to stoop a bit as they walked through the tunnel but Tobias, who was short and wiry, stood at full height as he led the way.

"It's more dangerous for you than for me," Abraham continued. "I'm a Roman citizen who got trapped in the city, and Titus has promised us safe passage. So if I'm captured, I would have to return home, which means I couldn't stay to help you and Rivka, but I wouldn't be killed."

He left unspoken his fear that Tobias, if captured, would be crucified in the daily display of terror the Romans conducted for the Zealots' benefit. Jews caught outside the city were offered a chance to defect; if they refused—which most of them did, fearing what would happen to their families in their absence—they were deemed to be revolutionaries and executed by crucifixion. Dozens met a similar fate every day, and Abraham had watched the rebels drag the families of those being crucified to the top of the city walls to watch the spectacle below. "This is what happens to traitors," the Zealots warned the terrified citizens. It was an effective recruiting tool; some joined the revolutionaries willingly after that, but a few jumped over the walls and took their chances with the Romans.

Reaching the spot where the aqueduct emptied out under the wall, Abraham and Tobias stood and looked through the overgrowth to the outside. Dismayed by what they saw, neither one spoke for a long time.

"It's too late now," Tobias finally said. "We should have done this last week."

"We weren't as desperate last week. We still had corn to eat." Abraham gazed forlornly at the bare hillside. The Romans had cleared several acres when they built their camp; now they had deforested the entire area. Every tree had been cut down, and the grass was completely trampled. There was nothing left to forage.

"This must be where the timber came from to build the new siege towers."

Abraham had seen the movable wooden structures Tobias referred to. The siege towers were immense, seventy-five feet tall, and allowed the Roman archers to shoot at the rebels defending the walls at close range.

"I don't know how much longer the city can hold out," Tobias said sadly.

"The longer it holds out, the more innocent people will die, and the more vengeful the Romans will be when they finally do take it. The rebels have no realistic hope of defeating the Roman legions; they never did."

"No, but they will not give up one square inch of the territory they hold—not until the last one of them is dead. And for what purpose? Most of us were content living under Roman rule. It wasn't always pleasant but it was not usually oppressive. For the most part we paid our taxes and lived in peace."

"If the war continues at this rate," Abraham said, "no one will be left alive to enjoy the peace that follows—whichever side eventually prevails." He supposed a miracle was possible, but the rebel factions were vastly outnumbered, poorly organized, and prone to fighting among themselves.

"I guess we wouldn't have gotten far outside the wall today, anyway," Tobias said. "See how closely the camp is guarded." He pointed toward the tents of the Tenth Legion, a few hundred yards in the distance. A Roman sentry was posted about every ten feet around the southern perimeter, the part of the camp visible from their vantage point.

"We'd better head back." Abraham put a hand on Tobias's shoulder and urged him to turn around.

Tobias did not move. "They're well fed, the soldiers. The perimeter is guarded, but if we could just slip past the sentries, the camp would be virtually empty." He spoke as if picturing every step of an imaginary assault on the camp. "We could find the mess tent easily enough. It's probably that large one about a third of the way in. They would never miss whatever we could carry out—"

"You can't be serious! There is no way we could make it through all those guards undetected."

"I have a wife and child who are going to die soon if I don't bring them something to eat." Tobias had a wild look in his eyes that alarmed Abraham. "And there is food in that camp."

"Tobias—"

"I know," he said bitterly. "There's no way to get to it." He turned and sighed. "We'd be killed, and then my family would starve for certain."

"Perhaps we can find another abandoned house with a bit of food hidden away," Abraham said. "That's how God blessed us with the corn."

They walked the short distance back through the aqueduct and Abraham gave Tobias a hand as they climbed out over the dirt and rubble to the street. As soon as they got their footing on level ground, a group of Zealots rounded the corner and headed their way.

"Have you been outside the walls?" one of them demanded.

"See if they have food," commanded another.

Abraham and Tobias exchanged a brief glance, wondering what to do. The two were unarmed and they had no food, but that didn't mean the half-dozen ragtag soldiers would let them go.

"Run for it," Tobias urged.

Abraham tore down the street as fast as his legs would carry him, with Tobias pounding the pavement right behind him. The Zealots were in hot pursuit, daggers drawn, shouting, "Stop! Traitors!"

His leg muscles burning with the uncommon exertion, Abraham turned onto a street he recognized and jerked his head backward, still running at full speed. The soldiers were gaining on them.

"Left!" Tobias shouted, his arms flailing wildly as his short legs tried to match Abraham's frantic pace.

Abraham turned left into the alley Tobias had indicated, and a few yards ahead he saw a street. He couldn't consult Tobias about their route, so he darted in that direction. The footsteps behind him were not quite as thunderous, and Abraham thought that he and Tobias might be able to outrun the rebels. Instinctively, he darted into first one alley and then another one, his feet seeming to know where to carry him.

He concentrated so hard on finding landmarks that it took him a few moments to notice the footsteps had not followed him after his last turn. Slowing enough to brave a glance backward, he discovered he was alone on the street. *Tobias! What happened to Tobias? He was right behind me.*

Abraham heard shouts and the sound of running from the next street over, so he changed direction and followed the noise. But the narrow streets and alleys were like a maze, and no matter how hard he tried or how fast he ran, he could not manage to find Tobias and his pursuers. After a few minutes he could no longer hear them at all, and he slumped against a stone wall, his heart pounding and his chest heaving like a blacksmith's bellows. Sweat dripped off his face and stained his clothes.

Perhaps Tobias eluded them, he thought. Tobias knew the Lower City well and might have spotted a hiding place, a narrow passageway he could squeeze into while the soldiers ran past him, unaware. Or perhaps he was talking his way out of the situation this very moment, if they had caught up with him. Tobias was stubborn and feisty and quite persuasive.

He was being optimistic, he knew, but Abraham did not want to consider the other possibilities. After catching his breath, he began to try to find his way home. For more than an hour Abraham wandered, turning down one blind alley after another and then backtracking. He never fully recognized where he was, but he finally reached a street he knew would take him back to the Upper City.

Walking into the late afternoon sun, he shielded his eyes with his hand, and as he climbed the hill, he prayed he would find Tobias at home with Rivka, entertaining her with a highly colorful but carefully edited version of their adventure.

Tobias was not at home, however.

"I got lost," Abraham told Rivka. "I guess I wasn't paying enough attention and I, uh, got separated from Tobias. It took me a long time to find my way back." That much was true, but he left out the part about being chased by a pack of Zealots at the time they'd been separated.

Rivka's eyes widened in fear. "But Tobias wouldn't get lost, so why isn't he here by now?"

"Perhaps he's still searching for food." Abraham averted his head to avoid looking at Rivka as he spoke. "We hadn't found anything yet when I got lost," he explained.

The baby cried weakly in her arms, and Rivka tried to soothe him with a soft "Shhh, shhh, shhh."

They sat in the courtyard until nightfall settled around them like a close dark shroud. Rivka tried to comfort her hungry infant as she watched the door anxiously, while Abraham prayed silently and tried valiantly to console her.

His mind explored dozens of possible scenarios, trying not to think about the brutally murdered man in the streets and trying not to imagine what the soldiers might have done to Tobias when they caught him. The one thing he was sure of was that Tobias had not outrun them; if he had, he would certainly have made it home.

He would start searching for Tobias at dawn, Abraham decided.

7

THE NEXT MORNING ABRAHAM RETURNED to the Lower City and attempted to retrace his steps, searching for any sign of Tobias. He had not slept well, tossing and turning all night. Once, when he had dozed off for a few minutes, he dreamed of tripping over Tobias's mutilated body in the street. He woke up vowing he would not let that happen to his cousin. If Tobias had been killed, he would find his body and give him a proper burial.

Abraham combed the streets but did not find a body. He looked up and down the alleys for a fresh bloodstain, a lone sandal, a torn bit of cloth—he remembered Tobias had been wearing a faded blue tunic—but he found no clues, no evidence that Tobias might have been beaten or killed. He went all the way back to the opening of the aqueduct, finding the place where he'd last seen his cousin racing behind him. But there was no sign of what had happened to Tobias.

Of course, the revolutionaries could have killed him and dumped his body in a deserted building. But Abraham focused on another alternative: perhaps Tobias had been forced to join the revolutionaries to fight for the city. He would never have joined their army willingly, but if captured, Abraham thought, Tobias would do it to spare his life, in the hopes he could eventually escape and be reunited with Rivka and Joel. Abraham gradually accepted the fact that he might never know what had happened to Tobias, but he chose to believe his cousin was still alive, and that's the scenario he painted for Rivka when he returned that evening.

Over the next few days he scoured the city for food. The most successful strategy, he had discovered, was to look for abandoned houses that appeared to have been ransacked. He would sneak inside to see if the thieves, most likely the rebel forces, had left anything behind in their haste. No morsel of bread was too moldy for him; he treasured every crumb. Occasionally he found a few kernels of wheat. Even if they'd been crushed, he gathered them to take to Rivka and the baby, who were both slowly starving.

One day he mistakenly entered a home that was still occupied, and the owner, near death, protested feebly and incoherently. Abraham mumbled that he had the wrong house and scrambled back into the street, cringing at the realization that he had stooped to burglary. But he was not a common thief, he told himself; he would not steal food from anyone living.

The dead were another matter. He entered another house where bodies had been stacked against the walls like firewood. Desperate, he held one hand over his nose to stifle the odor while he searched the makeshift mausoleum. He was rewarded for his efforts with a handful of barley.

Every day he brought his collection back to Rivka, offering the meager provisions to her and the baby. She always insisted he take a few bites for himself.

"What will happen to us if you starve to death?" she asked. "You must eat something too, Abraham."

Little Joel's cries were growing weaker and more infrequent, and Abraham realized that Rivka was no longer able to nurse her baby. Her milk had failed as her body struggled to sustain itself, and she tried to keep Joel alive on water and tiny spoonfuls of gruel she made from a few grains of boiled wheat. The child was frightfully thin, yet his stomach was swollen and distended.

Rivka's once-beautiful olive skin was now sallow and stretched taut over hollow cheeks, and her dark eyes appeared sunken and list-less. She became animated only when talking about what life had been like before the war, which she and Abraham sometimes did to keep their minds from dwelling on their desperation. She brought Jerusalem to life for him—Jerusalem the way it had been in its glory, not the war- and famine-ravaged city he experienced every day. They also talked of their spiritual journeys, and how they had each come to believe in Jesus of Nazareth.

Every evening, even in the midst of starvation, they gave thanks for their few bites of food—if they had any. They prayed for Tobias and for their deliverance from the iron yoke of the Roman Empire. Abraham often wondered if God heard their prayers or if He had turned a deaf ear to the Holy City and all its inhabitants.

On one of the nights they'd had nothing to eat, Abraham couldn't sleep. His stomach twisted in pain, and his legs cramped. He was walking farther each day with fewer results, and it was taking a toll on his body. Weary of lying in bed and willing sleep to come— without success—Abraham got up and went to the courtyard.

It was a clear, mild night, pleasant after yet another endless, fruitless, oppressively hot day. He stretched out on a stone bench, his hands clasped behind his head, and looked up at the canopy of stars. The heavenly bodies twinkled like diamonds against a black velvet canopy. They were untouched by the fighting, the bloodshed, the hunger, and the mind-bending terror.

The words of a psalm came to his mind:

> *When I consider Your heavens, the work of Your fingers,*
> *The moon and the stars, which You have ordained,*
> *What is man that You are mindful of him,*
> *And the son of man that You visit him?*

Are You really mindful of man? Abraham wondered. *Do You even know who I am—where I am right now? Do You hear the cries of a starving infant?*

A slight breeze blew across his face, and it seemed to stir something in his heart. He heard no voice, felt no hand on his shoulder;

nevertheless he sat up suddenly, feeling compelled to follow some unseen presence that beckoned him.

He slipped quietly out of the house and stood on the street in front of the main door. The full moon cast a pale light on the cobblestones, and the eerie stillness of midnight welcomed him. *Which way?* he wondered, and instantly he knew. He walked about a hundred feet and when he came to a cross street, he again knew which way to turn. At the next intersection he paused, and a bony hand reached out and clutched his arm.

"What—?" Abraham sputtered and spun around, startled by the sudden appearance of an elderly servant woman on the street.

She said nothing, but her steel-gray eyes urged him to follow. She took a few steps and then turned and looked back at him, silently entreating him. For reasons he could not have explained, Abraham felt no threat from her, so he followed.

The frail, stooped woman led him into an alley and then opened a door into the courtyard of a sizable home. Leaves skittered across the tiled floor as they walked toward a stairway. She paused at a table by the doorway and motioned for Abraham to pick up a small lamp that was burning there. He looked at the clay saucer for a moment and wondered if he was dreaming. Rivka had quit lighting the lamps months ago, to extend their supply of olive oil. He passed his hand over the wick and felt the warmth of the flame. This was no dream.

Abraham followed the woman down the stairs into the cellar. The home had been plundered, and they had to step over broken shards of pottery scattered all over the floor. He spied some trampled kernels of wheat and instinctively bent to pick them up, but she stopped him, taking his arm and leading him to the corner. Smiling, she pointed to several items the looters had missed: two clay jars filled with olive oil, a small sack of flour, and a plentiful supply of unground wheat. Actually, it was no more than a wealthy family would consume in a day or two, but it was more grain than Abraham had seen in one place in many weeks.

Excited, he turned to start asking the questions tumbling through his head: How had she found this place? Did she live here? Work here? Why did she want to share this bounty with him?

The old woman was gone.

He held the lamp high and searched the shadows of the dark cellar. Her shawl was on the floor beside him, right where she had stood, but the woman was no longer there.

Using the discarded shawl as a knapsack, he bundled up the wheat and the flour. Then he tucked the jars of olive oil under his arm, picked up the lamp, and walked noisily over the debris and up the stairs. He glanced around the courtyard, but the woman was not there, either. The door to the alley was ajar. Had they closed it when they entered? He couldn't remember.

For a moment Abraham thought about searching the rest of the house, but he somehow knew he would not find her. He was not even sure now whether the woman had been real or an apparition. But the supplies he was carrying were real, and he rejoiced over them.

There was no need for the lamp in the bright moonlight, so he blew it out. But he took it with him as he left the house; the oil it still held was valuable.

Humbled and heartened, Abraham was near tears as he traveled the few blocks back to Rivka's house. *What is man that You are mindful of him?* he quoted silently. *And the son of man that You visit him?*

The stars shone brilliantly in the heavens as the truth sank into Abraham's consciousness: he had been visited. God knew who he was, and where he was. And He had heard their prayers.

❧

Rivka rationed the olive oil, using a small amount to make griddle cakes with the flour. Every day she swallowed a spoonful of the oil and fed Joel as much as he would take. She crushed the wheat and boiled it into porridge. Abraham ate a daily portion of the porridge, but he would not touch the olive oil; in his mind, the oil was for Rivka. He remembered the widow of Zarephath, whose one jar of oil miraculously was not depleted during a long drought because she had fed the prophet Elijah, and he prayed God would do the same for Rivka.

Eventually, however, the oil ran out, and their spirits with it. The baby no longer cried, and Rivka became lethargic, sitting for hours on end with Joel pressed to her chest, her mouth forming words but making no sound. Abraham thought she was praying, but when he spoke to her, she looked at him blankly and did not answer his questions.

One day toward the end of July, Abraham left the house to wander the city, half-dazed. For the last few days he'd had only a few kernels of wheat. He ate them raw because they seemed to last longer. They were crunchy—like seeds or nuts, he told himself.

The specter of starvation hung over the city; he saw it everywhere he looked. Gaunt men gnawed shoe leather in their hunger; others made a meal of straw. When he saw a woman digging in the dust of the street for a crumb, Abraham's first impulse was to pity her and his second was to fight her for it. It was a fleeting thought and he resisted it, but he was no longer amazed that such desperation occurred to him.

He walked the streets aimlessly and finally grasped the fact that he had meandered too close to the fighting when he found himself stepping over a body in the street. A large stone whistled by his head, then another. They came from a Roman catapult. The Temple Mount, straight ahead of him, seemed to be where the battle was raging. *The rebels are making their last stand,* he realized, *fighting for their holiest shrine.*

Preoccupied, Abraham did not hear the sounds of an approaching party of revolutionaries until it was almost too late. He ducked into a narrow crevice between two stone buildings. It was a tiny space in the tightly packed quarter of the city, a space he could never have squeezed into when he first arrived in Jerusalem. *If I lose any more weight,* he thought with an untimely touch of amusement, *maybe I'll become completely invisible.*

He had definitely not achieved invisibility yet. One of the soldiers had seen him and now reached into his hiding place and grabbed a handful of Abraham's tunic, bringing his face halfway out of the shadows.

Tobias! Abraham's mouth fell open, but he caught himself before he spoke the name aloud.

"Rivka? The baby?" Tobias asked in a hoarse, anguished whisper. His eyelids were purple and heavy, and his face was lined with exhaustion.

"Alive, but barely."

"What have you found?" one of the soldiers shouted in their direction.

"Nothing!" Tobias shoved Abraham roughly against the stone wall. "This one has no food, and he's too weak to fight."

Abraham crumpled to the ground. Blood trickled down his face from a gash in his scalp. He looked up at Tobias and nodded almost imperceptibly when he saw the unspoken apology in his cousin's eyes.

"Then let's go!" another soldier called, anxious to move on.

Tobias knelt over Abraham and reached for his belt, pretending to search for a wallet. "I'll never make it out of this alive," Tobias murmured. "Save them . . . if you can."

Abraham saw the silent pleading in Tobias's eyes, which filled with tears at the reference to his family.

"And if you can't," he added, "then save yourself." His voice choked with emotion, he stammered, "F-f-find a way out."

"Tobias, what are you doing?" The soldier's voice was angry, and a scowl twisted his face.

"I thought he might be carrying money."

"And what would there be to spend it on?" the other man asked bitterly.

"Freedom," Tobias whispered, giving Abraham a final look that held the significance of a shared understanding. "God be with you, Abraham."

"And with you," Abraham replied softly. There was so much he wanted to say that his heart ached more than his head, and as Tobias turned and left, Abraham knew with a certainty that it would be the last time he ever saw his cousin. He also knew that Tobias had spoken the truth: he would never survive the final battle for the heart and soul of Jerusalem; Tobias would die a reluctant martyr to the cause.

Abraham remained motionless on the ground as the soldiers departed. He watched them step over several bodies heaped in the street, casualties who'd been allowed to die where they lay. When the group was finally out of sight, he sat up and touched his head gingerly. The wound was not deep and the bleeding had stopped. A large lump was rising and he had a raging headache, but he would be fine. He bore no ill will toward Tobias for the injury, for he knew it was an impulsive attempt to spare Abraham the same fate Tobias had met. And it had worked.

Light-headed but heavyhearted, Abraham made his way slowly through the deserted streets back to the house, debating whether to tell Rivka. Would the news that Tobias was alive renew her strength and revive her will to live? Or would it only throw her deeper into despair, knowing his chance of living through the final battle was virtually nonexistent?

His internal debate turned out to be an exercise in futility. When he reached the house, he found Rivka sitting against the wall, her eyes closed, her breathing shallow. She still held the baby clutched tightly to her chest, but Abraham perceived instantly that something was drastically wrong.

He knelt down beside Rivka and reached over to touch Joel, stroking the baby's cheek lightly with the back of his index finger. The child was cold and clammy and unresponsive. Abraham gently closed the lifeless eyes, which had been fixed on his mother's face. One pitifully small hand held on to Rivka's sleeve, and Abraham carefully pried the tiny fingers loose. Judging from the stiffness, Abraham surmised that Joel must have been dead for several hours.

Abraham started to lift the child, but the motion roused Rivka and she opened her eyes. *No.* Her mouth formed the word silently.

"Rivka . . ." He didn't know what to say. Did she not know the child was dead? Could she not comprehend what had happened or could she just not accept it?

Rivka's arms moved from side to side ever so slightly, and a faint sound escaped her lips. Abraham leaned closer, his face only inches from hers, and listened. She was trying to hum.

He lost his composure then. He sat back and leaned against the wall beside her, letting the tears fall down his dust-streaked face. *Why?* he silently asked God over and over, begging for an answer to his unanswerable question.

After a few minutes, he noticed that Rivka had fallen asleep again. He took the baby from her arms and carried him into the bedroom. Rummaging through a storage chest, Abraham found several yards of linen fabric and tore off a long strip to use as a shroud. He wound it tightly around Joel's tiny body and then wrapped the cloth over the baby's old-man face, the visible hallmark of starvation. Abraham emptied another small chest and laid the baby inside. There was no place to bury him, and Abraham didn't know what to do next. He finally decided to place the chest in the *mikvah*, the small bath used for ritual cleansing in the wealthier Jewish homes.

Rivka nodded her approval later when Abraham told her what he'd done. "Thank you," she said weakly. "For everything."

He held a cup to Rivka's lips and gave her small sips of water. That evening he crushed the last few kernels of wheat and tried to feed them to her, but she could no longer swallow.

For the next two days Abraham never left Rivka's side, watching helplessly as her life ebbed away minute by painfully slow minute. When it was finally over, he wrapped her body with the

rest of the linen and laid her in the *mikvah*, next to the chest where
he had placed Joel's body. Then he broke down and sobbed like a
baby.

He kept thinking of Tobias's words: "Save them, if you can."

I tried, Tobias. God knows I tried to save them.

At last, when he was able to speak, Abraham said the *kaddish*,
the traditional prayer of mourning for the dead. He had not witnessed a funeral since he had become a Christian; therefore he did
not know what the proper burial custom for a believer should be. So
after the *kaddish* he added an extemporaneous prayer for Rivka and
Joel, asking the Lord to raise them up on the last day.

☙

Freedom. Abraham could still see the look in his cousin's eyes. *That's
what Tobias said he would do with money.*

Abraham understood Tobias's meaning: take the money and
leave. "Find a way out," Tobias had told him. Abraham wondered if
there could possibly be a way out of the city now.

Months earlier the two of them had talked about trying to leave
Jerusalem, had even planned what they would do. "We could sail to
Ephesus," Tobias had suggested.

"Why Ephesus?" Abraham asked. He knew it was a large, important city—the third leading city in the Empire—but he had no idea
why it would appeal to Tobias.

"There's a thriving Christian community there, headed by the
apostle John. He's the last living member of the Twelve, you know.
It was one of John's disciples who led us to Christ several years ago."
Tobias had recounted for Abraham his and Rivka's conversion, and
they had talked at length about John and the church at Ephesus.

"I have plenty of money for the trip," Tobias had informed him.
He had taken Abraham to a small room and revealed the place where
he had hidden a small fortune in gold coins. Tobias's usually cheer-
ful demeanor turned completely serious. "If anything happens to me

before we can leave," he said, "I want you to use this to take Rivka and the baby to safety."

Something *had* happened to Tobias before they could leave, but by that time access in and out of the city had been completely closed. When the siege had started in earnest, just prior to Tobias's capture by the revolutionaries, the Romans quickly built their own wall around the city, constructing a five-mile-long fence in just three days and sealing the fate of Jerusalem's inhabitants.

Abraham often wondered why he had stayed in Jerusalem through the war that was about to destroy its very foundations. In the early days he could have left at any time, before the danger of staying behind enemy lines became so great. Even after that, he could have managed to see Titus or perhaps Tiberius Alexander, the general's chief adviser, and convince the authorities of his citizenship and loyalty to Rome. Had he done that, he could be home right now, dining at his father's table, his belly stuffed with the finest food instead of racing rats for a few grains of corn or wheat.

Perhaps that was one of the reasons he had stayed: to spite his father, to rebel against having his entire life planned for him. It had been his father's dream for Abraham to study rhetoric and embark on a law career as a prelude to political advancement. True, he had been gifted at it, and he enjoyed the study of law. The practice of law, however, was a different matter. Cherished ideals, Abraham had discovered, easily bent to corruption and manipulation. The system worked for the wealthy and well-connected but not the plebeian, and Abraham had no desire whatsoever to become embroiled in the hierarchy of political power and intrigue for the rest of his life.

Reluctant to return home and confront his father about the future, he had stayed in Jerusalem in spite of the risks. And once Tobias had been captured, Abraham could not bring himself to leave Rivka and the baby, knowing they would face starvation without someone to care for them. Ultimately, though, they had died in spite of his best efforts, and his failure to save them weighed heavily on him.

Save yourself. Tobias's words echoed in his mind. But how? Could he get out of the city before it fell to the might of Rome? And what would he do if he managed to get beyond the walls?

Instantly he decided he wanted to pursue the course he and Tobias had originally discussed: sailing to Ephesus. It was as good a plan as any. He wanted to meet the last surviving apostle, someone who had actually walked and talked with Jesus of Nazareth. John had known Him personally, intimately, and Abraham wanted to see Jesus through John's eyes.

His plan would mean a daring escape through the impenetrable siege of the Roman legions, then walking all the way to Caesarea, on the Mediterranean coast. The journey would take several days under the best of conditions. With no food in his stomach, and no prospect of a meal for the foreseeable future, he would be too weak to travel that far.

But staying in Jerusalem was certain death, and Abraham was not ready to become another corpse on a Roman cross.

8

HAVING DETERMINED TO ESCAPE FROM JERUSALEM and flee to Ephesus, Abraham retrieved Tobias's money from its hiding place with considerable trepidation.

What if by some miracle Tobias survives the war? He hesitated, then put one of the two bags of coins back in the wall. *But if I leave it here,* he reasoned, *looters will find it, and then what good will it do Tobias?*

Abraham did not ponder long. He took both bags of gold and fastened them securely around his waist, under his tunic. He also took the razor-sharp dagger he found with the money, then he draped his cloak over his shoulder and tied his belt over it. It was far too warm to need the cloak for normal wear, but it helped disguise the bulky treasure of gold under his clothes, and he could wrap himself in the outer garment at night. If—no—*once* he made it outside the city, he would be sleeping on the ground.

It was late afternoon when Abraham was ready to depart. He planned to head for the old aqueduct and explore the area just outside the original stone wall. Perhaps under cover of nightfall he could skirt the southern edge of the city, heading away from the camp of the Tenth Legion. Then he would have to find a way past the wooden wall the Romans had hastily thrown up to surround their enemies, while avoiding the camps of the Twelfth and Fourteenth Legions at the northwest corner of Jerusalem.

Before leaving, he stopped briefly in the *mikvah* and silently paid his last respects to Rivka and Joel, regretting yet again that he'd been unable to save them or to bury them properly. His grief tasted like bile as he swallowed hard and blinked back tears of exhaustion compounded with great loss. He tried to imagine the extent of Tobias's grief, and he wondered if he would ever live long enough to have a wife and child of his own.

Outside, the scorching August sun beat down on Abraham. He quickly realized that the source of the intense heat was not confined to the heavens: the city was on fire! It had not yet spread to the Upper City, but it would, and he prayed he had not waited too late to make his escape. Immediately below him the Lower City blazed in a wall of crimson fury. From a distance he could hear the cries of thousands of people as they fled their homes.

Like a moth drawn to a flame, Abraham turned to stare in the direction of the Temple Mount. The most sacred spot in Jerusalem— the most sacred spot in the world, its inhabitants would argue— burned like a massive torch. He stood transfixed, watching the conflagration for a few minutes. The magnificent structure—the place of worship King David had conceived and his son Solomon had built, that Zerubbabel had rebuilt when the exiles returned from Babylon, that Herod had restored and enlarged to an incomparable scale, the house of prayer that Jesus of Nazareth had purged of its corrupt money changers—had, in one form or another, occupied this piece of holy ground for a thousand years. Now it would soon be gone, an incomprehensible loss.

A stomach cramp broke Abraham's trance and propelled him into action: if he were going to survive the carnage that was bound to accompany the destruction of the city, he had to get moving. He headed for the southern border of the Lower City. That route would take longer for him to reach the aqueduct but would, he hoped, allow him to stay ahead of the rapidly spreading fires.

The streets were in total chaos. People were shoving and clawing their way through the terrified crowds. Smoke stung Abraham's eyes and made him cough as he picked his way through the alleys, keeping track of the position of the sun to make sure he was heading in the right direction. Once or twice he headed down a blind alley and had to backtrack, and once he was pushed hard, fell to the ground, and narrowly missed being trampled to death.

The smoke thinned out as he reached the southern wall of the city, but complete panic ruled the streets. Some people were committing suicide or begging someone else to kill them, so they could escape being sold into slavery or raped by the Romans.

A number of people were trying desperately to scale the massive stone wall with their bare hands. A hopeless endeavor, Abraham knew. If by some miracle a man managed to reach the top, there was no place to go from there. The wall was built on a cliff that dropped steeply into the Hinnom Valley—a precipitous fall that surely no one could survive. If someone ran along the top of the wall in either direction, he would soon come under fire by the Roman troops. The valley was where Abraham wanted to be, but he knew it was impossible to reach by going over the wall; that's why he planned to go underneath it.

Abraham leaned against the nearest building to catch his breath for a moment and to survey the area. From here he would turn east and follow the wall a short way until it curved north, and then, he estimated, he would be a quarter- to a half-mile south of the entrance to the aqueduct. He filled his lungs with air and forced his weary legs, already shaky, to keep going. Most of the people were headed in the opposite direction, and as they streamed around him, a few of them looked at Abraham as if he had lost his mind.

The sun was sinking low in the western sky as he reached the part of the eastern wall where Tobias had found the abandoned water channel. The crowd was not as dense here, but he slowed down and waited, not wanting anyone to follow him into the aqueduct. It would be hard enough escaping notice by himself; he didn't need hangers-on to contend with. A few yards away from his target, he sat down by the wall, hoping to appear too exhausted to go farther; in reality he was closely watching the melee in the streets.

In a few minutes, several looters started arguing over something they had stolen, and a fight broke out. Abraham seized the opportunity afforded by the distraction to scramble down the short embankment and behind the brush and debris covering the entrance.

Once inside the stone tunnel he sat down, both to rest and to make certain he had not been followed. With no cushion left on his bones, Abraham found the bedrock hard and uncomfortable, but the stone was cooler than the streets and afforded shelter from the bedlam aboveground. The shouting from the streets now sounded muffled, and after a few anxious minutes of watching and waiting, he leaned his head back and allowed his eyes to close. Gradually his breathing returned to normal, and he relished the solitude of his hiding place.

Fearing he might doze off if he relaxed too much, Abraham stood to his feet and stretched.

"Ouch," he muttered as he rubbed the top of his head. He had forgotten that the aqueduct would not quite accommodate his full height.

At the end of the tunnel he pushed aside some dead branches and debris and peered into the shadows outside. It seemed a lifetime ago that he had stood here with Tobias, but it had been only a few weeks. *So much has happened in such a short time*, Abraham thought. *So much tragedy. So much death. So much unspeakable heartache.*

He stepped gingerly into the open, having observed no activity from the direction of the Roman camp on the Mount of Olives. Then he turned and craned his neck to look up at the inferno that was Jerusalem. He was approximately a hundred feet below the top of the wall, but he could hear the sound of slaughter emanating from the city above. The cries of the desperate and dying reverberated all the way to the valley. As Abraham had feared, the battle for Jerusalem was culminating in a bloodbath. He supposed he should be grieving or shocked or panic-stricken, but he was none of those. He was simply numb—too exhausted, too hungry, and too disaster-weary to fully appreciate the significance of the events he was witnessing.

At nightfall the armies would be returning to their camps, so he hurriedly began the descent to the valley floor, wincing as the tangled vines and thorny bushes clinging to the rocky hillside scratched his arms and legs. He headed west, skirting the walls of the city in the opposite direction he had just traveled. As he reached the southwest corner of the city and turned north, twilight was deepening the shadows. With dismay Abraham realized he would not be able to make it past the northern suburbs before night blanketed the valley, which meant that he would have to sleep somewhere in the vicinity of the main Roman camp at the northwestern corner of the city. He prayed for a clear, moonlit night so he could travel as far as possible.

Suddenly, when he was below Herod's Tower, he heard shouts and saw combatants burst through an opening in the stone wall where it had been breached during the siege. Abraham threw himself to the ground and crawled on his belly toward cover. The hillside was so bare, there wasn't much left to hide behind, but the shadows were deep, and there was a tangled knot of dried vines that hung from an outcropping of rock. He tried to slide underneath it and prayed the approaching darkness would protect him from notice.

Soon he realized that Roman soldiers had chased a handful of revolutionaries outside the walls.

"Coward! Where is your courage now?" one of them shouted as an unarmed rebel begged for his life, babbling that he had never wanted to fight in the first place.

Abraham thought of Tobias, who had also been forced to join the battle against his will, and he stifled an outcry as he watched the slaughter in front of him. Not content to have run the coward through with his sword, the attacker pulled it out and swung it high. Then he swiftly brought it down with a powerful two-handed stroke against the man's throat. A spurt of blood arced up from the rebel's neck as his head was severed.

Two Roman tribunes on horseback came up from the south, riding past Abraham toward the skirmish. By the time they arrived, the rebels had been butchered and the Romans were sheathing their swords.

"What's going on?" the taller one asked as he quickly dismounted. "Do we need more troops in this area?"

"No," one of the soldiers replied. "Just some stragglers we chased all the way from the temple. They were trying to remove some of their precious treasures."

"Good work," the shorter tribune said as the soldiers searched the bodies for the spoils of war. Abraham reckoned the man was barely above the military's minimum height requirement of five feet, eight inches. But what he lacked in height he evidently made up for in callousness. The officer walked around the bodies of the fallen revolutionaries, kicking the severed head to turn it over and laughing hoarsely. "You startled this one. His eyes were about to pop out of his head."

The first officer ordered the soldiers to return to their camp, saying that the two tribunes were headed to the general's headquarters. The legionnaires tramped off wearily, complaining of how long the Jews had held their ground and how glad they would be to get out of this backwater outpost and return to civilization now that Palestine had been completely conquered. They passed within twenty feet of Abraham but did not notice him, and he exhaled slowly as they disappeared down the hill.

The taller tribune prepared to mount his horse, but the other man placed a hand on his arm to stay him. "Are you sure you want to go through with this, Claudius?" Twilight was fading rapidly and Abraham could not quite make out the expression on the scrappy tribune's face, but the threat implied in his voice was unmistakable.

The tribune named Claudius did not flinch. "I did not make the complaint against you, Damian, someone else did. I just happen to be the one Tiberius Alexander sent to fetch you," he said, his disgust for the other officer obvious. "Frankly, I'm surprised it took this long for you to come to his attention."

"The Jews themselves set fire to the porticoes," the tribune named Damian protested, "and Tiberius knows that."

Claudius did not back down. "General Titus had commanded that the fires be allowed to die out so the temple itself would be spared. Evidently someone saw you throw a torch directly into the temple."

"I was unaware of the order."

"I doubt that, but I'm not the one you have to answer to."

The two men glared at each other silently for a moment, until Claudius finally said, "You're not under arrest, Damian. The commander simply wants to hear your side of the story."

The tension was so thick between the two men that Abraham could feel it where he lay in the shadows.

"Are you going back with me willingly," Claudius continued, "or shall I report to Tiberius that you refused and let him send a search party for you?"

"No need for that," Damian replied sarcastically. He reached for the reins of his horse as if he were preparing to mount, but Abraham saw the subtle movement of Damian's other hand feeling for something at his waist.

The moment Claudius turned and put his foot in the stirrup, Damian whirled around and grabbed him from behind. Before Claudius could utter a protest, Damian had plunged a knife into the vulnerable spot between the tribune's helmet and his chest armor. A low gurgle issued from Claudius's split throat, and he slumped to the ground as Damian released his hold on him.

Abraham was stunned. Watching the death of the rebels had been one thing; it's what happened in a war. But this was cold-blooded murder. He'd never witnessed such ruthlessness, and was horrified at the barbarous conduct of a Roman officer against one of his own comrades. But then, the man was apparently guilty of arson as well. Fear gripped Abraham, knowing he was now alone on the hillside with this vicious killer.

His fear rose as Damian took a few steps in his direction, and Abraham worried for a panicky moment that he had given himself away. But Damian soon turned and walked back. He leaned down, apparently checking to make sure Claudius was dead, then he stood up and lifted his tunic. Damian relieved himself on the bodies of the tribune and the fallen rebels, cursing the renegade Jew Tiberius Alexander, who served as the Roman commander's chief adviser.

His desecration complete, Damian mounted his horse and galloped off in the direction of the Tenth Legion camp. Abraham wondered if the villainous tribune would ever face the consequences of his crimes, but somehow he doubted it. Arson against the temple would be hard to prove, given the firestorm of the final battle for Jerusalem; most of the city was in flames. And whoever found Claudius's body would assume he was a casualty of war, not a murder victim.

Abraham waited until he could no longer hear the hoofbeats of Damian's horse, then he stood stiffly. He was scratched and scared, but still in one piece. It was completely dark now, which was probably the only reason he had been able to remain hidden.

He heard a snorting sound nearby and froze, then he realized it was Claudius's horse.

The horse! he thought, his spirits rising. *I need that horse.*

He inched toward the sound, not wanting to frighten the animal, and not wanting to stumble over the carnage. Abraham got close enough to smell leather and sweat and blood, then close enough to detect a dark, hulking object directly in front of him. The warhorse was nudging his master's body, waiting for a command.

Abraham reached up and patted the horse's muzzle, speaking softly to calm him as he felt for the bridle and reins. "Come on, boy. Let's get out of here."

∽✕∾

As the moon rose, Abraham was able to make out the shape of the Roman wall barricading the city to his left and the original stone wall to his right. He let the horse have free rein, knowing it would head toward the army camp to the north. That was the direction he needed to travel to reach the road that would take him to Caesarea, although he intended to steer clear of the camp itself. But first he had to find a way past the second wall, and as the horse ambled across the valley, Abraham searched for any sign of an opening.

He could see the fires still raging in the city above him, could smell the pungent aroma of burning wood and human flesh, could hear faint cries of terror and pain. *Hundreds of thousands must have lost their lives today,* he thought. *Many of them pilgrims, just like me.* He gave silent thanks to God for preserving his life and prayed for protection on his journey ahead.

Progress was slow. The horse was tired and Abraham didn't quite know where he was. Although he wanted to hurry, he did not urge the horse to gallop, fearing he might encounter another group of soldiers.

A half hour too late, it dawned on him he should have taken the dead tribune's sword and helmet. Abraham knew he would never be mistaken for a soldier up close, but from a distance the helmet might have made him appear to be a Roman officer returning to camp. As for the sword—well, he had no scabbard, so carrying it would have proved difficult, but it might have come in handy for defense. If anyone, soldier or otherwise, suspected he was escaping Jerusalem with a fortune in gold tied around his waist, Abraham would be in grave danger. *At least I have the dagger I took from Tobias's house,* he reminded himself.

The pale sliver of a moon was straight overhead when he caught a faint gleam of metal ahead on his left. Shortly after that he felt a change in the airflow around him. *It's a gate, an open gate!* Abraham was jubilant at the discovery, but his enthusiasm faded when he realized that a cart pulling a large catapult was blocking the opening. He dismounted and felt his way around the heavy equipment. It was leaning precariously to one side; one of the cart wheels had broken under the weight. Enough space was left between the wreck and the wall that he could easily pass through to the other side, and Abraham thought the horse could make it out as well, if he could persuade the animal to step over the splintered wheel. He'd have to be careful to avoid the projecting corner of the catapult; it could slide completely off the cart and crush them.

Abraham walked through the gate, holding the horse's reins behind him. He turned and cajoled the huge beast into the opening.

"Ho! Who's that?"

The shout startled Abraham, and he dropped the reins. The horse, halfway through the gate, reared on its hind legs and then hurtled over the broken wheel as three soldiers rushed toward Abraham, drawing their weapons as they ran. He hadn't seen them as he had approached the catapult. Were they supposed to be guarding the open gate? Repairing the cart? Where did they come from? Why hadn't he heard them?

Abraham had a fraction of a second to decide whether to make a run for it or to stay and fight. On foot, in the pitch dark, he wouldn't have a chance. He wasn't sure what his chances were against three armed soldiers, but that was the decision he made, and instantly the dagger was in his right hand.

Abraham had never been a brawler or a soldier, but he had always been athletic, and in spite of his fatigue and hunger, his reflexes were keen and as quick as a cat's. He saw the first soldier's movement a split second before he heard the sword slice the air. Abraham dodged, grabbed the man's arm, and kicked him in the shins. Thrown off balance, the man swung his sword aimlessly toward Abraham. He ducked, avoiding it easily, then felt another soldier try to stab him from behind. Abraham jerked away so fast that the man's dagger merely cut through his cloak and tunic but did not break the skin. With one arm he pried himself loose from the man's grip on his shoulder, and with the other hand he stabbed blindly. His dagger struck the man in the forearm, and the soldier dropped his weapon as blood gushed from an artery in his wrist.

The third man was coming toward him, as well as the first, back on his feet now. Abraham gauged their distance and as they neared, he lunged and rolled, knocking them into each other. The first man fell back on the ground but the other one managed to stay on his feet. The rolling tackle had winded Abraham, and he didn't move fast enough this time. The legionnaire's sword caught him at the ear and slashed along the jawline to his chin. A burning pain seared his face as he tried to roll away, and suddenly two men were on top of him.

The soldier he had stabbed was bleeding profusely but wielding his dagger with a vengeance. Feeling what must have been a supernatural burst of strength, given his condition, Abraham caught the man's arm and wrestled the weapon away from him, while landing a kick to the groin that doubled another soldier over in pain.

The third soldier was still after him, however, and when Abraham looked up, he saw a sword poised over his midsection. He was about to die. He had survived the famine and the fires, only to lose his life just when he thought he had finally escaped.

At that moment the horse whinnied loudly and reared, his slashing front feet landing a hair's breadth away from the soldier standing over Abraham, distracting his attacker just long enough for Abraham to get to his feet. He was surprised the animal had not cantered off, but the warhorse had not been frightened away by the fighting.

With one motion Abraham grabbed the reins and leaped onto the steed. As if knowing what was expected, the horse raced into the night, trampling one of the soldiers in the hasty departure.

Abraham never looked back.

❧

Two days later he arrived in Caesarea. He was famished and weak, having eaten nothing but a handful of dried grass since his escape. He had found plenty of water, though. The horse had sniffed out a stream, and after watering his mount, Abraham had drunk his fill and then cleaned his wounds as best he could.

He lay in the cool grass by the creek bank to dry off, basking in the warmth of the sunshine and the exhilarating freedom of fresh air.

Freedom, Tobias. I made it out—and with your money, I'll make it to freedom.

He transferred a few of the gold coins from the money bags under his tunic to a leather wallet secured to his belt, and he silently thanked his cousin for the gift of his freedom as he resumed his journey.

At the outskirts of Caesarea, Abraham spied the Roman garrison. He dismounted and affectionately patted the horse that had saved his life. "They'll feed you well there, old friend," he said, "and you'll serve another soldier as honorably as you served poor Claudius." Then he shooed the horse in the direction of the fort.

When he reached the city, Abraham entered the first inn he came to, eager to consume his first real meal in months.

"What happened to you, traveler?" the innkeeper asked, pointing to Abraham's numerous scrapes and scratches.

"I fell into a ravine," Abraham replied in a voice that indicated he did not wish to be questioned further.

The serving woman, probably the innkeeper's wife, brought his food and then watched Abraham warily as he ate. *I must be quite a sight,* he thought, *especially if I look as horrible as I feel.* Abraham forced himself to eat slowly, aware that trying to eat too much after having been empty for so long could make him sick.

After his dinner, he asked for directions to the harbor and inquired about any ships that might be sailing to Asia. The innkeeper obligingly produced the name of someone to see at the harbor. Then he said, "You really should tend to that cut first. It looks like that 'ravine' you encountered was carrying a sword."

Before Abraham could refuse, the innkeeper's wife was pouring wine into the wound on his face, blotting it gently with a cloth. Abraham winced in pain and tried not to yell.

"When it quits stinging," his would-be nurse said with a smile, "it will feel a lot better."

Abraham was too happy to be alive to harbor a grudge for long. As the liquid fire dried on his face, the woman poured olive oil onto the cloth and dabbed it along the cut.

"There, doesn't that feel better?" she said. "You don't want to let a wound like that fester."

Abraham paid his bill, thanked his hosts, and then walked to the harbor. He was overjoyed to find the captain the innkeeper had recommended and to learn that the grain ship he piloted was about to sail for Asia.

"Yes, we put in at Ephesus, and yes, I have room on board," he said in answer to Abraham's rapid-fire questions. He named a price and Abraham gladly counted it out and tendered it.

"An hour later, and you'd have missed me," the captain said. "We're ready to cast off. This must be your lucky day—and from the looks of you, it appears you could use some luck." He smiled broadly at the new passenger and Abraham realized belatedly that he should have bargained for the fare. He didn't care about the cost, however; he was too relieved to have reached safety.

Forty-eight hours after he fled Jerusalem, Abraham was in the hold of a ship headed for Ephesus. He could scarcely believe the tumultuous events that had transpired over the last few weeks and months. According to his calculations, he had been in Palestine for 123 days. He had found and lost two of the dearest people he'd ever known. He had survived famine and what must have been one of the bloodiest wars in human history.

There has to be a purpose, he thought as the sound of the water lulled him to sleep, *some reason God allowed me to survive when so many others didn't.*

Abraham wasn't sure what that purpose was, but he believed he would find it in Ephesus.

9

ABRAHAM BLINKED AND DAMIAN'S REVOLTING FACE swam into focus. At close range, he could see that the years had taken their toll on Damian. His face was lined and the skin under his eyes had the telltale bags that come with age. His sharp beak of a nose reminded Abraham of a bird of prey. *How like a vulture he is,* Abraham thought.

Damian was simply the chief predator, it now seemed to Abraham as he surveyed the hundreds of other vultures wearing red tunics and leather armor; there were almost as many soldiers as spectators in the crowd assembled around the colossal statue and the stone altar at the Temple of Domitian.

Lowering the purloined bowl he had held aloft for Abraham's inspection, Damian turned to the crowd. "Here is what's going to happen today," he said. "This is a simple test of loyalty to the Empire. As you know, Rome does not care what gods you believe in as long as you pay homage to Caesar. I am proud to serve Emperor Flavius Domitianus"—he gestured to the gigantic statue—"in the important capacity of facilitating the expression of your loyalty and worship."

You serve the emperor as a hired thug, Abraham longed to say.

Damian swaggered in front of his audience, informing his captives and instructing the onlookers on the requirements of the mandatory sacrifice. "It's very easy," he said. "You toss a pinch of incense into the fire on the altar and say, 'Lord Caesar.' Although you may say more, no eloquent speech is required. Just two simple words: *Lord Caesar.*

"Failure to do so constitutes treason and will result in swift punishment." Damian paused for effect. "Now, I am a reasonable man. A merciful man—"

Merciful! Abraham bit his lip, wanting to scream that Damian was anything but merciful.

"So as long as everyone remains calm and there is no public disturbance or destruction of property," Damian continued, "then instead of the death penalty, I will be content to impose the penalty of banishment to the island of Patmos—Devil's Island, as it's called." His mouth lifted in a malicious grin at the nickname.

"Of course, all of your possessions will be confiscated, but your life will be spared. You will spend the rest of your days as a Roman prisoner, toiling in the rock quarries on Devil's Island. It's, ah, rather difficult work."

Damian appeared to be salivating at that thought, and some of the spectators murmured their approval at the news that the Christians who refused to sacrifice would be sentenced to Devil's Island. The penal colony there was home to the dregs of society—robbers and rapists—as well as political prisoners and atheists.

"Now that we have the preliminaries established, let's get down to business." Damian turned and walked toward Abraham again, but he stopped farther back than he had before, Abraham noted. He almost smiled when he realized the reason: the closer Damian got, the more obvious it was that he had to tilt his head up to look Abraham in the eye.

How that must gall him, Abraham thought, determined to keep his back ramrod straight in order to emphasize his height.

"I had intended to start with you, Abraham, because we have something of a history, you and I. But it would be more fitting, don't you think, to begin with the . . . the elder statesman, if you will, of your illegal sect. The 'Apostle,' I believe you call him. After all, he sets the example for your kind.

"Bring them here," Damian ordered his troops, waving in the

direction of the vehicle that had delivered John and Jacob. Two husky soldiers leveled their spears at the pair standing by the carriage and marched them toward the altar.

"I went to great trouble to find them, Abraham, and get them here for this occasion. I had to send two centuries—150 men—to scour the countryside. Did you think I wouldn't track them down?"

What Abraham thought was that Damian enjoyed this game of cat and mouse: he delighted in toying with his victims and prolonging the inevitable just to increase their anxiety.

Jacob's eyes flashed a silent greeting to his father as he reached the altar. He was only a few feet away now, and Abraham eagerly observed the son he had missed so much. The black eye and the scrape on his face were minor; they would heal quickly. But the wound Damian was about to inflict would last a lifetime, and Abraham's heart ached for his boy.

John appeared not to have suffered any injuries when he had been arrested. While the elderly man's body looked weak, his eyes blazed fire. Abraham had seen that cantankerous look many times over the years and often found it entertaining—when he wasn't on the receiving end of it. All he felt now was worry. John had been a friend as well as pastor, and Abraham cared for him deeply.

"So we begin with you, *Aposssssstle.*" Damian drew out the word, making a mockery of the title.

He extended the bowl of incense toward John, who looked at it briefly, then closed his eyes and raised both of his hands in the position he used when praying or pronouncing a benediction over a gathering of the church.

"*Shema Yisrael,*" John intoned. "*Adonai eloheynu, Adonai echad . . .*"

Abraham recognized the ancient Jewish confession of faith, the monotheistic creed to which Christians adhered as well: *Hear, O Israel: the Lord our God, the Lord is one.* He had recited the Shema daily for as long as he could remember, and without conscious effort his lips moved silently along with John as the Apostle continued in Hebrew:

"You shall love the Lord your God with all your heart and with all your soul and with all your strength . . ."

"Stop that babbling!" Damian's anger erupted suddenly, and he swatted one of John's upraised hands as if he were reprimanding a two-year-old. "Speak clearly, old man. Will you make the sacrifice or not?"

John pushed aside the bowl Damian held in front of him. "I will not take your incense, and I will not make your sacrifice. There is *one* God, and His name is *not* Domitian." He jabbed a gnarled finger at Damian's face. "It is Jesus Christ. *He* is the King of kings and Lord of lords, and at *His* name every knee shall bow—"

"Enough! There will be no sermons today. And as for bowing your knee," Damian said gruffly, "you *will* bow to Rome. Devil's Island will bring you to your knees, I guarantee."

Abraham watched with dismay as Damian called for leg irons. John winced in pain as one soldier pinned his arms behind him and another stooped to fasten the chains around his ankles, but he did not cry out, not even when the soldier tightened the shackles until the blood trickled down his legs onto his feet.

Appearing satisfied with the suffering he had caused the Apostle, Damian turned his attention to Jacob. He smiled, signaling that he had checked his anger again—for the moment, anyway.

"They say the apple doesn't fall far from the tree, Abraham, and it's obvious this one is your son. Same hair, same eyes, same obstinate jaw—he looks just like you. Too bad he didn't follow in your footsteps, though. I understand he's become a preacher, like the demented Apostle here."

Abraham could tell that Jacob was restraining himself with effort. His son would love to crush Damian's face right now, and with his greater size and strength, Jacob could physically punish Damian easily. But it would bring swift, and probably fatal, retaliation from Damian's minions.

"You heard the warning, boy. No sermons." Damian took Jacob's hand and plunged it into the container of incense. "There's the altar." He motioned with his head and then slowly released Jacob's wrist.

Jacob pulled out a pinch of the imperial incense but remained where he was. Slowly rubbing the powder between his fingers, he dusted the ground with it, saying firmly, "I will not sacrifice to Caesar. My loyalty is to the Lord Jesus."

Abraham's chest constricted. He was both proud and heartsick. He saw Elizabeth, one arm still around Rebecca, bring a hand to her mouth while the soldiers shackled their son. Jacob did not resist or protest as a grim-faced legionnaire roughly pushed him away from the altar. The chains around his ankles clanged as Jacob took a few shuffling steps, adapting to the new restriction of his movement with the agility of youth. Abraham knew the indignity and the injustice of his punishment would be far harder on Jacob than any physical restraint.

It will be my turn next, Abraham thought. *What will I do?*

An internal war waged in Abraham's mind. He was furious with Damian and would do anything to protect his family from this monster's savagery. But could he deny Christ? Abraham heard an inner voice say, *If you deny Me before men, I will deny you before My Father in heaven.*

He tried to ignore the voice. *Peter denied Christ,* he told himself, *and he was forgiven. If I made the sacrifice—if I threw the incense into the fire and said those two little words—wouldn't God's grace cover my sin?*

Thinking of the apostle Peter reminded Abraham of his son Peter, and he searched the crowd frantically. That's who was missing! He couldn't see Peter anywhere and he wondered what had happened to his frail, easily frightened son. How had he escaped this nightmare? Or had Damian already captured or killed him?

Damian turned toward Abraham, but before he could extend the incense and demand the sacrifice, Naomi stepped forward. Shivering in her semiundressed state, she quickly walked up to Damian. A good two inches taller, Naomi stared at him boldly and said, "Look, I told your henchmen that I was not one of these religious fanatics. I'm cold and I want to go home, so let's get this over with."

Naomi's shapely feminine form was clearly visible beneath her thin sleeveless tunic, and Damian looked her up and down.

"What spirit you have," he said approvingly.

"And common sense," she replied. "A trait the rest of my family does not seem to possess."

Damian gave a snorting laugh at her bluntness. "How true, how true."

"May I?" Naomi asked, reaching for the incense.

"As you wish."

She took a pinch of the incense and then walked officiously to the altar. With a dramatic flair Naomi flicked the incense into the fire. As it sparked and sizzled, releasing its aromatic fragrance, she said, "Hail, Caesar Domitian, Lord and God."

Damian smiled triumphantly. "Well done," he said, bowing slightly in her direction. "If you'll wait in the carriage, I'll have someone drive you home."

As a soldier helped Naomi climb into the carriage, Damian avidly watched her every movement. "Smart girl, Abraham. And quite attractive. You must be very proud. Or very ashamed. Which is it?"

Damian didn't expect a reply, and Abraham kept silent, his mind spinning. He realized that Naomi's action had probably saved the family fortune. Surely Damian would not dare confiscate his estate if one of his heirs had proved loyal to the emperor. *But*, he thought, *Damian may try to get his hands on my wealth through my daughter.* Abraham had noticed the way Damian had looked at Naomi. And even if Damian were unsuccessful—which was likely, given Naomi's fiery temperament and deep disdain for most men—Abraham could not trust his oldest daughter to use his money wisely. Naomi had proven yet again that she would act only in her own self-interest.

It's not that I love riches, Abraham rationalized. But protecting his family was paramount, and he was accustomed to using the power

of wealth to move the machinery of government. There *had* to be a
way around Damian's machinations. There always was, if you had
enough money. If the emperor had given an order, the emperor
could rescind it. And all it took to get to the emperor was money,
Abraham was convinced of it. He could always go to Rome and
make a personal appeal to Caesar.

As if he were making a simple business decision, Abraham mentally ticked off a list of factors to consider. One son had just been condemned to hard labor, another son was missing, his oldest daughter
was intent on wasting her inheritance, and his youngest daughter was
terrified at the prospect of Devil's Island. And Elizabeth, his beloved
Elizabeth. He could not stand by and watch his wife be put in chains.
He couldn't.

Surely God would understand, he told himself. But if God understood, why was he so tormented by his decision?

"Your other daughter is even more beautiful." Damian had
turned his attention to Rebecca. "Just like you, Elizabeth."

Damian's back was to Abraham, so he couldn't see the look on
Damian's face. But he saw the reaction clearly on Elizabeth's—fear,
loathing, and a flicker of anger.

"What a pretty young thing." Damian reached out and grabbed a
handful of Rebecca's long dark hair, pulling her toward him sugges-
tively. "Fortunate indeed the man who makes a woman out of you."

"Damian, please." Elizabeth's voice was ragged.

"How nice to hear you say my name, Elizabeth. It brings back
such fond memories."

A decidedly dark memory surfaced in Abraham's mind, and he
reached the limit of silent endurance. He had to stop this now,
whatever it took.

"Damian!" he shouted. "Bring me the incense."

Damian's sarcastic laughter echoed off the stone altar as he dropped
Rebecca's hair and whirled around. "Why, Abraham. Has your faith
crumbled so quickly?"

10

ELIZABETH WATCHED IN HORROR as Damian offered the incense to her husband. *No! Please, God, don't let him do it,* she prayed silently. *Abraham doesn't mean it. He's mistakenly trying to protect me.*

She recognized the look on Abraham's face—that dogged determination, that ardent desire to right an injustice. And she knew the way Abraham's mind worked. He had always protected her and provided for her. It was one of the reasons she had fallen in love with him. Her husband didn't look the part—he was big, tough, and sometimes gruff—but he was a nurturer. He sometimes didn't understand his children, but he loved them; there wasn't anything he wouldn't do for them. Or for her.

But to deny the Lord . . . surely he wouldn't go that far, she told herself.

Damian had looked almost gleeful when Abraham asked for the incense. Now Elizabeth watched numbly as Abraham dipped a meaty hand into the bowl of incense.

God, have mercy on his soul, she prayed desperately.

Abraham turned toward the altar and raised his hand over the flame. He hesitated for the briefest of moments, then released the incense. "Lord Caesar," he said. Abraham's voice was clearly audible but cracked slightly as he pronounced the two blasphemous words the emperor had commanded.

Rebecca gasped, "No!" and reached for Elizabeth's hand.

When Abraham turned around, his face was ashen, and Elizabeth was filled with an indescribable sadness. Part of her refused to believe her husband had caved under the pressure; another part understood and forgave, even as she prayed God would understand and forgive.

"Damian." Abraham's voice was stronger now, Elizabeth noted, as he walked purposely toward his adversary. "I made your abominable sacrifice. You got what you wanted, so let the others go. Your quarrel is with me, not my family."

"My *official* business with you is concluded, Abraham. For the moment. But you're right—we have some unfinished *personal* business to resolve." Damian gestured to the other prisoners standing behind Elizabeth. "However, we shouldn't keep all these church members waiting while you and I settle an old score. They must have the same opportunity to prove their loyalty to Caesar.

"Besides," he continued, "my quarrel is not with you alone. You forget that I also have an outstanding dispute with your lovely wife." The word *wife* sounded somehow indecent as it rolled off Damian's tongue.

"Our dispute can be handled in private," Abraham insisted.

"Oh, I certainly intend to spend some private time with your family. Or at least some of them." Damian looked pointedly at Rebecca and then turned to Elizabeth.

"What do you think of your hero now?" he asked. "Did you ever imagine your husband would turn out to be such a coward?"

Elizabeth looked at her husband reassuringly, trying to signal her love and forgiveness. *Abraham's love for me has always been his blind spot,* she thought with a rush of tenderness mingled with deep regret.

Surprisingly, she was not afraid of Damian this time. She'd always known the man was evil, had recognized it even as a girl. And when, after all these years, he had reappeared in their lives, she had known intuitively that Abraham could not protect her from Damian this time.

Not like before.

As she steadfastly regarded the man poised to destroy her entire family, Elizabeth let her mind wander to the long-ago conflict that could have culminated only in this moment. She recalled the first time she ever laid eyes on Abraham . . .

❧

"I found him on the pier," Quintus told Elizabeth. "He'd been staggering around for hours, stopping people and asking for directions, mumbling that he had to find 'the last apostle.' After I heard him say that a few times, I finally realized he meant John."

Quintus was tall for his age, but the teenager was as thin as a reed, all arms and legs. Elizabeth could not imagine how he had managed to get the heavy man draped over the donkey and up the steep hills to John's house.

"The harbormaster thought he was drunk or crazy and wanted to throw him in jail for creating a disturbance." Quintus huffed with the effort of trying to get the man, who was lying facedown across the saddle, his arms and legs almost touching the ground on either side of the animal, to his feet. "At first I thought he was out of his mind too, then I realized he was sick. Look at that wound on his face."

Elizabeth cringed when the two of them got the man upright and she saw the jagged line down his jaw. It was red and swollen and oozing. Infected, no doubt.

"He doesn't look as if he would be this heavy," she said as she draped one of his arms around her shoulder and helped Quintus drag him inside. "He's skin and bones. Half-starved, it looks like. And burning with fever."

"Do you think I did the right thing?" Quintus asked when they had laid him across John's bed. "Bringing him here, I mean?"

"Of course. John would never turn him away. And he might have died in jail—he's very sick." Elizabeth looked around John's sparsely furnished bedroom. She knew where everything was because she visited John frequently—not only to make sure he had something to eat regularly but to help around the house. Cooking and cleaning were not a high priority for John. With an adequate household staff at home, Elizabeth was not needed there, and she found satisfaction in serving the Apostle in mundane matters so he could focus on the ministry.

"Get another tunic from that chest," she told Quintus. "And an extra cover for the bed. I'll go get a basin of water. We'll clean him up as best we can and try to get his fever down."

When Quintus undressed the sick man, they found out why he was so heavy. "Look at this," he said as Elizabeth returned. He upended a leather bag and dumped its contents onto the bed. Gold coins spilled all over the blankets he had piled over the stranger. Quintus cupped his hands together and scooped the coins up, then let them fall again, smiling as the gold pieces clinked together in a heap. "There's another bag just like this one. They were tied to his waist, underneath his tunic. Have you ever seen so much money?"

Elizabeth had seen that much money before, but only in her father's bank. The man Quintus had rescued was carrying a small fortune in gold coins. If he had survived jail, it would have been as a pauper; someone would certainly have robbed him. It was likely that Quintus had saved not only the man's life, he had saved his wealth as well.

As she sponged the cool water onto his face, the man began to rouse. He grabbed her hand and clutched it tightly, his strength surprising her. "Do you know where I can find John?" he asked, his voice a feverish croak. His eyes did not quite focus on her as he muttered, "John knew the Lord."

"You're in John's house," she told him. "He'll be home soon. In the meantime, we'll take care of you." The sick man couldn't seem to keep his eyes open for very long, and he groaned as she sponged the water over his wound.

"Quintus, bring me a cup of fresh water, please."

Elizabeth studied the man's face while Quintus was gone. He must have been handsome before all this happened to him. She had seen bruises and scrapes on his arms and legs, as well as the horrible cut on his jaw, and he had obviously been near starvation. His eyes fluttered open again, and she blushed at being caught staring at him.

"You're so beautiful," he rasped. "Are you an angel?"

Before she could reply he drifted off again.

When Quintus returned, Elizabeth said, "Help me hold his head up."

They dribbled water over his parched lips and the sick man managed to swallow a few sips. Then he fell back, exhausted.

"He came from Caesarea," Quintus offered. "In Palestine."

Elizabeth's head jerked up. "He told you that?"

"No, but the only ship to dock this morning had sailed from Caesarea. You know, there's a war going on there."

"The war is over," she told him. Quintus looked surprised, so she added, "My father just got a letter from . . . from someone who was there."

Elizabeth was not happy that the war in Palestine was finally over. In fact, she was desperate at the news. That's why she had come to see John today. To tell him about the letter, and to ask for his advice.

But when John returned, there was no opportunity to speak to him about her problem. Two of the church elders were with the Apostle, and one of them, a retired legionnaire named Acacius, had some medical training.

"Looks like a sword cut," the former legionnaire said. "Saw plenty of them in my day." He lanced the man's wound, draining it and cleaning it, then poured wine on it.

"Let this air out a while," he told Elizabeth. "Then apply olive oil to keep it soft."

She nodded. "I can also come back tomorrow to check on him."

John and the elders anointed the injured traveler with oil and

laid hands on him, praying that the Lord would restore him—
whoever he was.

⌒⤫⌒

When Elizabeth returned the next day, the stranger had improved a
bit. His fever had gone down and he was even a little hungry, he said
in answer to her queries. So she made some soup and then sat by the
bed, slowly feeding him a spoonful at a time.

"You were here yesterday, weren't you?" he asked when he had
finished the bowl of soup.

"Yes. You were incoherent from the fever." She smiled at the
memory. "You thought I was an angel."

His eyes caught hers and held them for a moment. "I still hold
that opinion."

She blushed and looked away. "I brought bread and more vegetables with me today, but is there anything special you'd like? I can
get it at the market for you."

His eyes misted over, and he shook his head weakly. "Nothing special," he said after a moment. "I'm grateful for food of any kind. Just
having enough to eat would be a blessing." He cleared his throat. "But
I should give you some money, so you can buy additional supplies for
me and John. He said I could stay as long as I needed. I told him I
would pay my own way . . ."

Panic twisted his face as he began to pat his waist frantically.
"Oh, no! It's gone! Something happened to my—"

"No, it's not gone, it's all right," Elizabeth said quickly, once she
realized what he was looking for. "Quintus found the gold you were
carrying. It was quite a sum. We were afraid to leave it lying around
the house—John is often gone, sometimes for days at a time. So we
took it to my father."

"You took it? Your father . . ." He tried to rise but was too
unsteady on his feet.

Elizabeth helped him back in bed. "My father is a banker," she explained. "Your money will be safe."

The look on his face was skeptical, so she said, "Wait here a minute. I'll be right back."

Elizabeth retrieved her basket from the kitchen and returned with a piece of paper. "Here. It's a receipt. I made sure all the gold was counted carefully and recorded accurately."

He examined the paper and frowned. "It says the money belongs to someone named Elizabeth."

"That's me. I'm Elizabeth. I didn't know your name, you see, and we couldn't leave it blank. So I opened the account in my name. But you don't have to worry. You can trust me." She knew she was starting to ramble, but she wanted to make sure he understood that he hadn't been robbed. "When you're well enough, I'll take you to the bank and we'll transfer the account to your name. I didn't know what else to do—"

"Thank you," he said, placing a hand over hers. "Thank you very much, Elizabeth."

The way he said her name made her cheeks flush. "You're welcome . . ."

"Abraham. That's my name."

"Abraham." It was strange; she felt as if she had known him for a long time, yet she had just now learned his name. And he didn't know her, either, but he seemed not to be angry that she had taken it upon herself to handle his considerable fortune. "Then you trust me, Abraham?"

"I've learned to trust angels," he said softly, a distant look on his face, as if he were remembering something. Then he fell quiet.

"Shall I bring you more soup?"

"Since you own me now, I guess I'd better do whatever you say." Abraham smiled broadly and then flinched when the movement stretched the long cut on his jaw.

Elizabeth's heart was beating rapidly as she went to the kitchen, and she hummed a happy tune. For the moment, she had forgotten all about the dreadful letter from Jerusalem.

∽◦∾

Over the next few weeks, Elizabeth came to see Abraham every day. Gradually, he began to regain his strength and to lose his hollow look.

They sat and talked for hours each time, and she eagerly looked forward to their visits. He told her about his unforgettable sojourn in Jerusalem, about Tobias being forced to fight in the army, and about Rivka and Joel dying from starvation. Sometimes he would pause when recounting an incident, and she got the impression he was editing out certain details. But from what he did tell her, she knew it had been a horrific experience.

He also told her about the voyage to Ephesus. "I was so exhausted that I slept a lot. I had brought provisions with me, so I stayed below-decks most of the time and kept to myself. Eventually the food I'd bought ran out, but by that time I had gotten so sick I couldn't eat anyway. I could have asked one of the crew members to tell the captain I was sick, or asked one of the other passengers for help. But I was afraid someone would discover I was carrying a lot of money and rob me." He paused and looked sternly at her. "And someone did—you!"

"I did not—" she said, then relaxed as his dour face dissolved; he had been trying to suppress a smile. "You're teasing me, Abraham."

"Yes. I'm teasing." He laughed merrily then, and she loved the sound of it.

A moment later he grew sober again. "It's a good thing Quintus was there on the dock when I arrived. No telling what might have happened if he hadn't found me and decided to help."

"He's a good sort. Very conscientious and responsible." Now she filled him in on Quintus's background. "A year ago, when he became a Christian, his father disowned him. One of the families in our congregation took him in. And I persuaded my father—who is not a believer, but he's a good man—to help Quintus get a job. One of my father's financial clients owns a small shipping business, and he hired Quintus as a stevedore. It's hard work, but he never complains."

"Hard? It's backbreaking work. He doesn't seem to be built for it."

"The poor thing eats like a horse, but he just keeps growing taller, not wider. Everyone wonders if he'll ever fill out."

Elizabeth also told Abraham about the other church members and how some of her family's household servants had become believers. "That's how I learned about Jesus," she said. "Through them. My father hasn't accepted Christ. Not yet. I'm still trusting God to open his heart to the truth."

When John was home, he discipled Abraham, not just teaching him the doctrines of the faith but sharing stories about Jesus and His ministry—the very thing Abraham had come to Ephesus to learn. John regaled them with anecdotes, and Elizabeth enjoyed hearing the stories even though she had heard many of them before. Somehow they seemed fresh each time John told them, as if they had happened yesterday and not four decades earlier.

One day, about a month after Abraham had arrived in Ephesus, Elizabeth took him to the bank to straighten out his account.

"There," she said when the paperwork was complete and she had signed her name with a flourish, "I don't own you anymore."

"I wouldn't be too sure about that," Abraham replied as he put a hand on her elbow and steered her outside.

It was a warm sunny day in late September. Summer had lingered like a favorite friend reluctant to leave after an extended visit. As they stepped out of the bank into the bright sunlight and she saw the expression on Abraham's face, the light of understanding finally penetrated Elizabeth's mind. He was looking at her with such open affection and longing that it startled her.

She was dismayed. *When did the teasing turn into something more?*

she wondered, scolding herself silently. *This is impossible. I should never have let myself get so close to him. Never.*

Abraham was in no hurry to return to John's—"I feel fine," he informed her, "and it's a great day to be outdoors, especially with you"—so they strolled leisurely through Ephesus while she pointed out the places of interest. They stopped in the *agora* for a snack— "All this walking has whetted my appetite," Abraham said—and he insisted on buying all sorts of delicacies for Elizabeth to enjoy.

She clapped in delight when she saw the candied orange slices. "These are my favorite treat," she said. He popped one in her mouth and then laughed when she sighed rapturously and said, "They're so sweet and tart and utterly delicious."

Elizabeth tried to keep the conversation light and, for the most part, avoided looking directly at him. *If things were different . . .* she thought, then quickly stopped herself. Things weren't different, and it was no use pretending otherwise.

It was late afternoon when they returned to John's house and she gathered her belongings.

"I should go now," she said, "so I can get home before dark." She didn't want to leave, didn't want their carefree time together to end. It had been one of the most wonderful days of her life, one she knew would not be repeated.

"I'll see you tomorrow," he said, opening the door for her.

She hesitated, then stepped outside, knowing she needed to put some distance between them—permanently. "I'm not sure I can come back tomorrow."

"Is something wrong?"

Something was dreadfully wrong, but she couldn't tell him. "No," she said. "It's just that you're so much stronger now, and you don't really need me anymore." She could read the protest in his eyes, so she continued hurriedly, before he could object. "You've accomplished what you came to Ephesus to do—find the last apostle and hear what he had to say about Jesus. And now that I've returned all the money I stole from you"—she risked a tentative smile at him—"you have no reason to stay here. I imagine you'll be leaving soon . . ."

Elizabeth stopped. Her eyes filled with tears and gave away her distress.

"I have every reason to stay here," he said softly. "At least I hope I do." He crossed the threshold to stand beside her, then reached for her hand and held it tenderly.

"Abraham—"

"No. Let me say what I've wanted to say all day long."

With her tiny fingers engulfed in his massive but gentle hand, she felt powerless to object.

"When I escaped from the nightmare that was Jerusalem," Abraham said, "I knew God had spared me for a purpose. Not knowing what to do, I came to Ephesus looking for John. I not only found John, I found you. And when I found you, Elizabeth, I found my purpose."

With his free hand he tilted her chin so she could see his face. "I love you, Elizabeth. I want to marry you."

Her chin quivered in his hand and a large tear spilled over her lashes and splashed onto his thumb. "I can't marry you," she said morosely. "I'm engaged to someone else."

Abraham took a quick step backward, as if she had slapped him. Then Elizabeth turned and fled down the hill into the fading light of an enchanting day that had suddenly lost its golden glow.

11

ELIZABETH DID NOT RETURN TO JOHN'S HOUSE. Two days later she sent Servius with a basket of food and her apologies.

"What shall I tell John?" the faithful household retainer asked.

"Just say that I'm indisposed." Elizabeth ran her fingers wearily through her tangled mop of curls. Exhausted from not sleeping, she felt certain she looked indisposed, and Servius seemed satisfied with that excuse.

She had lain awake the past two nights, lamenting the fact that she'd allowed Abraham to fall in love with her and berating herself for having such deep feelings for him when she was promised to another man. Now she was miserable, Abraham was miserable, and she had no one to blame but herself.

Elizabeth knew she should have talked to John, as she had intended, about the letter from her fiancé. It had arrived the same day as Abraham—probably on the same boat. As soon as her father had read the letter to her, she had rushed to John's house, panic-stricken. While she waited for the Apostle to return, Quintus had arrived with Abraham, and nothing had been quite the same since.

She could have talked to John at any time during the last month, but she had enjoyed her daily visits with Abraham so much, she kept putting off the conversation. She'd become an expert at putting things off, especially *this* detestable thing. She had gotten used to not thinking about her engagement—had almost convinced herself, in fact, that it was not a reality.

In Abraham's presence, it had been easy to forget her dilemma.

But it hadn't gone away, and now she had caused a disaster by her procrastination.

After a week of moping, Elizabeth told herself it was time to snap out of it. Her future was sealed, and that's all there was to it. She might as well accept it with whatever dignity she could muster and get on with her life. She had to put Abraham out of her mind once and for all, and she had to reconcile herself to the prospect of marriage to a man she didn't love, a man she almost feared.

For the first time in days, she took pains with her grooming, dressed in her favorite tunic, and greeted her father pleasantly at breakfast. She consulted the cook about menus, directed a serving girl in the preparation of baskets of food for the needy, and sent her father's cloak for mending, so it would be ready when the weather changed.

By midmorning Elizabeth had convinced herself that life was almost back to normal, but that illusion was shattered when an unexpected visitor arrived. Servius was nowhere to be found, so she crossed the courtyard and answered the insistent knock at the door herself.

"Abraham . . ."

"May I come in?"

"Of course." Her hand was shaking so much, he had to help her latch the door behind them.

"May I offer you some refreshment?" Her tone was cordial but formal.

Abraham refused with a shake of his head. Ordinarily, she would have invited her visitor into the dining room, but she was so flustered by his sudden appearance that she simply motioned him to a seat in the open atrium. He probably wouldn't be staying long anyway, she figured.

Whatever the purpose for his visit, Abraham couldn't seem to bring himself to speak. He just kept staring at her as if it had been seven years, not seven days, since he'd last seen her.

"I heard you were leaving town," she said, deciding at last that he must have come to say good-bye. She hadn't expected a farewell visit, not after the way she'd treated him.

"I was . . . I am," he corrected himself. "But I wanted to see you first." Abraham hesitated, then with an obvious effort at self-control, he said, "I think you owe me an explanation, Elizabeth. And I want to hear it."

She bowed her head in shame. "You're right," she said softly. "I owe you that." She didn't know where to start, however.

He filled in the silence. "My better judgment tells me I should just cut my losses and leave, but for some reason I have to know why you let me fall in love with you when you're going to marry someone else. I thought you had the same kind of feelings I did. You came to see me every single day, and you seemed so happy to be with me."

"I was," she whispered so faintly that he missed it.

"Day after day you sat in my room, with the sunlight streaming through the window, making your hair look like a flame-kissed halo. You hung on to every word I said, and your laughter . . ." He bit his lip and looked down for a moment. "Your laughter was like the music of heaven to my soul. My very own angel—"

"Abraham, stop. Please."

"Why did you do it?" He was angry now. "Why did you keep coming back? Was it just to torment me? In all that time, didn't you realize I was falling in love with you?"

"I didn't let myself think about the possibility," she said unevenly. "And when I finally realized it, it was too late. I'm sorry, Abraham. You can't imagine how sorry I am. I never meant to hurt you, I didn't."

"Well, you did hurt me. And I suppose there's nothing to be done about it now." He stood up and turned to face her. "You helped heal the wound on my face, but you've left one in my heart."

"Please forgive me, Abraham. *Please.*" Surely he could hear the anguish in her voice and know how truly remorseful she was.

But he did not offer his forgiveness. "I just hope he makes you

happy, Elizabeth. I would have spent every moment of my life making you happy, and I hope to God he does the same."

"He won't make me happy," she protested. "He'll make me miserable, and I don't want to marry him, but I have to." She wished
she could make Abraham understand.

He sat back down on the bench. "Am I going to have to drag it
out of you, or are you going to tell me the story?"

"You're still speaking to me?"

"Well, I still love you, so I guess I can tolerate hearing your voice
a little while longer. Besides, if you really don't want to marry this
man, maybe there's something I can do to help."

"H-help?" She hicccuped when she tried to speak, tears beginning
to flow in spite of her effort to stop them.

"You have to stop crying first, though."

She nodded her head yes.

"Promise?"

"Yes," she said finally. "I promise."

"Let's go inside," he suggested. "Someplace a little more private."

Elizabeth led Abraham from the atrium into the adjoining dining room. "We'll be comfortable in here," she said. "And we can talk
freely." They arranged themselves on the long sofas, and Elizabeth
dried her eyes on one of the large linen napkins draped over the
edge. Then she related the story of her engagement.

❧

She had just turned sixteen when she accompanied her father, Rufus,
on a business trip to Rome. It was by far the most thrilling adventure
of her life—a whirlwind of exciting new places and people—and she
had loved every minute of it.

Well, almost every minute. While in the capital they made frequent visits to the home of Senator Lucius Mallus Balbus. Elizabeth
had found the senator pompous and boring, and she thought even
less of his eighteen-year-old son, who had quickly become infatuated

with her and wanted to monopolize her time. As much as she disliked the boy, she was unfailingly polite; his father was a valuable business associate.

"Young Mallus is quite taken with you, Elizabeth," her father said one night as they returned from a dinner party at the senator's home. Rufus seemed pleased.

"The feeling is *not* mutual." Elizabeth frowned but quickly added. "Don't worry. I'll continue to be nice. I know his father is a very influential man."

It was not easy to be nice, however, especially after the day she and Drusilla, the wife of Senator Mallus, had returned early from a shopping excursion. From an upstairs window of the villa, Elizabeth had observed a disturbing scene: the senator's son had kicked a dog for no reason, sending the poor, defenseless creature halfway across the courtyard. The sight had sickened her, and she confronted him about it after dinner that night.

He denied the incident. "It wasn't me," he said. "Must have been someone else."

"I was upstairs," she said. "I saw you."

"It doesn't matter what you think you saw," he said. "I did no such thing."

His defiant look intimidated Elizabeth. She knew he was lying simply because he could get away with it; no one challenged the senator's son.

As much as she had loved Rome, she hated her visits to the Mallus family, and Elizabeth was both disappointed and relieved when it was time to depart.

In spite of several hints from her father, Elizabeth had remained oblivious to what was going on behind the scenes. It wasn't until their ship was almost to Ephesus that she learned her father had concluded more than one business deal in Rome: he had signed a marriage agreement with Senator Mallus and had promised a spring wedding for his daughter and the senator's son.

"I can't believe you did it without consulting me," Elizabeth said when Rufus finally told her. Distraught, she paced the deck of the ship.

"And I can't believe you're so upset about it," her father replied. "It's a good match, with a good family. A powerful family."

"Is that all that matters to you? Marrying me off to a powerful family to advance your career?"

"Elizabeth, you're of marriageable age. It's my responsibility to find a suitable husband for you. Young Mallus is a fine young man, and he—"

"He's perfectly dreadful, that's what he is!"

"Now, Elizabeth—"

"Well, he is. I can't stand to be in the same room with him, let alone spend the rest of my life with him. How could you do this to me?"

"Tell me, daughter, just what you find so objectionable about him."

Her father sounded as if he was losing patience with her, but she didn't care; too much was at stake to hold her feelings inside. "What about him *isn't* objectionable?" she shot back. "He's rude and arrogant. Swaggers around like everyone should be in awe of him."

"Perhaps the boy is still somewhat immature and full of himself, but he'll settle down. He has an excellent military and political career ahead of him."

"He's cruel. And he lies."

Rufus sighed with annoyance. "Elizabeth, what are you talking about?"

"He hurts helpless animals." She shuddered, recalling what she'd witnessed from the window, and she told her father about the dog.

"Not everyone loves animals as much as you do, child. I'm sure he didn't mean any harm by it."

"Then why would he lie about it? And if he'll lie about kicking a dog, what else would he lie about? You've taught me to value honesty and integrity, Father. And now you want me to marry a man who has none."

"I think you're exaggerating the situation, Elizabeth."

She knew she wasn't exaggerating, and she knew this marriage would be a horrible mistake. What she didn't know was how to convince her father of that fact. She stared over the rail at the ocean, thinking she might as well throw herself overboard; it would be preferable to a lifetime with a man she detested.

"You have to trust me to do what's best for you," Rufus said.

"Is it really best for me to marry a man I don't love or respect?"

"After you're married, you'll grow to love your husband. Wait and see."

For the first time in her life, Elizabeth did not believe her father. She felt as if she had received a death sentence, and she couldn't shake the feeling no matter what she did.

By the time they got home, she could not eat at all and could barely sleep. Day after day she stayed in her room and cried, thinking that if her mother had still been alive, she would never have agreed to this marriage. *Mother would have seen "young Mallus" for what he was,* Elizabeth told herself. *And she would never make me go through with this.*

Rufus prepared for the impending nuptials, but Elizabeth couldn't bring herself to cooperate. Justina, Servius's wife, started sewing a wedding dress, but by the time she was finished with it, the dress hung loosely on Elizabeth because she'd lost so much weight.

She could not talk her father out of it, but she did finally persuade him to postpone the wedding for a year. "I'm too young," she told him, "and not ready to be a wife. Surely you can give me one year to get used to the idea. Just one year. Then the Mallus family can have the rest of my life."

Reluctantly, Rufus wrote Senator Mallus and told him. The senator wrote back and said that he was not at all happy about the postponement but that his son, now a tribune, had just received a commission. He was being sent to Palestine, where a rebellion had broken out. The senator said the army would quash the uprising quickly—in no more than a few months—and that they could delay the marriage until then.

But the war in Palestine was not over in a few months. Instead, it dragged on and on, and for the next four years, Elizabeth felt as if she'd been given a reprieve. She put the engagement completely out of her mind and went on with her life.

Then one day the letter had arrived. "Jerusalem has finally fallen," her fiancé wrote. "We have some minor cleanup to take care of, then the troops will return to Rome with General Titus by the spring."

And then he would come to Ephesus for the wedding, he said.

The tone of the letter was repugnant. "Tell Elizabeth she'd better be ready this time. She's not a little girl any longer."

Elizabeth nearly fell apart as she read and reread the letter. It was the news she had been dreading for four years.

"You're lucky he still wants you," her father said. "There will be no arguments this time—no more delays."

❦

As they reclined comfortably in the dining room, Elizabeth finished telling Abraham the story of her engagement. This time, he was the one who listened intently.

"I used to pray the war in Palestine would never end," she told him with an apologetic look. "I'm ashamed to admit that, especially after you told me about all the suffering.

"Can you believe I did that? I knew it meant more people would die, but I prayed for the war to continue."

"I think God understood your heart," Abraham said gently. "You didn't want to have to face a future you couldn't fathom."

"All that time, I put the engagement out of my mind. As long as the war was going on, I didn't have to think about it. Then, the day you arrived, my father received the letter from Damian."

"Damian." Abraham frowned. "That's his name? Your fiancé?"

"Yes, Damian. Lucius Mallus Damianus." She pronounced the full name with disgust, noticing that Abraham had a strange look on his face.

Just then Justina entered the room, carrying a tray. "I had the cook prepare a light lunch for you and your guest," she said.

"Thank you." Elizabeth rose as Justina placed the tray on the table between the sofas. "I'll serve," Elizabeth told her, wanting to continue her conversation with Abraham in privacy.

When the servant left, Elizabeth poured the wine and filled a plate with cold cuts for Abraham, who attacked the meal with relish. It gladdened Elizabeth to know that he had fully recovered his appetite; he bore little resemblance now to the half-starved stranger she had met at John's house.

"Tell me what this Damian looks like," Abraham said after a few bites.

She couldn't imagine why Abraham would want to know what his rival looked like, but she complied with his request. "He's not very tall, maybe three or four inches taller than me. Dark, wavy hair. Rather slight for a soldier, but physically strong and tough. Very intimidating.

"Just being around him gave me an eerie feeling. He would get this mean look in his eyes, the meanest look I've ever seen."

"Did he ever do anything to hurt you?" Abraham asked.

She shook her head. "No, but sometimes I remember hearing that dog yelp and scurry off with his tail between his legs, and I can't help wondering if Damian will someday kick me."

Abraham set his cup of wine down on the table so hard that it splashed over the top.

"I'm sorry, Abraham. I've upset you again."

"No, this Damian fellow upset me. If he ever laid a hand on you . . ."

Elizabeth was surprised at the dark glower that crossed his face.

She had never seen Abraham look so fierce, and she didn't know what to say.

"You can't marry him, Elizabeth. You belong with me." He spoke with such sincerity that it squeezed her heart. She wanted desperately to belong to him but knew she belonged to someone else.

"I can't do anything about it," she said, her voice starting to shake again. "I have to go through with it."

"If you were married to someone else, then you *couldn't* marry Damian."

"Don't talk that way, Abraham. I can't go back on my word. I promised."

"No, your father promised."

"Yes, but I promised my father I would abide by the agreement. I couldn't break the contract and hurt my father like that. His reputation would be damaged. And Senator Mallus might do something to get back at him."

"Let me tell you what it's like in Rome." Abraham pushed his plate back and wiped his mouth. "Betrothals are broken all the time; getting engaged and then unengaged is almost a sport among the upper classes. Marriages are dissolved on a whim, and it's not uncommon for a man, especially a prosperous, powerful man such as a senator—or a senator's son—to divorce and remarry three or four times."

"Even when there's a marriage contract? You can do that?"

"Yes." He smiled. "A lawyer isn't worth his salt if he can't come up with a way out of a seemingly ironclad contract. And marriage contracts are not that difficult to get around. I've done it before."

She gasped in surprise.

"Not for me," he quickly amended. "For a client."

"Oh, I see." She was buoyed by his words—she'd prayed for a way out of this marriage from the beginning. But she was also disturbed by the casual attitude toward marriage he had described. "I thought marriage was supposed to last a lifetime," she said.

"It *is* supposed to last a lifetime—and it will with the right person." His voice rang with conviction. "Damian is *not* the right person for you, Elizabeth. I'm persuaded of that beyond a shadow of a doubt."

"And I suppose you're going to tell me that you're the right person?"

"I know it as surely as I know my name."

Her smile was fleeting, as she thought how happy she would be married to Abraham, then quickly dismissed the idea. "I've never broken a promise before, Abraham. My father—"

"I ordinarily wouldn't recommend going back on your word. It's not something I take lightly. But this is . . . Damian is . . . It's just . . ." He scowled again, so upset that he had trouble finding the right words.

"Let me talk to your father," he finally managed. "If I can persuade him that Damian is all wrong for you, if I get him to agree to set aside the marriage contract, then will you marry me?"

By that time she could have forced the sun to rise in the west more easily than she could have refused Abraham. "Yes," she said eagerly. "Oh, yes."

Over the next three days Abraham was closeted with her father for hour after hour. They also conferred with John. She never knew exactly what transpired in their lengthy discussions, but two weeks later she and Abraham were standing before John to solemnize their wedding covenant. She wore the dress Justina had made four years earlier and was never happier than the moment Abraham slipped a gold band on the third finger of her left hand.

12

THE SWEETNESS OF THE MEMORY was palpable, but it was tinged with bitterness now. Elizabeth had just watched her husband make the sacrifice to Caesar, and she couldn't help thinking she was the reason he had committed the horrendous sin.

Now she faced the same choice: sacrifice or exile. Damian was standing in front of her, and Elizabeth forced herself to listen to what he was saying. Something about Rebecca . . . *No!*

Elizabeth blanched. She saw the way Damian was looking at her daughter. It was the same lustful way he had looked at her when he'd arrived in Ephesus that spring, a few months after she'd married Abraham. Just now he had touched Rebecca with the same evil intent . . .

Elizabeth slammed the door of her mind shut on that frightful memory.

It will all be over today, she told herself. One way or another, Damian would get his revenge—the retribution he'd waited twenty-five years to accomplish—and there was nothing they could do about it. Elizabeth no longer worried what Damian could or would do to her; her only thought was for her daughter.

Somehow she had to protect Rebecca.

~◌~

Abraham instantly knew he had made the wrong choice. He'd felt it the moment he dropped the incense into the fire, felt an indefinable loss, and he knew the presence of God had departed from him. In its place a dense cloud of darkness had descended.

He caught Jacob's eye, and the look of deep disappointment on his son's face pierced Abraham's soul. Nevertheless he shoved his conscience aside and focused on Damian, who now turned from Elizabeth and offered the incense to Rebecca.

He's saving Elizabeth for last, Abraham realized with a chill.

"It's your turn, pretty one," Damian informed Rebecca. "I wonder if you have the same mettle as your spirited sister," he said with a smile. "I suggest you follow her example and avoid the consequences of breaking the law."

Rebecca made no move to take the incense he offered. Abraham did not know if she was paralyzed by shock and incapable of movement or if she intended to defy the emperor's order.

"I'm sure you have your father's permission, since he just made the sacrifice himself." When Rebecca still did not move, Damian grabbed her hand and led her forward. "Time's wasting, Rebecca."

Elizabeth reached toward Damian, begging for mercy. "Please, don't do this. Why should her life be ruined because of your hatred for me?"

"Whatever feelings I might have for you, Elizabeth, have nothing to do with this. I'm simply upholding the law. Your daughter must make the sacrifice or pay the consequences, just like everybody else."

Damian escorted Rebecca the few remaining steps to the altar. Still, she hesitated, her gaze drawn to the carvings around the base of the huge limestone block. Figures from Roman mythology, she guessed. Symbolic representations of the glory of the Empire. She had walked across the large open pavilion outside the Temple of Domitian before but had never approached close enough to see the altar's intricate artwork.

As she stared at the softly glowing coals on the surface of the altar, Damian taunted her. "You won't fare well on Patmos, you know. You've led a spoiled, pampered life, secure in your father's mansion. I doubt you'll find the accommodations on Devil's Island to your liking. And the work in the quarries is backbreaking, lifting heavy rocks and carrying them in a basket strapped to your back. You haul the rocks to the harbor, and then go back to the quarry and start all over again. Lift, carry, haul, lift, carry, haul—from sunrise to sunset. Then you return to the cold dark cave you'll call home.

"Is that the kind of life you want, Rebecca? The sweat and pain of hard labor? The terror of being an innocent young woman in a camp full of soldiers? You'll never recline at a sumptuous meal again. Never marry or have children. Everything you've known before will be gone in an instant, unless you make the sacrifice to Caesar—now!"

Rebecca took a pinch of the incense and held it over the altar. She turned and looked at her father.

Abraham had never been more anguished in his life. He did not want Rebecca to make the same mistake he had, and yet he couldn't bear the thought of her punishment. Couldn't stand to think about the danger and the deprivation she would face on Devil's Island. Couldn't bring himself to wonder whether she would be tempted to commit suicide as so many prisoners there did.

Rebecca closed her eyes and opened her hand. The incense sizzled on the coals.

"Say the words," Damian ordered in a guttural tone. "Say it, Rebecca!"

"Jesus is Lord!" Rebecca shouted the words, then she turned and stared at Damian. "I know no other lord," she said firmly.

Damian erupted in rage. "Seize her!" he screamed. "Get her out of my sight!"

Everything spun out of control for Abraham. Instantly two soldiers grabbed Rebecca and clamped circles of iron around her hands and her delicate ankles. Before he could form a word of protest, before his brain could tell his feet to move, Abraham saw his wife react. Exploding with the fury of a mother whose young was being devoured by a wild beast, Elizabeth ran toward the soldiers restraining her daughter.

One of the centurions intercepted Elizabeth and blocked her way.

"Get your hands off her, you animals!" Elizabeth cried as she tried to sidestep the centurion. "She's a child, not a criminal!"

Elizabeth's fists pounded frantically against the centurion's armor, but he did not budge.

Abraham's heart lurched in terror. It was a crime to attack a Roman centurion; Elizabeth could be put to death for it. He screamed, "Stop, Elizabeth! No!" and then began running toward her. He had taken only a few steps when one of the numerous soldiers patrolling the temple area knocked Abraham in the head with the blunt end of his spear.

The blow sent him reeling, but he stayed on his feet, still yelling for Elizabeth to stop. Another legionnaire rushed to strike Abraham with a club, and he sank to the ground.

Abraham's vision blurred and dimmed. He continued to hear the voices around him, but they were distorted, as if the speakers were in a well. As he faded in and out of consciousness, chaotic scenes from the past merged with the present in his jumbled mind . . .

∽◦∼

"Stop it, Elizabeth!" Abraham sounded stern as he grabbed his bride's arm. Elizabeth shrieked in delight and tried to twist away from him. The little minx had tormented him ever since she had discovered he was ticklish.

She slipped out of his grasp and stood at a safe distance, leaning forward with her hands resting on her knees. They were both out of breath from climbing the hillside and from their silly games. With her joyous laughter ringing in the wildflower-scented air, there was no way Abraham could stay peeved at her. As far as he was concerned, Elizabeth could tickle him whenever she wanted; the sheer pleasure of her touch far outweighed the irritation.

When she had caught her breath, Elizabeth removed a light woolen blanket from the large basket and spread it in the clearing at the top of the hill. They had chosen the scenic spot, which over-looked the harbor, for their first picnic.

"What a glorious day," she said as she sat down. "Spring is my favorite season. Emerging beauty. The promise of new life. A season filled with hope." She smiled and patted the blanket beside her, inviting Abraham to join her. "What's your favorite time of year?"

"Any time I'm with you," Abraham quipped. He sat down behind Elizabeth and put his arms around her. She leaned back against him, and for a minute they silently watched the clouds billow across the sky like moving mountains of cotton.

"Remember the first time you came to my house?" Elizabeth asked.

He grunted, and she took that for a yes. "I don't know what you said to my father that day," she continued, "but I'm awfully glad you persuaded him to let me marry you. These last six months have been the happiest of my life."

She turned around to face him. "Are you happy too, Abraham?"

"I didn't know it was possible to be this happy." He brushed a loose curl away from her forehead and traced the curve of her cheek with a finger.

Abraham certainly recalled the conversations he had had with her father that day, and for several days afterward. Rufus had not been receptive when he first approached him.

"I suspect you have an ulterior motive for telling me Elizabeth shouldn't marry young Mallus," Rufus had said.

"It's true. I admit I want to marry Elizabeth myself," Abraham had replied. "But please hear me out. I have some information about this man you should know—information that will change your mind about the suitability of this marriage."

Abraham had told Rufus then about seeing Damian murder another tribune in Jerusalem. Rufus, who was nervous by nature, wrung his hands in despair at the startling revelation. "Elizabeth is my only child. I can't let her marry a murderer, but what can I do?

The Mallus family is very powerful—the senator could make life miserable for me."

"And his son could make life miserable for Elizabeth," Abraham responded.

After several days of strategizing, Rufus had written a letter to Mallus, breaking the marriage contract. He had sought legal counsel, he told the senator—not telling him, of course, that his lawyer would be the man Elizabeth was going to marry instead of the senator's son. Rufus also said that his lawyer was holding a signed affidavit from an eyewitness who had seen Damian murder a fellow officer. "Should it be necessary," Rufus wrote, "we will turn this information over to the authorities. But because of your status in the Empire, and in regard for our longtime association, I would rather keep this matter private and let you handle it with military officials in Rome as you see fit."

It was blackmail, pure and simple: "Cancel the marriage contract, and I won't brand your son as a murderer."

Abraham—who was both the legal counsel and the eyewitness—knew that proving a case against Damian would be difficult, if not impossible. But he had assured Rufus that the senator would want to avoid any hint of a scandal. It was a calculated risk, but one worth taking. And one that had paid off.

Senator Mallus had responded with a short but gracious letter, thanking Rufus for his discretion. By the time his letter had arrived, Elizabeth and Abraham were newlyweds.

Sitting here now, with Elizabeth in his arms, enjoying the sunshine and the solitude and the spectacular view of the mountains and the harbor, he was indeed a happy man.

"Abraham, are you listening to me?" Elizabeth interrupted his train of thought.

"I'm sorry," he said. "I was distracted by thoughts of marital bliss." He smiled broadly at his lovely wife. "What were you saying?"

"I said, I have something important to tell you. You've been so busy, we haven't had much time together, and I've been waiting for just the right time."

"I apologize, sweetheart. I know I've neglected my beautiful bride, but there's so much to do with getting a new enterprise off the ground." Rufus had made a wedding present of a small shipping business that had been unable to navigate some choppy financial waters. The inexperienced owners had not repaid their loans and had walked away from the business, leaving Rufus's bank holding the notes. With good management, he'd told Abraham, it could be a very profitable venture. Abraham was determined to turn the business around and expand the fledgling company's trade route.

"So what is this important matter you've been waiting to tell me?" *It must be good news,* he thought. She had never looked happier.

"Abraham!" The reedy voice was followed a moment later by a view of Quintus's head. He cleared his throat as he crested the top of the hill. "Abraham, I'm sorry to interrupt you . . ." The gangly teenager reddened and looked embarrassed.

Abraham sighed. "What is it, Quintus?"

Elizabeth shifted her position and looked away, her mouth set in a tight line.

"There's a man at the office who wants to see you—"

"Can't Decimus handle it?" Abraham's voice betrayed his impatience. He'd left explicit instructions with his foreman, who by now should have been capable of handling anything that came up this afternoon. It was the first time in months Abraham had managed to steal a few daylight hours with his wife.

"Decimus assured the man we could handle his business, but he insists on talking to the owner personally." Quintus paused. "Decimus said to tell you the man is a wealthy merchant from Troas. Says he has a thousand barrels of wine sitting in his warehouse, and he just found out the shipper he's been using has cheated him for years. He needs to start moving the wine right away, he said, and with that much inventory, well . . ."

A thousand barrels of wine. A regular customer with that kind of volume could be the linchpin for a shipping company, especially a new and expanding one. Abraham looked at Elizabeth guiltily. For days he'd been promising to take a few hours off to have a picnic with her. And she had wanted to tell him something important. He didn't want to disappoint his wife, but he couldn't afford to pass up an opportunity to land an account that could make or break his new business.

"Elizabeth," he said, "I'd better see about this."

She stood and brushed off the skirt of her tunic. "We haven't even eaten our lunch yet," she said, her lip twitching.

Abraham rose and tried to put his arm around her, but she wouldn't let him. "Honey, I'm sorry," he said.

Without saying a word, Elizabeth bent down, opened the lid of the basket, then reached for the blanket.

"No, leave it." Abraham grasped her hand to stop her from folding the blanket and putting it away. "Wait for me here. I'll see the man for just a few minutes, as a courtesy, and then tell him we'll have to finish our business later. I can be back in less than an hour. And then we can have our picnic—and talk."

Elizabeth appeared slightly mollified and offered her cheek for a brief kiss before he left with Quintus.

When they had walked down the hillside a ways, Quintus said, "I hope Elizabeth will forgive me for dragging you away. She looked angry."

"She'll forgive you," Abraham said quickly. "I'm the one she's upset with right now, but I'll make it up to her. I wouldn't have let you interrupt me if it hadn't been something important." Already he was mentally calculating cargo space for a thousand barrels of wine, and speculating on the destination ports.

"When Decimus asked if I knew where you were, I couldn't lie. I said I knew, but that I had promised not to tell anyone. He kept badgering me until I finally said I'd deliver a message to you. I think he was mad that I wouldn't tell him."

"Decimus is probably just mad because you don't answer to him anymore; you work for me now." When Abraham had taken over the shipping business, he'd discovered that Quintus, who had worked for the previous owner, had a good head for numbers. Quintus was not only bright, he was industrious and loyal. So Abraham had moved him off the docks and into the office, where he had no official title or job duties. He simply did whatever Abraham asked him to, and Quintus had quickly proven himself invaluable.

It took about ten minutes to wind their way down the hill into the city, but when they reached Harbor Street, the two of them quickly picked up the pace. Abraham was eager to find out how he could help the wine merchant, and eager to conclude his meeting with the man so he could get back to Elizabeth. He was excited as they walked down the broad avenue, ignoring the vendors who vied for business along the colonnade. Except for the time it took him away from his bride, Abraham didn't mind the long hours he was putting into the business. He loved the challenge, and he loved the noise and the bustle and even the smells of the harbor.

Seagulls scavenging for crumbs scattered when the two men walked up the four steps from the street to the wooden pier. With the long stride of tall men, they walked the length of the pier— *Someday I'll move to larger quarters in the very center of the harbor,* Abraham thought smugly—and entered the cramped office of his shipping company.

The wine merchant was not there.

Quintus went in search of Decimus, who returned to report sheepishly that he didn't know where the man had gone. "I got called out on the dock just after Quintus left. I excused myself, said I'd be right back, and I left him here in the office. Couldn't have been gone more than a couple of minutes, but when I got back, the merchant was nowhere to be found."

Abraham was both disappointed and aggravated. "He just left without saying anything? I thought he had insisted on seeing me."

"Oh, he did," Decimus said. "He was adamant about it. I wouldn't have sent Quintus to get you otherwise."

"Did he leave his name or say how I could get in contact with him?" In his mind Abraham saw all those barrels of wine sitting in a warehouse in Troas, just waiting to be loaded on his ships— the account was his!

Flustered, Decimus scratched his head. "Surely he told me his name. Let me think . . ." He paused and then shrugged. "Sorry," he finally said, "I can't remember now if he even said who he was. He wanted to see our operation, and I showed him around. Asked question after question about the business and its owner. Then I heard about all that wine sitting in his warehouse waiting to be shipped, and everything else left my head.

"I know he said Troas," Decimus added. "That I remember, because I have an uncle in Troas—"

"It's all right, Decimus." Abraham couldn't be too angry with his foreman; he had done the same thing. He had thought of what his net profit would be for shipping a thousand barrels of wine, and nothing else had seemed important after that.

"I'd better check on the loading crew," Decimus mumbled as he turned and left.

Quintus seemed as let down and as puzzled as Abraham. "But why would he leave if he really wanted to talk to you? It's not only rude, it just doesn't make sense."

"I guess the lesson to be learned is that if something sounds too good to be true, it probably is." Abraham chided himself for neglecting the most important person in his life—Elizabeth—to chase down something that had seemed urgent but turned out to be a waste of time. *If I'm lucky,* he thought, *she won't be too mad at me. Maybe we can recapture our earlier mood.*

They walked out on the pier, and Abraham was saying good-bye to Quintus when Rufus sprinted up to them. His wiry red hair flapped wildly over his forehead, and he was out of breath.

"Where's Elizabeth?" he asked. "She's not home. I went there first."

"What's wrong? Are you okay?" His father-in-law looked quite disturbed, Abraham thought.

"Where is she?"

"She's up in the hills, waiting for me. We were having a picnic."

"Is she all right?"

"Yes, she's fine." Abraham motioned for Rufus to enter the office. "Come in and tell me what has you so upset."

"Maybe I'm just being paranoid," Rufus said when he had taken a seat. "But something unusual happened while I was in a meeting with a client this morning."

Abraham smiled. Rufus did tend to exaggerate the dimensions of a problem. Whatever it was, Rufus had probably blown it out of proportion.

"A man came into the bank today," Rufus said, "and told my assistant, Junius, that he wanted to open an account—mentioned a large sum of money—but he wanted me to handle it personally. He was an acquaintance of mine from Rome, the man said. Junius entertained him while they waited for me to conclude my meeting."

"That's not too unusual," Abraham said. "I imagine personal referrals are a large part of your business." He was impatient to get back to his beautiful young wife, who was waiting to serve him a meal outdoors and tell him something important. "What does this have to do with Elizabeth?"

"He engaged in small talk with Junius while they waited, and he asked a lot of questions about me and my family. He seemed to know a lot about us, Junius said. Specifically, he remembered I had a young daughter, and that she was very beautiful. He even remembered her name, and he asked if Elizabeth was married yet. Junius said yes and told him about you."

Rufus stopped to catch his breath, and suddenly Abraham began to wonder if Rufus's paranoia was catching. He had a queasy feeling in his empty stomach.

"Shortly after that, the man left, saying he would come back tomorrow. Afterward, Junius got to thinking it was curious that he had asked so many personal questions rather than questions about the bank."

Taken by itself, the inquisitive customer at the bank wouldn't have amounted to much, but with the mysterious stranger disappearing at the shipping office, it seemed more than a coincidence. Abraham stood up and started pacing the floor. "He asked specifically about Elizabeth, whether she was married?" There was something disconcerting about that.

Rufus nodded. "I guess what worried me the most is the way Junius described the man—said he was not very tall, had a sharp nose, dark hair and eyes, and walked with a swagger. I couldn't help remembering—"

"That sounds like the wine merchant," Quintus interrupted.

"That's how Elizabeth described Damian. Swaggering." Rufus looked at Quintus. "Wine merchant?"

"Come on," Abraham yelled as he bolted out of the office. "We have to hurry!" If the wine merchant and the bank customer bore a resemblance to Damian, he was taking no chances.

Abraham ran down Harbor Street at a breakneck pace, overturning a vendor's cart in his haste. The tradesman cursed as his vegetables scattered over the pavement, and Rufus called over his shoulder, "I'll cover your loss later."

The trio sped across the city but had to slow down when they reached the hills. Abraham clawed his way up the slopes without bothering to follow the winding path he and Elizabeth had taken earlier. He climbed through a patch of thistles, not noticing how they scratched his ankles. All that mattered was getting to Elizabeth.

"I know where she's supposed to be," Quintus told Rufus as they followed a short distance behind Abraham. "We'll catch up with you," he yelled up the hill.

When Abraham reached the clearing, he saw the picnic basket

lying on the blanket, but Elizabeth was nowhere in sight. The sick feeling in his stomach exploded into panic, and he could scarcely breathe.

"Elizzzaaabeth!" he shouted frantically while praying silently, *Please, God, let her just be off picking wildflowers or something.*

Winded, Abraham stayed where he was for a moment and scanned the area. He could find no clue as to where she had gone. "Elizabeth!" he called again.

He heard a muffled scream and thought it came from a stand of laurel trees behind the clearing.

"Elizabeth!" Abraham's cry echoed over the hillside as he tore into the woods, his heart pounding.

He spotted them a dozen yards into the thicket. Elizabeth's tunic was torn at the shoulders and hanging down to her waist. Her back pinned against a tree, she was struggling against her attacker, who held one hand over her mouth and groped her roughly with the other. She shoved and kicked but could not break loose from his grasp.

It was Damian, no doubt about it. Abraham closed the distance between them in an instant. He reacted in blind rage, yanking Damian by the hair with such force that his feet dangled in the air. Abraham slung him to the ground and kicked him in the stomach. Damian's face turned ashen and he had no breath, but Abraham snatched him to his feet again, then drove a massive fist like a sledgehammer into Damian's face. The bones in his nose popped like dry twigs, and blood gushed down his face. As Damian staggered backward, Abraham grabbed him by the throat and slammed his head into the trunk of a tree.

Damian slid to the ground, but Abraham kept pummeling him until he felt restraining hands pulling him back.

"Abraham, stop! You're going to kill him." Quintus was half-apologetic. "You've stopped him. It's over. You can't just murder the man."

Abraham froze in position over Damian, his elbow drawn back and his fist ready to deliver another blow. "Why not?" For a moment

Abraham looked at Quintus in confusion, then he came to his senses. Damian was a murderer; he wasn't. But he likely would have been if Quintus hadn't stopped him.

He looked around for Elizabeth and saw her clutching her torn dress to cover herself. Rufus stood beside her, his arm around her protectively.

"Let him go," Rufus said. "I don't think he'll be back after the beating you've given him."

Abraham slowly stood up and looked down at Damian. Blood still poured from his nose and his face was purple and puffy from Abraham's fury.

In spite of his injuries, Damian spoke with defiance. "You're wrong, old man. I *will* be back—you can count on it. And next time, I'll take what is rightfully mine," he said with a despicable look at Elizabeth.

Abraham took a step toward Damian, his fist automatically clenching, but Quintus held him back.

Damian stared at Abraham unflinchingly. "And then I'll kill you," Damian said slowly. Finally he turned and limped down the hill.

Abraham unclenched his fists and walked over to Elizabeth, who fell against him, sobbing. For a few minutes he held her against his pounding heart, then he picked her up and carried her back to the clearing. The others followed.

"Quintus, you take the basket for me," he ordered. "But leave the blanket. I'll meet you at the house."

Quintus and Rufus started down the hill while Abraham carefully wrapped the blanket around Elizabeth. She was white-faced and trembling. Abraham picked her up again and began to slowly travel down the path back to the city.

In a minute, he stopped. Elizabeth was whispering and he leaned close to hear what she was saying.

"I'm going to have a baby," she murmured in a small voice, tears streaming down her face. "That's what I wanted to tell you."

13

REBECCA HEARD BLOODCURDLING SCREAMS as her father collapsed and, simultaneously, Damian unsheathed his sword and ran toward her mother, who was pounding furiously but futilely against the chest of a Roman centurion. The soldier shoved her away just as Damian reached her, and with a violent lunge, he impaled Elizabeth on his drawn weapon. Damian's sword pierced her chest and protruded from her back as she slumped to the ground.

The screaming grew louder and Rebecca thought it would deafen her. Even when she realized the screams were her own, she was helpless to stop them.

Jacob shuffled over to Rebecca and tried to calm her. "Stop screaming. Shhhhhh."

As Jacob kept speaking soothingly to her, she was finally able to still her screams. "It's all right," he told her. "Mother is in heaven already. Jesus is standing at the right hand of the Father, and He is welcoming her home even now."

For a long time Damian stared down at Elizabeth, then he knelt beside her. One of his men came to assist him, but Damian waved him off.

"It wasn't supposed to end this way, Elizabeth, but you chose to break the law." Damian's voice was cold and merciless. "You've always made stupid choices. You chose to marry Abraham when you could have had me." With a sneer, he pulled his bloodstained sword from the corpse. "Stupid choices," he repeated.

Rebecca bit her lip to keep from screaming again when Damian touched her mother's body as he removed the sword. She wanted to fall into her brother's arms, wanted him to hold her and comfort her, but they were both bound by chains. Jacob reached out and squeezed her hand, their metal cuffs clanging against each other. They silently watched as Damian used their mother's tunic to wipe her blood off his sword while the soldiers regained control of the crowd.

So much had happened so fast, Rebecca could scarcely comprehend it. She looked over at John. Tears streamed down the Apostle's face as he watched the gruesome scene.

After a moment Damian regained his composure and rose to his feet. *The man is insane,* Rebecca realized. *And my mother and father knew this madman. How? Why?*

Rebecca's whole world had turned upside down in one hour. Her mother had been brutally murdered; her father was injured, if not dead. And her father had done the unthinkable: he had denied the Lord Jesus. In her confusion, Rebecca had almost denied Him too, but at the last minute she had suddenly been compelled to speak the one bedrock truth she believed with all her heart: Jesus is Lord.

Her mind swirling, Rebecca watched as Damian marched the other Christians one by one to the altar of Domitian. Those who made the sacrifice were sent home; those who refused were put in chains and joined the group bound for Devil's Island.

Some of them, like old Servius, were household servants who had cared for her all her life. The soldiers treated him roughly when he refused to bow to Caesar, and as they manhandled him into the iron cuffs, Servius was knocked against the corner of the carved stone altar. His gray hair was matted with blood but his back was straight as he took his place beside Rebecca.

"Be strong," he whispered to her. She thought of their all-night vigil the night before and knew she would not have had the courage to endure if Servius had not called them all to prayer.

When the sacrifices were finally concluded, the soldiers lined up the prisoners, some two dozen who had been faithful to Christ, to begin a forced march to the harbor. "You'll board the ship for Patmos there," Damian barked. "Say good-bye to Ephesus," he said. "You'll never see home again."

If he's not insane, Rebecca thought, *he's the vilest man who ever lived.*

As they began to march, Rebecca looked at her mother's lifeless form for the last time and wondered what would happen to her body. She tried to get a final glimpse of her father but could not; the crowd was moving in the opposite direction, and she stumbled along with them to keep from being knocked down. As best she could tell, Abraham was still lying motionless on the ground. Rebecca fervently hoped he was alive and that she would see him again someday.

The midmorning march to the harbor was the longest mile Rebecca had ever walked. The leg irons bit into her flesh, and the cuts on her ankles seemed to deepen with each movement. The blood dripping over her sandals mingled with the dust of the street until her feet were a sticky mess. With every step she winced from pain.

Some of the spectators who had watched the mandatory sacrifices lined the street to jeer at the Christians marching in chains. Rebecca closed her ears to their shouts. As they filed past the columns marking the entrance to the temple pavilion and into the street, Rebecca spied her father's assistant in the crowd. *Why hadn't Quintus been with those required to sacrifice?* she wondered. Not all the members of their church had been arrested, she realized, but Quintus worked for her father and was close to her family. Surely the officials would have rounded him up with the others. Could he have been an informer? What an appalling thought.

Slowly the group made its way down the sloping Marble Street and then turned into the broad avenue that led to the harbor. Vendors left their stalls to watch the procession, and Rebecca searched for Galen as she passed his shop. She was relieved that he had been spared this nightmare, and at the same time wished he were with her. But he had left the day before to deliver a major order he'd just finished—a complete set of silver serving pieces—to a wealthy customer in Magnesia. He had been proud of his work and thrilled for the increase in business now that he was about to be a married man.

Abraham had finally spoken to Galen, and her father had given his consent to the union. Overjoyed, the couple had immediately started making plans for their wedding. Now their joy had been turned to mourning, and Rebecca didn't know if she would ever see Galen again.

Numbly, she marched on until they reached the harbor that had always been a vital part of her family's life. She loved the ocean, and she loved sailing. Rebecca breathed deeply, inhaling the tangy smell of salt water. It reminded her of her father. One of her earliest memories was crawling up in her father's lap when he came home from the harbor every afternoon. "You smell like the ocean," she would tell him, wrinkling her nose as she buried her face in his tunic, and he would laugh as he held her close.

She had never sailed without her father, she suddenly realized. *Why isn't he here?* she lamented. *If he hadn't made the sacrifice, he would be with me now, and I wouldn't be so scared.* At least Jacob was with her, and she took comfort in that thought.

As they filed up the steep plank to board the ship, she told herself, *I'll pretend we're boarding the* Mercury *for a voyage to Rome.* But she could not keep up the pretense for more than a minute. No soldiers had ever guarded the passengers on the *Mercury*. And no one in chains had ever boarded her father's beautiful ship, which was long, sleek, and elegant in every detail. The dilapidated boat they boarded now was squat and creaky, and it reeked of sweat and urine and rancid fish. Rebecca gagged from the smell as the soldiers herded them belowdecks.

As they got under way, the prisoners sat huddled together in a cramped area of the cargo hold. Some were crying, some were praying, and some, like Rebecca, were silent. This was certainly no holiday cruise on her father's ship; this old hulk was headed for the hell of Devil's Island, and fear gripped Rebecca's mind as she contemplated what awaited her there.

⁂

When the carriage deposited Naomi at the villa just before noon, she went straight to the kitchen to find something to eat. She supposed she'd have to prepare it herself, since the entire household had been apprehended and taken to the Temple of Domitian, and most of them were now on their way to Devil's Island.

As she searched the pantry, she made a mental note to find someone to repair the front door, which had been knocked off its hinges by the brutes who had stormed it early that morning. *After all, I'm the mistress of the house now,* Naomi thought with a small burst of pride followed by a pang of regret. Watching her mother be stabbed to death was a most unpleasant way to acquire the job, but Naomi knew she was capable of running a large household, and with her mother gone, someone had to do it. She would have to find more help immediately, though. Perhaps she would attend the next slave auction; she would inquire about it after the games this afternoon, she decided.

As she assembled a snack of fruit and cheese and bread, Naomi remembered that Peter had not been with them that morning. *He must be here somewhere,* she thought. *Probably still hiding.*

Poor Peter. If she had an ally within the family, he was it. Not that she could count on him in a crisis; he would vanish, as he had that morning. But at least he made an effort to see things from her point of view. And occasionally Peter even agreed with her in family discussions.

Naomi went from room to room looking for him, calling his name. "It's all right, Peter. You can come out now. It's only me."

It had not surprised Naomi that he had managed to hide so well that he avoided discovery. When they were younger, Peter had always been the best of the four at playing hide-and-seek. Rebecca was too eager to be found, too ready to be congratulated for finding such a clever place to hide. Jacob was fast, but too big and awkward to hide easily. What Peter lacked in speed and agility, he made up for in craftiness and patience. Peter always found the place no one thought to look in, and he would stay completely still and quiet even when the others were inches away from him. An hour or more after the others had all given up the game, Peter would still be hiding.

Now she found him in the library, dusting himself off. "Where were you?" she asked.

"In there." He pointed to a small storage closet under the staircase. "I rolled myself up in an old carpet."

"It's a wonder you didn't suffocate."

"After a while I crawled out of the carpet. But I stayed in the closet until I heard you just now." Peter stretched and blinked, his eyes adjusting to the sunlit room. He looked around nervously. "Where is everyone else? What happened?"

Naomi ushered Peter into the dining room and related the tumultuous events while they ate the impromptu meal she had thrown together.

"I can't believe Father sacrificed to the emperor." Peter's forehead wrinkled in astonishment. "It goes against everything he stands for."

"I know, but he did it." Naomi was oddly disturbed. On the one hand, she had thought he would be a fool *not* to make the sacrifice, and had repeatedly said so. On the other hand, she supposed she had harbored the thought that her father's faith was some kind of an anchor—one she had not held on to, but one she assumed would be there if she ever needed it. But if that anchor didn't hold even for her father . . .

I don't need a supernatural faith as an anchor at all, she reminded herself. She didn't have faith in the Christian God or any of the Roman gods. She didn't have faith in the Roman Empire. Naomi had faith in herself, and that was all she needed.

Peter broke down and cried when she told him about Elizabeth being run through with a sword. "And it was the strangest thing," Naomi said. "That Damian fellow *knew* Mother—he said she could have married him instead of Father."

Peter's hand shook so much that he put his spoon down without taking a bite. "I'm glad I wasn't there to see it," he said quietly. "What about Father? Is he dead too?"

"I . . . I don't know for sure." Naomi poured herself some wine and avoided looking at Peter. "Some of the soldiers beat him severely, and he was lying on the ground. He could have been unconscious, I suppose. But probably dead."

"You just went off and left them there?"

"What was I supposed to do, Peter? Jacob and Rebecca had marched off in chains. Hundreds of soldiers were still in the area when Damian ordered two of his men to take me home. Since their commander had just killed my mother for hitting a centurion, and their comrades had beaten my father for trying to interfere, I didn't think my escorts would take kindly to my stopping to inquire about my parents."

They finished the meal in silence, and Naomi was still sulking as she went upstairs to get dressed. Peter had touched a sore spot, but she would not admit it. As she had been driven off in the carriage, Naomi had fought a wave of guilt for not seeing about her father. He might have still been alive, and she knew she should have seen if he needed help, but she had wanted to put as much distance as possible between her and the painful public spectacle. And she had not been willing to risk any further embarrassment or jeopardy. So she had simply come home.

It would be much easier, it occurred to her now, if her father were indeed dead. *Not only am I capable of running this household,* she thought, *I can run the entire shipping business.* With her father out of the picture, there would be nothing—or no one—to stand in her way, and Naomi liked that idea.

As she meticulously dressed for the games, she put aside any lingering doubts. *I don't have time for guilt,* she told herself. *I have a life to live.*

14

BEFORE HE OPENED HIS EYES, Abraham tasted the dust and grit of the cobblestones where he'd been lying since the soldiers had struck him down. His head was pounding and his ears ringing. His body was trembling so much, he felt as if someone was shaking him.

Someone *was* shaking him, he finally realized, trying to wake him up. He opened one eye and then the other. His vision was blurred, and the man's face swam in front of him, becoming two faces and then merging together again.

"Abraham," the man said. "Abraham, can you hear me?"

He couldn't recognize the face, but the familiar voice was easily identified. "Quintus," he mumbled, "is that you?"

"Yes, Abraham." Quintus put a hand under his shoulder. "Can you sit up? You've been hurt."

With Quintus's help, Abraham sat up slowly. He spit a pebble out of his mouth and brushed some of the dirt off his face.

"It's over," Quintus said. "The soldiers have cleared out."

Abraham gradually became aware of his surroundings, and then it hit him. "Elizabeth! Oh, God, please . . ." He crawled on his hands and knees toward his wife, trying to piece together the blurred images he recalled—Damian, the sword, Elizabeth falling. He'd seen it all in a haze and had thought—had desperately hoped—he was dreaming. Surely it was a nightmare, a delusion caused by his throbbing head.

But when he reached Elizabeth, he knew it was true: Damian had killed her. Abraham fell across his wife's body, sobbing.

"Pull yourself together." Quintus's voice was unusually stern. "We need to get out of here."

Abraham shook off the hand on his shoulder. "Leave me alone!" he cried.

Quintus persisted. "Come on, Abraham. We need to get Elizabeth home. We can't leave her body lying in the street."

That truth pierced through his grief and shock. Abraham summoned his strength to stand and pick up his wife's body. When he stooped over to lift her, a pain shot through his head and he felt as if the top of his skull would explode.

"Let me help you," Quintus said.

"I can do it," Abraham replied. He was determined not to leave Elizabeth on the streets like an animal, and he would get her away from this pagan temple if it was the last thing he ever did.

Quintus steadied Abraham as he stood and balanced Elizabeth in his arms for the arduous trip home. The journey of just under a mile seemed to take forever. It was uphill all the way, and because of his injuries and his tears, Abraham had trouble seeing the road beneath his feet. Twice he had to set Elizabeth down, wipe the tears from his eyes, and catch his breath. He was too stubborn and proud to let Quintus help him.

Abraham managed to control his grief until they reached the top of the last hill and he caught sight of their villa, the beautiful sprawling home he had built for his bride and their young children. For the last hundred yards, Abraham wailed at the top of his lungs, and when they finally stepped over the broken door into the courtyard entrance of the house, he collapsed with Elizabeth still in his arms.

࿎

Naomi heard the loud lament and ran to the window. From her upstairs bedroom, she looked out and saw her father carrying her mother toward the house.

He's alive, she thought. *Alive and brokenhearted.*

She allowed herself a brief moment of sympathy for her father. She knew what it was like to bury the person you loved most in the world, and to bury your dreams along with your spouse. Naomi quickly forgot her father's grief, however, as she recalled her own. She'd been far too young to lose everything in life that had been dear to her. All she had now were her memories and two bands of solid gold she kept in a velvet-lined box made of teak.

Naomi took the box out of the chest where she kept it. The top was inlaid with a trefoil-shaped mosaic of delicate wood veneers. She seldom looked at the keepsake box anymore; she had not allowed herself the luxury of mourning for a long time now. Three years earlier, when her husband died, she had spent all her grief early on and then determined to go on with her life, throwing herself into a whirlwind of social activities.

She filled her days with trips to the baths, the hairdresser, the dressmaker, the theater, the games, dinner parties, and visits to friends. She spent her evenings planning how to fill the next day. And in the odd moment when she actually allowed herself to think, it was only about the future, never the past.

Now she ran a slim finger over the trefoil inlay and the circle of gold leaf that surrounded it. The symbol of eternity, like the wedding bands, inside. *Eternity? Nothing lasts forever,* she thought bitterly.

For a while she had held on to the belief that she would be reunited with Crispin, but eventually she had discarded any belief in the afterlife—whether the Elysian fields of Roman mythology or the celestial heaven of the Christians—along with her faith.

The sound of her father's mournful sobs carried upstairs from the courtyard below. Naomi wished he would stop wailing. It was getting on her nerves. She put away the keepsake box and finished dressing, trying to muster enthusiasm for attending the games with Julia, but she was not able to shake her dark reflections.

There had been a time, she remembered, when her father was the person Naomi had loved most in the world. She was his little princess, whom he nicknamed Tyranna. He had doted on her, and she doted on being the center of his world.

Then, when she was almost five, the twins were born. It had been a difficult delivery and her mother had almost died. When she was older, Naomi had learned that the firstborn, Peter, had been in the breech position; he came into the world feet first, and one of his legs was twisted as a result. All his life Peter had been smaller and weaker than his younger twin, Jacob, and the birth injury had left him lame.

All Naomi knew then was that her mother was sick for a very long time. A nurse took care of the newborns, and Abraham started taking Naomi to the harbor with him every day. She played in her father's office, and in the afternoons Quintus taught her to add on the abacus and to scratch the alphabet on a clay tablet. Her father taught her to swim and even took her sailing with him. She grew up loving the harbor, the big ships, and everything about her father's booming business.

After Rebecca was born, two years after the twins, Abraham had built the big villa on the hill and hired a schoolmaster to teach Naomi. Her father still let her come to his office, though, after her lessons each day. But more and more, she noticed, he turned his attention away from her and toward her brothers. Her mother, preoccupied with the new baby and managing a large household, had little time for Naomi. Then when Peter and Jacob began their formal education at age seven, Abraham had started letting them come to the harbor every afternoon, and Naomi was told she had to stay home.

She was crushed. "But why? Why do I have to stay home just because Peter and Jacob are old enough to learn the business now? It's not fair!"

"It may not be fair," her father had said, "but that's the way it's going to be. After all, the boys will inherit the business one day. And besides, the harbor is not a proper place for a young girl, Naomi. Your mother has always frowned on it."

"Why isn't it proper? I like the office, and I've got a good head for business. I can copy the shipping manifests from your notes, and I've helped Quintus record the inventory. I can calculate as fast as he can! Well, almost. Anyway—"

Her father interrupted her. "The business world is a man's domain, and I've done you a disservice by letting you tag along with me into that world. It's time you learned to be a lady, Naomi. You're almost twelve, and in a few years you'll be married."

Naomi had been so disappointed, she cried for days. Gradually her tears had turned into hot anger, and her affection for her father had cooled and hardened into bitterness.

As she fastened a gold chain around her neck, Naomi looked in the mirror. *I became a lady, Father. Just as you insisted.* She pinned her long curls into a fashionable sweep. *A beautiful lady with many admirers.*

Naomi shut the door on her memories as she shut the bedroom door behind her. She allowed herself one final thought of the past before leaving for the games in honor of the emperor's birthday. *I'll never forgive you for shutting me out, Father. Never.*

◌⁓◌

Quintus went to the back of the house while Abraham remained seated on the tile floor of the atrium, cradling Elizabeth in his arms. He wept until his tears drenched his wife's blood-spattered tunic.

He finally stopped sobbing, but his voice wavered as he said, "What a fool I've been, Elizabeth. What a fool." Spent and bereft, he leaned back against the wall and closed his eyes. The pain in his head was nothing compared to the pain in his heart. How could his well-ordered life have disintegrated so suddenly?

After resting a while, Abraham struggled to his feet and carried his beloved wife, the mother of his children, his reason for living, up the stairs. He laid her on the bed where they had shared so many intimate conversations and spoke to her for the final time, pouring out his innermost thoughts to the only one he'd ever loved enough to reveal that much of himself.

"I'm sorry, Elizabeth," he continued in a tremulous voice. "I stupidly thought I could save my fortune and somehow save my family. Instead, I've lost you, and I've lost my soul."

A new wave of tears gushed out of eyes he had been certain were bone-dry. "I will love you forever, Elizabeth. There will never be another." He picked up a pale hand and kissed it. "I know you are in heaven listening to me, and I fear God will not forgive my treason. But I will beg God's forgiveness every day of my life so I can join you in heaven someday."

Slowly and reverently Abraham removed his wife's clothing, weeping with every tug of her blood-soaked tunic. The one who had brought warmth and sunshine to his life now lay on the bed, her bare skin as cold and smooth as alabaster. Touching her eyelids, he silently vowed he would give his fortune ten times over if he could see the sparkle in those lively green eyes just one more time.

Abraham washed her body in a final baptism, then anointed her with aromatic oils. When he had finished preparing Elizabeth for burial, he wrapped her in white linen.

Then Abraham cleaned himself up, changed clothes, and went outside to the grassy knoll where he had constructed a private mausoleum when the villa was first built. Rufus, Elizabeth's father, was buried there, as was Crispin, Naomi's husband. Elizabeth would be laid to rest in one of the niches carved into the hillside, then after a year, when the body had decomposed, her bones would be gathered and placed in a carved limestone ossuary engraved with her name.

Quintus had already opened the heavy door and was standing inside the crypt. "I was looking for this," he said, indicating the stretcher he had just picked up. "We'll need it to carry the body." The stretcher, made of heavy canvas covering two wooden poles, would be used as a funeral bier.

"There won't be much of a funeral," Abraham said brokenly. "Not with Jacob and Rebecca gone. And John." He paused. "John married us, you know."

"Yes, I was there," Quintus replied.

Abraham nodded, as if remembering. "I thought we'd bury the Apostle long before he had a chance to bury one of us. Now she's gone, and he's not here to do the funeral."

Quintus placed a hand on Abraham's shoulder. "I'm so sorry. Elizabeth was the kindest woman I've ever known."

"Help me bring her down, Quintus. I want to bury her before sunset."

They turned to go back into the house, but Abraham staggered dizzily and almost fainted. Quintus helped him inside. "When have you eaten anything?" he asked.

Abraham thought for a moment. "Night before last, I think."

"You need something in your stomach," Quintus said as they walked into the kitchen. "I'll find you something to eat."

"No, I want to bury Elizabeth first."

"You won't have the strength if you don't eat." In a reversal of roles, Quintus ordered his boss to sit down. He pulled a rough wooden stool up to the chopping block where the cook prepared the family's meals. A set of well-used pots and pans hung over the brick fireplace, but with no one to tend it, the fire had gone out and the coals were cold. The room was chilly.

Abraham watched silently as Quintus loaded two plates with an odd assortment from the pantry and filled a carafe with wine. "You couldn't exactly call this a meal," Quintus said as he sat across from Abraham, "but I didn't want to take time to cook you something."

"You can cook?" Abraham was surprised.

"Enough to keep from starving. You have to make do when you live alone."

Abraham had no appetite, but he forced down a few bites of bread and some dried figs. As they ate, Quintus told him about watching the morning's unbearable events unfold.

"The only reason I wasn't required to pledge my loyalty to Caesar with the rest of you," he said, "was the fact that I'd been out looking for you most of the night. If the soldiers came looking for me, which they probably did, I wasn't there. Servius had rousted me out of bed when you didn't come home. I searched the harbor area and across the city, and I felt sure you had been arrested, but didn't think it wise to pay a visit to the Roman camp alone, in the middle of the night, to verify that."

Abraham agreed with a nod of his head, a move he instantly regretted. He was feeling nauseated from the pain. "It would have served no purpose if you'd been arrested too," he said.

"Just before daybreak I finally gave up and headed here to say that I couldn't find you. I arrived as the soldiers were dragging everyone out of the house."

Abraham shuddered at the mental image that conjured up.

"I surmised they would be going to the Temple of Domitian," Quintus continued, "so I followed at a distance. I should have been with them, I kept telling myself. I felt responsible, as if there were something I could have done to prevent it, or something I could do to stop it; yet I knew there wasn't anything to be done. So I just watched, trying to mingle in with the crowd so I wouldn't be discovered. I felt like a coward."

It was unlike Quintus to carry the burden of conversation by himself; he was rather quiet most of the time. But he must have realized Abraham was unable to talk much and that he would want to know everything that had happened.

"Finally, I remembered something John had once preached: 'Don't seek martyrdom; if it is God's will, it will find you. But if God provides a way of escape, then take it.'" Quintus paused to take a drink of wine. "So I guess God provided an escape for me, although I don't know why."

Abraham pushed his plate away, unable to look at any more food, let alone eat it.

Quintus looked reflective for a moment. "I . . . I don't know what I would have done, Abraham, if I'd been forced to choose between Caesar and Christ. I like to think I would have been loyal to Christ, but I don't know. I just don't know."

"You would have made the right choice, Quintus. You're a man of principle. I thought I was . . ." Abraham stopped, unable to go on. The thought of his failure was more than he could take right now.

Quintus's face grew longer, as if pulled down by a weight. "Abraham, there's something that's been eating away at me for weeks. Ever since Damian arrived."

Abraham flinched at the name, but Quintus continued. "I can't get it out of my mind that I stopped you from killing him that day in the woods. And maybe if I hadn't, none of this would have happened. Oh, the emperor would have found someone else to carry out his persecution, but it wouldn't have been Damian. And if it weren't Damian, then Elizabeth would still be alive."

Both men started weeping at that thought. "She was like a sister to me," Quintus said. "And it will always haunt me that it's my fault she was killed."

"I've thought the same thing over and over," Abraham said hoarsely, "that I should have killed Damian when I had the chance. But that would have made me no better than he was—it would have made me a murderer. And Elizabeth would have despised me for it."

He shook his head sadly, thinking of what Elizabeth had said recently when she had discovered he was carrying a dagger: "I didn't marry a murderer." *No,* he thought now. *You married a traitor.*

"You helped me make the right choice then, Quintus. Today I made the wrong choice all by myself." Consumed by grief and guilt, Abraham knew that choice would haunt him the rest of his life.

15

THE LEG IRONS CHAFED AND PINCHED as Jacob stretched his long legs. He wanted to stand up and move around, but Rebecca had fallen asleep with her head on his shoulder and he didn't want to disturb her. The cargo area was too crowded for him to be able to walk much anyway, and the soldiers weren't about to allow him to go up to the deck for some fresh air; nevertheless he felt a restless urge to pace.

Jacob told himself it was an urge he would have to stifle for the time being. Patmos was only thirty miles from Ephesus. They would reach the prison camp soon, and after a few hours of working in the quarries of Devil's Island, he would probably long to be back in the bowels of this stinking ship with his aching back propped up against a rough wooden barrel.

Closing his eyes, Jacob tried to doze. In spite of his exhaustion, and in spite of the monotony of the gentle pitch and roll of the creaking old boat—it was as smelly as the belly of Jonah's great fish, but it was still seaworthy—he could not relax enough to fall asleep, so he tried to pray. But he could not keep his mind focused. He was still too dumbstruck over his mother's murder, still too angry at his father's betrayal. *How could he have done it?* Jacob wondered for the thousandth time. *My father denied his faith to save his fortune. My own father!*

He knew his father had been a genuine believer—of that he was certain. When Jacob was a child, Abraham had taught him Scripture verses and how to pray. His father had tried to raise his children to honor God and had demonstrated his concern for the body of

Christ by hosting the church in their home. Jacob knew his father had always loved and supported the Apostle—he had even financed the trip they had just taken, although, Jacob now reflected, that may have been as much to get him away from Ephesus and Damian as it was to support his ministry.

Jacob remembered the times he had argued with his father about the state religion and emperor worship. But Abraham had been primarily concerned about his son's safety, Jacob recalled; he certainly had never advocated sacrificing to Domitian. His father had agreed that worshiping Caesar was tantamount to treason against God and that such betrayal would involve eternal damnation. So if he knew it was such a cardinal sin, why did he do it? Could he really have been so greedy that he valued his wealth above his salvation? Yet Jacob could not remember a single instance when his father had demonstrated avarice; he had always been a generous man.

Jacob shifted his position slightly to alleviate the scraping of his shoulder blade against the barrel supporting him. Rebecca whimpered as she slept against him, her fear and grief finding expression even in her slumber.

Rebecca. How can I protect her? he wondered. *She's my responsibility now.* Jacob felt the weight of that responsibility keenly as he looked down at his sister. Long strands of chestnut hair fell across her face. *She's become a beautiful young woman,* he thought, *and now she's destined to be a slave for these brutes.*

He had seen how the sailors ogled Rebecca as the prisoners boarded the ship. The soldiers had leered at her too—but none so lustfully as Damian. Jacob had wanted to kill Damian when the commander had touched his sister. And then Damian had killed their mother while Jacob watched helplessly. Even now he wanted to avenge his mother's murder, and he knew that if he saw Damian again, he would have to fight the urge to crush his skull like a grape.

As Jacob thought about the perils Rebecca would face on Devil's Island and his desperate desire to protect her, he began to see his father's sin in a new light. It wasn't his fortune that had been his father's downfall; it was his desire to protect his family. Jacob understood that now. It didn't excuse his father's sin, but it explained why he had succumbed to the pressure to make the mandatory sacrifice.

If Father repents, will God forgive him and restore him? Jacob wondered. *Even for this sacrilege?* He would have to remember to ask John about that. For now, the Apostle had his eyes closed, and Jacob guessed he was either sleeping or praying. John often did that in the afternoons—started praying or meditating and then nodded off. Jacob offered a silent prayer for his father's soul and listened to the sounds of the old ship as it plowed steadily through the rolling sea.

It was late afternoon, Jacob estimated—he couldn't see the sun from the cargo hold—when they approached Patmos. Jacob could tell they were nearing land by the decrease in speed and the increase in activity above. He heard sailors scrambling over the deck and the sound of heavy ropes being readied for mooring.

He nudged Rebecca. "Wake up," he said. "We're almost there."

"Where?" she said sleepily. "Oh, Devil's Island," she added as she yawned and then wrinkled her nose. "At least we'll get off this smelly old barge. I can't believe I fell asleep."

In a few minutes several soldiers marched down the wooden steps into the hold and ordered the prisoners to disembark. "Single file up the steps," one of them said. "Assemble in rows of ten on the main deck."

Jacob stood and stretched, then helped Rebecca and John to their feet. With their legs and wrists shackled, it was awkward getting a sure footing, especially after sitting for hours in a cramped space.

Seeing the sunlight was a welcome relief, Jacob thought as they shuffled down the gangplank. Once they were on land, one of the prison guards unlocked their leg irons and handcuffs. Rebecca sighed with relief as the chains dropped to the ground. With anger, Jacob noticed her swollen ankles and the red streaks flashing up her legs. How could these barbarians expect a delicate young woman to survive such treatment?

"Stay in formation," a soldier ordered, brandishing his spear to reinforce the instruction.

Two men, whom Jacob later identified as the camp commander and the medical officer, strolled up and down the four rows of prisoners. "You!" the medical officer shouted at Rebecca. "Over here." He motioned Rebecca to a shallow inlet and told her to stand in the water.

"Why?" she asked, looking at Jacob as if afraid to be separated from her brother.

The officer's face softened momentarily as he leaned toward her. "Because you can't work on infected legs. The salt water will dry up those gashes." He straightened and then added sternly, "Now, do as you're told."

Rebecca took off her sandals and stepped into the water. She winced as the salt stung the cuts on her legs. Jacob listened to the camp commander's instructions while he tried to keep an eye on his sister.

"You've arrived too late in the day to work," the commander said. "So today you'll find a cave, which will serve as your living quarters. Tomorrow at daybreak you will report to the main camp for morning rations. You'll begin work an hour after daybreak. If you don't report for work, you will be flogged. Your work crew will have an overseer, and any violation of his orders will bring swift and severe punishment. An hour before sundown, work will stop and you'll receive your evening rations. Then you'll return promptly to your cave. No loitering around the camp."

After the commander barked, "You're dismissed," the soldiers distributed one blanket and a loaf of bread to each prisoner.

Rebecca stepped out of the water and into her sandals. "Thank you," she said with a tentative smile to the soldier who handed her the evening ration of bread.

"Don't get happy just yet, girl," he said with a snarl. "This place is not called Devil's Island without reason."

The prisoners began to disperse and one of the soldiers pointed them in the directions they were likely to find open caves. Jacob noted that most of the group, including Servius and the other household servants who had been banished with them, headed north or west to search out living space.

John made no move to leave, so Jacob prodded him gently. "Not so fast," the Apostle said. "Let's look around a minute."

John, Jacob, and Rebecca stood and surveyed the island. Jacob knew from his father's maps that Patmos was a small, rocky island about ten miles long and six miles wide, approximately thirty miles off the coast of Ephesus in the Aegean Sea. Because of its desolate and barren nature, Rome used it as a place to banish criminals. *No need for shackles here,* Jacob thought wryly. There would be no daring escapes from Devil's Island.

As the trio scanned the arc-shaped island, they noted that a very narrow isthmus divided it into two nearly equal parts, a northern and a southern. On the east side, on a stretch of level ground, were the harbor where they had arrived and the Roman encampment.

"This way, I think," John said, turning to the south.

"The steepest hills are in that direction," Jacob protested. He was concerned about the aged Apostle having to walk up and down the mountain every day. But then he didn't know how John could survive even a few days of carrying heavy rocks from the quarries in the hills to the harbor and back, regardless of where their cave was located.

"Humor an old man," John said. He smiled and clapped Jacob on the shoulder. "I have a feeling the cave we're supposed to have is that way."

They started up the southern slopes, and John stumbled a time or two over the rocky terrain. Soon Jacob spotted a strong, straight stick about five feet long. He picked it up and brushed it off, then gave it to the Apostle to help him walk across the volcanic wasteland.

About a mile from the harbor the Apostle finally stopped. "See that cave?" He pointed to an opening in the rock a dozen yards away. "Does it look as if anyone is living there?"

"I'll go see," Jacob said. He walked inside the cave and looked around. "Hello!" he called into the interior. The sound of his voice bounced off the rocks. There was no reply and no sign anyone had ever occupied the cave.

After a few moments Jacob went back outside and waved the others over. "It appears empty."

As John and Rebecca joined him, he turned to look where they had come from. The harbor and camp lay in the distance below them; the mouth of the cave had a commanding view of the entire island and the sea. *We're facing Ephesus,* Jacob realized. *Home.* Perhaps that was why John had wanted to come in this direction.

The mouth of the cave was wide and shaped like a funnel, gathering the breeze blowing in from the sea, which would be a welcome blessing during the heat of the summer but a burden in the colder weather. Jacob clutched the coarse woolen blanket he'd been issued; two months from now, when winter arrived, one blanket would not be much protection against the damp cold of the cave.

"I take it back," Jacob said as they walked into the cave and several large rats scurried across their feet and out into the fading sunlight. "It appears the place was occupied after all."

Rebecca screamed and Jacob couldn't help laughing. He reached for a rock and threw it at the rodents fleeing from their home's invaders.

"Not exactly the mansion you grew up in," the Apostle said to Rebecca, "but we'll try to make the best of it."

They walked deeper into the interior. About ten feet from the funneled mouth, the cave turned sharply left, forming a narrow passage wide enough for only one person to walk. The passage emptied into an almost perfectly shaped rectangular room of about 150 square feet.

Jacob was the first to enter the rectangular structure. John followed with a wide-eyed Rebecca, still searching for rats. Standing in the indirect light shining from the mouth of the cave, the Apostle spoke first. "I think we've found the perfect cave. Why other prisoners on this island haven't taken it long ago, I'll never know. Maybe God saved it just for us," he said thoughtfully. He paused and then said in a strong voice, "I feel something special is going to happen in this room. I feel it in my soul."

Rebecca seemed to perk up at his enthusiastic announcement. "This can be our bedroom," she said. "The soil is soft, and if we can find another blanket or a piece of fabric, we can curtain off the passage for warmth. It's not home, but it's bearable."

"Correction, Rebecca. This *is* home," John said softly. "You are not who you used to be, the privileged daughter of a wealthy and powerful man. Now you are a criminal for confessing Christ, an enemy of the State."

"And all three of us will die on this island for our confession of faith," Jacob added soberly. That thought had been nagging him since they arrived: they would never get off Devil's Island.

"Apostle, do you think God will let us die here?" Rebecca asked in a small voice.

John did not answer right away. "I don't know," he finally said. "It's possible. But we shouldn't worry about that. Our lives are in His hands, and only He knows the number of our days." He smiled broadly. "I never thought I'd live this long to begin with.

"I don't know about you," John continued, "but I'm starving. Let's go back to the mouth of the cave and have our evening meal as we watch the sunset." He held up his round loaf of bread. "Looks like Rome has spared no expense for a delicious dinner for its newest prisoners."

The elderly Apostle's infectious laughter echoed in the cavern and Jacob found himself smiling in spite of his worried exhaustion. "It occurs to me, John, that I have given my life—perhaps quite literally—to Someone I've never seen." His voice caught with a sudden emotion. "If I'm condemned to spend the rest of my life working as a slave for the Empire, at least I'm blessed to share the experience with the last eyewitness to His life."

"I've always loved hearing you talk about Jesus," Rebecca added. "And now I want to hear the stories all over again."

"After you," John said, indicating he would follow Jacob and Rebecca down the narrow passage back to the entrance. "I want to see the sea . . . that's where I met the Master, you know."

16

"YOU POOR THING," Julia cooed when Naomi met her at the entrance to the stadium. "I wasn't sure you'd be here . . . I mean, after what happened this morning."

Naomi wondered about the sincerity of Julia's sympathy. Although they were friends, Julia might not want to be seen with someone whose family had just been hauled before the authorities for being traitors to the Empire. *Perhaps I shouldn't have come,* Naomi thought briefly. It was coldhearted to leave her father and Peter alone with their grief, but she had been paralyzed with fear that the stigma of her fanatical family would attach itself to her, and attending a popular cultural event such as the games would prevent that from happening.

"What have you heard?" Naomi asked cautiously.

"That you and your father proved your loyalty to the emperor but that the rest of your family was sent to Devil's Island." Julia lowered her voice, and her thin, pinched face assumed a pained expression. "And that your mother was killed for attacking a soldier."

Naomi acknowledged the accuracy of Julia's brief report. "That's true."

"How perfectly awful for you."

"Yes, it was." Naomi's eyes were busy sizing up the crowd as she spoke, looking for friends and admirers and, as always, potential conquests. As several people nodded or waved in greeting, she began to relax. "I wasn't that close to my mother, you know. But it was unfortunate that she lost control of herself like that. What else could the commander do?"

"I suppose nothing. An attack like that could not go unpunished."

"Let's go inside," Naomi said. She did not want to talk about the morning's events, and now that she was here and had decided no one was going to ostracize her for her family's bizarre behavior, she wanted to find her seat and enjoy the program.

Naomi and Julia joined the throng of holiday enthusiasts jamming the arched entrances on either end of the elliptical stadium. They handed over their bronze tokens at the gate, and as they inched their way inside the arena, Naomi read the poster painted on the wall. It listed the occasion; the name of the editor, or manager, of the games; the program of events; and the pairs of gladiators in order of their appearance.

"He's not fighting today," Julia said, leaning close to Naomi's ear so she could be heard.

"What?" Naomi was startled by the comment.

"Gordius. That's whose name you were looking for, isn't it?" Julia smiled slyly.

Naomi nodded. She hated it when Julia read her mind—not that she cared if Julia knew about her attraction to the powerfully built, enormously popular gladiator. Naomi simply preferred to reveal her thoughts in her own words, when *she* chose to do so.

"You really should have an affair with him," Julia said as they finally broke through the arched stone passage and into the main part of the stadium. The sun was high overhead, but the temperature was mild—a lovely fall day, perfect weather for the games.

"I've thought about it," Naomi admitted. "But I wouldn't want it to distract me from my long-range plans."

"I know—Rome, a husband, untold wealth, influence." Julia wagged her carefully coifed head from side to side as she enumerated Naomi's well-known plans. "But it doesn't have to interfere. An affair is just a temporary way to satisfy an urge. It might do you a world of good—get your mind off . . . *things*," she said pointedly.

Naomi shrugged in reply. She knew Julia was referring to her family. That topic was closed, as far as she was concerned.

They passed the raised podium where the editor and dignitaries would sit and headed for the steps. "It makes me mad," Naomi said, "that the women's section is way up in the top tier."

"I know, but look at it this way," Julia said cheerfully. "As we ascend the heights, it's an opportunity to parade in front of an entire stadium of appreciative men . . . Just flirt your way to the top."

Naomi lifted the skirt of her tunic higher than necessary to climb the steep steps. Heads turned in her direction and she smiled coyly in acknowledgment. She thought about Julia's advice as they leisurely made their way to the top section of the stadium. Did she want to have an affair with Gordius? He was an *auctoratus*, one of the voluntary gladiators, and therefore not under strict supervision like the prisoners of war and condemned criminals consigned to the gladiatorial schools. Naomi had not met Gordius personally yet, but she knew she could arrange it if she really wanted to. All she had to do was say the word, and Julia would invite him to one of her dinner parties and make sure Naomi was seated next to him.

Recently, Naomi had seen him outside the arena and gotten a good look at him up close. Gordius had been entering the baths as she was leaving with Julia. Naomi had been so smitten with the professional fighter, she had almost suggested to Julia that they bathe again, just so she could get another glimpse of his rugged face and muscular body. Some of the women in their circles had had affairs with actors and gladiators. Perhaps Julia was one of them, the way she talked. Naomi had observed that Julia and Terentius, her husband, tended to go their separate ways.

The *hydraulis*, the stadium's large water-organ, had started the music for the opening procession by the time they reached their seats. Naomi loved the pomp and pageantry that began the games. The toga-draped sponsors, the public officials who financed the games, entered the arena preceded by attendants bearing symbols of their political office. Next were musicians playing fanfares on long straight trumpets, followed by four men carrying a platform on which a statue of Victoria, the goddess of victory, rode. The editor of the games entered next, with his assistants and referees trailing behind him. More trumpeters followed, these playing short, curved horns, and finally the afternoon's combatants marched into the arena in pairs, carrying their helmets under their arms. This was the only time the audience would see the gladiators' faces; later, the heavy bronze and tin-plated helmets with grated visors would cover them completely.

The spectators were noisy, as usual, and sitting so high in the stadium, Naomi sometimes had trouble hearing the music over the roar of the crowd. Special music—brass and reed instruments as well as the water-organ—announced the beginning of each fight and was also used to heighten the drama during the gladiatorial contests.

Today's program featured several novelty matches: two pairs of dwarf gladiators and a pair of female gladiators from Greece. It was the first time Naomi had seen women fight in the arena, and she applauded the idea, although she couldn't imagine why they would want to take up such an unusual, not to mention risky, occupation.

Naomi was bored by the other novelty event, the *taurocentae*. Several riders on horseback chased an equal number of bulls around the arena. When a *taurocenta* got close enough to his prey, he grabbed the horns of the bull from behind and swung off his mount onto the bull's back. The idea was to throw the bull to the ground, and the audience screamed its approval each time a rider felled one of the giant animals. Some of the unarmed sportsmen, however, could not maintain their holds. When they fell off, the powerful beasts charged the fallen riders, goring them and then tossing their bodies into the air until their blood splashed in the sand.

Also interspersed between the gladiatorial contests were the executions of several criminals condemned *ad bestias*, the severest form of death penalty that could be imposed by a judge. With no weapons, and naked except for a loincloth, the prisoners never had a chance against the beasts thrown into the arena to devour them.

Ordinarily Naomi enjoyed the games immensely and often made a small wager with Julia as a pair of gladiators entered the arena. Her enthusiasm waned as the day wore on, however. As the blood continued to spill on the sand of the arena floor, she kept seeing her mother's face and the blood that had gushed from her chest and saturated her tunic. Every time a stretcher left the arena carrying a dead or severely wounded combatant, Naomi thought of the carriage driving away and leaving her mother's dead body on the ground at the pavilion. The scene outside the Temple of Domitian had affected her more deeply than she cared to admit. The bloodshed she saw in the stadium was sheer entertainment, but her mother's blood had been personal, and she grew dizzy with the effort of trying to block it out of her mind.

The final match dragged on and on, both gladiators demonstrating their exceptional skill as swordsmen, and Naomi's attention wandered. When the crowd suddenly began to roar, she again focused her gaze on the fight. One of the gladiators dropped his shield and wearily raised a hand with his forefinger extended, indicating his capitulation. The referee stepped between the opponents to make sure the fighting stopped.

Instantly Julia was on her feet, waving the hem of her cloak and shouting for *missio*, the release of the vanquished gladiator. One aspect of the games that made them so popular was the opportunity for the audience to participate in the outcome. Whether a defeated gladiator lived or died at the point of surrender was technically the decision of the editor, who generally acceded to the wishes of the spectators. If a fighter had conducted himself with valor and skill, only giving up when the outcome was hopeless, the audience was usually sympathetic. In that case, the editor signaled the referee to release the loser, who left the arena alive, hopefully to fight again if his wounds were not too severe.

"Pugnax has been virtually invincible up until now," Julia said afterward, "and that is definitely the toughest opponent he's ever faced. He deserved to walk away, don't you think?" Julia had grown up attending the games and could identify each of the different categories of fighters as well as their weapons, and she knew the name and win-loss statistics of every popular gladiator.

Naomi agreed with a vague murmur, and Julia kept chattering. "Let's buy something," she said as they exited the stadium and passed one of the souvenir stands just outside the entrance.

The vendor's display held an array of sports-related merchandise. Naomi passed over the helmet-shaped terra-cotta lamps and the small stone figurines with removable helmets and swords—the kind of plaything Peter and Jacob would have loved as children but their mother would never have allowed in the house—and selected a small bronze mirror. She automatically checked her reflection in the highly polished oval; the other side featured an engraving of a gladiator in his battle regalia.

"You're coming for dinner tonight, aren't you?" Julia asked when they had made their purchases.

It was unlike Naomi to pass up such an occasion, and she didn't really want to go home to her family—what was left of it—but she did not think she could keep a smile pasted on her face throughout a lengthy dinner at Julia's. "Forgive me, no. It's been a very long day, and suddenly I'm exhausted—"

"Of course you are, dear friend," Julia said in her typically effusive manner. "Don't worry about it."

They said good-bye, and as Julia stooped to enter the litter waiting for her, she called out, "I'll see you at the baths tomorrow." Eight slaves lifted the two long poles extending from the enclosed sedan and balanced them on sturdy shoulders before merging with the traffic flowing back to the city.

Watching them depart, Naomi realized she had forgotten to ask Julia about the next slave auction. *I'll do that tomorrow,* she told herself as she began the walk home. In addition to buying slaves or at least hiring more household help, she was going to make other changes immediately—one of them being the purchase of a litter. *Imagine someone of my social status not even having a vehicle,* she thought, her indignation growing with every step. In spite of her father's considerable wealth, her family had lived quite unpretentiously. Abraham walked almost everywhere he went, but he resorted to a horse and carriage in inclement weather, or if traveling out of town. Her father thought a litter was a ridiculous affectation. "Don't give yourself airs, girl. Why do you think God gave you two strong legs?" he had said.

But all of the important women had litters, and plenty of slaves to serve as porters. Naomi decided on the spot that her days of walking across town were over. She deserved to travel in a style commensurate with her wealth and position in society, and by Jupiter, she would—starting tomorrow.

By the time Naomi reached the crest of Mount Koressos, the sun was sinking behind her. Torches were already lit at the entrance to the family mausoleum, she noticed.

They must be having Mother's funeral. The thought stopped her. She hated funerals and had already thought about death entirely too much that day. But in spite of her reluctance, she found herself walking toward the mausoleum rather than entering the villa.

She stood just inside the entrance, not wanting to be observed by the mourners. As her eyes adjusted to the dim light of the cave-like tomb, she could make out three figures standing in front of the bier. Abraham had his arm around Peter, who was sniffling and trying to stifle a sob, his hand over his mouth. Quintus had his hands raised. As he spoke, Naomi recognized the quotation; it was from a letter the apostle Paul had written while living in Ephesus many years before. John had read the same verses at Crispin's funeral.

"'Listen,'" Quintus recited, "'I tell you a mystery: We will not all sleep, but we will all be changed—in a flash, in the twinkling of an eye, at the last trumpet. For the trumpet will sound, the dead will be raised imperishable, and we will be changed. For the perishable must clothe itself with the imperishable, and the mortal with immortality. When the perishable has been clothed with the imperishable, and the mortal with immortality, then the saying that is written will come true: "Death has been swallowed up in victory."'"

Hollow words, Naomi told herself. *They're not true. Not true!* But her heart ached as she heard her father's broken voice join Quintus's.

"'Where, O death, is your victory?'" they said in unison. "'Where, O death, is your sting?'"

Unable to listen any longer, Naomi turned and ran toward the villa. She knew where the sting of death was. It was in her heart.

17

WITH JACOB IN THE LEAD, the three of them marched single file back through the cave's narrow passage and then went outdoors to watch the sunset as they ate their meal, such as it was. Rebecca spread her blanket on the ground and told John, "Use your blanket as a seat cushion. You'll be more comfortable." She held his loaf of bread and the crude walking stick while the Apostle sat down.

When the others had sat down beside him, John bowed his head and blessed the food. "Lord, You taught us to pray, 'Give us this day our daily bread.' We thank You now for this bread. May it be to our bodies as a sumptuous meal in the finest home, for wherever we are, You make Your home with us."

"Amen," Jacob and Rebecca said in unison.

It did not take long to eat their individual loaves of bread, and although it by no means filled him up, it was enough to stop Jacob's empty stomach from rumbling.

Rebecca brushed the crumbs from her stained tunic and asked, "Apostle, why did God allow this to happen? Why did He allow my mother to die? He could have stopped it, surely He could have." Her mouth trembled as she spoke. "I've always tried to be good, and I don't understand it."

"Pain is as personal and as inevitable as death, Rebecca. It comes to the young, the old, the learned, the ignorant, the rich, and the poor." John leaned back against the rock at the opening of the cave. "Suffering comes to *every* believer sooner or later. No one permanently evades it."

"But what is the purpose of it?" Jacob asked. "And how do we endure it?"

"Things always happen for a reason," John said. "It may be a part of God's plan for us that we can't see at the moment, but in time—or in eternity—it will become clear to us. Suffering need not be a wild, meaningless spasm of fate; if surrendered, it can become the most creative and redemptive force in life."

Jacob shook his head. "It's difficult to see anything creative or redemptive in this cruel place." As they had landed, he had noted the long leather whips carried by the prison guards. He knew they wouldn't hesitate to use them at the least infraction of the rules, and he dreaded the horror the next morning would bring.

"Our faith does not explain or remove suffering," John continued, his eyes on the camp below. "Faith does provide the inner resources for living through it, above it, and beyond it. We will suffer on Devil's Island for our faith in Jesus Christ, but God's grace will be sufficient for the journey."

He paused for a moment and then asked, "Do you remember the story of Joseph?"

Jacob and Rebecca nodded.

"Think about it," the Apostle said. "When Joseph's brothers sold him into slavery, he could not possibly understand that God was sending him into Egypt to prepare the world for famine. While there, Joseph was falsely accused of rape and sent to prison, but the Lord was with him. Eventually, when his brothers came to Egypt to buy grain to sustain their lives, Joseph understood why God had allowed him to be sold into slavery almost twenty years earlier. It had been part of God's long-range plan, a plan that Joseph could never have imagined. God not only spared Joseph's immediate family, He raised up a nation of millions out of a family of seventy-six people who had been saved because Joseph suffered unjustly as a slave.

"God may allow us to suffer on Devil's Island for a long-range plan none of us can see today. Perhaps He will do something through us on this island that will bless His church forever."

John spoke with such a quiet conviction that it was hard not to believe him. Jacob knew he would be pondering the story of Joseph in the days ahead and praying for God's purpose to be revealed. He would also pray, he admitted to himself, for their suffering to end sooner than Joseph's had. Jacob couldn't imagine twenty days on Devil's Island, let alone twenty years.

"You promised us a story about Jesus," Rebecca reminded the Apostle. "About how you met the Master by the sea."

John gazed out over the water, a distant look in his eye. To their left, the dying rays of the sun cast an orange glow on the horizon. "About this time every evening my brother James and I would be preparing to cast off from the shore in one of our family's fishing boats. We worked for our father, Zebedee, and we were partners with Simon Peter and Andrew."

"Wait a minute," Jacob said. "You fished at night?"

"The best fishing on the Sea of Galilee happened at night. We would take two boats with lanterns on the bow and fish along the bank. When we saw the water churning with fish, chasing the minnows in a feeding frenzy, we would jump out with our nets and seine toward the shore, trapping the fish against the bank. I remember this one time . . ." John paused to laugh at the memory. "It was not long after we first met Jesus, and we thought He must have been crazy."

"Why would you think the Lord was crazy?" Rebecca asked.

"Oh, I was a hotheaded teenager—about your age," he told Rebecca, "and you couldn't tell me anything I didn't already know. One day Jesus came out to the shores of the Galilee, where we were cleaning and mending our nets after fishing unsuccessfully all night. A crowd had followed Jesus, and there were so many people they couldn't all hear Him. So He got in one of our boats and asked Simon to put out a little way from the shore. Then Jesus sat down in the boat and taught the people. We listened while we worked on our nets.

"After He had finished teaching the people, He told us, 'Launch out into the deep water, and let down your nets for a catch.'

"When He said that, we looked at each other like He'd had a heat stroke. It was broad daylight. If there was one thing we knew about fishing on the Galilee, it was that you didn't fish in the daylight, and you certainly didn't fish in deep water.

"Simon Peter muttered under his breath, 'Jesus is a carpenter. What does He know about fishing?'" John chuckled and shook his head. "That Simon, what a mouth he had."

"Did the Lord hear him say that?" Rebecca's jaw had dropped.

"I don't know," John replied. "But Simon thought about it a minute and then said, 'Master, we've worked hard all night and haven't caught a thing. But because You say so, I'll do it.'

"We rowed farther away from the shore and let down the nets, thinking it was futile, yet not wanting to offend this young new rabbi. What a scene—I'll never forget it. It was as if the fish fought each other to jump into our nets. Before we knew it, the nets were full to the point of breaking, and we signaled for the others to bring the second boat out from the shore. We filled their nets with fish as well, and when we hauled the nets into the boats, the load was so heavy, I thought we might sink before we got back to the shore.

"We were rejoicing over the great catch, and then Jesus said something I'll never forget. He looked at us with eyes that pierced into our innermost beings. 'Follow Me,' He said, 'and I will make you fishers of men.'"

John shrugged as he summed up their reaction to the invitation. "There didn't seem to be anything else to do. So we left our nets and followed Him. We became His disciples full-time, and soon there were twelve of us."

Daylight was fading rapidly but none of them moved to enter the cave. It was the only time during that long, horrible day that Jacob had felt a moment of peace, and he didn't want it to end.

"What was your favorite miracle?" he asked John. "What moment of all moments did you most enjoy?"

John picked up his new walking stick and set it across his lap, twirling the stick as he thought for a moment. "It was another night on the Sea of Galilee," he said. "The time He came walking out of the darkness on the raging sea. I remember it like it happened last night."

"Please tell us," Rebecca urged. She leaned forward and placed a hand on the Apostle's arm. "I could listen to you talk about Jesus all night."

With bony fingers, John reached over and patted Rebecca's hand lightly. "You remind me so much of your mother," he said gently. "When she was about your age, she was so eager to hear the old stories. She would sit at my table and make me tell stories until I was hoarse. And so beautiful, she was. Just like you."

Tears welled up in Rebecca's eyes at the mention of her mother.

"That's where she met your father, you know. At my house. They would sit, one on either side of me, just like we're sitting now, and Elizabeth would beg me to tell a story, then Abraham would pepper me with questions. He was a new believer then."

Hearing about his mother and father stirred both sorrow and anger in Jacob, and he couldn't bear to listen to John's ramblings about his parents. "I thought you were going to tell us about the time Jesus walked on water," he said roughly.

"Oh, yes, I was." John laughed softly. "You'll have to forgive me. At my age, my mind tends to wander."

Suddenly two rats ran across their blanket toward the mouth of the cave, and with surprising speed John jabbed furiously at them with his walking stick. He managed to strike the tail of one rat against the rock, but the glancing blow was not enough to stop him. The animal simply squealed and streaked into the cave.

Rebecca had jumped up at the first sight of the rats. Now she screamed, "They went inside! Two rats just ran into our cave!"

"Two worthless, unwanted visitors," John said. "The first one I'll name Domitian, and the second I'll call Damian. I'll get them both someday." He exploded with laughter. "Your day of judgment is coming, Domitian. Yours too, Damian," he called into the darkness of the cave. "Don't get too comfortable in our house."

He reached up for Rebecca's hand. "Sit back down, child. I'll tell one more story and then we'll retire for the evening."

As daylight turned to deep shadow, the wind whirred around the rocks and stirred up the dust at their feet. Rebecca drew her cloak around her. "Do you want to go inside?" Jacob asked.

"Not yet." She shook her head, and Jacob wondered if she was simply prolonging the moment before they would have to lie on the damp floor of the cave and worry about Domitian and Damian crawling over them—*How like John to name the rats*, he thought— or whether, like him, she just wanted to stare into the distant sea in the direction of home. Soon darkness would completely obliterate their mountaintop view.

John stroked his scraggly white beard. "Where was I?" he asked Jacob.

"The Sea of Galilee," Jacob answered. "The night Jesus appeared in the storm."

"You've heard me tell this one before."

"Not fully. But you've referred to it in sermons, and it's in Matthew's Gospel. I want to hear your firsthand account now."

"All right," he said. "That day Jesus had fed five thousand men, plus their wives and children—but that's another story. After that momentous miracle, He told us to get in the boat and go to the other side of the sea, saying that He would meet us on the opposite shore later. Then He sent the multitude away."

"Why did He do that?" Rebecca probed.

"To keep them from following us. You have to remember that everyone He touched got well, and He cast out demons with a word. So huge crowds began to follow Him, wanting to see signs and wonders.

"The twelve of us got in the boat while the Master went up on the mountain by Himself to pray. It was about midafternoon when we shoved off from the shore and hoisted the sail. At sundown we were in the middle of the sea, when suddenly a vicious wind came roaring down the Jordan Valley. The mountains formed a perfect wind tunnel for any breeze blowing in the upper Galilee, and that tunnel emptied onto the sea. I lived my youth around that sea, and I've seen it as smooth as glass one minute and a terrifying tempest the next.

"But this night was different . . . very different. The winds were vicious, mean, and contrary to the laws of nature." John paused and looked from Rebecca to Jacob. "There is a lesson here. Sometimes the very thing that helps you—like the wind by which we sailed our boats—can suddenly turn against you. Sometimes the people you trust the most will betray you the quickest."

Jacob knew he was talking about his father's betrayal that morning.

"That night," John continued, "we couldn't believe the fierce winds that stirred the waves. The boat began to pitch and toss out of our control and to take on water, front and back. The sail was ripped completely off. We frantically tried to bail the water out of the boat as we prayed, but we knew death was near. Peter screamed so loudly, you could hear him above the howling winds and the crash of the waves against the hull. I was amazed the boat did not split in half."

"Where was Jesus?" Rebecca asked.

"That question was on every man's lips. We were in that storm for nine long brutal hours. Why didn't He come instantly? Why did He let us bail water and pray in panic most of the night?"

"Why do *you* think He waited?" Jacob too had wondered where God was during their long terrible ordeal that day.

"I think He did it to allow our self-sufficiency to reach its absolute end. Man's extremity is God's opportunity." John stifled a yawn. "You see, we had been in storms all our lives, but never one like this. We were professional fishermen—seasoned sailors with rock-ribbed confidence borne from years of fighting the sea for a living. That night we tried every trick we knew to keep our boat afloat . . . but nothing worked. Our self-sufficiency was gone. Our confidence completely failed. We believed we were beyond the help of the Master and we thought we were going to die."

"Where were you in the boat?" Rebecca asked.

"I was sitting on the last seat in the back with James. If I was going to die at sea, I wanted to die with my brother." The Apostle turned to Jacob. "Did you know that the fishermen who lived around the Sea of Galilee believed that just before you drowned you would see a ghost?"

"No, I didn't."

"That's what we'd always heard. So when we saw Jesus, we were terrified. We thought He was that ghost. Then the Master came walking across the water in the darkness of the night saying, 'Don't be afraid! It is I.'

"Peter was the first to speak—he generally was the first to open his mouth. He cupped his hands to his face and screamed to be heard over the howling winds. 'Lord, if it is You,' he said, 'command me to come to You on the water.'

"Jesus said one word, 'Come,' and Peter jumped out of the boat and started walking on the water as if it were made of stone. When he walked right over the waves and didn't sink, we wept and shouted for joy . . . and then everyone in the boat got deathly quiet."

"Why?" Rebecca asked when John paused. She was leaning forward with her elbows on her knees, listening raptly.

"Peter was sinking. Was it a cruel joke? Were we deluded fools for believing a man could walk on water? Peter looked down and then cried out in terror, 'Lord, save me!'

"Immediately, Jesus stretched out His hand and caught Peter, saying to him, 'O you of little faith, why did you doubt?'

"The two of them walked through the tempest toward us, and as soon as they were safely in the boat, the winds died instantly and the sea was smooth again."

Jacob slapped an insect crawling on his leg. "There's another lesson here, right?" He thought he knew what that lesson was, but he wanted John to reinforce it.

"Of course," John answered. It was too dark now to see the expression on John's face, but Jacob knew he must be smiling; the Apostle loved give-and-take with his disciples.

"The first time Peter walked on the water," John said, "he took his eyes off of the Master. He looked at the raging sea around him and started to sink. But the second time Peter walked on the water, he held the hand of Christ and made it back to the boat; then the winds stopped.

"When you focus on Christ and not the circumstance, the powers and principalities of darkness cannot touch you, much less defeat you. Learn this, both of you. In the storms of life on this island, never take your eyes off of Jesus."

"But why did Jesus rebuke Peter for his lack of faith?" Jacob chided. "He was the only one who got out of the boat. You and the others stayed put. At least Peter tried."

"That's exactly the point, Jacob. Action without faith is presumption. Jesus was letting us know again that without faith in Him, we could do nothing . . . nothing at all."

The stillness of the night surrounded Jacob as the three of them sat quietly in the darkness. Clouds obscured portions of the sky, and there was just enough starlight to make out John's white head next to his. "We really should go inside now," Jacob said as he stood up and offered a hand to the Apostle.

"Yes, we have a full day ahead of us tomorrow," John said without a trace of dismay in his voice.

They picked up their blankets and entered the cave, standing still for a few minutes to let their eyes adjust to the darkness. Then they held hands as Jacob led them into the narrow passageway, his free hand feeling along the wall of the cave as he guided them into their bedroom of solid rock.

Tomorrow night, Jacob thought, *we won't wait until it's completely dark before going to bed.*

They spread their blankets on the ground and lay down. Jacob wiggled his fingers in front of his face. The inner room of the cave was so dark, he could not see his hand.

Rebecca scooted closer to him. "I'm scared," she whispered in the darkness.

"Keep your eyes on the Savior," Jacob told her.

"I will . . . but can I hold your hand too?" She wove her tiny fingers through his much larger ones.

Jacob squeezed his sister's hand in reply, then closed his eyes. He was asleep almost instantly.

18

REBECCA WOKE TO THE SOUND OF SINGING. John's raspy off-key voice reverberated off the walls of the cave in one of his favorite hymns: "Wake up, O sleeper, rise from the dead, and Christ will shine on you. Wake up, O sleeper . . ."

Is it time for church? she wondered, half-asleep.

"Time to get up, Rebecca." This time it was Jacob's voice she heard, his hand she felt on her shoulder.

Suddenly she remembered where she was. *Devil's Island. I'm a prisoner!* she thought in panic. *My first day to work in the quarries.*

She sat up and looked around, unable to see much, although the darkness had changed from pitch-black to a charcoal gray. "Is it morning?" Rebecca asked, still somewhat disoriented.

"Almost daybreak," John said. "We have just enough time to walk down to the camp before roll call."

"And another delicious meal," Jacob said sarcastically.

"And water, I hope." Rebecca was ravenously thirsty. She realized with dismay that she couldn't wash her face or clean her teeth, let alone bathe. She could not even change out of the dirty tunic she had already worn for two days. Homesickness swept over her as she thought of her comfortable bedroom at home and the bathroom with its large marble basin and servants to draw the water.

Hastily she ran her fingers through her long hair—*That will be the extent of my grooming today,* she thought—and stood up. "Jacob, where are you?"

"Right here," he answered, reaching for her hand. "Let's go."

Once they had walked through the narrow passage from the inner chamber to the mouth of the cave, they could see better. As they exited, Rebecca noticed that the sun had not yet risen, but the level of gray had lightened considerably from the gloomy interior of the cave.

Silently, the three of them walked down the mountain in the early morning coolness. John led the way, his new walking stick firmly in hand as they carefully worked their way over the rocks. Halfway to the main camp, Jacob stopped Rebecca. "Where's your cloak?" he asked. "You're shivering."

Rebecca felt the gooseflesh along her bare arms in surprise. She had been so distracted by thoughts of what the day would hold, she hadn't realized how cold she was. "I must have left it in the cave. I had it spread over me, along with my blanket."

Jacob looked at the camp below and then back up the hillside, judging how long it would take him to double back to the cave and then make it down the mountain. "I'll go get it," he offered.

"No, we'll be late," Rebecca said quickly. "Besides, I won't need it when the sun comes up and I'm working."

"Are you sure?"

"Yes, I'm sure. Come on, we'd better hurry." She was terrified of what might happen if they reported late on their very first day.

"I wonder where we're supposed to go," Jacob said as they neared the main camp.

"Just follow the other prisoners," John replied. "They'll know the way."

It soon became obvious where they would report each morning. Several tables were arranged in a row outside a rather large weather-beaten building at the edge of the camp; at least a hundred prisoners were already lined up in front of the tables. Rebecca was wondering if it made a difference which line she stood in when a voice inter-rupted her thoughts.

"You're new." The gruff voice belonged to a grizzled character with wild, curly hair sprouting all over his head. From his tattered clothes and lack of equipment, she figured he was a fellow prisoner.

"Y-yes. How did you know?"

"I notice pretty things." The man grinned, showing a mouth full of crooked yellow teeth with some noticeable gaps.

Jacob whirled around and glared at the man, who held up a hand as if to halt any reprisal for his comment. "I was just going to tell you," he said, "that they got us listed by date of arrival. New ones on that end." He jerked a thumb toward the right, then walked over to the leftmost line.

While they stood in the line for newer arrivals, Rebecca listened to the prisoners ahead of her give their names to two clerks who were scanning a series of tablets laid out on the tables. When a clerk found the prisoner's name, he punched a mark in the clay.

After their names had been checked off the list, Rebecca, Jacob, and John followed the other prisoners into the makeshift building that served as a mess hall. Workers—*Other convicts?* Rebecca wondered—handed each prisoner a cup of water and a bowl of thin gruel. Their meal in hand, the prisoners found a place at one of the long wooden counters lining the walls and sat down on the rough benches provided for the diners.

"Give us this day our daily gruel." Jacob grinned in Rebecca's direction. He tilted the bowl of watery mush to his mouth and drank from it. "I guess they thought spoons might make us feel too civilized," he said when he had finished.

"More like too dangerous," John said. "You can be sure they won't put anything in your hands that could be used as a weapon."

Rebecca did not eat the gruel; she merely looked at her bowl. *This really isn't food,* she thought. *I don't know what it is, but it's not food.* Her stomach was empty, yet she had no appetite.

"Aren't you hungry?" Jacob asked.

"I don't think I can eat this." Rebecca thought of family meals in the *triclinium* at home, with her mother and father reclining beside her and the table in front of her spread with delicious food, and could not reconcile that image with sitting on rough-hewn benches next to common criminals who gulped down gruel from wooden bowls.

"Try," John urged. "You need to eat something before you work."

Rebecca took a few sips from her bowl, then set it down. The stuff was awful. She picked up her cup of water and drained it. "You take the rest," she said to Jacob as she pushed her bowl toward him. "That's all I can eat." When Jacob hesitated, she added, "Don't let it go to waste."

He downed the remainder of Rebecca's meal in a single swallow, then set the bowl down noisily on the counter. "Can you imagine how Naomi would chastise the cook for this swill?" he asked with a wink.

In spite of the apprehension that had killed her appetite, Rebecca smiled. She suddenly knew she could survive, as long as she had her brother with her.

"There you are, child." Servius appeared behind them, and Rebecca turned to greet him. "I was worried about you," he said, "when you got separated from our group yesterday. I thought you were right behind us as we started up the hill."

"John thought we should go in the other direction. We found a good cave. Did you?"

Servius nodded respectfully to Jacob and John. "Tolerable," he said. "It's crowded but has the advantage of being very close to the camp. Not as far to walk on these old legs." He turned to Rebecca. "I feel I should be taking care of you, though. If you need anything . . ."

"No, I'm fine." She wasn't fine, but her heart went out to the faithful old servant who had helped raise her. They were both con-victs now—equals—but he was still looking out for her. "I have John and Jacob to take care of me," she said. "You need to concen-trate on taking care of Servius for a change."

"On your feet!" The soldiers who guarded the prisoners walked through the room to round up the work crews. "Time to move."

Some two hundred prisoners stood and slowly filed toward the entrance, prodded by the guards, who tried to hurry them with shouts and threatening looks. As they went through the door, the condemned men, and the handful of women among them, handed their cups and bowls back to the workers who had doled them out earlier.

Rebecca stepped out into the sunshine, knowing she had crossed a threshold in her life, as surely as she had just stepped across the threshold of a rickety old door. There would be no going back to life as it used to be. With one pinch of incense she had gone from a privileged citizen of Rome to a criminal for Christ. Now her mother was dead, her father was an infidel, and she had been sentenced to hard labor for life. Her only consolation was that her brother was by her side.

༄

As Jacob marched toward the quarry with the other prisoners, he fretted over Rebecca. *Tomorrow I'll make sure she eats her gruel,* he promised himself. *She can't work all day on an empty stomach. And John . . .*

Jacob looked at the Apostle, who was walking a few steps ahead, beside Rebecca. He was having no trouble keeping pace with the crowd, his tall stick swinging confidently as he marched. *But how long can he last hauling rocks?* Jacob wondered.

The prisoner who had given them directions outside the mess hall stepped alongside Jacob. "Didn't mean no offense earlier," he said. "She your wife?" He pointed to Rebecca.

"Sister," Jacob answered.

"I got a sister too."

"I see." Jacob didn't know what to say, and he wasn't sure if talking was against the rules. Some of the others were carrying on conversations, but they kept their voices low and their eyes straight ahead of them.

Soon they passed the last of the ramshackle buildings that made up the camp. *These must be the barracks for the soldiers,* Jacob thought. They offered more protection from the elements than the standard army tent, but they looked none too sturdy.

"They call me Tonsorius," his new friend said.

"Tonsorius?" Jacob caught himself before he laughed out loud.

"Yeah. Used to be a barber." The man ran a calloused hand over his wild mane of hair. "Could use a haircut myself now."

"Mine's Jacob." It didn't seem appropriate to shake hands, so Jacob simply stated his name.

"What'd you and your sister do to get sent to this godforsaken place?" Tonsorius asked.

"We refused to sacrifice to Caesar."

"And they sent you to Devil's Island for that?"

Jacob nodded. "What did you do?"

"I was a little too good at my job," Tonsorius said with another gap-toothed grin. "Slit a man's throat."

Jacob jerked his head to look at the convict walking beside him. "You murdered him?"

Tonsorius shrugged. "Found out he had forced himself on my sister. He needed killing, I figured."

Jacob glanced at Rebecca and desperately wished he could yank his sweet innocent sister out of this gang of murderers and thieves and hide her someplace. She didn't belong here, and she wasn't safe here. Jacob knew that if someone forced himself on Rebecca, he could turn into a Tonsorius in an instant.

"I didn't charge him for the shave, though," Tonsorius added, as if that explained the situation to his satisfaction.

Jacob certainly did not know how to respond to that. After a while he asked, "Do you have any advice for a newcomer like me?"

Tonsorius beamed, obviously pleased with the question. "You saw

Brutus, the camp commander, when you arrived. He's tough and unbending, but not excessively cruel. Of course, he doesn't have to be—there's plenty of others ready to crack the whip for him. But you cause trouble, and he'll make trouble for you."

Just as Tonsorius warmed to his subject, he fell quiet for a minute. The guards were looking their way. Jacob kept his eyes on the dusty road as they trudged up the barren hill in silence.

"The trick is to work steady," Tonsorius said after a minute or two. "Work too fast, and you'll make enemies out of the rest of us. Work too slow, and you'll get the overseer's whip."

Jacob nodded soberly. He wasn't worried about working too slow; he was strong and sturdy. But what about Rebecca and John?

"When you do get the whip, Marcellus will patch you up if they hurt you too bad."

"Marcellus?"

"The medical officer. Good fellow. Not many like him around here."

Jacob saw huge boulders just ahead and knew they had reached the quarry. The prisoners in front were stooping to pick up what looked like baskets.

"One more thing," Tonsorius said. "Drink water every chance you get. You'll wilt like a daisy if you don't."

"Where—"

"They'll have water on the side of the road when we start hauling."

"Thanks for the help." Jacob gave the wild-looking man a final glance as they parted. *Tonsorius seems harmless enough . . . for a murderer, I suppose.* The reality of the situation hit Jacob hard. He was on a prison island with hardened criminals and probably would be for the rest of his life. In a few years he would look like Tonsorius, with rotten and missing teeth, unkempt hair, and filthy rags for his clothing. He might as well have received a death sentence—it would have been more merciful.

Keep your eyes on Christ and not the circumstance, Jacob told himself, remembering John's story from the previous evening. That was not going to be easy.

Passing in front of the lean-to where the equipment was stored, Jacob stopped to pick up one of the tightly woven straw baskets. They were odd-shaped containers with one side curved and the other side flat, so they would fit against the workers' backs. Instead of handles, the basket had leather straps that looped over the shoulders. He ran a few yards to catch up with Rebecca and John, who had already picked up their baskets.

They quickly fell into the work pattern. Huge chunks of stone had been chiseled out of the mountain and placed in massive piles some two hundred yards apart. Several prisoners at each pile used sledgehammers to break the boulders into smaller pieces, and the other prisoners' job was to load the split rock into their baskets and haul it down the mountain to the construction site at the harbor, roughly a mile away.

As he gathered rocks and loaded his basket, Jacob noticed there were almost as many guards as there were prisoners. The work crews would have to be carefully supervised, he realized, to make sure one of the prisoners did not use a hammer or pickax as a weapon.

One of the guards saw Rebecca pick up her half-full basket, as if testing to see how heavy it was. "Fill it to the top!" the guard shouted. "Make every trip to the harbor count." With that he cracked his well-oiled leather whip in the air over their heads, the sound echoing off the walls of the quarry. Rebecca flinched and immediately went back to loading rocks under the glaring eye of the guard.

Tonsorius was right, Jacob thought. *The overseers are eager to use their whips.* He had a feeling they would use threats of force to drive the inmates beyond their physical ability.

"When your basket is full, start to the harbor immediately," another guard barked.

His own basket almost to the brim, Jacob slowed his pace to allow

Rebecca and John to catch up with him. Rebecca sneezed several times from the dust they stirred up as they worked, and Jacob fought down another wave of anger. *She doesn't belong here.* The phrase echoed in his head along with the sound of the overseers' whips, which they cracked regularly for effect.

Soon all three of their baskets were full. "Time to go," John said. With a great effort, he tried to swing the heavy load up and over his shoulders. As John grunted and tried again, Jacob realized there was no way the Apostle could lift it. Quickly, Jacob lifted the basket of rocks and placed it on John's back, then did the same for Rebecca, and the trio began their maiden voyage toward the harbor.

The sun was already bearing down, and in spite of the mild temperature, the exertion caused the sweat to pour from their bodies. With only a bowl of gruel in his stomach, Jacob felt his strength already being drained. The basket straps dug into his shoulders, leaving his arms numb. He grew angrier with every step they took, knowing it was a major effort for John and Rebecca just to walk under the weight of the loads on their backs. John used his walking stick for balance; even so, Jacob feared he would topple over any minute.

Every few yards along the road a guard stood watch to make sure no one tried to escape or waste time. Jacob looked ahead of him down the mountain. The long line of criminals trudging toward the harbor under their heavy burdens looked like ants in single file marching toward a jar of honey. There would be nothing sweet at the end of this trail, however.

How do I keep my eyes on Christ and not the circumstance? Jacob asked himself. He started to ask John, then decided to wait until later; he didn't want the elderly man to have to answer while he struggled to carry his basket.

Finally they arrived at the harbor, emptied their baskets, and started back for another load. Apparently they didn't start fast enough. The crack of a whip filled the air. Already Jacob had become so accustomed to the sound, he didn't immediately realize that the tail of the whip had caught John from behind. But when John stumbled and then righted himself before falling, Jacob noticed the bright red line that appeared at the back of the Apostle's neck. It was a glancing blow, not a direct hit, but it unleashed the fury Jacob had been struggling to suppress.

Without thinking, Jacob growled his anger and dropped his basket, starting for the guard who had used the whip. Just as quickly, John grabbed his forearm and said, "Stop it! Don't give him a reason to kill you."

Jacob trembled from the effort to stifle his emotions. Rebecca, pale and frightened, looked at him pleadingly.

"Pick up your basket," John said. "Let's go."

Jacob knew John had just saved his life, but he still had trouble calming himself as they started back to the quarry. *Only one load,* he thought, *and I'm ready to explode. Rebecca's too delicate. John's too weak. And I'm too angry. We're never going to make it.*

As they walked the mile back to the piles of rock to repeat the whole process, Jacob noticed prisoners wielding large jugs stationed on the side of the road. He hadn't noticed the water carriers earlier. The three of them stopped for a quick drink from the common cup. Rebecca drank and then poured some of the water over her hands, which were dry and red.

She doesn't belong here. We don't belong here.

The noise of the quarries was monotonous—the hammers seemed to fall into a pattern, punctuated by the staccato of whips slicing through the air. Occasionally there was a muffled cry when a whip found a human target. The work was mindless and strenuous—and seemingly endless.

Stoop down, pick up a rock, toss it in the basket. Stoop, lift, toss. Stoop, lift, toss.

When they had refilled their baskets, Jacob again hoisted John's and Rebecca's on their shoulders, and they made another round-trip down to the harbor and back up to the rock piles. Jacob's shoulders

and back ached, and his feet were almost numb, but he estimated he
was in much better condition than the others. Before long, Rebecca's
hands were raw and bleeding, which simply fueled Jacob's anger
because he was helpless to do anything for her.

It was late afternoon, he guessed, when they made their third
trip to the harbor. He was worried about Rebecca, who had hardly
spoken all morning—*What was there to talk about, anyway?* he asked
himself—and John appeared on the brink of physical exhaustion,
yet he smiled gamely as Jacob removed the basket from his stooped
shoulders and dropped the rocks into the water.

"These rocks are heavy," John said as he rubbed a shoulder, "but
we will survive because we are standing by faith on the Solid Rock—
Christ Jesus."

Jacob frowned. He knew what John said was true, but he was in
no mood to hear a sermon. He had tried keeping his eyes on the
Savior and not their dire situation, but he couldn't see Christ anywhere on Devil's Island. This was living hell.

As Jacob turned to go back to the road leading up the mountain,
he noticed a new ship in the harbor. The old hulk they had sailed in
on yesterday had departed, and in its place at the dock was a much
larger, newer ship. In a split second Jacob took in the scene: sailors
lowering the gangplank, guards herding shackled prisoners into rows
on the main deck—twice as many as had been in their group—and
a soldier in a red-plumed helmet swaggering in front of them as if
he were Caesar himself.

Damian. Jacob froze at the sight. *He's here with a boatload of prisoners.* Jacob knew without being told that they were Christians,
probably from the towns around Ephesus, and that they had been
subjected to the same ordeal his family had been through. *That mur-
derous snake,* Jacob thought, as the image of his mother falling under
Damian's sword flashed through his mind and stabbed his heart.

"Get a move on!" a voice shouted.

"Jacob, the guards . . ." Rebecca tugged on her brother's arm, a worried look on her weary face.

He immediately turned around and started up the hill with her and John. "Did you see the new arrivals?" he asked.

She shook her head no.

Good, he thought. He did not want the knowledge of Damian's presence to add to his sister's trauma. Damian had leered at his beautiful sister earlier—did the monster have his sights set on her?

Surely Damian wouldn't be staying, Jacob told himself. He was probably just dropping off another group of his victims. But why did he accompany that ship personally? Damian hadn't traveled to Patmos with their boat. So what was he doing here?

As he wearily put one foot in front of the other, Jacob continued to stew over Damian's arrival, Rebecca's safety, and the injustice of their imprisonment. But when the forced laborers reached the quarry again, thoughts of Damian left Jacob's mind as he gave himself over to the mind-numbing, backbreaking work.

19

ABRAHAM COULDN'T SLEEP. He had just buried his wife of twenty-five years and knew he would never recover from the overwhelming loss. After the simple, very private funeral, Abraham had put off going upstairs as long as possible. Even after the rest of the household had gone to bed, he remained downstairs. Quintus had sat with Abraham, so he wouldn't have to be alone.

Finally, when he saw Quintus was about to fall asleep sitting straight up, Abraham told him, "You don't have to keep me company; go on home." But when Quintus stood to leave, Abraham had second thoughts. "No, it's too late," he said. "You should stay here tonight. Take Jacob's room." A lump had formed in Abraham's throat as he thought of the two empty bedrooms upstairs that belonged to Jacob and Rebecca. *I want my children back,* he thought forlornly.

Abraham had gone upstairs with Quintus and shown him to Jacob's room, then entered the master bedroom, feeling more alone than he had ever felt in his life. He could not bear to sleep in the huge, carved bed without his wife, so he had removed the bedcovers and spread them on the floor.

Now he lay sleepless on the cold, hard floor, haunted by memories. He had forgotten to light the charcoal brazier—one of the servants usually did that, but most of them were gone now—and the room was chilly. Suddenly he couldn't stand the thought of Elizabeth lying in the tomb, unprotected from the elements, and he wanted to take a blanket to the mausoleum for her. *I need to cover her up,* he thought irrationally. In cooler weather she would always sleep in two tunics at night, snuggling against him to share his body heat. And if he got up in the mornings before Elizabeth, he always tucked the covers around her so she would stay warm.

Abraham was not only haunted by memories of his wife, he was haunted by his sin. He remembered the words of King David, "My sin is ever before me." *That's how I feel,* he thought. *There's no way I can put it out of my mind.*

His thoughts drifted to Job, the biblical figure who had lost all his children as well as his fortune. *I managed to keep my fortune,* Abraham thought, *but I lost my wife and two of my children.* He had never thought his life would parallel that of Job, but now he had a better grasp of Job's suffering. Abraham remembered how, in the midst of his catastrophes, Job's wife had told him to "curse God and die." Job had complained and questioned, but he had not cursed God. While Abraham hadn't cursed God, he had denied Him—and right now he wasn't sure there was a difference.

For a long time Abraham lay trapped in his spiraling thoughts, and then finally, toward dawn, he closed his eyes . . . and promptly opened them in hell.

Abraham felt the flames lick at his body and heard bloodcurdling screams. Damian's countenance—or was it Satan?—appeared before him. "Welcome to my kingdom," the floating face said with a roar of fiendish laughter.

The flames were far hotter than any fire on earth, and the pain they inflicted was beyond bearing. Uncontrollable screams of agony bellowed from Abraham's mouth. He looked down at his hands, now scorched and blackened, as demons surrounded him, mocking and taunting him. "Your money won't help you here. Caesar can't deliver you from this pit."

He had never been so thirsty. His mouth was parched, his lips were swelling, and his tongue was so thick, he could not swallow. "Water, *please,*" he cried out. "Just a drop of water."

"There's no water here—and no mercy. This is your eternal reward."

The smell of human flesh burning without the relief of death was a gut-wrenching stench. Abraham looked down a dark, unending corridor of human bodies on fire, screaming, writhing, and cursing. This was suffering on a scale his mind could not grasp. He screamed, "Why am I here . . . Why?"

Then he remembered: he was a traitor. He had denied Christ and worshiped Caesar.

From his waterless inferno, Abraham looked across an immeasurable divide and saw the throne of God, brilliant in its splendor. A river flowed from beneath the throne, and Abraham knew he would never touch a drop of its clear, sparkling water. Instead, he would burn in this agony of pain for all eternity, out of reach of the river, separated from God.

Then came a pain far greater than the physical pain, an unimaginable anguish. He saw Elizabeth standing beside the river. How beautiful, how radiant she was in her robe of white, her burnished golden-red hair adorned by a martyr's crown. Abraham extended his arms toward her and shouted with all his might, "Elizabeth . . . Elizabeth . . . Elizabeth!"

The sound of his own screams woke him up. The nightmare had left the blankets twisted and his clothes soaked with sweat. His head was pounding, and he gingerly touched the knot where the soldier's club had caught him just above the ear.

Abraham got up and opened the shuttered window. As daylight streamed into the room, he blinked and rubbed his sleep-swollen eyes. *It must be almost noon,* he realized. He gripped the windowsill, visibly shaken by the graphic dream. In Scripture, God had often spoken to men in dreams, warning them or even foretelling their future. Had God sent this dream? Was God going to send him to hell?

In the distance Abraham could see the blue-green waters of the sea, and he suddenly remembered a verse from one of the ancient

Jewish prophets: "You will cast all our sins into the depths of the sea." *But surely not this sin,* Abraham reasoned. *I denied the Savior. I broke the first commandment.*

In broad daylight he seemed to see things more clearly. Abraham realized he had left his first love, Christ. All those years ago he had fallen in love with Jesus; that love had taken him to Jerusalem and then brought him to Ephesus—had brought him to Elizabeth. It hadn't been wrong to love Elizabeth; it was wrong to love her more than he loved God, however. Over the years Abraham had let his profound love for his wife and children overshadow his devotion to God, and at the very moment it had mattered the most, he had been loyal to them rather than to his Savior.

It was also wrong, he realized now, to think he could resolve situations that were out of his control. "I'll fix this," he had told Elizabeth when Damian arrived in Ephesus with his legionnaires. *What made me think I could manage things that only God could control?* he wondered.

Abraham knew the answer now: pride. He had trusted his own strength more than he had trusted God. But this hadn't been a business crisis he could settle with skillful negotiation or an influx of cash. This had been a spiritual test, and he had failed it miserably.

Abraham hung his head in anguish. Was there forgiveness for him? He wished he could talk to John, ask the Apostle to pray for him. Abraham didn't think he could pray for himself, and if he could, he wasn't sure God would listen to the plea of a traitor.

His gaze fell to the open peristyle below his bedroom window, and he remembered something John had said as the church met there one Sunday. Abraham had been sitting on a bench in the garden while he watched the white-headed preacher pace back and forth on the colonnaded porch, gesturing as he spoke.

"If we claim to be without sin," John had said, punching the air with his forefinger, "we are deceiving ourselves. The truth is not in us!" Then the Apostle had suddenly stopped and opened his arms expansively. "But if we confess our sins, He is faithful and just and will forgive us. He will forgive us," he had repeated for emphasis, "and cleanse us from all unrighteousness."

John had known the Lord's faithfulness for more than six decades; he knew what he was talking about. Encouraged by his memory of John's words, Abraham began praying aloud.

"Father God—Lord God of Abraham, Isaac, and Jacob—I confess my sin before You and humbly ask Your forgiveness. Cleanse me by the power of Your blood, and restore to me the joy of my salvation. As You gave Samson a second chance, give me a second chance to prove my love and loyalty for the Son of God. I have sinned a great sin, but please forgive me, heavenly Father. In Jesus' name I pray. Amen."

Abraham felt the stirrings of a fragile peace, the first peace he had felt in weeks. He still felt an immense burden of sorrow, but the torment that had accompanied it was gone.

As he bathed and dressed, Abraham decided he would still go to Rome and appeal to Caesar. He would try to win Jacob's and Rebecca's release from Devil's Island—and John's too, of course. But Abraham knew now that *God* would have to be the One to bring an end to their imprisonment. Abraham would put the appeal in motion, and this time he would leave the results to the sovereign Lord of the universe.

❦

As soon as he went downstairs, Abraham's peace was in jeopardy.

Without Servius, the household staff was in disarray. Abraham had to wander from room to room to find someone to prepare a meal for him; when the food finally arrived in the dining room an hour later, it was inedible.

Then Quintus appeared, wearing his I-really-don't-want-to-tell-you-this look, the one he always wore when there was bad news to report. Abraham led him out into the peristyle, where they could talk privately as they strolled.

"Naomi was at the harbor this morning . . ." Quintus hesitated a moment, waiting for Abraham's nod. When it came, he continued, "To see Kaeso."

"Kaeso?" Abraham was instantly alert. Naomi was hatching a scheme of some kind; he could feel it.

"He came to see me as soon as she left. Her visit didn't sit well with him."

"What did she want?"

"She told Kaeso to prepare the *Mercury* to sail for Rome—tomorrow. The captain informed Naomi that he took orders only from you, no one else. She said she was acting on your behalf, that you were going to appeal to Caesar for Jacob and Rebecca, and that if you were too ill to sail, she would be going alone."

Abraham had not mentioned his plan to Naomi, and he suspected that was not her true motive at all. What she really wanted to do was to go husband-shopping in Rome, but that wouldn't have sounded important enough to convince Kaeso to sail. She had guessed what her father's next move would be and then tried to manipulate the situation to her advantage. *Would she really have sailed without me?* Abraham wondered. It didn't matter now; she wouldn't have the opportunity.

"I told Kaeso I'd check it out with you," Quintus added. "Did you send her to make the arrangements with Kaeso? Are you going to Rome?"

"No, I didn't send Naomi as my messenger, but I am planning to go to Rome. And the sooner, the better."

"But the shipping season is over. All of our ships are going into dry dock in a few days."

"The *Mercury* is much faster than any of our commercial ships. We should be in Rome before the storms arrive. And if not, well, it's a risk I have to take." Abraham thought of what was at stake. Thought of his young daughter living in a prison camp with hardened criminals—men who were more like savage animals than humans. Thought of his son condemned to a life of hard labor. And he knew the risk was well worth it.

"It's something I have to do, Quintus. If God is in this plan, then He will preserve me through any storm. And I believe God is with me."

Abraham paused, thinking of his nightmare, the morning's introspection, and his prayer. "I repented, Quintus. I asked for forgiveness, and I believe I received it."

Quintus nodded slowly. "Good. I'm glad."

The two men walked in companionable silence for a minute. "I don't know how long I'll be gone," Abraham said. "Probably until spring. Watch over the business for me. I trust you to make whatever decisions might be necessary in my absence."

"I'll do my best, sir."

"And make sure Peter is all right. I hate to leave him alone . . ." Abraham would take Naomi with him, he decided. Perhaps the best thing for her would be to get married and live in Rome; it seemed to be what she wanted more than anything. He wished Peter would go with them but knew he would refuse; Peter was simply too afraid of sailing.

"I'll check on him regularly."

When they walked back through the house to the door, Quintus appeared reluctant to leave.

"Is there anything else?" Abraham finally asked.

Quintus shook his head. "No, just . . . I just wanted to say that I'll pray for you." He extended his hand. "Godspeed, Abraham."

Abraham choked up as they clasped hands, suddenly feeling it would be the last time they would ever see each other. "And God be with you, friend."

20

AFTER TWO DAYS ON DEVIL'S ISLAND, Jacob's entire existence had been reduced to a pile of rocks. He was aware of nothing but dust, sweat, pain, thirst, and gut-twisting fear of the unknown.

Behind him Rebecca sneezed, but Jacob avoided looking in her direction. He couldn't stand it anymore. It broke his heart to see her face and arms covered with with marble dust, her hands and feet caked with blood and dirt.

It was late afternoon and John was slowing down. Jacob could tell the Apostle was trying not to groan as he bent down and then straightened up—over and over and over again. The old man had to be near the point of complete collapse.

We don't belong here.

Jacob's basket was two-thirds full again when he heard horses galloping through the entrance of the quarry. He had forgotten that Damian's ship had arrived yesterday; now he saw the crimson plume on one of the helmeted riders and recognized his family's persecutor. The other man on horseback was the commander of the prison camp. Brutus appeared to be showing Damian around the quarry, pointing in different directions as their horses sauntered slowly through the giant dust bowl hollowed out of the rocks.

The guards had noticed the visitors on horseback too, and while their attention was diverted, Jacob switched his almost full basket with John's nearly empty one. John gave him a grateful look, and they both went back to work.

Damian's presence was like an invasion of the Prince of Darkness.

It galled Jacob that their mother's murderer enjoyed freedom, while he and his sister had been sentenced to slavery on this rocky wasteland simply for their religious beliefs.

They were almost ready to begin yet another trip to the harbor when Brutus and Damian rode close to the area where they were working. Suddenly Rebecca dropped the rock she was carrying, and Jacob knew by her startled reaction that she had finally recognized Damian. John appeared not to notice the men on horseback; he worked without looking up.

"Well, well. The old Apostle and the rich young preacher-boy." Damian held the reins loosely in one hand as he raised the other in greeting. "And the beautiful, sweet, innocent little sister."

Jacob deposited a final rock in his basket, then straightened up to look Damian in the eye. Rebecca, trembling, held tightly to her basket and kept her eyes on the ground.

Like a cocky little rooster, Damian crowed from his horse, "Military oversight of this work camp now falls within my jurisdiction, so I'll be paying personal attention to you." He smiled expansively. "But don't let me distract you from your new career here on Devil's Island. Carry on."

Jacob choked back a curse as he watched Damian laugh and motion in their direction, then lean over to say something to Brutus privately.

"Time to go." John placed a hand on Jacob's arm to get his attention. "Help me with my basket," he said quietly.

Jacob hoisted the basket as John turned his back and extended his arms toward the shoulder straps.

"What are you doing?" Damian shouted at Jacob. "Put that basket down."

Jacob obstinately held the heavy basket in front of him. "But it's full." He glared at the man the emperor had put in charge of Devil's Island. "Our job, as you well know, is to fill the baskets and carry them to the harbor."

"I said, put it down! *Your* job is to carry *your* basket—not his."

"I'm just putting it on his shoulders. He'll carry it down the mountain—then I'll carry my own basket." Jacob's voice rose with his anger.

"Put it down, now!" Damian's voice was a screech. "Now!" He nudged his horse closer to Jacob and the Apostle, cracking the whip over their heads. "Every man carries his own weight on this island."

Jacob set the basket down, feeling an inner rage he didn't know a human could feel.

Damian smirked at John. "Now pick up your basket, old man."

John stood silently, making no move to pick up the basket. He'd been unable to lift it from the very beginning, and Jacob knew it was pointless for John even to try now.

As Jacob heard the leather weapon whistle through the air again, he reached down and picked a rock out of the basket. He watched as Damian's whip struck the Apostle's back full force, once and then again. He saw the blood spurt, saw John drop to his knees and fall facedown in the dirt, heard him moan in agony, heard Rebecca scream. And then Jacob drew back his arm and unleashed all his pent-up fury in a single throw of his powerful arm, hurling a stone the size of an orange at the object of his rage.

The missile found its target. The rock crushed into Damian's head with such force that his helmet buckled like butter and he fell off his mount, unconscious.

Instantly Brutus dismounted. "Guards!" he called unnecessarily.

Jacob had already been surrounded by soldiers with their swords drawn. While the swordsmen held him at bay, another soldier grabbed him from behind, pinning his arms behind him, and yet another held a dagger to his throat.

Brutus held up a hand. "Wait!" he ordered the guards, then he addressed Jacob. "What's your name, prisoner?"

Jacob swallowed hard before answering the commander. He knew his life was over, yet he didn't regret his action.

"If this officer is dead, Jacob, you will be crucified today as an example for every criminal on this island. If he's merely unconscious, you'll be sentenced to serve at the oar of a Roman warship for life."

Brutus knelt down and turned his attention to Damian.

∽⚬∾

Rebecca reeled and almost collapsed at the proclamation. No matter what happened to Damian, she would lose Jacob forever. Perhaps John too. The Apostle had moaned once when he was struck, then he fell silent; his eyes were closed and he hadn't moved. Rebecca couldn't tell if he was still breathing. Was there no end to this horror?

She watched as Brutus pried the dented helmet from Damian's battered, bloody head. He lifted Damian's eyelids one at a time and examined the pupils, then he felt the wrist for a pulse. Finally the camp commander stood and announced, "He'll live."

Rebecca gasped in relief. Her brother would not be crucified.

Brutus walked in front of Jacob and angrily pointed his long forefinger at him. "Rome will use those strong arms of yours to row their warships for the rest of your life." Then he ordered the legionnaires, "Take this prisoner to the brig and chain him there. I'll ship him out of here tomorrow."

"No, you can't!" Rebecca screamed, and Brutus whirled around.

"What do you mean, I 'can't'? And who are you?" he demanded.

"I'm his sister." Rebecca took a deep breath and then her words poured out in a desperate torrent. "Please don't send him away. He was just trying to help an eighty-four-year-old man, a man who was too old and weak for this kind of work. And the officer he threw the rock at—" She almost choked on the words. "That monster killed our mother—ran her through with his sword and left her in the streets. And just now he was beating an old man for no reason. No reason! He's not a soldier, he's a butcher—"

"Watch your tongue," Brutus ordered.

The commander stepped toward her, and Rebecca saw the veins

pop out on his grimy forehead. He was tall, like her father, and towered over her. Unlike her father, however, his presence was a threat to her survival. Nevertheless, she continued to plead for her brother's release; she had nothing to lose.

She raised her gaze to meet the commander's. "Please don't send him away," she said earnestly. "He's all I have left of my family. I can't make it without him."

Brutus started to speak and then hesitated, and Rebecca thought her words had reached whatever humane impulse might remain in the hardened officer. Then he looked around at the guards, who were gauging his reaction, and the prisoners, who were gaping openmouthed at her audacity.

"Get back to work," he shouted. "All of you." He turned and walked away without looking at Rebecca.

The guards handcuffed Jacob and led him away, then Brutus mounted his horse and started barking orders. "Get a stretcher up here for this prisoner," he said, pointing to the Apostle, who was still lying facedown in the dust. "If he's alive, take him to the camp hospital."

"We don't need to wait for a stretcher," one of the guards said. The beefy man leaned down and picked up John, then threw the frail man over his shoulder like an old rug. Blood dripped down John's back and ran into his snowy hair as he hung silently over the soldier.

"Put the tribune on his horse," Brutus ordered, "and get him to Marcellus immediately."

Two soldiers lifted Damian and draped his body over the saddle. One of them took the reins and led the magnificently groomed horse out of the quarry and onto the rocky road to the harbor.

Rebecca watched in shock as first her brother and then the Apostle were taken away. She felt cut off, abandoned, utterly alone in the most godforsaken place she could ever imagine. She was hungry, thirsty, and bone-weary—and she wanted nothing more than to drop to the ground and die.

"You heard the commander," one of the overseers said. "Get back to work."

Rebecca looked at the basket at her feet. It was full of rocks. If she didn't pick it up and start carrying it to the harbor, she would hear the whip crack over her head. Tears rolled down her face as she stooped over and reached for the handles. She managed to lift the basket but couldn't get enough leverage to swing it up to her shoulders. Jacob had done it for her each time they'd loaded their baskets before. What would she do now?

"You!" One of the overseers called a prisoner over. "Help her get that basket on her back, then get your loads down to the harbor. Now!"

When she glanced at the prisoner sent to help her, Rebecca realized it was the wild-looking man she had seen outside the mess hall their first morning. It seemed a lifetime ago now.

Without a word, he picked up her basket and she put her arms through the straps, then he walked beside her as they left the quarry with a dozen or so of the others whose baskets were full. There was steady foot traffic in either direction on the harbor road.

"Sorry about your brother," the man told her.

Rebecca nodded her thanks, tears coursing down her cheeks. Jacob had told her the man's name last night and she tried to think of it now, but her mind wouldn't cooperate.

"The old man, was he your grandfather or something?"

"My pastor."

"Pastor?" The man looked puzzled, as if he didn't understand the term.

"A spiritual leader," she told him. "We're Christians."

"Oh, Christians." He nodded thoughtfully. "I've heard of them but never met any before. Of course, we don't get to meet too many people around here."

He reached up and scratched his head, and when Rebecca saw

the movement of his hand against the unruly tangle of wiry curls, she remembered. *Tonsorius—a barber. That's his name.*

"Except criminals," he continued. "But I guess you are a criminal or you wouldn't be here. Except you and your brother don't seem like criminals . . ." Tonsorius left his thought unfinished, as if the mental exertion of talking could not be borne at the same time he was carrying such a heavy physical burden.

When they got close to the harbor, Rebecca asked, "Do you know where the brig is, Tonsorius? Could I get to see my brother before they ship him out?"

He shook his head. "Can't help you there. They'd never let you get close enough, anyway."

"But I have to see him one last time. I have to." The tears she thought had stopped began to flow again.

Tonsorius regarded her for a long time. "Talk to Marcellus. Maybe he can help you." He looked doubtful, but he gave her directions to the camp hospital and wished her success.

After they dropped their rocks at the harbor, an overseer informed them there was not time to make another haul before sunset. He appeared supremely disappointed as he said, "Go ahead and report to the mess hall for the evening meal."

As hungry as she was, Rebecca did not go with the others to the mess hall. She waited until the guards were looking in the other direction, then she slipped into the main part of the camp, following the directions Tonsorius had given her to the hospital.

Used to the limestone and marble of the public buildings of Ephesus, Rebecca thought the rough wooden structures of the prison camp all looked alike. They were dark, drab rectangles, and if their weather-beaten boards had ever seen paint, it had faded years ago. She found the building marked with the staff of Asclepius—a rod with a serpent coiled around it, the symbol of healing—and knew she had found the hospital.

Inside, she scanned the row of cots. Most of them were unoccupied, but a man was bending over the last one, and she recognized the white-haired patient he was tending—John. *The Apostle is alive!* she thought with a brief flash of joy.

"How is he?" she asked when she had crossed the room.

"Unconscious still." The man looked at her curiously as he spoke, and Rebecca realized she must look a fright.

"Will he be all right?" She looked at the Apostle lying so still on the cot. He was on his side, but she could tell that his face was bruised where he had fallen. She shuddered to think what his back must look like after the lashing he'd received.

"It's too early to tell. In a younger man his injuries would not be fatal, but at his age . . ."

Rebecca struggled to remain calm. There was nothing she could do for the Apostle now. She needed to see her brother, and Tonsorius had said this man could possibly help her.

"Are you Marcellus?" she asked. When he nodded, she said, "You made me stand in the water when we arrived."

"How are your legs?"

"Better." She hadn't thought about her chafed ankles all day. After working in the quarries, there wasn't any place on her body that wasn't sore.

"Let me see your hands," he demanded.

"Why?" She didn't want the doctor to examine her, she wanted to ask him to help her find Jacob.

"Because they're bleeding." Marcellus sounded impatient.

Rebecca finally looked down at her hands. They were not just filthy; her knuckles were bloody, several nails had split, and there was caked blood on the palms of her hands where blisters had formed and then burst open. *No wonder they hurt so much,* she thought.

Marcellus made her sit on a supply table while he carefully cleaned her hands and applied some ointment. As he worked, she talked to him about Jacob and asked how to find the brig.

"Your brother is lucky," Marcellus told her. "He could have killed that officer. It so happens he was simply knocked out cold for a while. Then he came to, yelling and screaming."

"He's okay?" she asked, fear crawling up her spine as it suddenly dawned on her that Damian was somewhere in the camp, maybe in the hospital right now. She did not want to run into him.

"With a knot like a goose egg on his head, he won't be able to wear a helmet for a few days. But he'll be fine." Marcellus noticed her looking around. "He's not here anymore," he said, then went back to work.

When he finished with her hands, Marcellus used the ointment on her legs. "I can tell you where the brig is," he said finally, "but it's useless to go there. You would need Brutus's permission to see your brother, and he won't give it."

"But I have to ask him—I *have* to see my brother. I can't let him go away forever without saying good-bye." Rebecca struggled not to cry as she thought about never seeing Jacob again.

Marcellus turned away, an angry look on his face. He busied himself with the supplies on the table, then after a moment said, "I admire your courage, young woman, but you really should go back to your quarters. It's dangerous for you to be out after dark—"

"It's not dark yet," Rebecca protested. "And I have to see him." It was all she could think about. She didn't know what she would do after that, but Jacob was her lifeline, and she couldn't just let him go.

"Very well." Marcellus sighed and told her where to find Brutus. "But be careful. Prisoners are not supposed to be walking around the camp."

Rebecca slipped off the table and said good-bye to the Apostle, leaning down to kiss his forehead. Then she left and followed Marcellus's instructions for navigating the camp.

Soon she came to the building he had described as the camp headquarters. As she approached the door, she heard voices coming from an open window. Something told her to stop before she crossed in front of it, so she did. As she listened, she recognized that one of the speakers was Damian.

Rebecca closed her eyes and leaned back against the outside of the building, her heart pounding. She started to run but then realized they might be talking about Jacob, so she stayed.

"And you underestimate the importance of keeping discipline," Damian was saying. "It was necessary to establish my authority."

"Discipline is one thing," Brutus countered, "brutality is another. If you kill the prisoners, how can we keep the work going?"

"Prisoners are expendable. I can bring you an unending supply. And don't forget, *you* answer to *me* now. You'll run this place the way *I* see fit."

They weren't talking about Jacob, Rebecca decided, so she started to leave. But when she heard Brutus's next question, her feet refused to move.

"Is it true you killed that boy's mother in Ephesus?"

"Where did you hear that?"

"The young woman prisoner, his sister."

Damian's voice expressed his scorn. "You'd take the word of a convicted criminal over mine?"

"No," Brutus replied evenly, "that's why I'm asking you."

"She's just a hysterical girl. What I did or did not do in Ephesus is none of your business. I carried out my assignment from the emperor, and that's all that matters."

"Did your assignment call for murder?"

"The woman struck a centurion." Damian was shouting now. "I simply carried out her punishment on the spot. And that's the law around here too, Brutus. Any violation of the rules will bring *immediate* punishment. Do you understand?"

"Yes . . . sir." Brutus sounded none too pleased to be answering to Damian.

Rebecca heard footsteps and realized Damian was about to leave Brutus's office. Immediately she turned and sprinted down the main street of the camp, running as fast as her exhausted feet would carry her. She didn't slow down until she had passed the mess hall and had come to the spot where the path started up the southern slope to their cave. Her breath came in deep gulps as she leaned against a rock to rest.

She looked back and saw Damian walking toward the mess hall. *I have to get out of here before he sees me!* Panic overrode her exhaustion, and Rebecca began climbing the rocky path up the mountain. She didn't look back, but she didn't hear anyone following her, so she gradually slowed her pace. Her feet were screaming from the miles she'd carried a heavy load, and in spite of Marcellus's ointment, her raw hands burned with pain.

Halfway up the mountain, Rebecca realized she was headed back to the cave alone—totally alone—and suddenly she was terrified of spending the night by herself in that dark rat-infested hole in the rock. She turned around and looked back at the camp, hesitating. But what choice did she have? If she went back down the mountain . . .

Servius! He had said if she needed anything—and she did. She needed to be with someone, someone she knew and loved. But she didn't know where to find Servius. Yesterday he had said they'd found a cave not far from the camp; that's all she knew.

The hospital. Marcellus had been kind to her. Perhaps he would let her sleep on one of the cots in the medical building. But if Damian found out, he would punish her severely, and Marcellus would also pay a price for breaking the rules. She couldn't ask him to risk that, and besides, if she walked through the camp again, one of the guards was bound to see her. *"No loitering in the camp,"* Brutus had told the prisoners when they arrived. That was one of the rules, and Damian would make sure that Brutus enforced it.

The sun was low on the horizon now, and shadows fell across the mountain. Rebecca thought she saw movement on the path below her, then concluded that her mind was playing tricks on her as she strained to see into the twilight.

It will be dark soon—I have to decide. Which way do I go? she asked herself.

Rebecca shivered. The temperature had begun to drop as the sun went down. She had left her cloak in the cave that morning—this time intentionally—and now that garment seemed of immense significance to her. Not only did it represent warmth, it was her only possession, her only tie to her former life.

Not knowing what else to do, Rebecca turned around and started back up the mountain. When she had safely reached the cave, she went inside. While there was still enough light to see inside the dim interior, she went through the narrow passage to the inner chamber they had used for sleeping and retrieved her cloak and all three of their blankets. Then she went back to the wide funnel-mouth of the cave. She would pass the night here, she decided, just inside the entrance; she couldn't stand to be in the cave's inner room all by herself. It would feel like a tomb in the pitch darkness.

Still shivering, Rebecca wrapped herself in the cloak and the blankets and sat against the wall of the cave, watching the moon rise as darkness completely overtook the mountain. She was beyond tears now—starving, aching, feverish, and more alone than she had ever been.

She was afraid of what would happen if she went to sleep, so she remained sitting upright. In spite of her efforts to stay awake, however, exhaustion eventually closed her eyes and her head drooped to her chest.

Suddenly she snapped her head up. *What was that?* She listened to the sounds of the night and heard a rustling nearby.

The rats, she thought. *It's probably the rats.* John had named them Damian and Domitian, she remembered as she drew the blankets tighter around her.

But it wasn't the rats, she realized a second later. It was footsteps. Someone had entered the cave. As soon as she heard the footsteps, she heard the sound of heavy breathing and smelled alcohol.

Rebecca threw off the blankets and jumped to her feet. "Who's there?" she asked frantically, wondering if she could make it outside the cave before the intruder came any farther. Or should she try to hide in the large chamber of the cave?

She didn't have a chance to decide. As the stranger moved toward Rebecca, he stumbled and brushed against her. Rough hands grabbed her, and she couldn't pull loose from their hold. The man was drunk but strong.

"Stay still, and I won't hurt you."

Rebecca recognized her attacker then, and her fear escalated.

With a savage motion he pinned her against the wall and lifted her tunic, slurring his words as he expressed his evil design. "We have some unfinished business, Elizabeth."

Rebecca's screams pierced the night, but there was no one to hear, no one to save her as her mother's murderer brutally raped her.

21

JOHN THOUGHT HE HAD BEEN DREAMING, but when he opened his eyes and felt the sunlight on his face—and the fire of the wounds on his back—he realized the beating had actually happened, although he couldn't quite remember the details. He was lying on a cot, not on the ground of their cave, but close to an open window in what must be the camp hospital. He closed his eyes again as he recalled the sound of the whips, the struggle to lift an impossibly heavy load onto his back. Hoofbeats—there had been horses . . .

Damian. It started coming back to him. Damian had shown up in the quarry and had stopped Jacob from helping John with his basket. The next thing John knew, he had been struck from behind. Now he remembered the staggering force of the whip, the searing pain, and landing facedown in the dust. He remembered hearing Rebecca scream, and then he must have passed out.

Cramped from lying in one position for so long—*How long have I been here?* he wondered—John wanted to turn over. But he could not figure out how to roll onto his other side without first lying on his back, and he didn't want to risk the pain; he hurt enough as it was, so he continued to lie on his side, now and then glancing out the window. He couldn't see any activity, but he could hear the distant sound of tramping feet as workers arrived at the harbor to empty their baskets.

After a few minutes, an officer in a red tunic came into the infirmary. This soldier wasn't wearing the leather armor of the prison guards or the other camp officials, John noted. As he drew nearer, John recognized him as the medical officer.

"I see you're finally awake," Marcellus said. "That's good."

"What day is it?" John asked hoarsely.

"Sunday."

The Lord's Day, John thought. He knew they had arrived on Patmos on a Thursday. But was that three days ago, or longer? He had no idea.

"They brought you in yesterday," Marcellus said, answering the unspoken question. Then he pulled the thin blanket covering John down to his waist. "Let me look at your back."

John winced as Marcellus examined his wounds and applied ointment to his back. After a minute, the stinging began to subside and the medication felt cool and soothing.

"Get some more sleep," the medical officer told him. "When I come back, I'll bring some food, if you're able to eat."

"I'll be able," John said confidently, then promptly fell asleep again.

Later that day, when Marcellus returned, he helped John sit up, then handed him a bowl of the thin gruel served to the prisoners. "It's not much," he apologized, "but it will keep you alive . . . I think." He smiled tiredly. "Tomorrow I'll try to find something a little more nourishing."

"That's very kind of you." John sized up the medical officer as he sipped the watery mush. Not only did Marcellus not wear armor like the other soldiers, he did not seem to have the impenetrable interior defenses of the typical military man.

"I hear you're a preacher," Marcellus said. "Not the usual type we get around here. And definitely older than most of the other prisoners."

"I'm older than almost everybody. Eighty-four." John finished the gruel and handed the bowl back to Marcellus. He was beginning to feel better, now that he had eaten something. "I don't know why the good Lord has kept me alive so long." John often wondered why he was still around when all the other apostles had paid with their lives for their service to the King of kings. It was a mystery, but one he had come to accept.

"Evidently they've started sending more atheists here—Christians, I mean. Another group arrived yesterday."

"Have you ever known any Christians?" John asked. Marcellus shook his head. "Do you even know why we're called 'Christians'?"

"I know that you follow some man named Jesus. One of the many messiah-types from Palestine."

"*The* Messiah," John said emphatically. "That's what *Christ* means, the Anointed One, or Messiah. Jesus of Nazareth was—and is—our Savior."

"I see," Marcellus said as he straightened the medical supplies on the table under the window. The supplies had been arranged in an orderly fashion before Marcellus began toying with them, and John realized his attention to them now was simply a way of looking busy while he talked about a subject that could possibly get them both in trouble. There were no other patients in the infirmary, however, so they appeared to be free to talk.

"Anyway, this Christ has been dead a long time." Marcellus turned away from the window; perhaps he had been looking to make sure no one was outside. "Must have been fifty or sixty years ago—before I was born," he added.

"Sixty-five years, to be exact. I know—I was there."

"When He died?" Marcellus asked, incredulous.

"And when He was resurrected." John paused to let that soak in. "I knew Jesus personally. Maybe I'm the last one alive who did. Outside of the children, that is. He loved children, and some of His youngest followers are probably still around. But I was one of His original disciples."

Marcellus looked thoughtful. "When you say 'resurrected' . . ."

John was tired and in pain, but he ignored his physical weakness as his spirit stirred within him. He was still a fisher of men, and unless he was mistaken, Marcellus was his next catch. The soldier's open questions signaled his spiritual hunger, and John began to cast his net.

"Tell me, have you witnessed many crucifixions?" he asked the medical officer.

The question seemed to surprise Marcellus, and he thought a moment before answering. His eyes narrowed as he said, "I've seen enough."

"How many survivors have you treated?"

"Survivors? None." Marcellus was clearly puzzled by John's questions. "It's a death sentence."

"Exactly—and the soldiers make sure the condemned man is dead. I watched them crucify Jesus. Then I watched as the soldiers verified His death. One of them even stabbed Jesus in the side, and I saw water flow out with the blood."

Marcellus looked at the Apostle intently, still waiting for an answer to his question.

"He was dead, and He was buried. Then, three days later, His tomb was empty. I saw the burial linens lying on the ground, and I saw His prayer shawl, which had been wrapped around His head before burial, according to our custom, neatly folded and placed to one side.

"And later that night, He suddenly appeared in the room where the disciples were staying. I saw the scars in His wrists. Right here"— John pointed to the inside of his wrist, poking an arthritic finger in the space between the two bones of his lower arm, just above the point where they connected with his hand—"where He had been nailed to the cross. Jesus still bore the marks. And He was very much alive."

"Forgive me," Marcellus said, "but I'm not sure I can believe you." He looked uncomfortable, but he was not antagonistic.

John smiled. "We had a little trouble believing it ourselves at first. Then we began to remember things Jesus had said, prophecies that He would be raised after three days. We hadn't understood what He'd meant earlier.

"And then we saw Him again. And again. He was with us for forty days—hundreds of people saw Him during that time. After that, He ascended into heaven—disappeared into the clouds. I was an eyewitness to that too."

In spite of his desire to keep witnessing, the conversation had drained John, and Marcellus noticed it. "You should lie down now," he said. He helped John get comfortable on the cot, then covered him with the blanket. "Perhaps we can talk more later."

"You can count on it." John nodded and closed his eyes.

When he opened them again, it was twilight. Marcellus was standing nearby, placing a lamp on the table near John's cot. "I thought I would check on you one last time before I retire. I brought some water," he said, indicating the cup in his hand. "You haven't had much to drink today."

John drank the water in a few quick gulps and thanked Marcellus, who then began to put more ointment on his wounds.

"I see you have some old scars in addition to your recent injury."

"This was not my first run-in with the law," John said matter-of-factly. "But Caesar hasn't been able to kill me yet." He laughed softly, then groaned as Marcellus probed his tender flesh.

"Actually, your wounds look very good so far. I'll discharge you in a day or two." Marcellus paused, as if weighing a decision. "But I'll put you on medical leave. Indefinitely."

"What does that mean?"

"You won't have to report for work until I say so. I have a certain amount of discretion in this area, and I'm careful not to abuse it. But there are times when a prisoner simply is not able to work. And you weren't physically capable of this kind of work even before you were beaten."

John saw Marcellus's scowl in the flickering lamplight and was touched by his concern. "God bless you," he said.

"Well, good night." Marcellus started to leave and then hesitated. "Is there anything else I can do for you?"

"Yes, actually, there is. Two young people arrived from Ephesus with me: Jacob and Rebecca. Is there any way you can get a message to them, to let them know I'm all right?"

Marcellus didn't answer right away, and John began to feel uneasy. "Is something wrong?"

"Jacob is no longer here," Marcellus finally said. "Brutus shipped him out today."

"What? He was released?"

"No," Marcellus said quickly. "He was sentenced to the oar on a warship. They transferred him out of here early this morning."

John's heart sank. "But why?"

"After Damian whipped—after you were injured," Marcellus corrected himself carefully, "Jacob threw a stone at Commander Damian. It hit him in the head with such force that it knocked him off his horse. He was only knocked unconscious, so Jacob's life was spared. But now, instead of working in the quarry, he'll be rowing on a warship."

John remembered having to stop Jacob from retaliating against one of the overseers their first day in the quarry. No one had stopped Jacob the second time—and it had been Damian he had gone after. John understood all too well the struggle to control an outburst of temper, especially in the face of such injustice; his own volatile emotions had once earned him the nickname "Son of Thunder."

"What about Rebecca?" John's dismay at Jacob's fate was suddenly outweighed by a gnawing concern for her safety. Without Jacob, she would have been all alone in their cave last night.

"I saw her late yesterday," Marcellus said. "Right here. You were still unconscious. She was attempting to see her brother before he sailed. I tried to discourage her, but she was determined. I don't know if she managed to get permission to see him, though. It's not likely."

Both of them were silent for a moment. John thought of Rebecca working in the quarry without Jacob, who had lifted her basket each time, just as he had done for John. How would she manage? He thought of her walking up the mountain after work—alone, unprotected. Rebecca had probably never been alone in her life; she was used to being surrounded by family and friends who doted on her.

"I have to find her," he told Marcellus suddenly. John braced both hands on the wooden bar of the cot and slowly stood to his feet. "Where's my tunic?"

"You can't leave—"

"Not dressed only in this undergarment, I can't." John felt stronger as he stood and took a few steps around the room. "What happened to my clothes?"

"I sent them to be washed—but that's beside the point. You're not well enough to go looking for anybody."

"And *that's* beside the point. *Somebody* has to find her. She can't be left all by herself in this place!" John's voice rose tremulously.

Marcellus was looking at John as if he were crazy. *And maybe I am,* the old Apostle thought. But he suddenly knew that Rebecca was not only frightened, she was facing grave danger.

"I'll try to find her," Marcellus finally said. "Maybe she's still in the mess hall," he said doubtfully, looking out the window at the fading light. He turned around and motioned for John to get back on his cot. "Stay put. I'll be right back."

John sat down on the side of the cot and held his head in his hands. He prayed earnestly while Marcellus was gone, but the overwhelming sense of dread did not dissipate.

A few minutes later, Marcellus returned, a solemn expression on his face. John looked up at him questioningly.

"The mess hall was empty except for a few workers. All the inmates had left." Marcellus leaned back against the table, scooting the bowl-shaped lamp to the far edge. "No one remembered seeing the new woman prisoner."

John shook his head sadly. "I'm afraid something's happened to her." He shivered, but he didn't know whether it was from fear or the fact that he'd been sitting close to an open window in a state of undress.

"You'll catch cold in this night air," Marcellus said gently. He helped John back to bed and then shuttered the window. "I'm worried about her too," he admitted. "But it's too dark now to go looking for her. I'll check the dining room in the morning, and if Rebecca doesn't report for work, I'll see what I can find out."

Marcellus went to a cabinet and brought back an extra blanket for John. "Maybe she's with some of the other prisoners who came from Ephesus," he suggested. "Didn't she know some of them?"

"Yes." John brightened at the thought. "She knew the other Christians arrested with us—a number of them were household servants for her family."

But as Marcellus left and John tried to fall asleep, his darkest fears returned. He was not ordinarily a worrier, so the apprehension he felt now must be for a good reason. He believed Rebecca was alone and needed help—and he was powerless to do anything for her at the moment.

"Heavenly Father, I place her in Your loving care," he prayed. "Keep Your hand upon Rebecca, wherever she is."

22

ROME. EXCITEMENT. ADVENTURE. Naomi tilted her head back and let the sea mist spray her face. The wind blew her long auburn hair behind her back as the *Mercury* skimmed over the water. They had sailed at sunrise, so she had not taken the time to pin her abundant tresses in the elaborate style she usually wore. For the moment she didn't care about her appearance; there was no one to impress except her father and the crew, and they weren't worth the effort.

She opened her mouth in an exhilarated laugh. The gay sound was muffled by the roar of the sea and the wind. Nothing else mattered to Naomi now that she was headed to the destiny that awaited her in Rome.

Her only regret was that they hadn't departed two days ago, as she had planned. She had been to see Kaeso on Friday, and the obstinate old sea captain had insisted on getting her father's approval before making any arrangements to sail. That evening, when her father had confronted her, Naomi had been prepared with her arguments. Most of them, it turned out, were unnecessary. He had already decided to make an appeal to Caesar, as she had guessed, and even though her father seemed none too happy at the prospect of having her along, he had agreed she could travel to Rome with him.

"And you can marry a senator, if that's what will make you happy," he had said with a frown.

"Oh, it will!" Naomi glowed with anticipation.

"I still have a few acquaintances within the senatorial ranks, and I'll make some contacts for you while I'm there."

"Thank you, Father," Naomi had said rather demurely. *But that won't be necessary,* she thought. She didn't trust her father to find a suitable husband, and she especially did not want the taint of her family's religious convictions to hurt her chances for marriage. Naomi was confident she could take Rome by storm and meet a wealthy, marriage-minded senator within days of her arrival; then it was only a matter of using her considerable charm to get him to put a ring on her finger.

"I know you'll be busy with the appeal," she told her father. "I wouldn't want to take your attention away from that."

Abraham had looked at her in disbelief, as if he had read her mind. She didn't care what he thought, as long as he allowed her to go to Rome.

The appeal made sense, she supposed. While she was not in the least motivated to win the release of her fanatical brother and sister from Devil's Island, her father certainly was; it seemed to be his only reason for living at the moment. Caesar had the power to rescind their sentence, so it was natural that a man of her father's status would seek a personal audience with the emperor.

Once she was married again, Naomi decided, she would have little contact with her family. She would try to maintain a cordial relationship with her father, but from a distance. Naomi didn't want to alienate him completely; she was the oldest child and stood to receive a vast inheritance. She guessed that her father would not leave the shipping empire to her, but with Jacob out of the picture, and with Peter incapable of running the business, Naomi was the logical choice to succeed her father—and she was determined to make that happen as well.

After her father had announced his intention to go to Rome, Naomi spent the next two days packing and planning for the trip. On Saturday, while Abraham paid a visit to his banker and Kaeso bought provisions, Naomi had gone to a slave auction. With Julia's help she had bought a pair of slaves, a brother and sister originally from Egypt. The two were young, attractive, healthy, strong—and strong-willed, evidently. Lepidus and Fulvia had lived in Rome most of their lives. When their owner decided to sell them, they had run away rather than be separated. Eventually captured, they had been bought and sold twice before winding up in Ephesus. Naomi had paid a premium for the pair, but she was drawn to their sullen good looks and thought their having grown up in Rome might be an advantage to her.

On Sunday morning, Naomi had been annoyed to encounter church members arriving at the villa. She pulled her father to one side. "I thought we were leaving today. What are these people doing here?" she asked, obviously provoked.

"We'll sail in the morning," Abraham had replied. "This is the Lord's Day, and we're going to have church." He calmly removed her hand from his forearm and went to greet their guests.

Naomi was not only irritated at the delay, she was perplexed. So in a few minutes, she followed the group out to the peristyle. She leaned against an archway, remaining at a distance from the worshipers seated in the garden. About fifteen people had shown up— a much smaller crowd than normal. But that was understandable, seeing that quite a few of the regular attendees had been shipped to Devil's Island. She noted that Galen was there, looking disconsolate without Rebecca by his side.

Her father stood to address the assembly. "Yesterday," he said, "I asked Quintus to gather what was left of the church here today, as usual—although the circumstances are far from usual right now." He paused to clear his throat. "I want to thank you for coming."

"I wasn't sure we should," someone said, "after what happened. We didn't know what to think, but Quintus said you'd had a change of heart."

Abraham nodded. "I have."

A few people murmured their approval, but one older man stood and confronted Abraham. "Because of your bad example," he said harshly, "some of the weaker brothers also made the sacrifice to Caesar—and they'll burn in hell for it! What good is your change of heart now?"

Quintus rose and put his hand on the man's shoulder, quietly urging him to sit back down.

Naomi watched as her father bowed his head, clearly in turmoil. "I deeply regret," he said after a moment, "that my sin caused others to go astray. I will carry that shame to my grave." Raising his head, he looked out at the congregation and spoke earnestly. "I wanted to confess my sin to you today and tell you that I have repented. I have asked God's forgiveness, and I want to ask yours, as well."

Tears rolled down Abraham's face as he continued. "I also want to ask for your prayers as I go to Rome on behalf of my children, Jacob and Rebecca, and our beloved Apostle. We should pray for all the believers who have been sent to Patmos. I've heard that the same thing is happening in other cities nearby, and that more Christians have been sentenced for refusing to make the mandatory sacrifice."

Naomi was disgusted at her father's show of emotion—a grown man standing there, crying like a schoolboy. She was also disturbed at his change of heart, and worried that he would get the family in trouble with the authorities if it became known that he had recanted his loyalty to Caesar. As soon as her father sat down, Naomi slipped out of the service and returned to her room. She did not want to be around when they started singing hymns; it always set her teeth on edge.

Now, standing on the deck of the *Mercury*, laughing into the wind, Naomi remembered the previous day's church service and her father's public confession. She filed that knowledge away, thinking it might come in handy someday. *I'll use it against him, if need be,* she thought. If she could find a way to tell the emperor that her father had recanted, there would not only be no release forthcoming for Jacob and Rebecca, her father would likely be imprisoned himself.

Naomi ran her hand over the smooth, highly polished railing of her father's private ship, bitterness rising like a bad taste in her mouth. He didn't want her to have the "indulgence" of riding in a litter, but he had splurged on this floating palace of luxury. It was necessary for his business, he'd always claimed.

But if he were in prison, Naomi thought, *the business would be mine to run—and so would this ship.*

∽✠∾

When John woke up the next morning, Marcellus was standing over him. "I brought you some food from the officers' quarters," the army doctor said as he placed a bowl of stew—with chunks of meat in it, John saw—and a small round loaf of bread on the supply table.

John smiled at the sight of the metal spoon resting in the wooden bowl of stew. "Aren't you afraid I'll try to poke your eye out with that weapon?"

Marcellus grinned when he realized John was pointing at the spoon. "I think I can overpower you, if need be." He went across the room and brought a stool back to the supply table so John could eat there. "While you eat your meal," he said, "I'll go to the mess hall and see if I can find Rebecca."

"Thank you," John said, grateful both for the food and Marcellus's concern. The medical officer had been the one ray of hope in this aptly named place; it was the devil's own island, indeed. Although Marcellus was not a believer—at least not yet—John knew God had placed the military doctor there to be available in John's hour of need.

The stew was not a great culinary accomplishment, but it was a considerable improvement over the prisoners' fare, and John felt strengthened by the first substantial food he had had in days. Marcellus had not returned by the time he finished his meal, so John stood and stretched his legs, then walked around a bit.

The hospital ward was a long, rectangular room with two large windows on either side of the main door, which was squarely in the middle of one of the long walls. Twenty cots were evenly spaced across the length of the room, ten on either side of the entrance. The building was probably a standard army design, John reckoned as he paced the length of the room. Erected near a battle-field, such a hospital would need several of these wards to treat the wounded. Here, however, the beds were empty, although John vaguely remembered Marcellus treating another prisoner while he was dozing off and on the day before. The man's hand had been crushed when a heap of rocks fell on him. Marcellus must have released the prisoner after patching him up, because he had not spent the night there.

Walking seemed to strengthen John further, and he thanked God for sparing his life and asked his heavenly Father yet again to reveal the purpose for which he had been sent to Patmos. Perhaps it was merely to witness to Marcellus, and for John, that would be enough. Yet he felt there was another, even deeper purpose. *Be patient,* the Apostle reminded himself. *That will come in time.*

John also prayed for Rebecca, and for Marcellus's success in find-ing her. He had been gone longer than John had thought would be necessary, and that was troublesome.

When Marcellus finally returned, John could tell at a glance that the news was not good.

"She wasn't there," Marcellus confirmed. "I stood just outside the mess hall and watched all the prisoners leave for the quarry; Rebecca wasn't among them." The medical officer sat down on the stool while John returned to his cot. "Evidently my presence aroused suspicion," he continued, "because one of Brutus's chief aides-de-camp approached me and asked what I was doing. I did some quick thinking and told him I had been curious about a prisoner I'd seen in the hospital on Saturday. 'The prisoner was injured,' I said, 'but didn't return for treatment. I just wondered what happened.' Then I shrugged as if it really didn't matter.

"It wasn't a complete lie, you know," Marcellus said sheepishly. "Rebecca *did* come to see me on Saturday, and she *was* injured—

well, her hands and feet were bleeding and I doctored them. I could tell that her heart, more than her body, was battered and broken . . ."

Marcellus was leaning forward on the stool, his forearms resting on his knees, as he talked to John. He dropped his head and fell silent for a moment. John wanted to prompt him to continue but felt checked; Marcellus was either remembering something or thinking things through, and John felt he should give him some time.

"Anyway, the aide wasn't convinced that my interest was merely casual. He demanded to know the prisoner's name, and I reluctantly told him. We walked over to the roll-call station and checked the records." He raised his head and looked at John again. "Rebecca didn't report for work yesterday or today."

John felt sick at heart. The apprehension he'd felt the previous night swept over him anew. *Something is terribly wrong.*

Marcellus stood and fiddled with the supplies on the table, glancing out the window. In a moment he turned back to John. "The aide was furious that Rebecca had been absent for two days. 'I know who she is,' he told me. 'Her brother is that troublemaker Brutus got rid of yesterday. These Christians are going to be nothing but problems,' he yelled." Marcellus shot John an apologetic look to signal his disagreement with the aide's assessment.

"The aide said they would send out a search party immediately. 'We'll find her,' he told me emphatically." Marcellus hesitated, looking out the window again. "And when they do . . ."

"What will they do to her?" John coaxed Marcellus to continue, almost afraid to hear the answer.

"He said that if she's dead, they'll bury her. And if she's alive, they'll punish her." Marcellus closed his eyes momentarily, as if pained by the thought. "A severe flogging—up to thirty-nine stripes—is the usual punishment. They have to set an example for the other prisoners."

"We have to find her first," John said, rising from his cot. "No," he corrected himself. "*I* have to find her. I can't prevail upon your kindness any further. You could get in serious trouble for helping me."

Marcellus nodded. "Yes, I could. But I can't let you go off looking for her on your own. You've improved remarkably fast for a man your age, but you're not recovered, by any means."

"God will give me the strength to do what I need to do," John replied firmly. "You could help me, though, by finding me some clothes to put on."

Marcellus walked through the door opposite the main entrance into another room. *That must be his office or private quarters,* John surmised. The medical officer returned in a moment, carrying the tunic John had been wearing when he arrived. It was clean and neatly folded.

"About the only luxury that's part of this assignment," Marcellus said, "is having someone to do my laundry. Most of the prisoners here die on the job, but occasionally some grow too old and feeble to work in the quarries. Then they're reassigned to menial jobs around the camp," he explained. "I sent your tunic to be cleaned with some of my uniforms."

Marcellus quickly examined John's back before he donned the tunic. "Very nice," he muttered. "The wounds are already beginning to close."

Thank God I was wearing an old tunic, John thought as he pulled the garment over his head. New fabric would have felt rough on his raw back, but this tunic had been washed so many times that it was soft as well as faded.

When he had dressed, John extended his hand to Marcellus, to thank him and wish him farewell. Marcellus looked at him a long time without taking his hand. Finally, he said, "I may be going out on a limb here, but I want to help you find Rebecca. You don't know your way around, and you're not supposed to be walking around the camp by yourself anyway."

"I don't think she's anywhere in the camp," John said slowly. "I have a feeling she went back to our cave. That's where I want to look first. I think she's either too frightened, or perhaps too sick, to come out."

"Then let me go find her. You shouldn't do a lot of climbing—and if she is in the cave, and she's sick, you couldn't get her back here without help."

"Are you sure you want to do this? Why?"

"Yes, to the first question. And I'll answer the second question when I get back."

"You can answer it on the way," John said. "I'll go with you to show you where the cave is. You'd never find it on your own." He smiled ruefully. "I don't know what possessed me at the time, but we went in the opposite direction from everyone else when we went looking for our new home. We walked quite a ways up the mountain too, before we found a cave. It has a spectacular view and is quite isolated, which makes it very private. I thought that would be nicer for Rebecca and Jacob rather than being crowded in with all the riffraff."

Marcellus shook his head appreciatively as John continued, "But the drawback is that if she is in the cave, and if she's sick or injured, there would be no one to call for help. She would be all alone."

"We'd better go quickly," Marcellus said. "Are you sure you can make it?"

"No, but I'm determined to try. And with God's help—and yours—I'll do so."

With work having started in the quarries, the main part of the camp was almost deserted. The Apostle and the medical officer walked through the camp without any observers, and when they had passed the mess hall, John pointed up the southern slope. "That direction," he said.

They had not climbed very far up the path when John stopped and looked around. "Are you all right?" Marcellus asked.

"Yes, but it was a lot easier when I had a walking stick. Jacob found it for me the first day, and I don't know what happened to it—got left in the quarry, I guess."

"I'll look around for something," Marcellus said.

"No, let's keep going," John said. "But keep your eyes open for a long sturdy branch."

"You sure are a tough old bird—a lot of pluck left in you," Marcellus said admiringly as they started up the hillside again.

John's wrinkled face lit up. "Aye, there is. A lot of pluck," he said with a chuckle.

About halfway up the mountain, they stopped to rest and let John catch his breath. His back had started stinging again with the exertion, and the Apostle knew that supernatural strength was the only reason he was able to climb the mountain at all; he never would have made it otherwise—no matter how much pluck he still had left.

While John sat down to rest, Marcellus found a thick branch suitable for another walking stick. As he pulled small twigs and leaves off the branch, he said, "About that second question you asked . . ."

"I was wondering when you would get to that."

"I have a daughter," he said, studying the branch in his hand. "She would be about Rebecca's age, I guess."

"Where is she?" John asked.

Marcellus shook his head. "I don't know. I haven't seen her since she was six years old." He went back to working on the branch, concentrating as carefully as if he were operating on a patient. When he had finished, he handed the stick to John and leaned back against a tree. "I didn't intend to get married and have a family. It's not really compatible with a soldier's life. But I fell in love with a girl when I was stationed in Cappadocia, and she became pregnant, so we got married. Then I got sent off to war, and my daughter was almost a year old before I saw her for the first time. What a beautiful little thing she was," he said wistfully.

John saw on Marcellus's face the emotional impact of his memories. "What happened to your family?" the Apostle asked gently.

"The army happened. My wife couldn't handle the long absences. I was away much more than I was home, and eventually there wasn't a home to come back to. Just after Livia—my daughter—turned four, I was sent to another battlefront. When I got back to Cappadocia, more than two years later, she was calling another man 'Papa.' My wife had divorced me and married someone else while I was off fighting for the glory of the Empire.

"I can't really blame her," Marcellus said sadly. "I couldn't be there for her, and I couldn't be a father to Livia. That's what I regretted the most, not seeing my little girl grow up."

"You never saw her again?"

"No, I thought I should let them get on with their lives, and I requested another assignment. Before I knew it, I was in another part of the world, and I've never been back." Marcellus pushed away from the tree and reached out to help John up. "It's been a long time, and I don't think about it much anymore," he said. "But something about Rebecca reminded me. She looked up at me with those big brown eyes, her lip quivering as she tried not to cry, and insisted that she had to find her brother. I could tell he was extremely important to her.

"I could also tell she was from a fine home, and I couldn't help wondering about her family. Then I thought about my own daughter being in an infernal place like this . . ." Marcellus left his thought unfinished as he gestured angrily toward the camp. As he turned and started up the mountain path, he said, "Anyway, you asked why I would risk getting involved. That's the answer: for Livia."

The two men climbed in silence. There was a deep wound in his new friend's heart, John realized, and Marcellus had honored him by revealing it.

It took John longer to make the climb than it had a few days earlier, and he was weak and trembling by the time they reached the cave. He sat down at the mouth of the cave, panting, while Marcellus went inside and quickly came back. "Nobody's in there," he reported.

"Look in the other room," John said in between gulps of air. "On your left, about ten feet in, there's a passage. It leads to the large chamber where we slept."

Marcellus was gone several minutes; when he returned, he was carrying Rebecca wrapped in a blanket. "She's been hurt," he told John. "It's too dim in there. I need daylight to work."

Dropping to one knee, the medical officer carefully placed Rebecca on the ground just outside the cave. "By the gods . . ." Marcellus swore as he saw the extent of her injuries.

John shifted to get a better look at Rebecca, and he blanched. Purple and black bruises covered her face. Her lip was cut and swollen, and John thought he saw a bite mark on her neck. Marcellus tried to pull the blanket away to examine her further, but she clutched it tightly, her eyes wide and frantic.

"She's conscious," Marcellus whispered to John, "but I couldn't get her to say anything. I thought she might recognize me out here in the light." He touched her hand gently. "Rebecca, I'm the medical officer, Marcellus. Do you remember me?" She offered no response. "You've been hurt and I need to examine you. Would you let me open the blanket?" Still no response.

John moved closer so Rebecca could see him. "It's me, Rebecca. The Apostle. What happened? Who did this to you?"

At the sound of his voice, Rebecca turned her head and focused on John, then she started crying soundlessly. Finally, her hands relaxed their hold on the blanket, and Marcellus moved it away from her body.

Both men gasped. Her clothes had been ripped to shreds, and her body bore multiple contusions. John looked away quickly, shocked at her suffering, and wanting to afford her a bit of privacy while Marcellus looked at her injuries. When he finished the brief exam, Marcellus wrapped the blanket around her and motioned for John to stand.

They walked a few feet away from Rebecca. Marcellus's jaw was set in a hard line. "She must have fought like a tiger," he said. "There's dried blood under her fingernails, so whoever attacked her will be wearing some deep scratches."

Marcellus's eyes turned to flint, and he softly said, "She was violated. Raped."

"Whoever did this is a wild animal, worthy of death," John said. He had difficulty comprehending that a human being could have pummeled Rebecca so savagely.

John's hand went to his chest. He felt the pang as keenly as if he had been stabbed in the heart. He stood with his head bowed for a long time, grief-stricken at what had happened to this dear innocent child, this precious girl he had loved all her seventeen years. *Dear God,* he cried out silently, *I can understand how there could be a purpose in sending a worn-out old preacher to this damnable place. But what purpose could there possibly be for this young woman, with her entire life ahead of her, to be sentenced to a life of cruelty and then to be so brutally attacked?*

When he turned back around, John saw that Marcellus had picked Rebecca up and was carrying her in his arms.

"I have to get her to the hospital," Marcellus said. "I'll come back and help you down the mountain after that, all right?"

"I got up here on my own," John said gruffly, "and I'll get down the same way." He stooped down to pick up his new walking stick. "Lead on."

23

JACOB'S HEAD POUNDED WITH EVERY STRIKE of the hammer. His position on the lower level put him in close proximity to the barrel-chested oarsmaster, who set the beat for the rowers by banging a heavy mallet on top of a sturdy oak beam projecting upward from the ship's floor. With each earsplitting *thwack*, Jacob reflexively pulled back on the oar. After three long days as an oarsman on the *Jupiter*, Jacob no longer bothered to watch the oarsmaster. Even with his eyes closed, Jacob could see the man's biceps bulge with every downward swing, see the impact of the hammer send a rippled response back up his muscular arm.

Just one week ago I was a free man, Jacob thought as he rhythmically rowed in unison with his shipmates. His temples throbbed and his back ached, but he never missed a stroke. Jacob could scarcely believe it had been only a week since he had been dragged to the Temple of Domitian and ordered to sacrifice to Caesar. The intervening seven days had seemed like seven years, so much had happened.

When they had left Patmos on Sunday morning, Jacob was unaware that Damian had boarded the transport just before it sailed. By nightfall the ship had made port at Smyrna, and early the next morning, Jacob was transferred to the *Jupiter*.

Standing on the dock, his legs shackled and his hands cuffed, Jacob had watched Damian disembark and stride imperiously into the city. *Will he wreak destruction on the church of Smyrna as he did in Ephesus?* Jacob had wondered. He breathed a prayer for Polycarp and the other Christians he had met when he'd visited Smyrna a few weeks earlier, when he and John had sailed there on the *Mercury*.

John had sought out Polycarp as soon as they arrived, and the Apostle's two protégés had quickly established a rapport. Like Jacob, Polycarp had been a disciple of John from a young age; now, at twenty-six, Polycarp was a leader in the church at Smyrna. The three of them had spent hours talking about the problems facing the church. After John retired one evening, Jacob and Polycarp had stayed up talking about the significance of the times in which they lived.

"Some of our church people don't believe in the Lord's return anymore," Polycarp had said, "even though I have always preached it. But it's been more than sixty years since Jesus made that promise, so they have a hard time believing it will come to pass."

"I guess I've been around John so much that I've never doubted it," Jacob had replied.

Polycarp smiled. "I know what you mean. John was an eyewitness to everything that happened—he heard Jesus make that promise personally. It's all still so real to John, there's no room for doubt. And when you're with him, that confidence is contagious."

"I wonder why, though, the Lord hasn't returned. Why has He left His church here to endure sadistic persecution?"

"I don't have an easy answer for that," Polycarp had said, "and it's a question I hear frequently. Especially when so many in our congregation are suffering."

Polycarp described for Jacob some of the difficulties the believers in Smyrna had endured. They couldn't get business permits or jobs because they were Christians, although that was never the stated reason. Some flimsy excuse always accompanied the denial, but it was discrimination, and they knew it. They also feared that official persecution was coming.

"We're not a wealthy church to begin with," Polycarp had said, "and with so many of our people going through hard economic times, it's been difficult." Worse than the financial struggles, though, were the doctrinal differences that threatened to divide the church. "I continually have to combat the teaching," Polycarp said, "that true believers don't have to suffer—that if you suffer, it's the result of sin in your life, or you don't have enough faith. Some believers have even advocated compromise with the Roman government and society. They think it's all right to attend the games and to host dinner parties at pagan temples."

That sounds like Naomi, Jacob had thought.

The next day, John had invited Jacob to preach at a gathering of the church. He was excited as he stood in front of the congregation to bring the Word of the Lord. It was a heady feeling, being part of the inner circle around John and being accepted among his peers in the ministry. But Jacob also felt the burden of preaching to people he knew were suffering for their faith. He decided that being the shepherd of a flock was a far cry from the evangelistic work he had done in Ephesus, and Jacob was sure that pastoring was a burden he hoped God would not ask him to carry.

At the end of the service, John had laid hands on Polycarp and anointed him as bishop. Then the Apostle admonished the congregation to follow Polycarp's leadership as he followed Christ and encouraged them to be patient in suffering.

Patient in suffering. Those words came back to Jacob now as his powerful arms continued to pull the wooden oar methodically through the water. He hadn't been very patient in suffering, and his impetuous response to difficult circumstances had landed him in the bowels of a warship.

Jacob would not have believed he could miss Devil's Island, yet he did. Mostly he missed Rebecca and John, and he worried how they were faring in the quarries without his help. But Jacob also missed working in the fresh air and sunshine, missed the privacy of their cave, and missed the ability to stand up and walk around— even if the price of such unrestricted movement had been carrying a heavy load of rocks all day long. Here, the work was equally mind-less and backbreaking, but it was carried out in the dark hole of a floating cell block. Only a few rays of sunlight filtered through the small opening where his oar reached into the water mere inches below his seat.

In his short time as one of the *Jupiter's* 170 oarsmen, Jacob had learned a lot about the ship and the imperial navy. The *Jupiter* was a *trireme,* so designated because of its three different levels of rowers. Each oarsman sat on a short wooden bench and pulled a single oar. The two upper banks of oars were stacked on the outrigger, a rowing frame attached to the hull, and staggered to allow the oars to dip into the water at different angles. The lowest bank of oars, where Jacob was stationed, passed through the hull itself. Built long and narrow—roughly 110 feet long and only twelve feet wide—the *trireme* was lighter and faster than the older *liburnicae.* With the oarsmaster set-ting a swift beat, the *Jupiter* could accelerate from standstill to half-speed in under ten seconds, and could hit top speed—eight knots—in about thirty seconds.

One thing Jacob did not miss about Devil's Island: the threat of the overseers' whips. Here, no patrolling guards used force to moti-vate or manipulate the workers. For one thing, the *Jupiter* carried a relatively small crew in addition to the oarsmen, plus a detachment of only fifteen to twenty marines; that's all the ship would hold. Moreover, cracking the whip would not have worked on board a warship: a single injured rower unable to maintain the stroke could cripple the ship during a crucial moment.

Jacob had learned something else about life on a warship, some-thing that gave him a faint glimmer of hope. His presence on the *Jupiter* was something of a fluke. Because of the necessity of a highly skilled and motivated crew, the imperial navy rarely used slaves or pris-oners on a *trireme* anymore, resorting to such measures only during wartime emergencies. With the Empire at peace for the moment—except for a few minor skirmishes on the northern frontiers where the army remained to solidify the borders—there was no state of emergency. However, with an aging peacetime force, the navy found itself shorthanded and had struck a deal with several penal colonies, like the one on Patmos, to take the occasional troublemaker off their hands—as long as the troublemaker was reasonably young and powerfully built. Jacob had fit the bill.

What gave him hope was the custom of offering freedom to prisoners or slaves serving as oarsmen before an impending battle. The warships still plying the Mediterranean enforced the *Pax Romana* against potential marauders, keeping the seas free for commercial traffic. The only battle Jacob was likely to see would be an encounter with the occasional pirate ship, and he didn't know if the wartime tradition of granting freedom would apply in that situation. But he had begun to pray that a foolhardy gang of thieves would challenge the *Jupiter* so he could find out.

Meanwhile, he rowed. And rowed. Hour after hour. Day in, day out.

The steady fall of the hammer and the swing of the oar had an almost hypnotic effect; sometimes Jacob's mind completely shut down while his muscles continued to move. He closed his eyes now, and the words in his head began to take on the rhythm of the oarsmaster's hammer . . .

Patient . . . in suff'ring . . . Patient . . . in suff'ring.

∽⚮∼

John sat on a stool by Rebecca's hospital cot. It was at the end of the row, by the supply table under the window—the bed he had occupied a few days earlier. The swelling in her face had gone down, he noted as he patted her hand, willing her to respond. Rebecca turned and looked at him, but she didn't speak. She had not uttered a single word since they'd found her.

That was Monday, John thought. *Three days ago.*

Rebecca closed her eyes again. She did not appear to be in pain;

John thought it was more a matter of being unable to face the world. He stood and began to pace the length of the room. He was still pacing several minutes later when Marcellus entered and looked at him, a question mark on his lined face. John shook his head to indicate there had been no change.

Marcellus walked to the far end of the room and bent over his other patient. John watched as the medical officer examined the man briefly and then stood back up.

"I don't think he's going to make it," Marcellus said wearily. "His internal injuries must be too severe."

A rock slide in the quarries had crushed two convicts to death several days earlier. A number of other prisoners had been hurt in the accident. Most of their injuries had been minor; Marcellus had treated and released them. This man, however, still hovered between life and death. John had stood by his cot and prayed for the man several times.

"Do you think she'll ever speak again?" John asked now, motioning toward Rebecca. "Does some injury prevent her from talking?"

"No, she's physically capable of speech. I've heard her cry out in her sleep." Marcellus wrinkled his brow with a look that conveyed both worry and frustration. "I suppose her silence is a result of the trauma. We have to give it time. Her body will heal . . . I just don't know about her spirit."

"God can heal her spirit," John said. "He can make her whole again—body, mind, and spirit." He straightened and smiled at Marcellus. "No reflection on your medical skills, but Jesus is the Great Physician. And I've consulted Him about our patient."

Marcellus nodded and a fleeting smile crossed his face. "Good. Maybe He can finish the work I've tried to start."

"He will, friend," John said softly. "He will."

John passed the rest of the morning sitting by Rebecca's side. Sometimes he prayed silently, at other times he prayed aloud. He quoted psalms and Scripture passages to her, knowing that the proclamation of the Word had healing power.

Hoping she could hear, John rambled on and on with stories about Mary and Martha and how he had been there when Jesus had raised their brother, Lazarus, from the dead. Rebecca's eyes never strayed from John's face as he spoke, but she still did not respond.

That afternoon, when he had grown hoarse and Rebecca had fallen asleep, John stood and stretched his legs. He looked out the window and wished he could take a short walk in the sunshine, but he wasn't supposed to wander around the camp. So he contented himself with strolling the length of the hospital ward again.

The door into Marcellus's quarters stood open, and as he passed it, John heard someone enter from the back of the building.

"Marcellus, I need a word with you."

John recognized the voice: it belonged to the camp commander. Quickly, John stepped away from the door.

"I'm in my office, Brutus," Marcellus called in reply.

John listened as the commander said he had heard the new woman prisoner was in the infirmary. "Although there's been no report that she was injured on the job. In fact," Brutus said, "she hasn't reported for work since Saturday."

Marcellus didn't reply, and John wished he could see what was going on. He wondered what explanation the medical officer would give.

"Is the rumor true?" Brutus demanded to know. "Is she here?"

"Perhaps you should sit down," Marcellus said.

John felt not a twinge of remorse for eavesdropping. *It's not my fault the door was left wide open,* he thought as he lay down on the cot nearest the door and pretended to nap. He spread a blanket over him, figuring he could pull it up to hide his face, if need be.

"And the old man—the one they call the Apostle," Brutus said. "Is he here too?"

From his cot, John peeked through the doorway into the other room. Brutus was sitting with his back to the door, so John couldn't read the expression on his face. But he could tell Brutus was angry by his tone of voice.

"Yes," Marcellus said with a slow exhale. "They're both here."

"The explanation had better be good," Brutus threatened.

"I put John on medical leave. He's too old and feeble to work in the quarries, and you know it."

"That's not my problem."

"Well, it's *my* problem. I still have a conscience, even if you don't."

"I have to run this place—*you* don't!"

John listened to the heated exchange, praying silently.

"And I don't envy you that," Marcellus said, lowering his voice.

Brutus matched the softening tone when he spoke. "You're going to leave this hellhole in a year. I do envy you that."

"Less than a year. My term of enlistment is up in three hundred and twenty days." Marcellus sounded as if they couldn't pass fast enough to suit him.

"What are you going to do after that?"

"I haven't let myself think about it. Don't much care where I land, just as long as it's far away from here."

"Sometimes I think we officers have been sentenced to Devil's Island as well as the convicts." Brutus laughed dryly. "What gods did we offend to draw this assignment?"

Marcellus drummed his fingers on the desk, then got back to the purpose of the visit. "Look, John is eighty-four years old. He never did anything wrong except believe in Jesus of Nazareth. He shouldn't be here."

"No, but he is here. And so is the young woman." Brutus returned to the question Marcellus had yet to answer. "Why is she in the hospital? Are you trying to protect her? Hide her?"

"I wish I could have protected her . . ." Marcellus's voice dropped off, and John knew he was remembering the day they'd found her in the cave. "She was raped," Marcellus finally said. "Brutally beaten and left for dead."

Brutus sighed. "Is she going to recover?"

"Physically, yes. But she may never be the same mentally. She hasn't spoken since it happened."

Evidently Brutus took a moment to think about the situation before speaking. "In a few days we can reassign her to the laundry or the kitchen." He ran his fingers through his hair and swore. "I just don't want the others to think I've gotten soft."

"No, we wouldn't want to show too much humanity," Marcellus said bitterly. Then he waved a hand apologetically. "Sorry," he muttered. "I appreciate it. We'll find something for Rebecca to do as soon as she's able."

Brutus stood and started to pace back and forth in front of the desk. John could see him now and then when he passed the open door.

"For the time being," Brutus said, "it's better if they just go back to their cave. Maybe—yes, *now*," he emphasized. "They should leave the hospital now."

"But why?"

"Because Damian returned today with another boatload of Christians. He's herding them here like cattle." Brutus spoke softly and John strained to hear. "If he sees Rebecca, it might remind him of her brother, and the old man, and that whole episode in the quarry—and I'm afraid of what he might do. Damian is a madman. I don't want to do anything to rile him."

"Do you think he did this to Rebecca?" Marcellus asked the question point-blank.

That was exactly what John had wondered, but he hadn't said anything to Marcellus about it.

Brutus didn't answer for a long time. "He's capable of it."

"She fought her attacker," Marcellus said. "There was blood under her fingernails. Whoever did this got quite a scratching—and depending on where she scratched him, the marks would be visible."

Brutus plopped back into the chair across from Marcellus.

"Damian has a trail of faint scratches down his face and neck, and I immediately thought of fingernails." Brutus's voice grew cold. "I joked with him about it. He winked and told me he had tangled with a wildcat. He likes to brag about his women. I thought he'd gotten into some rough play."

Marcellus exploded. "Would you like to see for yourself just how rough he 'played'?"

"No. I'll take your word for it." Brutus lowered his voice again. "But if Damian did do this—and I'm not saying he did—then she's not safe here. She's not safe anywhere on this island."

"So even if Rebecca goes back to their cave . . ." Marcellus paused. "Still, she would be safer there than here. I think he left her for dead; if so, he won't go looking for her."

"Except for the fact that at least a few people saw you bring her here. If I heard about it, Damian will too."

Marcellus hesitated, and John rolled to the edge of the cot, listening intently. "Then I'll make sure he thinks she *is* dead," Marcellus said. "I'll say she didn't recover from injuries sustained in the rock slide. If I put 'deceased' on her official records, then no one will have a reason to go looking for her."

"If Damian ever found out . . ."

"Then we'll have to make sure he doesn't." Marcellus looked meaningfully at Brutus as they stood facing each other, both within John's narrow line of vision. He could see the firm set to the medical officer's jaw. "I'll take care of the details," Marcellus said, "and you won't have to know about it. You can say, truthfully, that you never saw her when you came to the hospital."

"As far as I'm concerned, we never spoke about this."

Marcellus nodded soberly.

As Brutus turned to exit through the back door, John briefly glimpsed the scowl on the commander's face. In that single expression were etched anger, a desperate desire to be rid of Damian, and the degradation of the job he'd been assigned on Devil's Island. John breathed a sigh of relief that Brutus had left without having set foot inside the ward.

John had folded the blanket and was placing it neatly back on the cot when Marcellus walked in, a surprised look on his face. "I didn't realize the door was open."

"I'm glad it was," John said. "I heard everything." He started walking toward the window. "I'll wake Rebecca. We'd better go."

"Not so fast," Marcellus said, following John. "I don't want anyone to see us leave." He stopped John with a hand on his shoulder. "Let's move both of you back to my room, where you can wait. Then when night falls, we'll go back up the mountain. In the morning, I'll file my report."

"You're taking an even greater risk this time. I heard you say you'll be out of here in a matter of months." John was torn. He desperately wanted Marcellus's help to protect Rebecca, but he hated the thought of putting the man in jeopardy. What if Marcellus were arrested for falsifying records and had to stay on Devil's Island—as a prisoner?

"It's a risk I'm willing to take, for Livia. I couldn't live with myself otherwise." Marcellus spoke with conviction driven by quiet desperation. "I've given the army almost twenty years of my life. And in the process, I've given Caesar my soul. I want it back now."

24

On Sunday morning John stood at the mouth of the cave and watched as the sun emerged on the horizon and the sea began to glow with the promise of another dawn. For decades he had watched the sunrise as often as he could; it was a perpetual reassurance that God was still on His throne and that His mercies were new every morning. Lifting gnarled hands toward the sky and opening his heart toward God, the Apostle recited a psalm:

> *Blessed be the name of the Lord*
> *From this time forth and forevermore!*
> *From the rising of the sun to its going down*
> *The Lord's name is to be praised.*

Then he thanked God that Rebecca had finally spoken. It had been only one word, but John knew it was the breakthrough he had prayed for.

After Marcellus had helped them up the mountain Thursday night, he had returned twice on Friday, bringing extra blankets, a jug of water, a supply of wheat and corn, olive oil, a small cooking pot, a clay lamp, and several flints for starting fires. "All the comforts of home," he had joked. Marcellus had also brought a small ax with him, and he chopped wood while John gathered kindling.

"You can come down to the mess hall for bread and to refill your water jug," he told John, "but don't let Rebecca come anywhere near the camp. She mustn't be seen."

"I hate to leave her alone. Not yet, anyway."

Marcellus nodded. "That's probably for the best. I'll be here frequently to check on you. But I don't want to come so often that I raise suspicions."

When Marcellus returned to the hospital, John had felt a slight letdown. He not only appreciated the medical officer's help, John enjoyed his company. They'd had more opportunities to talk about the Lord over the last few days, and John knew in his spirit that Marcellus was close to becoming a believer.

On Saturday afternoon Rebecca had finally ventured outside the cave. She walked slowly, evidently still sore from the attack, as she moved to join John. He was sitting on a tree stump a few yards outside the cave, basking in the sunshine and watching the seagulls as they circled and then dived for food in the pounding surf surrounding the island. The blue-green water beat relentlessly against the rocky shore.

Rebecca sat on the ground beside John and laid her head in his lap. He stroked her hair idly as he watched the aerial combat along the shoreline. Her sudden cry startled him, and at first John thought it was simply the screeching of the gulls. Then he recognized the plaintive wail as distinctively human.

"Whyyyyy?" Rebecca began to sob as she repeated the single word over and over.

"Only God knows the answer to that question," John had said as he tried to comfort her. "But you're in good company. We've all asked it at one time or another."

For most of the afternoon, John held Rebecca and spoke soothingly. He knew her tears would be cleansing, knew she had to pour out her grief, her shame, her rage until she was empty. "Let it all out, child," he told her.

At sundown he'd started a fire and made a bit of porridge. Rebecca's breathing was still ragged from weeping and she didn't speak again, but she had eaten all the porridge. And she had slept through the night, without crying out or jerking in her sleep.

Now, satisfied that the sun had indeed risen on God's creation yet again, John went back to the interior chamber of the cave. Rebecca was still sleeping soundly, and he didn't want to disturb her just yet. Because it was the Lord's Day, John decided to spend more time in prayer. He leaned back against the wall of the cave, wishing he had his scrolls and parchments with him so he could read and contemplate the Scriptures. Much of the Word of God was stored in his heart, however, and he meditated on it now as he sat silently in the dim rock chamber that had become his home.

Suddenly a brilliant light, brighter than a thousand suns, flooded the room. John blinked and raised a hand to his eyes, and then he heard a loud voice behind him. As powerful and majestic as a trumpet, the voice said, "I am the Alpha and Omega, the First and the Last. What you see, write in a book and send it to the seven churches in Asia."

Startled, John turned toward the voice, and the walls of the cave seemed to fall away. He saw seven golden lampstands, and standing in the middle of them was a figure resplendently clad in a long robe with a golden sash. His hair was like the whitest wool, and His eyes were like flames of fire. His feet appeared to be glowing brass in a refiner's furnace. Was He real or an apparition? John wondered as he fell to his face like a dead man. Then the figure laid His right hand on the Apostle and said, "Do not be afraid. I am He who lives, and was dead, and behold, I am alive forevermore."

The risen Christ. He is here. John tried to speak. "My Lord and Savior." He formed the words but wasn't sure if any sound came out. It didn't seem to matter as Jesus raised him to his feet and began to reveal the purpose of the supernatural visitation.

"The seven lampstands are seven churches," the Lord explained. Then He gave John a message for each of the churches: Ephesus, Smyrna, Pergamum, Thyatira, Sardis, Philadelphia, and Laodicea.

After He had given His beloved disciple these messages, a door opened and John saw into heaven. "Come up here," Jesus said, "and I will show you what must take place after this."

Immediately John was transported before the throne of God. Circled by a rainbow of emerald, with a sea of glass, as clear as crystal, extending outward, it was like nothing he had ever seen, nothing he could have imagined. Flashes of lightning emanated from the throne, accompanied by the rumbling of thunder.

Around the throne were four living creatures covered with eyes, even under their wings. They were crying, "Holy, holy, holy is the Lord God Almighty, who was, and is, and is to come." As the creatures gave glory and honor, twenty-four elders laid their crowns before the throne and fell down to worship Him who lives forever.

With supernatural insight John watched the scene unfold before him, and listened with spiritual ears to the words of the angel who explained what was about to take place in heaven and on the earth. John saw plagues and pestilence beyond his mortal comprehension, yet his understanding was enlightened. And afterward he saw the indescribable glory of the Holy City, the new Jerusalem coming down out of heaven.

The loud voice like a trumpet said, "Now the tabernacle of God is with men, and He will dwell with them. They will be His people, and God Himself will be with them. He will wipe every tear from their eyes. There will be no more death or mourning or crying or pain, for the old order of things has passed away."

Then the One who sat on the throne said, "Write this down, for these words are true and faithful. He who overcomes will inherit all this."

John had entered eternity, and time had no significance. His entire being was consumed with the revelation, and the final words of Jesus reverberated in his spirit: "Surely I am coming quickly."

Even so, come, Lord Jesus! The words sang repeatedly in John's mind as the overwhelming brilliance gradually faded. Slowly, John's eyes became accustomed to the normal illumination of faint sunlight streaming into the cave, and he saw Rebecca sitting a few feet away from him, her arms wrapped around her knees. She was studying his face intently. "Are you all right?" she asked, her voice steady and sure.

John opened his mouth but couldn't quite speak, so he settled for a nod. It occurred to him that he should have been amazed and overjoyed to hear Rebecca asking that question. But after what he had just witnessed, John was not at all surprised that she seemed to be speaking and acting normally while he was the one who was suddenly speechless.

"You've been sitting there for the longest time," Rebecca said. "Your eyes were open, but you couldn't see or hear me. I started to get worried, and I was going to shake you and try to wake you up—except you weren't really asleep . . ." She wrinkled her forehead as she struggled to express what had happened. "And then I felt a calming presence, almost like a hand on my shoulder. Then all my fear just disappeared. *All* my fear," she repeated, and John understood that she meant more than the concern she had felt when he hadn't responded to her; Rebecca had been freed from the terror that had gripped her since the night she had been attacked.

"V-v-vision," John finally stuttered. "I had a vision."

Rebecca's eyes grew wide. "A vision? What did you—"

"Parchment," John interrupted. "I have to find parchment so I can write it down. It's a message for the church . . ." He looked around frantically, the recognition slamming into him that he was in a cave—as a prisoner—and that he had no writing materials of any kind.

But this is why it happened, he realized. *God sent me to Patmos so I could receive this revelation.*

"Marcellus will have parchment." Rebecca started to rise. "I could go ask him—"

"No, I'll go!"

"But I'm feeling much better," she protested. "I could make the trip down the mountain easier than you."

"Rebecca, promise me you won't set foot outside this cave!" John's voice was unusually stern, and she looked upset at his command. "You're supposed to be dead, remember?"

"Not really." She shook her head. "I vaguely recall you and Marcellus talking about it, but nothing about the last few days is very clear."

John quickly related how Marcellus had helped them get from the hospital back to the cave and the plan he had come up with for hiding her.

"So if I'm supposed to be dead, then I won't have to report for work in the quarry," she said with a long sigh of relief. "That's the only good news I've had since we arrived."

"The other good news is that I have an answer to your question—at least a partial answer. God *does* have a purpose for us here, Rebecca. I'm not sure why you had to be a part of it, but I know God allowed me to be a prisoner so He could speak to the church through me one more time."

"You mean the vision."

"Yes. I'm supposed to write it down, along with the messages to seven churches in Asia—some of them are the churches Jacob and I recently visited."

"Because you felt something terrible was about to happen. And it did."

He nodded. "But far more terrible things are in store, and that is why God gave me such an important revelation. To warn His people, and yet to encourage them."

John stood and began to pace as he thought out loud. "Consider this. Damian meant to kill me, or at least hurt me badly, yet God meant it for good. The injuries Damian inflicted are what caused Marcellus to put me on medical leave. As a result, I was here, in this cave, on the Lord's Day, ready to receive the revelation of Jesus Christ."

His eyes gleamed with a fervent zeal for the commission he'd been given. "And because I don't have to report for work, I will have all the time I need—and the solitude—to write down the vision."

"I could help," Rebecca said eagerly as she jumped to her feet. "I don't have to report for work, either. And I'm well educated, you know—I can write clearly. You could dictate to me, and spare these dear old fingers." She picked up one of John's thin hands and kissed it. "Perhaps that's why *I'm* here," she said softly. "To help you."

"Perhaps you'll be the one to carry my letters to the churches," John suggested. "God will have to provide a way for us to get His Word off this island. I don't know how, and I might not even live to see it, but He will make a way. I'm sure of it."

The elderly Apostle, invigorated with fresh strength for the task ahead, lifted Rebecca's hand into the air with his and began to offer praise to God.

> *O God, You have taught me from my youth;*
> *And to this day I declare Your wondrous works.*
> *Now also when I am old and grayheaded,*
> *O God, do not forsake me,*
> *Until I declare Your strength to this generation,*
> *Your power to everyone who is to come.*

25

THE SEA WAS ANGRY, and Abraham knew it even before he saw Kaeso's worried frown. They'd been sailing for two weeks and still had not reached Sicily, the large island just off the toe of the boot-shaped mainland of Italy. By now they should have rounded the western shore of the island, at which point they would bear north–northeast toward Ostia, the closest port to Rome.

"The wind's picked up, and it's shifted direction again," the captain informed him, pointing forward and upward. "A few minutes ago it was blowing from the southeast."

Abraham lifted his head and studied the wind flag; the breeze was coming from the northeast now. A sudden gust of wind plastered Abraham's clothes to his body and sent his hair flying wildly. The sleek bow of the *Mercury* no longer sliced the clear blue-green water silently and smoothly; the ship had begun to pitch and roll, and the water now reflected the murky violence of an approaching storm.

Abraham had hoped to be in Rome before the bad weather hit, although he had known that even at top speed the *Mercury* could not have reached its destination before entering the period known as *mare clausum,* the "closed sea." From mid-November to mid-March the waters of the Mediterranean became too unpredictable for safe navigation because of frequent gale-force winds and poor visibility.

He'd taken the *Mercury,* built not only for personal comfort but also for speed, intending to get to Rome as quickly as possible. Also, because it was smaller and lighter than his commercial ships, the *Mercury* could dock at Ostia, and from Ostia they could transfer to a barge for the short sixteen-mile trip up the Tiber River to the capital city. Now, however, Abraham wished he'd chosen one of the hefty, broad-bottomed cargo ships in his fleet. That would have meant docking at one of the larger ports and then traveling to Rome by an overland route, lengthening their trip. But the broad hull and greater weight of a cargo ship would have meant more stability on rough waters.

And a raging sea was what they were facing. Not ten minutes after the wind had shifted directions, it shifted again. Now it was blowing from the northwest. *Circular motion,* Abraham thought. *From southeast to northeast to northwest.* The winds were beginning to swirl in a circular pattern, a movement that could drive timid waves into furious mountains of water.

Following Kaeso's shouted directions from the tiller, the crew scrambled to secure the hatches. In the space of a few minutes, the velocity of the wind picked up exponentially, driving the waves higher and higher. Several sailors tried to lower the huge main sail, anchored to the thirty-six-foot-tall mast at midships, but they could not maintain their hold on the halyard and had to abandon the effort. The storm had simply come on them too fast.

"Do you think it's a full-blown hurricane?" Abraham leaned toward Kaeso and yelled to be heard over the whistling wind.

"No doubt about it. You shouldn't be out here," the captain shouted back through cupped hands. "Get inside—now!"

Without further question, Abraham gripped the handrail and walked slowly along the deck, leaning into the wind. He was not offended by the order, knowing Kaeso was motivated by concern for his safety. Soon the captain and crew would have to vacate the deck themselves and wait out the storm below.

As Abraham made his way to the deckhouse, he heard the sound every sailor learned to dread. When a gale reached hurricane force, the winds vibrated the long ropes anchoring the sails until they uttered a moaning sound, as if the ship were mourning its coming death. He glanced up at the main sail, already strained to the point of bursting, and the smaller foresail, called the *artemon,* which flew from a forward-leaning mast at the bow of the ship. The *artemon* was decorated with the traditional Roman *oculus,* a large painted eye. Abraham preferred to think of it as the all-seeing eye of God, and he breathed a prayer as he struggled to open the door of the deckhouse against the wind.

Once inside, he quickly descended the steps to the level where his stateroom was located at the very back of the stern. He steadied himself by keeping a hand on the wall as he walked. Even for a man with experienced sea legs, he found it hard to keep his balance as the bow of the ship rose and fell against the water with a violent thud.

Abraham had sailed through rough seas before, but never a hurricane. He had heard about rogue waves that seemed to come out of nowhere, forming a thirty-foot wall of water that could sink the mightiest of ships in mere seconds. The phenomenon occurred in a storm when several ordinary waves happened to synchronize their fury and force, combining into a powerful, unstable column of water. The resulting rogue wave forced the bow of a ship into a steep trough—mariners called it a "hole in the sea"—a dive so deep the bow could not recover before the next wave hit the stern and snapped it into splinters.

When Abraham reached his stateroom, he found Naomi huddled in the corner, her head on her knees. She'd never been prone to seasickness before, but then she had never sailed through a storm like this. Naomi appeared almost green as she looked up and asked, "Are we going to die?"

Abraham did not want to unduly alarm her, but he did not want to lie, either. "We're in great danger. This ship was designed for speed, not tunneling through mountains of water." He sat down and put his arm around his daughter. "We're sailing into a hurricane, and only God can save us."

Naomi shrugged off his arm and stood shakily to her feet. "Why would God save *you*?" she demanded angrily. "You chose Caesar over Christ, remember?"

Abraham winced at the blunt reminder. "Yes, but I repented."

"Quite conveniently, it seems. Don't tell me you wouldn't do the same thing again tomorrow if it meant saving your fortune. And then, I suppose, you'd just repent all over again."

"Naomi—" Abraham stopped his protest. He was not about to debate the sincerity of his confession with his rebellious daughter.

Naomi walked across the stateroom as she continued badgering him. "You know what I think you are? You're a Jonah. Maybe if you were thrown overboard, the sea would become calm."

Now Abraham was the one sitting on the floor with his head in his hands. "If I'm thrown overboard, maybe God will have a giant fish ready to swallow me and spit me out on land."

"You're just stupid enough—or crazy enough—to believe that."

Abraham did not respond as Naomi kept up her harangue. His daughter seemed to be raging as furiously inside as the hurricane that threatened outside. Abraham tried to tune her out for a moment, then began to listen more closely as he heard her scream, "I hate you! It's all your fault—you should have been the one to die."

"What are you talking about?"

"Crispin. You should have died, not him." Naomi grabbed onto a heavy table bolted into the wall. The bow of the ship rose higher and higher, then tilted on the crest of the wave and dived. The stern cantilevered out of the water as the bow plunged and smacked the sea with a shuddering crash.

She blames me for her husband's death, Abraham realized as the impact sent him sliding. He bumped into the built-in bed and grasped its sturdy frame. *But why? Because it was one of my ships?*

Naomi quit yelling but started to sob—whether in anger or terror, he wasn't sure. Abraham was stunned by her declaration that he was to blame for Crispin's death. He thought back to the circumstances surrounding his son-in-law's demise and remembered a crucial fact: *he* was supposed to be on the ship that went down. But at the last minute Crispin, whom Abraham had taken into the shipping business, had offered to make the trip for him.

Abraham recalled it all now. Rebecca had been sick for days with a high fever, and Crispin knew how worried he was. Abraham did not want to leave on an extended business trip when his youngest daughter could be seriously ill, and he had been grateful when Crispin, who was very competent and whom Abraham trusted implicitly, had volunteered. Rebecca recovered in a few days, but Crispin was lost at sea.

Weeks later Abraham learned that the ship, with its full crew and cargo, had gone down off the coast of Rhodes. He sailed there to locate any remaining traces of the wreckage; the only evidence had been a few planks of the hull, bits and pieces of cargo, and two badly decomposed bodies that had washed ashore. Abraham would never have been able to recognize the bodies, but he identified one of them from the engraved gold wedding ring on his left hand: it was Crispin.

And now he knew that Naomi blamed him for her loss—not only blamed him, but wished he had died in Crispin's place. *That's why she's so bitter,* Abraham thought. *She blames me for not being on that doomed ship, and she probably blames Rebecca for getting sick.*

Father and daughter continued to ride out the storm in silence, clinging precariously to the securely fastened furniture in the ship's luxurious stateroom. The violent tossing had Abraham's seaworthy stomach in knots, and when he closed his eyes, he could picture the giant waves battering the ship.

He was not surprised when the bow lifted and seemed to hang suspended in the air indefinitely; then it plunged deeper and deeper . . . and deeper still.

A rogue wave. He imagined it would blot out the whole horizon—a massive, vertical wall of water with no curling crest, just a thin white line along the entire length. *And we've hit it.*

As the *Mercury* plunged into the killer wave, Abraham's bulky body flew through the air, smashing the stateroom door, which blasted open on impact. The whirling wind snatched him from the room and flung him through the hole in the stern into the angry sea.

So this is how it will end, he thought as the churning water swallowed him.

∽⚮∾

Naomi stood on deck and watched as the badly battered *Mercury* limped toward the port of Ostia. The tattered remnants of its majestic sails hung pitifully from what was left of the masts, which had been snapped in half like twigs by the hurricane. The ship now inched along on manpower.

A sailing vessel, the *Mercury* had only a short row of oars on either side that could propel the ship forward in an emergency. The storm had been over in three hours, disappearing as suddenly as it had arisen, but it had taken more than a week to complete the voyage. The crew was utterly exhausted, and there had been times Naomi wondered if they would ever make it to Rome.

Naomi also wondered how she had survived the storm; most of it was a blur. She remembered seeing her father swept into the swirling water through the hole that had opened in the ship's stern. She remembered being more terrified than she had ever been in her life. But she had not been aware how long the storm had lasted or how she had managed to keep from being thrown overboard with her father. Eventually Kaeso had found her, and she remembered him trying to pry her away from the heavy table—the only part of her father's stateroom that had been left intact. Naomi had wrapped her arms and legs around one of the table legs and held on to it so tightly that her arms and legs were black with bruises for days afterward.

Kaeso had offered Naomi his cabin, and he moved to the crew quarters. The captain, who had worked for her father for more than twenty years, was polite but subdued. She knew he was grieving for his friend and employer, and she also knew he did not trust or respect her. Naomi couldn't care less, as long as he understood she was in charge now.

And I am *in charge,* she thought happily as she glimpsed workers on the dock staring slack-jawed at the crippled ship slowly approaching. As soon as the sailors had secured the ropes and lowered the gangplank, Naomi disembarked and ordered Lepidus, one of her new slaves, to hire a carriage. "I'm not floating up that smelly river on a barge," she muttered to his sister, Fulvia, who waited beside her on the dock.

"No, ma'am," the young Egyptian dutifully replied. "Not a lady of your status."

Naomi loved hearing the quick, deferential response and thanked the stars that she'd had the good sense to buy the brother–sister pair before she left Ephesus. "Load what's left of my things on a barge," she told Kaeso, "and have them sent to my father's villa."

Unsmiling, the captain nodded his acquiescence. "You can reach me through your father's office in Rome if you need me. I'll await your instructions on the repair of the *Mercury.*"

Among other things, the two of them had clashed on whether her father would want to restore the *Mercury* right away. They had also clashed on how to notify Abraham's Rome office and bank about his death. Naomi had wanted to wait and tell them in person, making sure they realized that she was taking over her father's business; that way she would have a chance to gauge people's reactions. But Kaeso had insisted on immediately sending a message by carrier pigeon, and she had relented when he agreed to say in his note that Abraham's oldest child would be arriving shortly in Rome to handle his affairs.

Lepidus returned with a splendid carriage, and Naomi smiled. She would arrive in style, as she had intended. She made sure Fulvia was carrying the small valise Naomi had personally packed and then settled into the carriage for the short trip to Rome. Inside the valise were two items, a wooden box and a leather pouch, which she had found locked inside the drawer of the table that had saved her life. The box held enough gold coins to meet their immediate expenses, and the pouch contained a document from her father's bank at home. Naomi was not sure what the technical term for the document was, but she understood its purpose: to make available for his use in Rome a vast sum of money, guaranteed by funds available in his account in Ephesus. All she had to do was present the letter to his banker in Rome, and the money would be hers.

I'm a very rich woman, she thought as the wheels of the carriage sang over the pavement. *Tomorrow will be the day I've lived for all my life.*

26

NAOMI TRIED TO CONCEAL HER FRUSTRATION as she spoke to the portly, balding banker. "I don't think you understand," she told Cassius, willing herself not to laugh at his ridiculous lisp. She did not want to insult the man—not until she'd secured her father's funds in her own name, that is.

Once again she went over the details, thinking that perhaps this time her words would penetrate his thick skull. "You acknowledged that you received the message saying my father had drowned at sea and that I would be handling his business affairs. And here is the letter from his bank in Ephesus authorizing you to release funds. I'm sure you've handled this kind of transaction for him before."

"Yes, of course, and I'd gladly do it again—for him."

"Then you'll do it for me. I'm his legal representative now." Naomi did not hesitate to make the claim, even though it might be a stretch. She was not familiar with the legalities of inheritance, but she knew she was her father's rightful heir. The man was simply being stubborn because she was a woman, she decided. It wasn't unusual for a woman to inherit a fortune, but it was out of the ordinary for her to attempt to exercise complete control over it. Some men couldn't handle the concept of a competent woman, and this fool of a banker was evidently one of them.

"Actually, there's some question about that," Cassius said, whistling the words through his teeth.

Naomi bristled visibly. "What do you mean?"

The banker appraised her carefully before he spoke. "A few days

after we received your message from the *Mercury*, we received a con-
tradictory message from your father. You see, he's not dead, therefore
you cannot be his legal representative."

"That's impossible." All the color drained from Naomi's face. "I
watched him drown." She stifled a moment of panic at the thought
that her father had not actually perished when he'd been hurled from
the ship. It couldn't be! Kaeso had said there was no way her father
could have survived in the open sea; even if he hadn't succumbed to
the raging waves of the hurricane, they were too far from shore for
him to swim to safety. After the storm had died down, Kaeso had
tried to search for Abraham, but there had been no sign of him.

"Perhaps you'd like to see the message. It originated from the
harbormaster's office at Syracuse." Cassius pushed a small square of
parchment across the desk, and Naomi's heart almost stopped as she
read it.

> Rescued at sea. Will arrive in Rome within the week.
> Let no funds be transferred from my account for any reason.

The note, written and signed in her father's bold, artistic handwriting, bore the harbormaster's seal. *Rescued at sea.* She couldn't believe
it—wouldn't believe it.

"It's obviously a forgery," Naomi said, her voice rising. "Some
impostor wants to get his greedy hands on my father's estate." She
was on the verge of tears, and she hoped the banker would think
it was from grief, not the deep despair that threatened to over-
whelm her. She had been terrified when her father was swept overboard, but afterward, she had not been devastated by the fact of his
death. Rather, it had seemed fitting—a matter of justice. After all,
he should have been the one lost at sea three years ago. She reasoned that Abraham had simply cheated destiny for a while before
finally meeting his intended fate, and she refused to feel guilty for
not mourning him.

"An impostor? That could be," Cassius said. "But you understand that I can't legally transfer any funds until we get this sorted out." His tone was placating, but the puffy black eyes were cold. Naomi could not tell whether he was convinced the message was authentic, or whether he was simply holding on to her father's assets with a banker's tightfisted reflexes.

This can't be happening, she thought, looking around the opulent office she had entered with such confidence, believing she would be a wealthy woman—in her own right, not in her father's name—when she left. Naomi knew she was far from destitute. She had a roof over her head—a magnificent roof, actually; her father's villa was small but lavish. And she had the wooden box with its stash of gold coins. But how long would that sustain a household? A few months, perhaps, if she were frugal. She did not want to count every coin and worry how she would live until her father's estate was settled, however. She had come to Rome to find a prominent husband, and that would require the right wardrobe. It meant being seen in the right places by the right people, and that required money—and plenty of it.

Naomi squared her shoulders as Cassius rose and walked around the desk. She had survived the stigma of her fanatically religious family in Ephesus, and she had survived a monstrous hurricane at sea. She didn't care if Cassius happened to be the most powerful official at the most prestigious bank in Rome, which he was—she'd be hanged before she would accept defeat from this overbearing lump of lard.

Cassius offered Naomi a pudgy arm, clearly indicating that their meeting was over. "Why don't you come back in a few days," he said, "after your father—or whoever sent this message—has had time to arrive in Rome and contact me."

Almost trembling with fury, Naomi stood but refused Cassius's arm. "Very well," she said in her haughtiest tone, "but you can rest assured that when this matter is resolved, I will transfer every last *denarius* of my father's assets to another bank."

"I wouldn't be too hasty to make any changes, if I were you."

She noted with some satisfaction that the banker had blinked before he spoke; she had gotten his attention with her threat.

"I could be of great assistance to you," Cassius continued. "I've handled your father's account for many years, and a woman in your position—alone in this delightful, but dangerous, city—might need the advice of an astute businessman such as myself."

She despised his patronizing tone, and she despised leaving his bank empty-handed. As she followed Cassius to the door, she resolved to find out who had sent that message. It had looked like her father's large, dramatic scrawl, Naomi thought, but she had examined the note only briefly. Someone familiar with his handwriting could have cleverly forged it—her father's string-bean assistant, for one. Quintus probably signed Abraham's name to correspondence as a matter of routine. Her father ran one of the largest shipping operations in the Empire, so there would be samples of his handwriting scattered from Mauretania to Arabia. *It could have been anyone,* she told herself.

When Cassius opened the door to escort her out, Naomi spied his assistant cowering before a tall silver-haired man who was demanding to see the banker immediately.

"Senator," Cassius called out in his ingratiating lisp. "I do apologize for keeping you waiting. Something unexpected came up."

The tall man turned and started to respond. When he saw Naomi, he stared with obvious interest. "If this is the 'something unexpected' that detained you, it's quite understandable," he said smoothly.

Even without Cassius's greeting, Naomi would have known the man was a senator: he wore the distinctive white toga with the broad purple stripe and the short boot stamped with the letter *C,* standing for *centum,* a reference to the original one hundred senators of the former Republic.

"Introduce us, Cassius, so I can make the lady's acquaintance."

The compliment earned the senator a dazzling smile from Naomi. Cassius complied with the request, introducing them and briefly explaining that Naomi had just arrived in Rome after nearly being shipwrecked. With the way Cassius lisped, Naomi couldn't quite decipher the man's name. All she knew was that she had been in Rome only a few hours and she had already met a senator. What incredible good fortune!

Her dark mood vanished instantly as she quickly and surreptitiously appraised her first prospect for a husband. His curly silver hair was neatly trimmed and styled, and the well-manicured hand was not encumbered with a wedding ring. While he was older than her father, the senator was fit and well preserved for his age. And she could tell by the appreciative look in his eye that his interest in her was definitely not of the fatherly sort. Not particularly handsome, his patrician appearance was nevertheless attractive to Naomi. She knew immediately that he was a man who was used to getting what he wanted, and she determined that *she* would be exactly what he wanted for the moment.

"It's a pleasure to meet you, Senator." Her voice was silky, her gaze frankly admiring.

Cassius suddenly changed from a hard-nosed businessman into a congenial host. "Since Naomi is here alone, I've offered to look out for her while she's in Rome."

"I'm sure the lady will have no shortage of gentlemen wanting to look out for her," the senator said, "myself included." His eyes never left Naomi's face, and she felt a ripple of excitement as he asked, "Would you do me the honor of dining with me this evening?"

After a slight pause to give the impression she needed time to consider the request, she said, "I'd be delighted."

"I've been invited to the palace," he added casually, "and Caesar's banquet hall is definitely something you should see while you're in Rome."

"I've heard it's splendid." *The palace!* He spoke as if it were simply another tourist attraction. Her heart raced at the thought of actually dining in the very pinnacle of power. She wondered if the emperor himself would be there. Surely he would, if it was some kind of state event. Her thoughts immediately went to what she would wear, how she would arrange her hair . . . and then her face fell.

The senator noticed her distress and appeared concerned. "Is something wrong?"

"I'm afraid I have nothing suitable to wear. Most of my clothes were destroyed in the hurricane." If it took every gold coin in her possession, she vowed silently, she would buy an expensive new tunic and *stola* the minute she left the bank. There was no way she would miss an opportunity to appear at the palace on the arm of a senator. But she'd had a sudden flash of inspiration and gambled that she could use the situation to her advantage.

"You see, I intended to buy a new wardrobe immediately," she said with a scorching look at Cassius, "but I've just learned that all my funds are being held until a certain misunderstanding is cleared up."

The banker looked decidedly uncomfortable as Naomi launched into a description of the meeting they'd just had in his office. "So buying a new wardrobe today is out of the question," she concluded, "and I wouldn't want to be an embarrassment to you at Caesar's banquet, no matter how much I would enjoy your company."

She lowered her lashes and cast a look she hoped would convey just how very much she wanted to attend and how much she needed his help to intervene with Cassius.

"Even if you wore the rags of a common laborer, a woman as uncommonly beautiful as you would never be an embarrassment." Wilting the banker with a glance, the senator said, "There must be something you can do, Cassius. I'm sure this will all be straightened out in a few days. Why don't you give the lady an advance against her father's letter of credit?"

It was more of a demand than a question, and the banker knew it. He looked as if the senator were holding a sword at his throat. "I suppose the bank could advance a small amount," he said slowly.

"A *reasonable* amount." The senator named a figure in a voice that dared Cassius to challenge him. "And I'll stand good for it, if need be."

"Of course," the banker said, his face brightening at the senator's guarantee. "I'll direct my assistant to take care of the transaction right away."

"I suggest you handle it personally," the senator replied dryly. He placed a possessive hand on Naomi's arm. "In the meantime, my dear, let me take you to the best dressmaker in Rome. We haven't much time to find an outfit that will cause you to turn the head of every official who dines at Caesar's table. And I have no doubt you will."

"Senator," Cassius implored as they started to leave, "what about the financial matter you wanted to discuss with me?"

"Oh, that. It will keep until tomorrow," the senator said with a smile in Naomi's direction. "A personal matter requires my attention first."

27

ABRAHAM LAY ON THE SHORE, his cheek pressed into the sand, a long strand of seaweed twisted around his almost bare body. He was parched, sunburned, and famished—but he was alive. There had been no whale, he thought, yet God had miraculously placed him on dry ground, just as He had Jonah.

He wasn't sure how long he'd been in the water. About thirty hours, he guessed, exhaustion fogging his mind. Abraham closed his eyes and reexperienced the sensation of flying through the stateroom and shooting up the mammoth wave, then plunging into the depths of the sea. He'd held his breath until he thought his lungs would burst, then he finally broke through to the surface with a desperate gasp. He had the presence of mind to strip off his clothes immediately, so the weight of the water-soaked fabric wouldn't drag him to the bottom of the ocean like an anchor.

Over and over, the vicious waves flipped his large frame into the air the way a child tossed a rag doll. It was early afternoon, but the hurricane had turned the skies as dark as ink. All Abraham could see was water, dark green walls of water that churned and rolled and threatened to suck him under with every turbulent wave.

After a while his eyes had burned from the brine and his arms and legs had felt like lead. His head hurt from the deafening roar of the storm, and fighting to keep above the surface of the water became a battle Abraham could not win; the strength and fury of the hurricane were too powerful for a mere mortal to overcome.

Finally, he was sucked under water for so long that the urge to breathe became too great to resist. He knew he was about to lose consciousness if he didn't breathe, but he also knew that if he did breathe he would inhale water—not air—into his lungs, and then it would be over. But he could not hold out against the sea any longer.

His eyes had been open as he was pulled under by the wave, but Abraham could see nothing in the roiling water. Now, he closed his eyes and contemplated how the first gulp of seawater would feel in his lungs. Would he enter a dreamlike state between death and life? He thought of Elizabeth. Would she be waiting for him on the other side? Would God welcome him, a repentant traitor, into heaven?

Sinking in a watery grave, about to succumb to the desperate need to breathe, he suddenly felt a solid substance jammed against his body. It was a dream . . . or was it? He was dying . . . or was he?

Abraham did not consciously wrap his arms around the submerged object, but when it rose to the surface with the next wave, it dragged him up with it. As his screaming lungs finally found the air they craved, he comprehended that the object he was clutching was indeed real. It was huge, it was solid, and it was floating.

And so was he.

Abraham clung to his inanimate rescuer. The object he'd encountered underwater and ridden to the surface was wooden, about twelve feet long, and so broad he couldn't completely get his arms around it. As his mind began to clear, Abraham realized he was holding on to a remnant of the main mast of the *Mercury*. The storm had snapped the massive oak timber like kindling and sent it hurtling into the sea after him. An object that size could easily have killed him; instead it had saved him, and the only conclusion he could reach was that God wanted him alive.

With a great effort, Abraham hauled himself on top of the wooden beam and stretched out along its length. Utter exhaustion claimed him then, and he lapsed into the bliss of unconsciousness. When he woke, the fierce winds had died and the water was as smooth as silk.

Cautiously, Abraham raised himself to a sitting position and straddled the mast. He wondered if the *Mercury* had ridden out the storm, or if the hole punched into the stern had capsized her. He looked around him, searching the water for any signs of wreckage. As far as he could tell, there was none. There was something else he looked for but couldn't see: land. Even before the storm blew in, Kaeso had been uncertain of their position because of continued rain and poor visibility for several days. Now, Abraham realized, he could easily be a hundred miles or more from land, but he had no way of knowing.

As darkness fell, he stretched out again, lying on his stomach. Stripped down to his undergarment, he shivered in the cold night air. He shivered, and he prayed. *Lord, if You spared me from the hurricane, surely it was not so I could die of exposure on the open sea.*

When morning arrived, there was still no sign of land. Abraham was a strong swimmer, and if he had seen land, he would have plowed his way through the water toward it. Instead, he lay on top of the mast and paddled, trying to set a course for the northeast; Rome lay somewhere in that direction.

By midday, Abraham was still chilled to the bone, yet the sun had started to burn his salt-soaked skin. His mouth was as dry as a boll of cotton, and his lips were cracked and sore. He longed for just a sip of water but knew that drinking the seawater would be deadly: the salt would further dehydrate him.

By midafternoon, figuring that another night in the water would kill him, Abraham began to despair of life. He'd already been in the water for more than twenty-four hours, and now, with no land in sight, and no sign of another ship, surviving seemed impossible. Abraham held out little hope for a passing ship; no one else would have been so foolhardy, or so desperate, to be on the ocean in the middle of November. He should never have tried to make the trip.

Finally, just as he was about to abandon all hope, Abraham spotted land. He uttered a hoarse shout for joy, then began to swim as hard as he could. It had taken the last ounce of his strength, but he managed to reach the shore.

For a long time he lay on the beach, thanking God and marshaling his survival instincts. The only possible purpose for his deliverance, Abraham reasoned, was the appeal to Caesar for the lives of Rebecca, Jacob, and John. Abraham counted his own life as worthless, but if something could be done for his children, and for the Apostle, then he must find a way to do it—with God's help.

The danger to them would be even greater, he realized, if the *Mercury* had weathered the storm and Naomi made it to Rome. He knew now that his oldest daughter was not just rebellious; she was heartless. She hated him, and she would probably go to any lengths to destroy him. And what could destroy him more than thwarting his attempt to free her brother and sister?

If she had the opportunity, Naomi would do just that; she certainly wouldn't lift a finger to help them. And if she found a way to get her hands on his fortune, Abraham thought, she would bleed him dry. He would have to find a way to get to Rome before she managed to do that. Of course, there was always the possibility she hadn't survived the hurricane; he simply didn't know.

Standing to his feet, Abraham brushed off as much sand as he could and looked around. He had to find shelter before nightfall. Seeing a few buildings in the distance, he realized he was close to a small village. As he approached it, he came across an old fisherman mending his nets. The man's eyes nearly popped out of his head when he looked up and saw a huge, half-naked sea urchin walking toward him.

"I was tossed overboard in the storm," Abraham explained.

"A bad one, it was," the man said with a slow nod.

"Where am I?" The man gave the name of the village, but Abraham didn't recognize it. "What is the nearest port?" he asked the fisherman.

"That would be Syracuse." The old man's fingers deftly worked the strands of rope with which he made his living.

Syracuse. The capital of the province of Sicily and a major Mediterranean port. The *Mercury* must have been blown off course by a hundred miles or more, Abraham realized. Syracuse was on the eastern side of the island, and they had been headed for the western side. Still, it was good news. Abraham's ships had sailed in and out of the harbor there a number of times, and he was bound to find someone he knew in Syracuse, or someone who at least recognized his name.

"Can you help me get there?" Abraham asked.

"Aye. Tomorrow." The man brushed a strand of dingy gray hair off his forehead and glanced at the sun, now lying low on the horizon. Then he looked Abraham up and down, as if deciding whether the large man posed a threat. Evidently Abraham passed muster. "You'd better come home with me till then."

That night Abraham slept on a straw mat spread on the dirt floor of the fisherman's small house. The ground was hard, but the blankets were warm, and Abraham's stomach was full. The man's name was Donatus, Abraham had learned as they shared a meal of salted fish and bread and swapped stories about the sea. Abraham told the fisherman about his shipping business and a few details about his family, saying simply that he had been trying to reach Rome to take care of an urgent matter that concerned his son and daughter.

The next morning Donatus clothed Abraham in an old tunic. It was threadbare, much too short, and it stretched much too tightly across his broad chest. But at least it covered his nakedness—if he could manage to walk without bursting the seams. Donatus also fashioned a pair of sandals for Abraham's feet, which were much larger than his own, by attaching a few strands of hemp to two pieces of leather. They looked ridiculous, but it meant he would not have to walk the twelve miles to Syracuse on his bare feet.

Abraham was touched by the old man's kindness and tried to refuse when Donatus offered his cloak as well. "I can't take that," Abraham said. "You can't get through the winter without a cloak."

"I've got blankets," Donatus argued. "I'll cut a hole in one and throw it over my head, if I need to." He grinned and added, "You've probably noticed that I'm very handy at making do with what I have."

Abraham's eyes moistened as he thanked the generous fisherman. "I may not look it now, but I'm a wealthy man. And I will see that you are repaid for all your efforts to help me."

The walk to Syracuse took all morning. Abraham was worn out by the time he arrived, but his mood was optimistic. He assumed he looked preposterous rather than prosperous, but he was in his element at the immense harbor and therefore naturally confident. There was little activity on the waterfront because commercial traffic had ceased, but he knew that some shippers would still have inventory in their warehouses to be moved by land.

He walked up and down the docks for an hour, until he finally located the harbormaster's office. The master, who introduced himself as Felix, recognized Abraham's name immediately and recalled that his business was headquartered in Ephesus. But it took a great deal of talking on Abraham's part to convince Felix that the man in an ill-fitting tunic and absurd homemade shoes was actually a shipping magnate.

To counter the man's disbelief, Abraham gave quite a bit of detail about his operations across the Empire, hoping Felix would recognize the authenticity of his knowledge. Abraham explained that he'd been traveling to Rome on very urgent business when they'd been hit by the hurricane and he'd been swept overboard.

"What did you say the name of your ship was?" Felix suddenly asked.

"The *Mercury*," Abraham repeated. "I have a number of ships in my fleet, but we were traveling on my private vessel."

"That's a one-of-a-kind ship," the harbormaster said, a note of awe in his voice.

Abraham looked surprised. "You know the *Mercury?*" He was quite sure he had never sailed his private ship into the port at Syracuse before.

"My brother-in-law helped outfit that ship for the builder. He visited us afterward, and it was all he talked about." For the next few minutes Felix quizzed Abraham about the *Mercury*—its construction, its equipment, its speed.

Finally satisfied with the answers, he asked, "Now, how can I be of assistance?"

Abraham sighed in relief. "The first thing you can do is help me get a message to my bank in Rome."

Within minutes a pigeon was on its way with the message that Abraham had been rescued at sea.

I only wish I could get there as fast, Abraham thought, wondering yet again if Kaeso had managed to keep the *Mercury* afloat. And if he had, had he been able to reach Rome without the main sail? The storm had probably disabled the foresail as well.

Abraham supposed he'd know in a few days. In addition to sending the message, Felix had agreed to hire a carriage to take Abraham to Rome and to arrange credit for him to purchase some better-fitting clothes for the journey.

As he walked out of the harbormaster's office beside Felix, Abraham looked down at his ludicrous outfit and smiled wryly, thinking how appalled Naomi would have been to see him dressed this way. She put such stock in appearances. The thought of his daughter— who more than ever seemed to be a total stranger, if not his enemy— sent a wave of sadness rushing over him. Was she still alive? he wondered. And if so, would the breach between them ever heal?

Where did we go wrong with her, Elizabeth? he silently asked his departed wife. *Where did we go wrong?*

28

"I HAVE EXCELLENT TASTE IN WOMEN," Lucius said, beaming down at her, "and their wardrobes."

"I agree—on both counts." Naomi smiled and tucked her hand through his arm as they entered the palace. The senator had not only accompanied her to the dressmaker, he had quickly eliminated all but one of the gowns offered for approval: a low-cut, formfitting tunic of emerald green topped by an exquisitely sheer matching *stola* that shimmered with tiny gold threads. The draped *stola* gave the appearance of traditional modesty, while its transparency revealed her figure, leaving little to the imagination. His choice was stunning, Naomi thought now as they strolled past one of the reflecting pools with its multicolored mosaic design.

The Domus Flavia, the palace Domitian had built on the Palatine Hill, afforded grandeur on a scale Naomi had never seen. Even the smells were magnificent: the fountains in the courtyard were spiked with perfumes that released the aroma of roses year-round. As they made their way to the great dining hall, Lucius pointed out many of the palace's distinguishing features. The main structure, situated at the top of the hill, contained the rooms used for official purposes—receptions, ceremonies, and banquets—as well as the throne room. An illuminated stairway cascaded down the hill, leading to the private residence of the imperial family.

Lucius's earlier prediction about turning heads was on target. The couple created a stir when they entered the dining hall, and Naomi reveled in the admiring glances and the subtle pointing and

whispering as they mingled with the other guests. Before she ever
had a sip of wine, Naomi was giddy from the intoxicating atmosphere of power and affluence. Everyone Lucius introduced her to
was a senator or high-ranking official.

After they exchanged a brief greeting with the emperor, Lucius
asked, "What did you think of Domitian?"

"I think he has a lot less hair than his statues would lead you to
believe," she whispered.

The comment caused Lucius's shoulders to shake with laughter.
"I suppose the royal sculptors value their careers more than artistic
devotion to realism."

"And what is that thing he does with his eyes?"

"It's a nervous tic. He gets very jumpy at times, and it pays not
to upset him." Lucius spoke in an even tone, but Naomi imagined
he'd had some touchy dealings with the edgy emperor.

Naomi found Lucius to be an excellent dinner companion, and
throughout the evening he entertained her with amusing stories
about the royal family. He pointed out Domitia Longina, the
emperor's wife, and related how Domitian had divorced her years
earlier, then later reinstated her. "But he's kept her image off the
coins this time," Lucius remarked with a wry smile.

Naomi took a bite of something tasty before continuing the conversation. The imperial chefs' spectacular offerings were wasted on
her this evening; she was too excited to do more than nibble. "I hear
that Caesar is very fond of the games," she said.

"He sponsors them frequently—at great expense, which he
passes along to the taxpayers, of course." Lucius leaned closer and
whispered intimately. "But Domitian's favorite sport is what he calls
bed-wrestling."

"Bed-wrestling? . . ." Naomi paused and then giggled. "Oh. You're
not talking about sporting events in the arena."

"No, these are private matches. Most of them, anyway." He raised
an eyebrow in a look that had Naomi chuckling again.

The senator was delightful as well as powerful, she decided, and she intended to cultivate his friendship, and perhaps more. She reached over and brushed his hand with her fingertips, letting his gaze lock onto hers. "What about you, Lucius? Do you like to wrestle?"

His eyes darkened in what she recognized as a spark of desire. "When the woman is beautiful . . . and willing."

Naomi smiled and slowly stroked his hand for a moment. Then she took a sip of wine and demanded, "Tell me more about the palace intrigues."

Lucius cleared his throat. "Do you know about his niece, Flavia Julia?" When she shook her head no, he continued. "She was the daughter of his brother, the emperor Titus. Years ago Domitian seduced Julia and moved her into the palace with him—after conveniently executing her husband. Julia died four years ago. From an abortion he compelled her to get, it was rumored."

Hearing about Flavia Julia reminded Naomi of her friend Julia back in Ephesus. *I wish she could see me now,* Naomi thought. *Dining at the palace.*

In the days following the banquet, Naomi saw the senator often. He took her sightseeing and shopping for more clothes, and he escorted her to dinner parties at the homes of prominent friends. Then one night, about a week after they'd met, he brought Naomi to his home—which was a palace in its own right—and there he made a proposition after dinner.

The meal had been sumptuous, the wine exquisite, and the conversation light and amusing. After the servants removed the remains of the meal, a steward extinguished the flames of the wall lamps and the standing torchères, leaving the room illuminated by a single candelabrum on the square rosewood dining table in front of them. Naomi and Lucius remained lounging on the *triclinium,* a respectable distance apart.

"I'm giving a large dinner party in a few weeks," he said, handing her the wineglass he had just refilled, "for the Saturnalia. I'd like you to serve as my hostess, if that's agreeable with you."

"I'd love to," Naomi replied, thrilled both that he'd asked and that she would get to celebrate the festival for the first time; her father had never allowed it. December 17 was the happiest holiday of the Roman calendar, a day for feasting and exchanging gifts with family and friends. A Lord of Misrule was elected to preside over the Saturnalia, and public gambling was even allowed on the holiday.

"In fact, I'd like you to help me entertain guests here on a regular basis." His slate-gray eyes glowed with hope. "Your beauty and charm would be a tremendous asset, and I so enjoy spending time with you."

Naomi took a sip of the wine, then set the glass on the table and reached for his hand. "I enjoy your company as well, Lucius." His silver hair sparkled in the candlelight, and she thought how remarkably young and virile he looked for a man in his sixties. And how quickly he had fallen under her spell.

"What would you think about moving in here? Your father's villa is rather far away, and I'd like to be able to see you more often. Every day, even."

"I'd like to see you more too, but—"

"Or if you prefer," he said quickly, "I could arrange for you to have a place of your own nearby. I would pay all your expenses, of course, and I'd take good care of you." He brought her hand up and kissed her fingertips, then the inside of her wrist. "Very good care," he murmured.

"Lucius, are you asking me to be your mistress?"

"I am indeed." He pulled her closer to him on the sofa. "The idea has a lot of merit, don't you think?"

"It's a tempting offer, and I'm very flattered, but . . ."

"But what?"

"But I won't share your home—or your bed—unless I share your name."

A frown tugged at the corners of his elegant mouth, and he drew back slightly. "I thought you said you had abandoned the rigid moral principles of your family."

"Oh, I have. My refusal is not a matter of scruples. It's a matter of self-preservation."

Actually, she had no qualms about becoming his mistress; Naomi simply thought it was in her best interest to hold out for marriage. While she had planned on jumping into the whirlwind of Roman society and having a number of suitors to choose from, it appeared that she'd met the most eligible bachelor in the city as soon as she had arrived. Now, he was enthralled with her beauty and youth, and she was drawn like a magnet to his prestige and power; it was a good match, and it seemed pointless to drag things out.

"I came to Rome to find a husband," she explained. "I want to do more than host dinner parties in a magnificent home. I want security. I want status and influence."

"The mistress of a powerful man can wield a tremendous influence herself."

"Mistresses come and go. Wives are a little harder to get rid of." Naomi shrugged. "You see, I'm just being practical." She laughed lightly and reached out to trace his lower lip teasingly with her index finger. "But I do think we're well-suited for each other."

"And why is that?" he asked, a hint of amusement crinkling his eyes.

"For one thing, we're a lot alike. We both know what we want and we go after it—ruthlessly."

"True." He smiled and playfully nipped at her finger. "I'm not easily sidetracked."

"Neither am I," she said. "And we both want the same thing right now."

"What?"

"My father's wealth."

Lucius raised up on one elbow and with the other arm gestured toward the rest of the immense mansion he'd shown her before dinner. "Do you call this living in poverty?"

"Don't pretend you're not interested in the fact that I'm an heiress to one of the largest fortunes in the Empire," Naomi said. "I know you're wealthy and live lavishly. But I also know that being a senator is an expensive proposition, requiring huge cash outlays that can deplete your wealth. My father understood that, and he's helped a number of senators stay in power by making hefty contributions to their causes, so they could keep their own assets intact."

"An astute man. And an equally astute daughter." He lay back on the sofa and looked at Naomi intently, a new appreciation animating his face. "I'm listening."

"You already know something of my problems in accessing my father's money. I could use your help—and I don't mean intervening with Cassius, although I appreciate that greatly. I need legal help, or political clout, or both, to secure my inheritance."

Naomi began to fill him in on the background. "I'm the oldest," she said, "but I also have two brothers and a sister. She's been sent into exile, along with one of my brothers, so they can't inherit—as long as they remain banished. My father was coming to Rome to try to get Jacob and Rebecca released."

"Which would have cut your share of his future estate in half."

"I'll admit, I was hoping he wouldn't be successful, and I'm relieved now that he won't have the opportunity to try."

"I've wondered why you didn't seem to be mourning your father's death."

"We've been estranged for some time."

"What if he's alive, as Cassius claims, and he makes an appeal on their behalf?" Lucius didn't wait for her reply but asked, "What crime did they commit?"

"Treason. They refused to sacrifice to Caesar."

"Your father couldn't get that overturned. Domitian has become a fanatic about loyalty. He won't be inclined to show any mercy," he said emphatically, "and the Senate won't challenge him on it, not in the foreseeable future, anyway."

"If Father tried to get the case before the Senate, could you prevent it?"

"More than likely, yes. I could work behind the scenes to undermine his efforts."

"I'm not ready to accept that he's alive. He should have arrived several days ago—if the message Cassius received was authentic—and he still hasn't shown up. But even if my father is dead, I'll still need help to take control of his assets."

"Your other brother, the one still in Ephesus—will he challenge the estate?"

"Peter has been sick all his life; he couldn't handle the responsibility. I'll make sure he stays in the family home, but I intend to take control of the business, and the money. If Peter tries to stop me, I'll find a way to have him declared incompetent."

Lucius whistled an appreciative sound. "You really *do* go after what you want, don't you?"

"I told you, we're a lot alike."

"Let's see if I have this right. You're determined to be your father's *sole* heir."

"Yes, and I'm offering to share his vast fortune with you, if you'll help me get my hands on it." She scooted closer to him on the sofa and placed a proprietary hand on his chest. "I have other assets I could share as well," she purred.

The senator responded by putting his arms around her and kissing her neck. Then he looked up and said softly, "Naomi, are you asking me to marry you?"

"I am indeed." She laughed and repeated what he'd said to her earlier. "The idea has a lot of merit, don't you think?"

29

"MY DAUGHTER DID *WHAT*?"

"She got married, sir. Yesterday."

Abraham sank onto one of the matching striped settees as the Egyptian slave—what was his name?—said he was there to pick up the rest of Naomi's things and take them to her new home.

Again, Abraham was reminded of Elizabeth. She was the one who had always remembered names, then whispered them in his ear.

Naomi certainly didn't waste any time, Abraham thought. He'd had several delays, and the trip from Syracuse had taken twice as long as he'd expected. Now that he'd finally reached his villa in Rome, he wanted nothing more than to collapse into bed, get a good night's sleep, and then visit his banker first thing in the morning. Instead, his arrival had been greeted with the news that his daughter had gotten married and moved out. And to think he'd been worried whether she was even alive.

Abraham sat in stunned silence so long, the Egyptian finally said, "If you'll permit me, sir, I'll leave now."

"Go," Abraham said with a weary wave of dismissal, then called him back. "Lepidus"—that was his name, Abraham suddenly remembered—"wait. Tell my daughter I want to see her. Here, tomorrow, at noon." He emphasized each word by stabbing the arm of the settee with his index finger.

Lepidus bowed politely and left. For a moment, Abraham remained seated, his thoughts alternating between the happy realization that the *Mercury* had survived the storm and worried curiosity about his daughter. Naomi had come to Rome to find a husband of her own choosing—fine. He just hadn't expected to be presented with a son-in-law after the fact. And as a father, he couldn't help hoping that she'd chosen well, and that she hadn't rushed into this marriage simply because she'd met a wealthy bachelor.

Had Naomi found the gold he'd brought on board the *Mercury*? Probably. Kaeso would have known where to look if she hadn't. Abraham had figured they would find the money and the letter of credit, and while he trusted Kaeso to use it wisely, he didn't trust his own daughter. That's why he had sent the message to Cassius. But what if Naomi hadn't found the money at all? What if she'd been broke when she arrived in Rome . . . ?

Such speculation would accomplish nothing, Abraham told himself. Naomi was smart and resourceful—even more resourceful than he had given her credit for, apparently. Tomorrow he would find out what she'd been doing in his absence. In the meantime, he would find the caretaker and make arrangements to get the house-hold running again.

As he walked through the villa—much smaller than his home in Ephesus, yet quite elegant—and outside to the cottage where the caretaker and his wife lived, Abraham kicked himself mentally. He had been so tired, not to mention surprised, that he hadn't even thought to ask Lepidus whom Naomi had married or where they lived.

Silvanus, the caretaker, and his wife, Clara, greeted Abraham warmly. They were the only full-time staff he retained at his home in the outskirts of Rome, because he usually stayed there only a few weeks or months each year. When Abraham arrived, they would hire additional staff while he was in residence. He asked the couple to take care of that for him now, and Clara insisted he share their meal.

As they ate, Abraham told them about finding Lepidus when he'd arrived and learning that Naomi had gotten married.

"From the time she arrived," Clara said, "that girl barely stayed around here long enough to sleep. And when she was here, she didn't say two words."

Abraham discerned from Clara's miffed expression that Naomi's "two words," whatever they were, had offended the woman. Knowing his daughter's tongue, Abraham wasn't surprised.

"Clara." Silvanus reproved his wife with a look. "I asked your daughter when you would be arriving," he said to Abraham, "but she didn't know. Then a few days ago she left and hasn't been back. We didn't know anything about a wedding."

Abraham did not ask any more questions about Naomi; it was obvious these two wouldn't have any idea what she'd been up to since she'd been in Rome.

"Did your wife make the trip with you this time?" Clara asked.

"No," Abraham said abruptly. Then he apologized. "I'm too tired right now. I'll tell you about it tomorrow." He excused himself, returned to the villa, and went straight to bed.

Elizabeth, he thought as he laid his head on the pillow, *I haven't had a decent night's sleep since you've been gone.* He'd assumed that the house in Rome, which Elizabeth had visited only occasionally, would not remind him of her the way their home in Ephesus had. Yet in every room he had encountered something that brought Elizabeth's face, her voice, her scent, back to him. It had been six weeks since she'd been killed, and he was beginning to think the desperate ache would never go away.

He'd also thought he was too strong, too tough, ever to cry himself to sleep; he was wrong about that as well. Abraham hadn't broken down and wept since the night he buried Elizabeth. But he'd been through too much, fought too hard, faced too many obstacles: now it suddenly became too much to bear. He not only grieved, for the first time he indulged in self-pity.

I can't deal with it anymore, he thought. *A man needs to have his children with him. And when he lies down to sleep, he ought to have his soft sweet wife beside him. I can't go on, Elizabeth. I just can't . . .*

The next morning, however, as he walked through the city, his outlook was brighter. He took hope from the glitter of the sun reflecting off the rich Italian marble of the buildings and monuments. He'd made it to Rome against impossible odds; now he would be just as persistent in his attempt to persuade the emperor or the Senate to intervene for his children's release.

When he arrived at the bank, Abraham learned that Cassius was taking a holiday, but the banker's assistant verified a key piece of information: Cassius had given Naomi an advance against the letter of credit, in spite of Abraham's instructions to the contrary. Abraham was aggravated, but getting to the bottom of the matter would require waiting until he could talk to Cassius. He was even more aggravated to think that Naomi must be up to something devious. Why else would she want to withdraw funds from his bank? If she'd found the gold coins, she would have had plenty of money to live on until he arrived.

After visiting the bank, Abraham went to his office, where he enjoyed a warm reunion with Kaeso. The leather-faced captain was almost speechless when Abraham walked in. "I'd about given up hope," he said, choking a bit on the words.

"Didn't you hear that I'd sent a message?"

"Yes, but then you didn't arrive. And Naomi said the note from you was a forgery. I didn't know what to think."

Abraham asked about the *Mercury*, and Kaeso described the repairs that would be needed. "I've been working night and day to get a complete estimate on what it would cost to make her seaworthy again," the captain said.

"I want her ready to sail as soon as spring arrives," Abraham told him.

"That will be pushing it, but I'll make it happen."

"The damage is not quite as bad as I would have imagined. Still . . ." Abraham could scarcely believe they'd managed to get the ship to Rome with both sails destroyed. "I want to give the crew a bonus."

"I was hoping you'd suggest that." Kaeso nodded his approval. "They put in a herculean effort to get us here."

The captain described the voyage of the crippled ship in detail, and Abraham told how a huge piece of the main mast had helped him survive on the open sea. He also described how he'd walked to Syracuse wearing a pair of homemade shoes and a tunic made for a man half his size.

Kaeso roared and slapped a weather-beaten hand on his knee. "Now, there's a story I'll be telling for a long time to come."

Before he left the office, Abraham gave instructions to send a messenger to Syracuse with a gift for Felix, the harbormaster, and a new cloak and two new tunics for Donatus.

Abraham was in a much better frame of mind after seeing Kaeso. But as he returned to the villa to meet his daughter, he recalled what Kaeso had said about Naomi thinking his message from Syracuse was a forgery. Why would she say that? Who else could have sent it? Who would even have known he'd been lost at sea and then used that information to say he'd been rescued? It didn't make sense.

Unless she wanted to believe the note was a forgery simply because she wanted him dead. Or she wanted everyone else to think so, because his death would have been more convenient for whatever she was planning to do. Abraham began to have a very uneasy feeling—a feeling that mushroomed into dread when he got back to the villa and found out that Naomi was not coming.

Instead, Naomi had sent Lepidus with a letter. Abraham sat at the desk in his bedroom and opened the letter with a sense of foreboding that burned in his gut. "Dear Father," she wrote—

I was relieved to learn you'd arrived safely in Rome. Forgive me for not coming to see you immediately, but I cannot spare the time. Because Lucius and I married rather quickly—

Rather quickly! Abraham shook his head and continued reading . . .

—without the fanfare of a large wedding, we are hosting a formal reception this Friday evening. With only three days left, I am working tirelessly to plan the kind of elegant event befitting my husband's position as a senator. Lucius is a wonderful man, and I hope you'll be happy for me, Father. I also hope you will attend the reception.

So she married a senator, Abraham thought as he laid the letter aside. *That was her idea before she ever set sail for Rome.* When Naomi made up her mind she wanted something, she didn't stop until she got it. Abraham had no doubt that the reception she was now planning would be spectacular, something the guests would talk about for months.

He picked up the letter again and glanced at the bottom, where Naomi had written her husband's name and the address of their home. The world came crashing in on him when Abraham read the name:

Senator Lucius Mallus Balbus

With an angry sweep of his arm, Abraham raked everything off the desk. A Grecian vase shattered as it hit the marble floor, but the sound was covered by the anguished cry that rose from his belly and roared out his throat.

The treacherous witch! How could his own flesh and blood do that to him? How could she marry the father of the man who had murdered Elizabeth and sent Jacob and Rebecca to Devil's Island? How?

Abraham did not just yell and scream, he raged. Damian had robbed him of the most precious things in his life, and now his daughter had married Damian's father. The betrayal pushed Abraham beyond the limit of what he could endure. As far as he was concerned, Naomi was no longer his daughter; he would disown her immediately.

And he would tell her immediately. He grabbed his cloak, stormed out of the room, and left the villa.

He had been walking for ten minutes, fuming silently and glaring at everyone on the street, when he realized he couldn't confront Naomi in the heat of his anger. If Mallus were there, Abraham feared he would kill the man with his bare hands. He did not want to let go of his anger, but he did not want to kill a man in a blind rage. Rationally, he knew that Mallus was not the one responsible for Elizabeth's death, but emotionally Abraham couldn't help blaming the man who had sired a murderer.

Abraham walked the streets aimlessly, not knowing what to do, then finally realizing there was nothing he could do. Naomi had made her choice.

Over the next few days, however, Abraham began to wonder if Naomi was actually aware of the choice she had made. He and Elizabeth had never talked to their children about having a connection with Damian in the past. And it was doubtful that Naomi had been aware of Damian's full name—Lucius Mallus Damianus—during the few weeks he'd been in Ephesus before arresting the Christians there. So it was possible she had never connected the man she'd married with her family's persecutor.

But surely the senator would have told her he had a son. How could she not know? Unless Mallus had realized who she was and deliberately kept the information from her.

On Friday Abraham finally decided that the only way to find out was to talk to Naomi, and that the best time to do it would be at the reception that night. With other people around, he would be less likely to give vent to his anger, and Mallus would be less inclined to make a scene.

∽✕∾

Naomi couldn't have been happier. Guests were arriving—they were expecting hundreds of luminaries, including the emperor—musicians were playing, and she was directing it all.

Lucius's home—their home, she reminded herself—was an architectural marvel. Built on different levels of the hillside, it was filled with priceless works of arts. A showplace home. And Naomi was the showpiece wife. She loved the role.

At each buffet table a steward steadily poured wine into an elaborate fountain. The wine flowed from the ornate silver bowl on top, decorated with clusters of gold grapes, into tiers of smaller leaf-shaped bowls before spilling into two dozen golden goblets circling the base of the fountain. As guests removed the full goblets, the stewards replaced them with additional goblets and repeated the process. The effect was delightful to watch and almost decadent in its extravagance.

The new gown she'd had made for the occasion was equally extravagant. The silk was the deep royal hue of lapis lazuli, and the bodice was decorated with tiny opals. Naomi wore a magnificent necklace of lapis and opals with matching earrings that dangled almost to her shoulders. The jewelry was a wedding present from her husband, who had bought it, he said, because the fire of the opals matched the fire of her hair.

It had taken Naomi several hours to get dressed for the evening. She had bathed in perfumed oils, and Fulvia, who was an expert in the use of kohl, had helped her apply cosmetics while a beautician curled and styled her hair. When he had seen the results, Lucius had been lavish in his praise, saying, "No woman in Rome can match your beauty, Naomi."

Now, as she stood by his side and greeted their guests, she smiled, recalling his words and the way he had fingered the stones draped gracefully around her neck. "You know," he'd said, "the ancient Romans believed that lapis lazuli is a powerful aphrodisiac."

"We'll test that theory later," she had promised with a laugh.

Her husband continued to introduce Naomi to a succession of dignitaries, including Marcus Cocceius Nerva, whom Lucius described as "an expert in the law and confidant to every emperor since Nero." Nerva had a thin face perched on top of a very long neck, and Naomi instantly guessed from his dour demeanor that the senator was staunchly conservative.

Soon, a rather large, overbearing senator dragged Lucius to one side to lobby for some proposal he wanted to bring before the Senate. Naomi found the intrusion rude, but she supposed that was the price of being a public official. Lucius winked at her over the top of the man's head, and she went to get a glass of wine.

Already flushed from the excitement, Naomi found that the glass of wine warmed her and lifted her spirits even further. She was searching for Lucius again when Lepidus approached and said that her father wanted to speak with her. She hadn't been sure her father would accept the invitation and was rather hoping he wouldn't, but she'd felt obligated to ask him. Well, she would treat him as graciously as the other guests, and she hoped he would be civil to Lucius.

Naomi followed Lepidus to one of the recessed alcoves off the wide hall to the banquet room. She'd almost forgotten what an imposing presence her father made; when she saw him now, he seemed to fill up the alcove.

"Father." She held out her hands and kissed him on the cheek. His greeting was polite but his posture aloof.

"You look radiant, Naomi. Marriage agrees with you."

His eyes did not match his words, she thought. He was trying to suppress a flare of anger.

"I know it's sudden, but please be happy for me, Father."

"You just met this man, Naomi. What do you really know about him?"

"Enough to know he's everything I wanted."

"So, tell me about him."

It was a command, not a request, and Naomi reminded herself to curb her tongue. She was determined not to let her father get her riled on what could be the most important night of her life. "He's a widower," she said. "He's older than I am—much older, actually. But I like that. He's very stable, and very influential."

"He's unscrupulous."

Abraham's eyes flashed as he spat out the word, and Naomi

nearly snapped back at him. But she kept her voice level as she said, "You haven't even met him yet, how can you judge him?"

"I know who he is, and I know what he is . . ."

"Let me introduce you to him. You may change your mind." Naomi started to lead him into the banquet hall, but he stopped her.

"Not yet," Abraham said. "I want to finish our conversation first. Please."

He appeared to make an effort to control himself, so she agreed.

"Does your husband have any children?" he asked.

"A son. I haven't met him yet."

"And what is his son's name?"

"I don't remember. He's in the military, off serving the emperor somewhere in the East." Naomi had no idea why he was questioning her like this, and her patience was wearing thin. "Father, I have guests to attend to. Won't you join me in—"

"I said, what is his son's name?" Her father shouted the question.

"I don't know! And I don't know why you're so upset."

Lucius suddenly stepped into the alcove. "Naomi, darling, I heard voices . . ."

"Lucius, this is my father, Abraham."

Abraham refused the hand Lucius extended, and his eyes continued to bore into Naomi as he spoke. "Tell her who your son is, Senator."

"My son? What has Damian got to do with this?"

"Everything! He has everything to do with this!"

Damian? That's his son's name? Naomi couldn't remember if Lucius had ever called his son by name. *But that was the name of—*

"His son is the homicidal maniac who killed your mother!"

Lucius took a step back as her father shouted and pointed a finger in his face.

This isn't happening, Naomi thought. *My father and my husband are about to come to blows at my wedding reception.*

"His son is the one who sent your brother and sister into exile."

"Father, please—"

"Did you know that when you married him, Naomi? Did you?"
She put a hand on her father's arm. "No, I didn't know that."
Her touch diverted his attention away from Lucius. "But now that
I know," she said, "it doesn't change anything. I married Lucius, not
his son."

"Your husband's son—your stepson—tore our family apart, and
it doesn't matter to you?" The veins in his neck bulged until Naomi
feared he would explode.

Lucius stepped forward. "Now, look here—"

This time Naomi put a hand on her husband's arm, telling him,
"Damian had no choice, really. Mother attacked one of his officers—"

"He didn't have to murder her on the streets of Ephesus," Abraham
said. "He could have formally sentenced Elizabeth instead of running
her through with his sword. But that's not his style, is it, Senator? It
wasn't his style twenty-five years ago, either, was it?"

Lucius's mouth dropped open. "Elizabeth . . . Ephesus." He turned
to Naomi. "When you told me about your family," he said slowly,
"I didn't realize who your mother was. She was engaged to my son
at one time, but her father broke it off."

"Tell her *why* Rufus broke it off," Abraham demanded.

"How could it possibly matter now—"

Abraham interrupted the senator. "He broke the engagement
because Elizabeth was frightened of Damian, and because Rufus had
received firsthand information that Damian had murdered a fellow
officer."

"That was a preposterous story, and I don't know why Rufus
concocted it—"

"It's a true story, and I know it's true, because I'm the one who
saw Damian murder the tribune in cold blood. Damian was a murderer then, and he's a murderer now!"

Naomi's head was spinning. She heard voices and looked around
to see that people had gathered around the alcove. She was morti-

fied that they had heard the commotion. Just then, a trumpet fanfare sounded from the portico outside, announcing Caesar's arrival.

Lucius signaled two servants who had approached with the crowd.
He pointed to Abraham and told them, "Escort this man off my property, and do not allow him to return under any circumstances."

"Now," Lucius said to his wife and their guests, "let's greet the
emperor." Naomi pasted a smile on her face, took her husband's
arm, and turned her back on her father.

30

REBECCA SET THE QUILL PEN DOWN and flexed her fingers. *Time for a break,* she decided. Whenever her hand or her eyes grew tired, she took a break; she did not want to make any mistakes as she painstakingly copied John's account of the revelation he'd received four months ago.

She took pride in her work, believing it was her purpose for being on Devil's Island. And without the work, she most certainly would have gone crazy by now. Rebecca hadn't been off the mountain in all those months, and the isolation had taken a toll on her.

Carefully, she picked up the makeshift writing desk—a piece of scrap lumber Marcellus had salvaged—that was resting on her lap. Then she stood and placed the desk on the folding stool she'd been sitting on. The stool was another contribution from Marcellus. The medical officer visited her and John at least twice a week, sometimes more, and he never came empty-handed. He not only brought food supplies, he tried to bring useful items that would make their harsh living conditions at least a bit more tolerable.

As Rebecca walked out of the cave, the brisk wind whipped her long hair across her face, and she reached up to tuck it securely behind her ears. It was cold outside, yet the sunshine felt good, and she blinked as her eyes adjusted to the change. No matter how bright the daylight, the interior of the cave remained dim. Even with the stool placed just inside the mouth of the cave, there were only a few hours each day she could work without lighting a lamp; by midafternoon there was not enough natural illumination for writing.

She tried to recall what day it was but couldn't. Sometime in early March—she'd have to ask Marcellus when he came. His visits were the only way she had of tracking time.

If I were home, I would be planning my wedding now, she thought as she looked out over the sea in the direction of Ephesus. She and Galen had planned to be married in the spring—probably in April, although they hadn't had time to set the date.

Thinking about Galen hurt too much, and she tried to shut him out of her mind. As always, she couldn't. Whenever she closed her eyes, he was there. Sitting on their favorite bench in the garden, the one by the fountain. Running across the hills with her, laughing together and holding hands.

The memories squeezed her heart until her chest ached. All her dreams were gone now. They'd been as fleeting as a glimpse of fireflies at twilight.

Such simple little dreams, but they were hers. Naomi had always had big dreams—marrying a senator, being the most beautiful, the wealthiest, the most powerful woman in the world. Rebecca had simply wanted to marry, make a home, raise children.

Children. That part of her dream was coming true, but it was more of a nightmare.

She ran a hand over her abdomen. She was pregnant, and it was finally beginning to show; her waistline had thickened slightly now that she was able to keep food down. For several weeks she had been so nauseated, she could barely think about eating.

Rebecca wanted to feel love for the child she was carrying, but it was difficult to disassociate the life inside her from the brutal manner in which that life had been conceived.

"I know the answer to the question, Naomi," she said softly, recalling the day Naomi had teased Rebecca for being ignorant of the relationships between men and women, and had asked if what Galen felt for Rebecca was love or merely lust.

Rebecca understood the difference now. Galen's desire for her had been pure and sweet. He had wanted her as his wife, and his love would have protected her, cherished her, satisfied her. Damian had been driven by an animalistic urge. He had wanted to use Rebecca and then discard her, even destroy her.

And now she was carrying Damian's child. The child of his lust.

The thought had terrified her at first. At times, it still did. But John had helped her accept the fact of her pregnancy, if not embrace it.

The dear old Apostle prayed for her daily, and one day he had prophesied over her and the baby. Rebecca recalled his words: "God has a message of comfort for you. The child you are carrying, a son, will become a great servant of the Lord. Satan has tried to destroy you, but God will preserve you, and in His time, He will exalt you."

Rebecca clung to the words of the prophecy because it gave her a glimmer of hope. And hope was a scarce commodity on Devil's Island.

"There you are, Scribe." John's familiar, raspy voice called to her from the mouth of the cave.

Rebecca turned and smiled at the use of his new nickname for her. "It's about time you got up from your nap. You're getting lazy on me," she teased.

John was anything but lazy. He had spent weeks writing down his revelation, agonizing as he put into words the inexpressible things he'd seen, and then revising what he'd written to make sure he had not omitted anything. Originally, the Apostle had worried that he would forget the revelation before he could write it down. But then he reasoned that God had specifically told him to write about the supernatural experience, and God had to know that would take time; therefore, John trusted the Holy Spirit would bring it all back to his mind until he'd finished describing it. And He had.

When John was finally through, Rebecca had neatly written an entire scroll from his notes. Now she was making an additional copy of this important message for the church.

"I was thinking about what you said yesterday," John told her. "That was an excellent observation, that the messages to the seven churches each contain both a commendation and a correction."

Rebecca was pleased that he had complimented her thinking, but she was modest in her reply. "I've copied the seven letters twice now, and I noticed that, each time, Jesus first praised the churches for what they'd done right, then He pointed out something that was wrong."

"Prophecy often contains a warning or a corrective measure. Also, when God brings a prophetic message to His people, it usually has both an immediate application and a future application. That's what I was thinking about just now."

"I don't understand," Rebecca said. "Please elaborate." They'd had many discussions about Scripture as they'd recorded John's apocalypse for posterity, and Rebecca loved learning from the Apostle.

"Obviously the seven letters are to seven specific churches in Asia. And the letters describe real situations those churches are facing right now—I know that firsthand from visiting some of them.

"But I also believe that the seven churches describe seven time periods, from the present to the end of the age. So that the last letter, to the church at Laodicea, describes the type of church that will exist just prior to Christ's return—lukewarm, neither cold nor hot . . ."

For the next few minutes, John expounded on his interpretation of the revelation while Rebecca listened avidly and asked questions. They were still discussing the topic when Marcellus arrived.

"Have I missed class again?" he asked with a grin. John had been discipling Marcellus, who often commented that he was learning so much, he felt like a schoolboy.

"I'll let you question him for a while," Rebecca said. "He's wearing me out."

"Actually, I'm worn out from standing out here so long. Let's go back inside." John headed for the cave, and the other two followed.

"I have some news," Marcellus said after John had positioned

himself on the stool. "Some sad news, I'm afraid." Like Rebecca, he
sat on the ground at John's feet.

"I'm not sure I can take any more sad news," Rebecca said.

"What is it, son?"

"One of the men who arrived with you from Ephesus—his name
is Servius—died last night."

Rebecca started crying and John explained, "Servius had been
part of Rebecca's household since before she was born." He reached
out to comfort Rebecca as he asked, "What happened?"

"It's been a hard winter," Marcellus said, "and he was getting up in
years. Working outdoors had weakened his body. He got very sick, and
by the time they brought him to me, there was nothing I could do."

"Why does everybody I love have to die or disappear?" Rebecca
asked, her breath ragged from weeping. Jacob had been sent away,
her mother was dead, and the last time she'd seen her father, he was
lying facedown by the altar at Domitian's temple; for all she knew,
he was dead. Now Servius.

Rebecca laughed hysterically even as she cried. "For that matter,
I'm dead too!" She rocked back and forth, her arms clamped to her
chest. "I'll never get off this island. According to the camp records,
I don't even exist anymore. I'll grow old and die here, and so will my
baby!"

Marcellus took a minute to calm her down, then he said, "I've
given that a lot of thought. Reporting you as dead seemed the only
thing to do at the time. It kept you safe, but it did create problems."

"You did what you thought was best," John said, "and we're very
grateful."

"My twenty-year term is up in late September . . ." Marcellus
hesitated for a moment, then plunged ahead with his plan. "The
baby will be about two months old then, and I could try to smuggle him off the island when I leave. Maybe take the baby to Ephesus,
to your family. I've already agreed to carry John's letter with me. I
could carry something for you too," he told Rebecca.

"What if Brutus saw you with the baby?" John asked. "Would he try to stop you? Or Damian? What if he found out?"

"Damian's visits have tapered off, so it's not as likely that he'd be here. As for Brutus—well, to begin with, he would be shocked speechless. Nobody has ever seen a baby in this place. And if I were caught, I . . . I thought I would say the baby is mine—if that's all right with you, Rebecca. Brutus knows you were raped and figures it was Damian. But if I claim the baby is mine, how could he prove otherwise? And if the baby is mine, then Brutus couldn't legally stop me from taking him with me."

"And then Damian wouldn't be able to claim the child was his," Rebecca said. "I've been worried that perhaps he would try to take the baby away." She had no idea what she would do when the baby was born, how she would raise a child while living in a cave, shut off from the rest of the world. Yet she certainly didn't want the child under Damian's influence.

"I doubt he would want a living reminder of what he did to you," Marcellus said, "although with Damian you never know."

Rebecca's maternal instincts were aroused for this child she hadn't wanted and hadn't quite grown to love, at least not yet. At the same time, she couldn't bear to think of something terrible happening to her unborn child—a child John had said would be a great servant of the Lord.

"But how could he survive?" Rebecca asked Marcellus. "How would you feed the baby?"

"I couldn't, except perhaps for a little water. But Ephesus is only about six hours away, and I could find a wet nurse as soon as I got there." He put a hand on Rebecca's shoulder. "I'd try to smuggle you off the island, Rebecca, if I could think of a way to disguise you. That would be a great deal riskier, though."

"Of course. How *do* you disguise a dead woman?" Rebecca smiled wanly. She was beginning to feel a bit better. The very fact that Marcellus was trying to figure something out encouraged her.

"I haven't told Brutus that you're going to have a baby. Actually, I haven't told him anything about you at all, and he hasn't asked."

"He doesn't want to be reminded, I'm sure," John said. "It's more convenient to forget about us."

Marcellus agreed. "But he's not entirely heartless. And he doesn't want any more trouble in the camp. I could try to appeal to him on that basis, tell him that if I take you and the baby with me, then he's rid of a problem."

"But that would leave you all alone," Rebecca said to John, tears suddenly threatening to spill at the thought. "I couldn't leave you here. I couldn't."

"Well," Marcellus said quickly, "we've got plenty of time to think about it. No need to make a decision right away."

"Yes, I have to give birth to this baby first." Rebecca sighed. She couldn't imagine having a baby without her mother being there to help.

"I'm studying up on that too. I have some medical texts in my office, but none of them discusses childbirth. That's a subject army doctors don't exactly need to know."

"I don't suppose there are any midwives on the island," John said.

Marcellus grinned. "Unless one gets sentenced soon, we're on our own . . . But how hard could it be?"

"Easy for you to say," Rebecca grumbled.

31

DISCOURAGEMENT WEIGHED DOWN ABRAHAM'S SOUL like the leather paperweight anchoring the open scroll on his desk. He picked up the lead-filled object and studied it intently, as if it held the answer to all his problems.

For months he had been trying to get his case before the Senate, but he couldn't find a sponsor to present it. Senators he had helped over the years, men who had courted his friendship and coveted his financial support, were mysteriously unavailable when he called on them now. Or, if he managed to get a meeting with them, they stuttered an excuse for not being able to help. He had worked through the winter and the spring without any progress; now it was June, and he was no closer to his goal than when he'd washed up on the shore after the hurricane.

Abraham guessed that Naomi's husband was using his influence to block the appeal; Senator Mallus was one of the most powerful politicians in Rome. Abraham had not seen his daughter since the night of the reception, when Mallus had thrown him out.

The heavy paperweight Abraham was staring at failed to hold his attention, so he set it to one side and unrolled the scroll it had held open. He'd read the long letter from Quintus at least a hundred times since it had arrived a month ago on the *Aurelia*, one of Abraham's cargo ships.

But because it was the only news he'd had of his family, he read it yet again.

"The business is doing well in your absence," Quintus wrote, "and we should have a successful season. I will keep you apprised of our operations whenever we have a ship bound for Rome.

"Peter has been helping me. You would be proud of him. The young man who always seemed so timid has matured through this crisis. He comes to the harbor every day, and he has taken over the bookkeeping and inventory so I can do, or try to do, your job.

"I give you this good news about Peter first, because the news about Jacob is not so good. He is no longer on Patmos but was sentenced to serve as an oarsman on a warship . . ."

Abraham quit reading and looked up for a moment. His heart always sank when he read that part and thought about Jacob spending the rest of his life rowing for the Roman navy. The only consolation was that being at sea would keep his son out of the reach of Damian.

"I learned this information," the letter said, "when I went to Patmos. The trip was Peter's idea. As soon as the seas opened, he said we should send a ship to Patmos with food and clothing for the prisoners. His intent, of course, was to provide for Jacob and Rebecca and the others from Ephesus; however, we assumed that we would not be allowed the privilege of seeing them or sending gifts to them personally, so we decided to send enough for all the prisoners.

"It was probably dangerous for believers to attempt such a thing, but Damian's troops had left Ephesus by then, so Peter approached your old friend Publius with the idea. Publius managed to get authorization for 'concerned citizens' to do 'charitable works' for the prisoners on Patmos. Other than Publius, who made a donation to the cause, the only citizens concerned enough to help the prisoners were the Christians remaining in Ephesus. I bought supplies of food and grain, and Peter collected clothing and blankets from the other believers. Then he packed up Jacob's and Rebecca's clothing, and most of Naomi's things as well."

Abraham smiled at the thought of Naomi's vast, colorful wardrobe being donated to convict laborers. She would never miss a single tunic, but she would despise the thought of the prisoners on Devil's Island wearing the clothes of an important society matron from Rome.

"I accompanied the boat to Patmos," Quintus wrote, "and showed our letter of authorization to the camp commander, whose name is Brutus. He was quite surprised and, I think, suspicious, even when I said the food and clothing were to be distributed among all the prisoners. He must have guessed I was interested in a specific prisoner.

"'There is women's clothing too,' I told him. Brutus said they had very few women there, but he would see that they got the clothing. Then I asked if he could give me any information about a young woman named Rebecca, who had been sent there from Ephesus with her brother Jacob, and others, last October.

"He remembered Jacob right away. That's when I found out he had been sentenced to a warship after a rock-throwing incident in the quarry. Evidently Jacob struck an officer and knocked him unconscious. Brutus would not provide any details, but I'm sure Jacob must have been provoked. I cannot imagine him becoming violent for no reason."

The officer had probably said or done something to Rebecca or John, Abraham guessed; he could easily picture Jacob coming to their defense and the situation getting out of control.

"Brutus refused to answer my inquiries about Rebecca and John. Then I mentioned that I had brought a case of fresh fruit for the officers and several bottles of vintage Italian brandy. He became a bit more cordial, and we discussed winemaking for a while. When I inquired again about Rebecca and John, he reluctantly said I should ask the medical officer about them.

"The medical officer, however, was not in the camp that afternoon, and no one knew where he was. I went to the hospital; John and Rebecca were not there, but perhaps one or both of them had been injured previously. Why else would Brutus refer me to the medical officer? I was unable to find out anything else before our ship sailed. We were not allowed to dock overnight, so we had to leave Patmos by sundown.

"I was very disappointed not to learn anything more about your daughter or the Apostle. I keep telling myself that they're all right, and I pray for them daily. Brutus must have hoped I would find something out, but he wanted the medical officer to be the one who told me. I feel I have let you down . . ."

Far from letting him down, Abraham thought, Quintus had done everything he could possibly do—more than anyone could be expected to do. And Peter . . . Abraham was so grateful that Quintus had shown such concern for Peter, and that his shy, withdrawn son had demonstrated some initiative both in the shipping business and for his family's welfare . . ."

Abraham rolled the letter back up and fought the urge to give in to despair. He couldn't stand not knowing how Rebecca was, but he stubbornly refused to think she was dead. At least he knew Jacob was all right, even though his sentence had shifted from one kind of hard labor to another.

Like Quintus, Abraham felt he had failed in his mission. He thought about sailing back to Ephesus and even trying to go to Patmos himself. But that wouldn't win Rebecca's release, even if he did manage to get more information out of Brutus or the medical officer. Kaeso had told him recently that the repairs were finished on the *Mercury;* they could leave at any time.

Should he stay and keep trying to make an appeal? Or should he give up and go home?

Early the next morning, at a meeting with other Christians in Rome, Abraham poured out his discouragement and asked for prayer. He had reconnected with a number of believers there and had told them all about the persecution in Ephesus and his concern for his children. The group had been praying regularly for a successful appeal; now they decided to fast as well as pray.

Ten days later, Abraham had a sponsor in the Senate. A member he had contacted before, Aulus Virius Horatius, came to see him.

"Several months ago," Horatius said, "I wasn't willing to risk taking up your case. Now I am."

"What changed your mind?" Abraham asked.

"My health is failing. I'll be retiring from the Senate soon, so I have nothing to lose politically. It occurs to me now that one of my last official acts could be to repay an old friend for his help over the years."

Something didn't ring quite true with the offer. Horatius had always been thin and pale; he didn't look any more sickly now than he had a few months ago when Abraham had solicited his aid. And Abraham had helped Horatius only once or twice over the years; the senator had not been a regular recipient of Abraham's largesse. But it was the only opportunity he'd been given, so Abraham seized it.

On the third Tuesday in June, Abraham entered the Curia with a mixture of hope and anxiety. He had spent many hours on his knees preparing for the one hour he would spend making his case before the Senate and the emperor. Abraham was about to plead for mercy from a ruler who was not known for showing mercy, but the ultimate outcome, he knew, would be a matter of divine justice.

The voices of the assembled senators echoed over the intricately patterned marble floor as Abraham walked toward the carved stone balustrade in front of the speakers' podium. The Curia Julia, the building where the Senate met to deliberate, had been commissioned 140 years earlier by Julius Caesar, but the massive fire that swept Rome during Nero's reign also damaged the Curia. Just two years ago, some thirty years after the fire, Domitian had completed its restoration to Julius's original design. Roughly sixty feet wide and ninety feet long, the Curia would seat some two hundred senators on the rows of benches lining the long sides of the chamber. Although it only took seventy senators to constitute an assembly, the hall was overflowing the day Abraham's case was heard.

The senators took their positions according to rank, with the most important members seated close to the podium and the junior members standing in back. Abraham saw Senator Mallus at the front, and he automatically clenched his fist; he still felt like hitting the man. Only Senator Nerva, a longtime power player at the palace, was seated closer to the podium than Mallus. None of the senators Abraham had contacted over the last few months acknowledged his presence, and even Horatius, who was responsible for getting his case heard, merely gave a perfunctory nod in his direction.

Arrayed in their purple-striped togas, the senators were an impressive-looking group, and during the period of the Republic, the Senate had indeed been a powerful institution. Beginning with the dictatorship of Gaius Julius Caesar, however, and throughout the succession of nearly a dozen emperors, the Senate's influence had been radically curtailed. While the senators would deliberate the case, their votes would be a mere reflection of the will of the emperor.

Abraham understood, therefore, that one man would determine the outcome of his appeal, and that man was already at the rostrum, dressed in full military costume. Domitian was popular with the troops—he had given them large pay increases to secure their support—and often wore a military uniform; it was a tacit admission that he could not stay in power without the full backing of the army.

After the assembly was called to order, Horatius presented an overview of the case and introduced Abraham. It was a bright, sunny day and the Curia was packed. When he mounted the podium, Abraham suddenly appreciated the airiness afforded by the sixty-foot-high ceiling; it would keep the room cooler, and he was already beginning to feel warm.

Almost as soon as Abraham began his carefully prepared speech, the members began to bombard Abraham with questions. He noted that the first questions, which dealt mostly with the facts of the case, came from allies of Senator Mallus.

Then one of the senators asked, "When your son and daughter refused to sacrifice to Lord Domitian, did they make the right choice?"

It had been decades—a lifetime ago, it seemed—since Abraham had practiced law, but he recognized the lawyer's skill behind the question.

"My children have no political quarrel with Rome," he said carefully. "They were simply following their conscience, and they meant no disrespect to Caesar by it."

Senator Mallus fired the next question himself. "I understand you were present when your son and daughter refused the mandatory sacrifice, and even though you also profess to be a Christian, you went ahead and offered the sacrifice to Caesar. Did *you* make the right choice?"

Abraham tried to hedge. "I did what I thought was best at that moment."

He didn't like where this line of questioning was leading. He also didn't like the fact that Horatius would not look him in the eye, even though his sponsor was in his direct line of vision.

A thought struck Abraham with the force and clarity of a flash of lightning that illuminates a stormy night: Horatius had been bought. As long as Mallus had opposed his efforts, Abraham could not get a single senator to sponsor his cause. It was Mallus who had had the change of heart; he had wanted Abraham's case to come before the Senate so he could set a trap, and he had paid Horatius to make it happen. And it must have been Abraham's own daughter who provided the information used to bait the trap.

The commanding silver-haired senator who had become Abraham's son-in-law paced in front of the podium; when Mallus stopped and placed a hand on the balustrade, the other senators leaned forward expectantly. "I also understand you later recanted your loyalty to Caesar," he said, "and you apologized to a group of Christians for making the sacrifice, which you described as 'a sin.'"

Mallus paused to look at the hushed crowd, then turned to Abraham and asked, "If you had it to do over again, would you worship Emperor Domitian as Lord and God?"

The emperor rose from his seat and walked toward Abraham. "Now, that's an intriguing question, and I want to hear the answer. Would you make the same choice today?"

It's all over, Abraham thought. *All these months, and it's finally over.*

Yet rather than despair at having fought a hopeless cause for so long, Abraham felt relief, and an unusual peace. He stared briefly at his malicious son-in-law and the despotic emperor, then he addressed the Senate.

"I came before this august body today to make an appeal to reason and justice on behalf of my son and daughter. But somehow I have been placed on trial—not for anything I have done or failed to do, but for what I believe. Rome has enjoyed a long history of religious tolerance, yet now it is unlawful for a man to follow his conscience in matters of religion. No matter how upstanding a man may be, he faces the loss of his liberty and his property simply for the crime of being a Christian.

"As followers of Jesus Christ, we are peaceable people who love one another and strive to help our fellowman. We are law-abiding citizens, we pay our taxes, we support and defend the Empire. The one thing we cannot do is offer our worship to anyone other than Jesus Christ."

A low murmur rumbled through the crowd, and Abraham raised his voice. "You ask if I would make the same choice today that I made eight months ago, and the answer is no. My loyalty is to the Lord Jesus Christ, who was crucified by Rome, resurrected by the power of Almighty God, then ascended into heaven. That same Jesus is coming again to rule and reign on the earth, and at His name every knee will bow in worship."

Abraham pointed at his chief accuser and then at the emperor.

"You will bow, Senator Mallus, and you, Caesar Domitian. And every man in this room will confess that Jesus Christ is Lord, to the glory of God the Father."

Chaos erupted in the Curia. Senators shouted and gestured, and Domitian signaled for the Praetorian Guard.

Abraham kept his head high as Caesar's soldiers arrested him and marched him down the long hall lined by the most powerful citizens in the Roman Empire. He had submitted his life to a power far greater than Rome's, and in that decisive moment, he knew no fear.

32

"WHICH NECKLACE? The gold-mesh choker or the emerald pendant?" Naomi held the two costly baubles in front of her husband.

Lucius sighed, then pointed to the choker. "We're going to the games, Naomi, not a gala."

"But we're sitting in the emperor's box this time." She turned around so he could fasten the clasp of the necklace. "And he's planned a special event for today, something that affects me personally. So I want to look my best."

He watched her primp for a minute, then said, "It happened exactly as you said it would, Naomi. Your father recanted his loyalty to Caesar, right there on the floor of the Senate."

"I wish I could have seen you question him. I'll bet you were wonderful."

"An inspired performance, if I do say so." Lucius's face relaxed in a self-congratulatory smile that quickly faded. "I thought the emperor would execute him immediately, quietly. Instead, Domitian waited for his next grandiose public spectacle. Are you sure it doesn't bother you? If you'd rather not watch . . ."

Naomi looked into the bronze hand mirror, gave her mass of lustrous auburn curls a final pat, then shrugged. "It's been a month. I've gotten used to the idea." She set the mirror down and turned to face her husband. "Besides, it's his time. He's cheated death before, but he won't now. And once he's gone, you can help me claim his fortune."

"You don't think he has disinherited you in his will?"

"If he has, then we'll get it invalidated. You have the power."

Naomi walked over to Lucius and tilted her head up for a kiss. When he dutifully obliged, she added, "And then, with my wealth combined with yours, we'll be as rich as Croesus."

"What will be left to consume your attention then, my dear wife?"

"I've been thinking about that."

"And what new idea has entered your pretty head?"

Her eyes sparkling with mischief, Naomi walked her index and middle fingers up his chest, then clasped her arms around his neck.

"We're going to kill Caesar, so you can be emperor."

❧

For one month Abraham had received free accommodations courtesy of the emperor. That's how he had come to think of his imprisonment.

His host had provided no amenities. The room was small and dark, and there was no bed; he slept chained to the stone wall. Yet in all of his fifty-one years Abraham had not felt such freedom.

And joy. He actually felt an unspeakable joy, and on occasion, he had even laughed out loud. The guards had called him a madman, but the truth was that Abraham was living in the presence of God.

The joy came from knowing he was truly forgiven. Like the apostle Peter, he had briefly denied Christ; but Abraham had genuinely repented and then boldly professed his faith before Caesar. Now, in the same way he had heard an inner voice warning him not to make the sacrifice—a voice he had ignored—Abraham heard the voice of the Spirit encouraging him: *Whoever confesses Me before men, him I will also confess before My Father who is in heaven.*

Abraham passed his days praying and thinking about his life. He thanked God for the twenty-five years he'd had with his precious wife and prayed he would be with Elizabeth soon. Almost hourly he petitioned heaven for Rebecca and Jacob, always saying, "Father, I commit my children into Your hands."

Sometimes he wished he could get another letter to Ephesus, to let Peter know he was in prison. Several weeks earlier he had written

Quintus to thank him for looking out for Peter and the business, and he'd also written a letter to his son. Abraham also hoped the believers in Ephesus would someday learn that he had belatedly taken the bold stand for Christ he should have taken that momentous day at Domitian's temple.

The one thing Abraham did not pray for was his release. He had a firm conviction that it was his time to die, and that thought did not disturb him. The calm resignation he had felt when he'd been arrested at the Curia had turned into joyful acceptance of his lot.

Weeks ago, when the soldiers of the Praetorian Guard had escorted Abraham to prison, they had passed through the Arch of Titus, a masterpiece of Roman architecture Domitian had erected to commemorate the victory his brother, the late emperor, had won in Jerusalem. A bas-relief on the stone monument depicted the sacred vessels of the Jewish temple being carried as spoils of war in a triumphal procession. Abraham had thought of Tobias then, and how his cousin had known, and accepted, that he would not survive the final battle for Jerusalem.

Now Abraham knew with a certainty that he would not survive Domitian's persecution, and it was strange to think that in some way it had all started back then, in Jerusalem. Events had been set in motion twenty-five—no, twenty-six—years ago that had culminated in his sitting in this depressingly dark, oppressively hot prison cell, waiting to be executed.

Seemingly unrelated events had merged, lives had been irrevocably intertwined, and while Abraham didn't fully understand it, he knew that somehow it had all happened as part of a divine plan. Inadvertently witnessing a murder in a faraway place. Traveling to Ephesus and marrying Elizabeth. Damian resurfacing after all those years. Who could have foreseen that it would all come together and end like this?

Finally, early one morning while Abraham was singing a psalm, the guards came for him.

"Today's your big day," one of them said.

They unfastened his shackles from the large hooks in the wall, and Abraham stood. He kicked one leg and then the other to untangle the chains still linking his ankles, then shuffled out of the cell, surrounded by four heavily armed guards.

Abraham hadn't seen daylight in weeks, and when they reached the street, he stumbled as his eyes readjusted to the outside world. When he could finally focus, he looked up and saw his destiny looming in front of him.

The Colosseum.

Now Abraham understood why Domitian had not already killed him: the emperor was staging his execution for the public's entertainment.

The official name of the place where he would die was the Flavian Amphitheater, but most people referred to the impressive elliptical structure as the Colosseum, after the colossal statue of Nero that had once dominated the site. Abraham had been inside the Colosseum once, not to watch the games but to try to make contact with senators who could help with his appeal.

Now he looked up at the beautiful columns representing the orders of Greek architecture—Doric, Ionic, and Corinthian—and the soaring arches of travertine stone, and he remembered how impressed he'd been at the ease with which fifty thousand spectators could find their assigned seats. Each of the eighty arches that opened into the stands was numbered, and the tickets for an event designated the entrance, row, and seat number for the holder.

Today, however, Abraham did not enter the Colosseum through one of the public entrances. The guards took him into a separate building, then down a flight of stairs and through a tunnel to the *hypogeum,* the underground complex of rooms and passages below the arena. The *hypogeum* contained storage rooms for props and scenery, dressing rooms for the gladiators, and cages for the wild animals.

As he waited in a holding area for condemned prisoners, Abraham heard the crowds begin to arrive. He listened to the sounds of stamping feet overhead and felt the walls around him vibrate as the throng of spectators climbed to their seats. He heard the gladiators arrive in the *hypogeum*, heard their managers shouting instructions.

Abraham's only moment of near-panic came when he distinguished a different kind of sound echoing from the rooms nearby. These were not human sounds but the sounds of animals.

Animals that paced and roared.

Hungry animals. Abraham knew that the beasts would not have been fed for several days, ensuring that they would viciously attack and devour their human prey.

Hurting animals. He also knew that before releasing them into the arena, the handlers would agitate the huge cats with hot irons, stirring them to savagery.

Abraham closed his eyes and tried to pray but couldn't concentrate because of the noise. It didn't matter; in the weeks of his imprisonment, he had reached a point where he could pray without words. Every breath he took was a prayer.

Finally, he managed to form a coherent thought, asking simply that he would be courageous and meet his death with dignity. That he would acquit himself as a man. And above all, that he would die as a Christian worthy of being called by the name of Christ.

For several hours, Abraham listened to the games proceed above him. He heard the trumpets announce the opening procession and listened as the gladiators marched around the arena to the deafening roar of the crowd. Then he waited through a series of matches, wondering how far into the program his execution would occur. Sometimes the fighting was directly overhead, and the ceiling—actually the wooden floor of the arena—thundered above him; then the gladiators would move to a different part of the arena, and he would strain to hear the distant clanging of swords. The arena floor was huge, almost three hundred feet long, so there were times he could only guess what was happening by the reaction of the audience.

By the time the guards returned to escort him to the arena, Abraham had counted himself as dead. He was calm when they unlocked his chains and removed his tunic. He did not resist as they tied his hands with ropes. And he did not cry out as a guard lashed his bare back with the whip, so the animals could catch the scent of his blood.

With his hands bound in front of him and a rope looped around his neck, Abraham was led out of the *hypogeum* by a contingent of ten guards. A man carrying a tablet announcing the nature of Abraham's crime preceded the group onto the sand-covered floor of the arena. As he circled the amphitheater, displaying the tablet for the crowd, the guards led Abraham to the center of the arena and tied him securely to a tall, sturdy stake.

Abraham looked up at the mammoth stretch of canvas that shaded the spectators from the bright afternoon sun. Domitian had permanently stationed a detachment of marines at the Colosseum just to operate the complicated rigging that rolled and unrolled the awnings. The emperor had spared no expense in providing for the comfort of the spectators who thrilled to the blood and gore of the games. He not only shielded them from the sun, he had installed spouts that sprayed cool, scented water into the air.

The stake where Abraham was tied was directly across from the emperor's box; he recognized it from the twin columns topped by gold eagles and the crimson banner hanging behind the ornate gold throne. Even from a hundred feet away, Abraham could plainly see that Domitian was enjoying the afternoon's entertainment. Abraham also recognized the couple seated beside the emperor—Naomi and Senator Mallus.

His daughter had betrayed him, Abraham knew. She had to have been the one who told Mallus about Abraham's tearful confession to the church the day before they'd left Ephesus.

While Naomi had betrayed him, she was no ordinary Judas; she would never have settled for a mere thirty pieces of silver. Abraham

knew she was after a much greater fortune—his estate—but he had
no time to wonder how she might try to acquire it.

Just then the loud clang of a metal grate alerted him that one of
the animal cages had been opened. Abraham looked toward the
sound and saw three lions charging into the arena. Head to head,
they sprinted toward him, their powerful paws ripping into the
sand, their tongues hanging out.

Blood from Abraham's back had drained down his legs and
dripped on the sand, and the scent of it propelled the huge animals
in his direction. Abraham's feet were about twelve inches off the
ground, his belly about three feet; the guards had positioned him to
make it possible for the lions to disembowel him with one pass.

The audience bellowed its approval as the huge cats raced forward. Abraham waited for the beasts to rip him to shreds, rejoicing
that he would soon be in the presence of Christ.

And then, less than ten yards away from him, the lions suddenly
thrust their paws into the sand as if they had reached the edge of a
steep cliff.

The lions slid to a stop and looked up at Abraham.

∾

Naomi stared in disbelief as the lions suddenly stopped, then backed
up and sat down.

When the crowd fell silent, Domitian turned to the editor of the
games and ordered, "Do something!"

"Shall I release more lions?" the distraught editor asked. "P-per-
haps the leopards?"

"Why? So they can lie there and lick their paws like house cats?"
His eye twitching madly, the emperor glowered at the man responsible for managing the games.

While Domitian was clearly displeased, Naomi thought she saw
her father smiling. She was infuriated that he appeared to be cheat-
ing death yet again.

"This is boring," one of the senators sitting behind them commented.

Higher up in the stands, in the section reserved for the poorer classes, a man shouted, "Great is the God of the Christians!" Some of the crowd picked up the chant, and others began to cry out for *missio,* the optional release of a defeated gladiator.

The dignitaries sitting to the right of the imperial box remained silent, waiting to see what their ruler would do. So did the Vestal Virgins, the priestesses of Rome, from their reserved seats at the left of the imperial box.

As the demands from the audience escalated, Domitian jumped from his seat and screamed at the editor, who then turned to his assistant, evidently relaying the emperor's instructions. The assistant left the podium and disappeared down the ramp leading underground.

Naomi couldn't stand not knowing what was happening. She looked at Lucius for an explanation, but he shrugged to indicate he didn't know, either.

When Domitian returned to his throne, Naomi boldly leaned over and addressed him. "Lord Caesar, the *missio* applies only to gladiatorial contests, not executions, doesn't it?"

"Yes, although the crowd seems to think otherwise." Domitian narrowed his eyes and appraised her. "I suppose I could always make an exception, especially for a woman of such striking beauty. I impose sentences and I can undo them; it's one of the benefits of being emperor."

His sly smile raised goose bumps on Naomi's arms. She was flattered by his attention, but the last thing she wanted was for him to make an exception in this case.

"Is *missio* what you want, Naomi? I've ordered the editor to remove the lions and prepare to send in the gladiators to finish the job, but there's still time to reverse my decision." He extended his hand, palm upward, toward her. "The editor is waiting for my signal. I defer to you."

With the crowd still shouting for her father's release, Naomi looked at the emperor. She slowly extended her arm and rotated her wrist until her thumb pointed straight down.

"Kill him," she said.

Domitian laughed, and with a look of stark admiration he mimicked her gesture, giving the thumbs-down signal to the editor. The white-robed Vestal Virgins followed suit.

Moments later, six animal handlers entered the arena wearing protective gear. The lions snarled as the men approached with their whips cracking. Working in pairs, the handlers returned the three lions to the cage.

From the other end of the arena, a dozen gladiators entered and marched in lockstep toward Abraham, swords at their sides, their faces invisible behind their visored helmets. The attitude of the audience changed with the appearance of the gladiators. Anticipating a spectacular kill, they began to yell their excitement.

At a signal shouted from the *hypogeum*, the gladiators simultaneously raised their weapons and attacked the condemned man. Abraham's body became a fountain, spouting blood onto the arena floor. The executioners slit his throat, hacked at his heart, and sliced open his stomach. They stabbed and carved and cut, and then stood back, satisfied with a job well done.

The spectators went wild. Domitian beamed at the sycophants surrounding him, then motioned for the editor to proceed with the next event.

Finally—finally—it was over. Naomi had scarcely breathed during the gruesome spectacle.

When the red-spattered gladiators departed, two workers carrying large hooks came to remove the victim. They untied the ropes that bound Abraham to the stake, then let his body slump to the ground.

As they dragged Abraham's lifeless form across the sand, Lucius laced his fingers through his wife's and gave her hand a squeeze. Naomi looked up at him and said something, but with the crowd already screaming for the next entertainment, Lucius could not hear. He leaned closer so she could repeat her question.

"What will happen to his body?"

"It will be dumped in the Tiber."

Naomi nodded. *The water.* That was fitting. *It's where he should have died in the first place.*

33

TERRA FIRMA. Solid ground felt good beneath his feet, and Jacob had enjoyed three days of it, even though it had involved the nastiest assignment of his involuntary naval career.

The *Jupiter* had made an unscheduled return to its home port of Misenum, which was also the headquarters of the imperial navy. The vast waterways of the Empire were organized into nine different regions, each with a fleet of warships that patrolled a designated area from the home port. The fleet based in Misenum, of which the *Jupiter* was a part, patrolled the Mediterranean Sea from the western coast of Italy to the eastern coast of Spain.

Jacob's ship had returned to the base because most of the crew had come down with dysentery. Jacob had been one of the fortunate few who had not suffered from the awful bouts of diarrhea and vomiting that had swept through the ranks of the oarsmen. They'd been far out to sea when the first men got sick; within two days half the crew was groaning with severe abdominal cramps and unable to row, and the *Jupiter* was sailing on wind power alone. With a serious outbreak of illness crippling his ship, the captain reversed course, but by the time the floating sick ward made it back to Misenum, nine out of ten oarsmen were out of commission—and they'd buried seven men at sea.

The unpleasant assignment that fell to Jacob—and the other dozen or so marines who managed to escape the illness—had been cleaning the ship after it docked. For two days Jacob had washed and scrubbed and mopped . . . and hung his head over the side to gulp in deep breaths of fresh air so he wouldn't heave from the stench.

But today he was working on the dock, in the sunshine, and it almost felt like being at home. Jacob had worked as a stevedore on his father's dock when he was learning the business. He'd hated the backbreaking work then, but he didn't mind it so much now. At least he wasn't in chains anymore, although someone was always around to keep an eye on him.

It was a clear day, still warm for the middle of September, and in the distance he could see the island of Capri. This was a popular resort area for the upper class, and many wealthy Romans spent part of the year in their villas around the beautiful Bay of Naples. Jacob recalled that the emperor Tiberius had died at his villa on Capri, with his successor, the evil Caligula, looking on. Over on the mainland, on the plain of Campania, was Mount Vesuvius, the volcano that had erupted and wiped out the cities of Pompeii and Herculaneum seventeen years earlier. Jacob's grandfather, Rufus, had told stories about it when Jacob was a child.

Jacob had always wanted to visit southern Italy, and now he wished he could be a simple tourist, wished he had the freedom to go sightseeing. He longed for freedom, period. He'd lost his, and had no reason to believe he would ever get it back.

He had tried to be patient in suffering, and he knew God had given him favor. First, he'd been moved from Devil's Island to the *Jupiter*. Then he'd been elevated from a lower oarsman to the top bank of oars, and at just the right time. Jacob had spent the winter months at his original position in the hull; it was dark and close, but protected from the elements. In the spring he'd been moved to the upper deck, and rowing in the warm sunshine, or even the occasional summer shower, was a vast improvement.

Now he was walking around on dry ground, and Jacob thanked the Lord for it while he worked.

During the eleven months Jacob had been at sea, the *Jupiter* had made port a number of times. The first time, the captain had confined Jacob to the ship. The second time, he had let Jacob off the ship but had kept him cuffed. But that meant Jacob couldn't help with the loading of supplies, so eventually the captain had let him work unrestrained, although closely supervised.

Each time they'd been in harbor those first few months, Jacob had prayed for a chance to escape. But every time he considered making a run for it, something kept him back. He supposed a part of it was fear; if they caught him, which was likely, he would be killed. But part of it was spiritual. It was a matter of submitting to God's will, and for some reason Jacob had yet to determine, this was God's will for him.

He kept remembering what John had said when they arrived on Patmos, how he had talked about Joseph being sold into slavery in Egypt, and how Joseph couldn't see at the time that it was part of God's plan to save his family. Jacob fervently prayed that God would use his imprisonment to save his own family—and that it wouldn't take as many years as it had for Joseph.

An unusual amount of activity was taking place on the dock today, Jacob noted, even though few ships in the fleet were currently in the harbor. One of them was a transport, which the prefect—the official with oversight of the entire fleet—had ordered to be loaded right away; he had assigned all available personnel to the task, and they'd been working for several hours.

There weren't enough men, however, to get the job done as fast as the prefect wanted—Jacob gathered that the transport needed to leave immediately on some important mission—and the crew was taking shortcuts Jacob didn't like. They had already loaded the food supplies, and the last items to load were some barrels of wine—the local Campanian wine favored by the Roman aristocracy and military officials.

Jacob frowned when he looked up from the dock to see one man pushing a heavy barrel up the loading ramp, followed in close proximity by another man. His father would never have allowed more than one stevedore on the loading plank at once, not when they were loading 250-pound barrels. Safety required that a man rolling a large barrel up the ramp reach the top and hand off his load to the workers on the deck of the ship before another man started rolling his barrel upward.

The prefect of the fleet was standing close by, talking to another officer on the dock, and Jacob was debating whether to point out the safety hazard when he heard a startled cry from the ramp. He looked up to see that the top man had lost his grip as he was hauling the barrel over the railing, and it came crashing back down on the ramp and slammed into the other man's barrel. The impact knocked the second man off the plank and left both barrels careening toward the dock . . . and the two officers.

Without stopping to think, Jacob made a flying dive toward the men, knocking the prefect to the ground and pushing the officer into the water. Jacob continued to slide on his stomach for a few feet, the rough wooden pier ripping his tunic and filling his chest with splinters. As he came to a stop, Jacob heard the runaway barrels crash on the dock behind him. Both containers burst open, drenching him with sixty gallons of fine wine.

For a moment there was pandemonium on the dock around him, with workers scrambling and shouting. The prefect stood up as two men fished the other officer out of the water and pulled him back up on the pier.

Hurrying over to the dripping man, the prefect called out, "Admiral! Are you all right?"

Jacob closed his eyes in dismay. He'd just tackled the prefect of the fleet—the highest-ranking official at his home port—and nearly drowned an admiral to boot. What next?

"I hadn't intended on going for a swim today," the admiral said. He shook water off his arms and then tried to wring out his tunic. "But I'm none the worse for it."

The prefect proceeded to upbraid the marines responsible for the mishap. "The admiral is scheduled to leave on this transport as soon as it's loaded, and there had better not be any further delays."

While the prefect issued dire threats to the crew, the admiral turned his attention to Jacob and the wreckage on the dock.

"Help that man up," he instructed a nearby sailor.

Jacob took the hand extended to him, and stood to his feet.

"You saved my life—I would have been crushed," the admiral said. "Thank you."

"You're welcome, sir." Jacob stood rigidly at attention, even though his chest burned from the scrapes. He knew he must look ridiculous in the shredded tunic—the only one he owned—and he smelled like a distillery after the accidental wine bath.

"What's your name, young man?"

"Jacob of Ephesus, serving on the *Jupiter*."

"Why aren't you in uniform?"

"I'm not a regular marine, sir." Jacob hesitated a fraction of a second, then explained. "I was transferred to the *Jupiter* from the penal colony at Patmos."

"I detest the practice of using criminals to fill the ranks of the navy," the admiral burst out, a scowl darkening his face. He bent down to shake the water out of his hair and then straightened up, studying Jacob closely. "You're not the usual sort that winds up at Devil's Island. An upper-class bearing . . . you speak well . . ."

"I'm fluent in four languages, and I come from a well-to-do family in Asia."

"What did you do that landed you on Devil's Island?"

"I seem to have made an enemy of the emperor, sir"—Jacob took a deep breath—"by refusing to make a mandatory sacrifice confessing Caesar as Lord."

The admiral kept his expression blank, but his eyes opened wider. "I want to hear more about this," he informed Jacob, "as soon as I dry off."

Moments later Jacob was following the admiral and his staff on board the transport. One of them directed Jacob to a small office adjacent to the captain's quarters, and in a few minutes a marine brought a basin of water so Jacob could wash off, plus a uniform and a pair of sandals.

"You can put these on after the doctor takes a look at you," the young sailor told Jacob.

"Doctor?"

"The admiral's personal physician always travels with him."

Jacob sat silently in the one chair in the room while the doctor removed the splinters and treated his scrapes. When he left, Jacob put on the uniform. He'd never worn a uniform before, and the knee-length tunic felt strange. But with his own tunic ruined, he had nothing else to wear.

About the time Jacob finished dressing, the admiral walked in and Jacob scrambled to stand at attention.

The admiral motioned for Jacob to sit, then he perched on the edge of the desk. "Did you know who I was when you tackled me and saved my life?" he asked.

"No, sir."

"I'm the ranking admiral in the imperial navy," he said. "My name is Flavius Juvenalis."

Jacob's eyebrows rose at the name and his stomach knotted up suddenly. The admiral was a member of the Flavian family? The imperial family?

"Yes," he replied in answer to Jacob's unspoken question, "a distant relation of Domitian. I despised him—"

The admiral started to say more, then apparently thought better of it. Jacob was stunned that he was sitting across from a man who was not only the highest-ranking official in the navy but a relative of the emperor. The emperor whose worship Jacob had preached against on the streets of Ephesus. The emperor who had sent his henchmen to persecute the followers of Christ. The emperor who had stripped Jacob of his freedom and devastated his family.

"I want to hear your story," Juvenalis said. "You were telling me that you're a prisoner of conscience."

"Yes, sir." Jacob didn't know what or how much to tell Juvenalis, but instead of fear he began to feel optimistic about this chance meeting with the admiral. In fact, he began to think it wasn't a chance meeting at all; perhaps it had been ordained.

"My family is Christian," Jacob began. He explained who his father was, then Jacob told the story of John preaching outside the Temple of Domitian, and how he had chased off a group of teenagers who were throwing stones at the Apostle. He told about the report of the incident that went from the local *concilium* to Rome. He told about Damian being sent by the emperor to enforce the mandatory sacrifice, and how Damian had killed Elizabeth and sent Jacob and his young sister to Devil's Island, along with other Christians from Ephesus. He told how Damian had beaten the elderly Apostle in the quarry and then he'd thrown the stone that hit Damian. Jacob told it all, and Juvenalis listened intently, stopping him now and then to ask a question.

"I'm traveling to Rome," the admiral finally said, "and you're sailing with me. I'll notify the captain of the *Jupiter* that I'm transferring you into my custody."

Jacob jumped to his feet, his heart leaping at the realization that God had given him favor again. He didn't know in what capacity Juvenalis would use him, but it had to be far better than being an oarsman on a warship.

"Whatever assignment you give me," Jacob said, "I'll give it my best, sir."

"Your assignment is to get your sister off that godforsaken island." The admiral's voice was gruff, and he didn't speak for a moment.

Jacob's mind was whirling. He couldn't believe what the admiral was saying. Go to Devil's Island and take Rebecca? "But how?" he finally stuttered.

"I'll have to leave the how up to you, son. What I *can* do is get the emperor to issue an edict of liberation for you and your sister."

"But Domitian is the one who sent us there . . ."

"I'm sorry. I didn't make that clear." He shook his head wearily and waved Jacob back to the chair. "Sit down, and I'll explain."

Juvenalis relayed the information that Domitian had been assassinated three days earlier. "That's why I'm going to Rome," he said, "to meet with the new emperor and his military advisers."

"And you think the new emperor will grant a pardon for us?"

"I think he'll be willing to do a personal favor for the ranking admiral in order to solidify the support of the imperial navy for his new regime."

Jacob was overjoyed at the possibility, and bold enough to ask that John be included in the favor. The admiral agreed.

"Domitian was widely hated," Juvenalis said, "and his memory will be vilified now that he's gone. Eventually, all the senators and nobles he exiled will be recalled, perhaps the prisoners of conscience as well. I intend to speed up the process in your case, to repay you for saving my life."

A marine came in to report that the transport was ready to get under way.

"I need to get a message to the prefect first. And the captain of the *Jupiter*," the admiral said on his way out the door.

When they left, Jacob dropped to his knees and put his head in his hands. Tears stung his eyes as he breathed a quiet prayer of thanksgiving and then petitioned heaven for favor with the new emperor, whoever he was.

Jacob was on his way to Rome, and—he dared to believe—freedom.

34

DOMITIAN WAS DEAD, Nerva was emperor, and Naomi was livid.

"You mean it was decided—just like that?" She snapped her fingers as she spoke, then resumed pacing in front of the dining table.

"I'm sure it was decided before he was killed," Lucius said, "otherwise it wouldn't have happened all at once. As soon as he was dead, the praetors presented Nerva as their choice for successor, and the Senate ratified him immediately."

"Nerva must have been behind it, then."

"I doubt he played an active part in the conspiracy, although he may have known about it in advance." Lucius looked up with a frown, his eyes following Naomi as she walked back and forth in front of him. "Sit down, Naomi. Your angry little parade is getting on my nerves."

She arched an eyebrow at him, then walked around the table to the *triclinium* and stretched out beside him. Lucius seldom spoke harshly to her, and she didn't like it.

"I'm sorry," he said. "I've had a very long, exhausting day."

Mollified by his quick apology, she prompted him to continue. "So, tell me everything that happened."

"As best I can reconstruct it, the emperor's wife enlisted Norbanus and Petronius Secundus, the new prefects of the Praetorian Guard, to help plan it. The man who actually stabbed Domitian was a former family slave; he was killed in the struggle."

"When I first suggested the idea, you said it was bound to happen sooner or later. I thought it might as well be us. Instead, someone else got to him first." Naomi wrinkled her mouth in a pout. *Six weeks of scheming to come up with a plan that would work—and for nothing,* she thought. Lucius had said it would be risky and that it would take a while to coordinate; they simply hadn't had enough time. She could have kicked herself for not coming up with the idea months ago.

"Domitian used to complain about assassination plots," Lucius said. "He often said it was an emperor's unfortunate lot that no one would believe the rumors about a plot against him until it had been successfully executed."

"Maybe if he had rereleased the coins with Domitia's image on them, she might not have had him killed."

Lucius laughed so hard at the droll remark, he nearly spilled his wine. "I don't think that was the reason, but it might not have hurt."

"Why *did* she do it?" Naomi couldn't conceive of an emperor's wife wanting to assassinate her husband. With her husband dead, she would no longer be empress—out of power—and why would she want that?

"He'd become extremely paranoid," Lucius said, "and he suspected everyone, including his wife, of disloyalty. I think Domitia worried that he would have her killed in order to prevent her from killing him, so to keep Domitian from killing her, she had him killed first. See how convoluted palace politics can become?"

"Do emperors always have so many enemies?"

"The bad ones do. Domitian had angered a lot of people in fifteen years, especially the last few years. He took over complete control of the membership of the Senate, and he had a penchant for getting rid of people he didn't like. He had executed or exiled a number of senators recently."

"I'm glad Domitian didn't get rid of you." What a dreadful thought that was; she pushed it aside quickly. "But I'm still mad that they picked Nerva to be emperor, and not you. Why him?"

Lucius shrugged. "Several reasons, I suppose. Nerva's popular, and

very stable—he's been around a long time. And he'll provide a coun-
terbalance to some of Domitian's more drastic measures."

"In other words, he won't make waves."

"No, we don't like waves in the Senate." Lucius smiled and set
his plate aside, then laid his head on the slope of the sofa. "Also,
Nerva has no heirs, so he can't start a dynasty. I'm sure that was part
of their consideration."

"You're taking this very well. Didn't you want to be emperor?"

"It was more your dream than mine, actually." He repositioned
himself so he could see her face. "Are you really disappointed, darling?"

"Only for you. I thought you deserved to be Caesar."

To be honest, she was very disappointed. And dissatisfied with
her life. But how could she explain it? Naomi wasn't sure what she
wanted anymore, just that she wanted to *be* somebody. Somebody
important in her own right. Not because she was her father's daughter. And not because she was a senator's wife, although she loved the
status it brought, and she had grown rather fond of Lucius.

Being Caesar's wife had seemed like the next logical step toward
an uncertain destination. Naomi would outlive Lucius by many
years, and she had figured that someday, as the widow of an
emperor, she would have the clout to do whatever she wanted—
when she finally figured out what that was.

"I learned something else today." Lucius paused and then
smiled when she quickly gestured for him to continue. "Domitian
had ordered Damian home. He wanted him for another special
assignment."

"Doing what?"

"I don't know. The emperor had signed the documents for his
recall, and I suppose he would have told Damian upon his arrival."

Naomi didn't want to think about Damian. Based on the one
time she'd seen him, she didn't like him. And she certainly didn't
trust him, although she had admitted he might be useful in their
abortive plot against Domitian. She and Lucius had talked about

enlisting Damian to help them carry it out—he certainly would not have had any qualms about it. But they had not arrived at a way to get Damian back to Rome without making Domitian suspicious.

As she thought about it now, Naomi decided that her first plan—the plan to take control of her father's business—was what she should have concentrated on. She hadn't abandoned the idea; she had simply gotten unexpectedly sidetracked with the notion of her husband becoming emperor.

"Lucius, I think we should go to Ephesus."

"Now?"

"Yes. After my father died, you managed to get a declaration that I'm the sole heir to the family fortune, didn't you?"

He nodded. "Domitian signed it several weeks ago. But it will probably have to be approved by a court—if your brother Peter produces the original will and challenges us. Not that we couldn't win; it would simply mean a legal battle."

"All the more reason we should start right away. I want to get that finalized, then I want to move the headquarters of the shipping business to Rome. That way I can run it from here."

"My wife, the beautiful entrepreneur." He leaned over and gave her a quick kiss, then said, "But I can't leave right away, Naomi. With the change in rulership, I have to be here to protect my interests. I don't think Nerva has a quibble with me, but I need to make sure the status quo holds in the Senate before I leave on an extended trip."

"But what about my interests? We have to protect them too." She knew Lucius was right, and she certainly didn't want to do anything to jeopardize his position. But Naomi was impatient, now that she had decided it was time to quit talking about taking control of her father's fortune and actually do it.

"You could go ahead without me," he suggested. "And I can join you later."

She brightened at the thought. The *Mercury* had been restored,

and if the weather cooperated, she could be in Ephesus in ten days—
two weeks at the most.

"I'll leave as soon as I can," she said. With Fulvia's help, it
wouldn't take her more than a day or two to get ready.

"I'll see that you have the document that names you sole heir,
and plenty of money to tide you over until I can arrive in the
spring."

"Spring? You can't come until then?"

"I might not be able to leave before the seas close in November."

Naomi frowned darkly. Spring was six months away; anything
could happen between now and then. "But what if—"

"I know," Lucius said suddenly. "When Damian arrives, I'll send
him to you in Ephesus. With Domitian dead, he won't have a new
assignment, and perhaps he could be of assistance to you until I can
get there."

She didn't like the idea, but she didn't resist it. No woman had
ever run a worldwide shipping operation before, and Naomi decided
she'd deal with the devil himself if it meant being the first one.

"All right," she agreed. "But promise you'll hurry, darling."

✐

Jacob wanted to run down the street shouting, "I'm free! I'm free!"
But he slowed to a walk, telling himself he couldn't afford to lose the
precious document clutched tightly in his hand—the document
that had put an end to almost a year of torment.

When the admiral had left early yesterday morning to meet with
the emperor, he'd told Jacob to wait on board the ship, which had
docked overnight at the port of Ostia. Juvenalis hadn't returned for
more than twenty-four hours, and Jacob had spent most of that time
pacing on the deck and praying. When the admiral finally showed
up, he had the edict of liberation he'd promised, and he had gener-
ously given Jacob the money to take a carriage from Ostia to Rome.

The carriage had deposited him at the Capitoline Hill, the heart of the city, and now Jacob was headed for his father's riverfront office on the Tiber. He hoped by some chance that Abraham might be there or at his villa. The office was closer, so Jacob had decided to go there first. He knew his father would have been trying to get him and Rebecca released, and that would necessitate a trip to Rome, so it was possible his father was in the city even now.

Jacob turned off the street toward the warehouses lining the river. Nothing much had changed since the last time he'd been here. When he got to the wharf, Jacob broke into a sprint, unable to contain himself any longer. And when he neared the part of the dock where his father's office was located, he recognized the man with salt-and-pepper hair sitting on a post at the water's edge, idly watching the barges drift by.

"Kaeso!"

The captain jerked his head around and stared. Then he stood, wide-eyed and wondering, as Jacob ran forward.

"Jacob? . . . Jacob!"

"It's me." Jacob laughed exuberantly and threw his arms around Kaeso. The old sailor was probably unaccustomed to such demonstrative behavior, but Jacob couldn't help it.

"The deep tan, the uniform . . . What did you do, boy? Join the navy?"

"No, I—it's a long story."

"I've got plenty of time to hear it. I've got nothing but time—"

"Is my father here? If you're here, then the *Mercury* must be here, and I knew Father would be in Rome trying to do something to . . ." Jacob's words tumbled over themselves in their hurry to escape his mouth, until he finally realized that Kaeso was silent and unsmiling. The news about his father must be bad, whatever it was.

"We'd better go inside and sit down," Kaeso said. "We have a lot to talk about."

They found a nearly empty corner of the warehouse and sat down on a couple of bales of cotton.

"Is my father alive?" Jacob asked.

Kaeso shook his head. "No. He died two almost two months ago."

Jacob doubled over, as if he'd suddenly exhaled all the air in his lungs.

Kaeso put a hand on his shoulder. "I'm sorry, Jacob."

"Why? *Why?*" Jacob wanted to break down and sob, but he wanted to hear about his father even more. "Tell me what happened," he demanded. "All of it."

Kaeso told him about the catastrophic voyage from Ephesus, how Abraham had survived the hurricane, and how Naomi had gotten married only a couple of weeks after they arrived. "She married some senator," he said. "And I don't know how to tell you this . . ."

Kaeso stood up and rubbed the back of his neck. "Naomi's husband has a son, and this son is . . . His name is Damian, and he's the one who killed your mother and sent you—"

Jacob exploded. "She married Damian's father?" Rage spilled out of him in red-faced volcanic fury, and he shouted, "I could *kill* her for that!"

"Abraham said she didn't know the senator was related to Damian before she married him, but she didn't leave him when she found out, either. It nearly broke your father's heart. He never saw Naomi again."

Of all the things Jacob had thought he might encounter in Rome, this was not one of them. His sister married to Damian's father.

"Anyway," Kaeso went on, "months later—toward the end of June, I guess—your father finally did get a hearing before the Senate." He told Jacob about Abraham's testimony at the Curia, and how he had been arrested.

"I never saw your father afterward," Kaeso said, "although I found out where they were holding him. I tried to see him, but the guards wouldn't let me in. I knew he was there, though, because I heard him singing."

"Singing?"

"Yes, and he sounded happy, strangely enough. Some song I

didn't know—about not being afraid even in the valley of the shadow of death." Kaeso sat back down on the bale beside Jacob. "Is that one of your Christian songs?" he asked.

Jacob nodded but couldn't speak until he'd swallowed the lump in his throat. "The Twenty-third Psalm."

"He used to talk about that kind of thing sometimes, but I never was interested in religion, and he didn't shove it down my throat. I just liked working for your father because he was a good man. An honest man. And he had the best boats in the business." He looked at Jacob and smiled briefly, then became reflective again. "Now I wish I'd listened more to what he had to say."

Jacob was quiet for a minute, trying to absorb everything Kaeso had told him. Then he finally asked, "How did he die?"

"In the arena," Kaeso said softly.

"He was condemned *ad bestias*?" The thought of wild beasts tearing his father's body apart made Jacob sick.

Kaeso nodded. "I was there that day. At the Colosseum. I didn't want to see it, and yet I couldn't stay away. I felt I had to be there for him." Kaeso told Jacob about the lions, how they had stopped and sat down before Abraham. And then he told him about the part Naomi had played in her father's death.

"I had spotted her earlier, from up in the stands. She was sitting right there in Caesar's box like she was some kind of queen. Then when those lions wouldn't touch Abraham, and all the crowd was yelling and screaming, I looked down and she had her arm straight out and her thumb down. I started screaming myself then, and cursing. Her own father! I couldn't imagine what kind of person would do that."

Jacob's tears fell uncontrollably. His mind was reeling, and he was almost beyond reacting. His sister betraying his father . . . It was too much to bear.

Kaeso finally told him about the gladiators killing Abraham, then he choked up and joined Jacob, weeping unashamedly.

Jacob fell on his knees and leaned over the bale of cotton, sobbing. Then he thought about Naomi, and his anger boiled over again. He pummeled the bale with his fists until his knuckles bled, and Kaeso had to stop him. Some of the workers in the warehouse came over to see what was going on, but Kaeso waved them away.

Later, when Jacob had calmed down, he told Kaeso everything that had happened to him, from Devil's Island to the *Jupiter*, and how the admiral had helped him get not only his freedom but a release for Rebecca and John as well.

"I have to get to Patmos right away," Jacob said when he'd finished the story. "Is the *Mercury* ready to sail?"

"The *Mercury* has already sailed." Kaeso put a steadying hand on Jacob's arm as he continued. "Naomi left yesterday. I refused to work for her, so she fired me and hired another captain. Had to hire additional sailors too, because most of the crew did the same thing I did. We were loyal to your father and not keen on the idea of his daughter being in charge now, which she seems to think she is."

It must have been quite a scene, Jacob thought. Kaeso was obviously still worked up about it; his voice had risen as he talked.

"I had already written a letter to Quintus," the captain continued, "informing him of your father's death and asking what to do about the business operations in Rome. Everyone here always assumed you would take over after your father was gone, but when he died you were, well . . ."

"What did Quintus say?" Jacob knew his father had wanted him to take over the business someday, but he had no idea if Abraham had made provision for it in his will. They'd been at odds over his career plans when Damian had arrived to enforce the mandatory sacrifice and their family was torn apart.

"There hasn't been enough time to receive a reply yet." Kaeso sighed and said, "Anyway, I didn't see how I could stop Naomi from taking the *Mercury*. If I'd known you were on your way, though . . ."

"Where was she going?"

"To Ephesus. Said she had business there. And if you ask me, she's up to no good, whatever her business is."

Naomi married to Damian's father. Naomi sailing to Ephesus. Rebecca still on Devil's Island. Alarm bells rang in Jacob's head.

"I've got to leave right away . . . A cargo ship. We can take one of Father's cargo ships. You have to help me, Kaeso. Please—"

"I will, I will. But we won't have a ship ready to sail for a couple of days. There's one of ours in the harbor, but it's still being unloaded."

"I don't care if it's unloaded or not, we have to sail *now.*"

Kaeso studied Jacob's face for a moment before clapping him on the back. "Then let's hurry to Ostia."

35

DEAD IN THE WATER. Naomi couldn't believe it.

The first few days at sea had been beautiful and uneventful. The *Mercury* was making top speed, they were halfway to Ephesus, and then—suddenly—the wind had died and the ship had stopped.

And here they were. Going nowhere.

For two days now, Naomi had been arguing with the captain she'd hired when Kaeso had refused to sail the *Mercury.* She had thought Kaeso was a stubborn old seaman, but this new captain, Gracchus, topped him.

Gracchus is so bullheaded, his name ought to be Taurus, she thought as she paced the stateroom floor. She didn't like being in this room, even though it had been rebuilt and refurnished after the hurricane. Too many memories still haunted it.

When Naomi had first realized the ship was stalled, she had ordered Gracchus to put the crew on the oars. He flat-out refused.

"Do you see that giant sheet of canvas?" he had asked, pointing to the main mast. "It's called a sail. This is a *sailing* ship," he'd informed her, as if she'd been an ignorant child.

Infuriated, Naomi had snapped, "It also has oars, and I happen to know they work—*if* somebody pulls them." She knew the *Mercury* was equipped with only a short row of oars port and starboard, and they weren't that effective. But they did cause the ship to move slowly through the water, and moving slowly would be preferable to this.

Above all, Naomi resented the captain's refusal to follow her order. And she despised not getting her way; it was simply unthinkable.

So, for the past two days—two full days—she had used every

weapon in her arsenal of manipulation. She had demanded, flirted, wheedled, cajoled, threatened, yelled, and even cried—all to no effect. Gracchus wouldn't budge.

Over and over he'd said, "Like I already told you: the wind will pick up in a day or two, and when it does, we'll be sailing again."

But the wind hadn't picked up, and they weren't sailing.

Now, sitting in her stateroom, frustrated beyond endurance, Naomi finally decided to do something she never did: swallow her pride. She would go to Gracchus and apologize for her contrariness. She would ask him nicely, calmly, and she would offer a bonus if the crew would row until the wind picked up again.

When she found Gracchus on the main deck, she arranged her face in what she hoped would pass for a contrite smile.

Gracchus took one look at her, folded his arms across his chest, and said, "We're not rowing."

It made her so mad, she exploded. "I own this business now—the largest shipping business in the Empire—and I'll see to it that you never work in the Mediterranean again!"

The captain didn't even blink. "Try it."

Naomi turned and marched back to the stateroom. *When we finally do get to Ephesus—and we will—I won't pay that mutinous man a single* denarius *for this trip.*

She closed the door of the room and leaned back against it. Suddenly, Naomi started to laugh. The last time she'd sailed, she had survived the gale-force winds of a hurricane. This time there wasn't even a wisp of a breeze. The forces of nature were conspiring against her.

Naomi's laughter quickly died. She couldn't control nature, and she had finally met a man she couldn't control.

❧

She wouldn't be going home. Rebecca had wrestled with the decision for days, but until this moment she hadn't been fully convinced it was the right choice. Now she knew.

"I can't leave," she said to Marcellus, who stood beside her on the rocky crest, looking out over the ocean, his hands clasped behind his back.

"You're sure?"

"John needs me, and I have to stay." It was as simple as that. John needed her. The baby would have Marcellus, and after that Peter, and plenty of others in Ephesus. But if she left, John would have no one.

She didn't know how they would survive, isolated on this mountain, without Marcellus's help; perhaps they wouldn't, but they would soon find out. His twenty-year term had been up several days ago, and Marcellus should have been gone by now, but the regular supply ship from Ephesus was overdue. As soon as it arrived, Marcellus would take the baby, and John's letter, and leave.

Marcellus had talked about her going with them. He had even tried to talk to Brutus about it, but the commander had been so busy coping with the overcrowding in the camp that Marcellus hadn't been able to find a private moment with him. It was just as well, Rebecca thought now, because she couldn't leave unless John did. She would not let the Apostle die on Devil's Island alone.

She would miss Marcellus; he had been like a father to her. And without him, they would never have survived as long as they had— almost a year now. Just as God had provided manna in the wilderness for Moses and the children of Israel, He had provided the medical officer for her and John.

And for Victor. Marcellus had brought the two-month-old baby into the world, and now he was taking him to freedom.

As John had prophesied, Rebecca had given birth to a son. Not that the Apostle had been much help when the baby had arrived.

Rebecca was still embarrassed to think about the delivery. She'd been distraught because instead of her mother, she had two men— men!—to help her through the ordeal of childbirth. Actually, only one man had helped, and the other had merely survived. During the long hours of labor, Marcellus had stayed with her in the inner chamber of the cave, while John had waited in the outer room and prayed. And he had prayed so loudly at times, Rebecca had decided he was not so much petitioning God for help as he was trying to drown out her screams.

She had never experienced anything like it. The pain. The fear. And then the joy. A fuzzy-headed, red-faced, mewling little gift of joy.

"I hear Victor," Rebecca said suddenly. She'd been lost in her thoughts, yet alert to the baby's cry; she responded by turning toward the cave.

Marcellus put a hand out to stop her. "I'll get the baby. I need the practice, don't you think?" He smiled and patted her arm.

She watched him walk back to the cave, then turned around and stared over the water in the direction of Ephesus, her thoughts returning to what would happen in a few days. The thought of being separated from Victor left a dead spot in Rebecca's heart. How could she stand it? Yet how could she keep her baby? She couldn't. It would be impossible to try to raise a child in a cave, hidden away from the world. Victor deserved a life, and he wouldn't have one on Devil's Island.

Her brother Peter would look after Victor. He wouldn't know how to take care of a baby, of course, but he would find someone to help. And Marcellus had said he would make sure Victor was provided for before he left for Smyrna, and Pergamum, and the other churches. He was excited about being the Apostle's emissary to deliver the revelation to the churches.

Marcellus had also promised to look up Galen, to tell him that she was all right, and that she would understand if he did not wait for her. That was another decision Rebecca had made: she had to release Galen from his promise to marry her. She couldn't hold him to it, not when she had no reason to think she'd ever get off Devil's Island.

And she didn't have a single reason to think she would. Except for John. He was convinced they would be released—said he knew it in his bones, and that his bones had been around long enough to know that kind of thing.

⸎

Jacob and Kaeso stood on the deck of the *Honoria*, studying the sky. When they had left Ostia, the wind was brisk, and the sails had unfurled with a noisy, welcome swoosh.

Now the sails barely flapped, and the powerful waves had turned to timid ripples. The wind was dying.

Jacob was worried. They were at least a day behind Naomi, and the *Mercury* was a much faster ship. The *Honoria* was a massive work-horse of the sea, designed to plow through the water slowly and methodically.

He didn't think Naomi would sail to Patmos—why would she want to? He couldn't imagine her wanting to visit Devil's Island out of concern for Rebecca. But he didn't trust Naomi. He'd been hit with so many surprises lately, he didn't think anything could shock him now—but he didn't want to find out. He wanted to get Rebecca and John safely off the island and back to Ephesus before Naomi had time to do anything. He had no idea what his older sister might be up to, but like Kaeso, he figured her intentions were evil.

"We have to dump the wax," Jacob told Kaeso. "It's weighing us down."

When they had arrived at Ostia, the *Honoria* had been unloaded, with one exception: a shipment of wax from Corsica. Jacob had insisted on sailing right away, without unloading the remainder of the cargo, and Kaeso had backed him up. The captain of the *Honoria*, Tiberius Durus, had worked for Abraham almost as long as Kaeso and had a similar regard for his late employer. Durus had agreed to leave port immediately.

"That's an expensive shipment," Kaeso pointed out.

"I know it will be a disaster economically, but I'll just have to make up the losses when I get back to Ephesus. Right now that wax is slowing us down, and we have to catch—"

Kaeso interrupted him. "If the wind isn't blowing, the *Mercury* isn't moving, either."

"But when the wind picks up," Jacob said, "we'll have to make up the time, and we can't do it loaded. In the meantime, we can toss the cargo overboard . . . and we can row."

Unlike the *Mercury*, the *Honoria* was equipped with a full bank of oars. It didn't have the multilevel banks of oars like a warship, but Abraham had built his ships with more oars than the standard merchant ship. His father's philosophy had been that cargo had to move whether the wind cooperated or not, and now Jacob was grateful for that foresight.

Kaeso and Jacob consulted with Durus about the plan. "The crew will be surprised at tossing the cargo," Durus told Jacob, "but they won't grumble. They know what happened to your father. We were all saddened at the news, and they'll want to help."

The crew worked the rest of the day and into the night unloading the shipment of wax. Jacob tucked his tunic into his belt and worked alongside them. He'd gotten rid of the naval uniform before they sailed; he didn't need any more reminders of that episode in his life. Heaving the heavy containers over the side was more difficult than pushing them down a loading plank, and the men were near exhaustion when the job was finally finished.

The next morning, Durus assembled the crew on deck and assigned the men to the oars, saying that they would row in shifts— "around the clock, if the sky remains bright enough to navigate by starlight."

Before they left the deck, Jacob stood up and addressed the crew. "I want to explain why it's so urgent to get to Patmos as quickly as possible." He told them the highlights of what his family had been through, and how the admiral had liberated him and given him the "assignment" of getting Rebecca off Devil's Island.

"I don't know what's happened to my sister in the last year," Jacob said, "but I imagine it's been a living hell. If you'll help me get there to rescue her, I'll double your salary for this trip."

An excited murmur rippled through the crew, and Jacob raised a hand to get their attention. "I also know a thing or two about rowing," he said, "having spent the last eleven months on a warship. So I'll take the oar with you."

Jacob turned and nodded at Durus, who dismissed the crew. Minutes later, when the first shift of rowers took their position at the oars, Jacob was with them.

The muscles across his broad back rippled like strands of rope beneath his burnished skin as Jacob pulled back on the oar rhythmically.

I'm coming, Rebecca. I'm coming.

36

WHEN THE FOUR BARREL-CHESTED STEVEDORES lowered the vehicle to the ground, Peter gingerly stepped out and walked toward the shipping office, trying not to limp. He was still not used to being hauled around in a litter, but it was the only way he could make the daily trip from the family villa on Mount Koressos to the harbor.

Quintus had suggested buying a litter several months earlier, and had come up with the idea of using some of the dockhands to carry Peter around in it. The men were accustomed to lifting heavy loads and appreciated the extra income for the job, and hiring them meant Peter would not have to rely on slave labor for transportation. Still, there was something unmanly about the conveyance, Peter thought, and he was embarrassed that he had to use it. He wondered if his father would approve.

All his life Peter had longed for his father's approval, but until recently he had received precious little of it. He understood that it had been much easier for his father to relate to Jacob. His twin brother was physically strong with a personality to match, just like Abraham. Peter had always been different, and that had been harder for his father to accept. It wasn't that his father didn't love him, Peter knew; it's just that his father hadn't quite known what to do with a crippled son. At an early age Peter had realized he could never measure up to his father's expectations, so he never really tried. Instead, he had sought to fade into the background as much as possible.

And then, not quite a year ago, everything changed. His mother was killed, Jacob and Rebecca were exiled, and his father and Naomi left for Rome. Peter was on his own for the first time in his life, and while it intimidated him, it also appealed to him. He had discovered a friend and mentor in Quintus, and now Peter enjoyed the challenge of working and trying to learn the shipping business.

And even if it had come a bit late, he knew that his father was proud of him. That's what Abraham had written in the letter Peter had received six weeks ago. "I'm very proud of what you've tried to do for Jacob and Rebecca," his father had said, "and I trust that with Quintus's help you will continue to look after the business for me. I'm depending on you, son."

Peter's heart swelled as he thought of his father's words—a father's final words to his son, it had turned out. Last week another letter had arrived. Kaeso had written to Quintus, informing him of Abraham's death and how Naomi's betrayal had caused it. Peter was still struggling with the news, even though his father had implied in his letter that the future was very uncertain, and had also included a codicil to his will.

Now Peter was the head of the family, or what was left of it, and he prayed every day that he would be able to do something to bring Jacob and Rebecca home. Prayer was another addition to his life. Peter's faith had been reestablished through this ordeal, and while he was still physically weak, he was becoming spiritually strong.

A seagull screeched and flew off as Peter awkwardly clumped down the few steps from the street to the pier. When he arrived on the dock, he found Quintus staring out to sea.

"We got a message from the *Valeria* this morning," Quintus said.

"The *Valeria*?" Peter looked up and down the wharf in confusion. The ship had been loaded yesterday and scheduled to sail this morning; it wasn't there now.

"She's gone," Quintus said. "Sailed less than two hours ago."

"Is there some kind of problem?" The cargo ships always carried messenger pigeons, but they were used sparingly; Peter couldn't imagine what had prompted an important communication so soon after the ship had sailed.

Quintus handed Peter the miniature scroll. It was a message from the captain of the *Valeria* saying that they had just sailed past Abraham's personal cutter, which was heading toward the harbor at Ephesus.

"The *Mercury*?" Peter's voice rose in surprise. "Kaeso's letter didn't say anything about coming to Ephesus. In fact, he asked what he should do with Father's ship, and said he would wait for our instructions."

"Exactly."

Peter mulled over the news for a moment, an uneasy sensation making his stomach flutter. The *Valeria*, which had just left port, was carrying Quintus's reply requesting that Kaeso bring the *Mercury* home. Why had the captain sailed without waiting? "Something must have happened to change Kaeso's mind . . ."

"Either that, or someone other than Kaeso is on board." Quintus kept his voice level, but his face had hardened into set lines.

"But who?"

"I can make a guess," Quintus said, "but we'll know soon enough. The *Mercury* should arrive any time now."

⌘

Jacob and the crew of the *Honoria* rowed around the clock for two days, then the wind began to pick up. They kept rowing for as many hours as they could each day, and with the combination of wind power and manpower, they reached record speeds for a ship of that size.

When they finally reached Patmos, only two weeks after leaving Rome, Jacob's mood was swinging between anticipation and anxiety. He knew the seamen were working as fast as possible, but they couldn't get the ship tied to the dock fast enough to suit him.

Yet when he set foot on the dock, he almost couldn't move; it was entirely too familiar. Shaking off the sense of dread that had come over him, Jacob headed straight for the camp commander's office.

When he learned that Brutus wasn't in, Jacob was almost

relieved. He knew the commander would remember him, and he was glad not to have to deal with that scene. Instead, Jacob spoke with Brutus's aide. He presented the edict of liberation, and the aide studied it for several minutes.

"I've never seen anything like this," the aide finally said. His wrinkled brow told Jacob that the aide hadn't wanted to see anything like it, either.

"It's signed and sealed by the new emperor, Marcus Cocceius Nerva, and Admiral Flavius Juvenalis. It releases me from the imperial navy, and releases my sister, Rebecca, and my friend, John, from Devil's Island."

"I suppose it's authentic, but I'll have to get Brutus to take a look at it before anybody leaves here."

"All right," Jacob said, not happy with that answer, but willing to admit it was a logical matter for the camp commander to handle. "In the meantime, can you tell me about my sister—about Rebecca?"

"When did she arrive? That's the easiest way to find the records."

"Last year, October twenty-fourth. So did John, the same day."

The aide searched the office for the records. When he found the right document, he removed the scroll from its cubbyhole and scanned it. "Here it is," he said after a minute. "Rebecca. From Ephesus. Arrived, October twenty-four. Died, November one."

"Died? . . ." Jacob's heart stopped. He'd come all this way— tossed valuable cargo, pushed the crew to the limit—to rescue his sister from this torturous place as quickly as possible, and she had died only a few days after he had been sent to the *Jupiter*. He fought to keep his emotions in check as the aide continued to read.

"From injuries sustained in a rock slide, it says."

"What about John?" He prayed silently, *Please, God, not him too.*

The aide quickly found John's name. "Hmmm. This is very unusual," he said after double-checking the entry. "Maybe I should verify this with the medical officer . . ."

"What does it say?"

"According to this, your friend has been on medical leave since October twenty-nine, last year—"

Jacob turned and bolted out of the office. "Where are you going?" the aide called.

"I know where to find him," Jacob replied over his shoulder.

෨⤳

When the *Mercury* sailed into the harbor, Peter and Quintus were waiting on the dock. Peter agreed with Quintus's guess that Naomi would be on board, and he was not looking forward to seeing his sister.

He stood stoically and watched as the crew skillfully moored the stately ship and then lowered the gangplank. In a moment, Naomi emerged from the deckhouse, followed by a man who appeared to be the captain. Naomi turned back to say something to the man— something that obviously displeased him, judging from the scowl on his face. The unknown captain bowed exaggeratedly and gestured for Naomi to precede him.

Naomi's eyes widened as she walked down the ramp. "Peter, what a wonderful surprise. I didn't expect to find you at the harbor."

His sister looked flummoxed, Peter thought, but she covered it quickly. "I'm surprised to see you as well, Naomi."

She turned to the captain with an imperious look. "Gracchus, I'll settle with you later, after I've had a chance to visit with my brother."

Quintus introduced himself to Gracchus, who also shook hands with Peter. Naomi appeared annoyed while the others observed the usual social amenities.

She took Peter's arm. "Let's go home and talk."

Peter didn't budge. He wasn't about to let her set foot in the villa, not after what Kaeso had written about her. "We'll talk here," Peter said bluntly. "In my office." He hoped Naomi noticed that he had referred to Abraham's office as his now; Peter wanted to keep her unsettled.

With a pointed look at Peter, Quintus said, "If you need me, I'll be next door." He offered to show Gracchus around, and the two of them went into the warehouse.

Peter accompanied Naomi into the large office—he'd called it his, but he actually shared it with Quintus, just as his father had—and motioned for her to sit down. He leaned back against the desk and stared at his sister for a moment. She looked even more beautiful, he thought, but as cold and haughty as ever, and it almost unnerved him. When he thought of what she'd done to destroy their father, however, Peter found his courage.

"What are you doing here, Naomi? Your life is in Rome now."

"I came home to deal with Father's estate—to help you with things," she amended. "I know it's too much for you to handle by yourself."

"It might have been at one time," he conceded, "but not anymore. Everything's fine. I'm running the business—with Quintus, of course—and I don't need any help from you."

Her conciliatory tone turned condescending. "Actually, you do need my help. You see, Father made me the sole heir of his estate."

"Oh, he did?" Peter almost smiled in amusement; he knew better.

"Yes," she said, "and I have a legal document to prove it."

"I don't know what kind of legal document you think you have, but it did not come from Father." Peter leaned forward and enunciated each word carefully. "He disowned you, Naomi, and I have the codicil to his will that proves it."

Naomi briefly looked as if she had been cornered, then she composed herself and stood up. "All right. Father did not appoint me his sole heir—the emperor did. You know Father committed treason, and that made his estate subject to confiscation by Rome. You should thank me that I used my husband's influence with Domitian to do something about keeping Father's fortune in the family."

Peter's confidence wavered. He knew he could prove that his father had disowned Naomi, but she had maneuvered the emperor into awarding her the estate. Where did that leave him? But wait a minute. Her legal document was signed by a dead emperor; perhaps there was hope in that fact.

He straightened and looked Naomi in the eye, willing himself to speak boldly. "There's a new emperor now, one who holds little respect for the decisions of the tyrant who preceded him. Your legal document will probably be worthless if I challenge it. And I will."

"Look, Peter, you and I should stick together. We're family." Naomi's voice was placating, her expression benign. "We'll devise an equitable distribution of the estate."

Peter laughed in scorn. "Equitable? Just what would you consider equitable?"

"Don't worry," Naomi said with a huff. "I'll see that you're well provided for. With Jacob and Rebecca out of the picture, there's only you and me. There will be more than enough for the two of us."

He might have buckled under Naomi's pressure, but when she casually dismissed their exiled brother and sister, Peter was outraged. "Jacob and Rebecca will not remain out of the picture forever," he told her. "Not if there's anything I can do about it."

With a new emperor—an emperor who would be more sympathetic to their case, Peter suddenly realized—perhaps there *was* something he could do. "In fact," he announced, "I'm going to Rome to try to accomplish what Father couldn't."

"You? Go to Rome?" Naomi fell back in her chair, convulsed with laughter. "That's preposterous. You get so seasick, you couldn't sail around the harbor, let alone to Rome."

"I'm finding out I can do things I never thought I could before. And I'd risk puking my guts up all the way to Rome if it meant bringing Jacob and Rebecca home."

Naomi stopped laughing and appraised her brother coolly. "If Jacob is ever released, which I doubt, he'll take over the business and you'll just fade into the shadows again. But we could work together,

Peter. You could run the office here in Ephesus, and I'll run the office in Rome."

"You're wrong. If Jacob returns, he'll be interested in ministry work, not in being tied to the business. And even if he does want to take over the business, he won't try to shut me out. You tried to shut us *all* out, Naomi."

Peter was yelling, but once he'd started, he couldn't stop. He unleashed the fury he'd been holding back. "You might as well have killed Father yourself," he shouted. "You didn't do anything to help him—you encouraged his execution!"

Naomi rose, trembling with anger. "I did what I had to do to protect myself, and to protect the family fortune. And now I'll do whatever I have to do to get my inheritance. I'm the oldest child, and I have a right to this business!"

"You forfeited that right," Peter said, calmer now. For a minute he silently watched Naomi pace the floor as she tried to gain control of herself.

"You don't know what it's like," she said suddenly. "Being told you can't do something because you're a woman. I could run this business better than you and Jacob put together. But Father would never consider that, simply because I'm a woman."

Peter knew it was true, both that Naomi was capable of running the business and that his father would never have allowed her to do it, even if Naomi had not turned against him. He actually felt a twinge of sympathy for his sister then, but it didn't last. She'd gone too far; she had destroyed any trace of the brotherly love he had once felt for her.

"I know what it's like to want to be something you're not," he said softly. "To want to be well when you're sick all the time. To want to be strong and courageous when you're always afraid. But I'm learning to be content with what I have and with what I am. That's a lesson I don't think you'll ever learn, Naomi."

He limped toward the door. "I want you to leave now," he said. "You're not welcome here."

Naomi stared at him and started to speak, then she backed away and walked out of the office. Peter's voice was clear and strong as he called after her, "And find another way to get back to Rome. You're not taking the *Mercury.*"

When she left, Peter sat down at the desk and sighed deeply. He was shaken from the unexpected encounter with his sister, but gratified that he had stood up to her. He didn't know what Naomi would do now, but Peter vowed that if she tried to claim their father's estate, he would battle her with everything in him.

37

JACOB RAN OUT OF THE COMMANDER'S OFFICE and through the camp. When he reached the southern slope, he started scrambling up the mountain as fast as he could. He had to stop a couple of times to wipe tears from his eyes, so he could see his way. His thoughts were a dark jumble, his heart burned in his chest, and he could barely get his breath—but it was more from anger than exertion.

As he climbed, Jacob thought about everything and everyone he had lost. His mother. His father. And now his sister.

"I've lost too much," he shouted up the mountain. "Do You hear me, God? It's too much!"

Near the top of the mountain, Jacob looked up and saw a patch of brilliant color moving in the area of the cave. It was a woman. A woman in a bright blue tunic. He suddenly remembered Naomi wearing a tunic that same color one day. He'd called it peacock blue because she had been strutting around, proudly showing off the new dress.

Naomi? Here? It couldn't be . . . could it?

He started running, then had to catch himself to keep from falling down the mountain.

⚭

"Did you hear that?" Rebecca asked.

John had just joined her outside the cave to enjoy the sunshine. "Hear what?" he said.

"I thought I heard someone shouting."

Rebecca hadn't slept well from the anticipation of being alone on the mountain with John. Marcellus would be gone in a day or two, and just knowing he would not be there to help anymore had left her jittery and highly alert to strange or unusual sounds.

Nervous, she scanned the hillside from right to left and back again, and finally saw a head pop over the horizon.

Then everything happened at once.

"I knew it! I knew it!" John shouted. "Oh, heaven be praised."

John recognized Jacob first. But then he'd been expecting someone to arrive, or something to happen—some avenue of escape; Rebecca hadn't. And she couldn't believe her brother was really there until he wrapped his arms around her. Then she burst into tears.

"Rebecca!" Jacob didn't just hug her. He clung to her and wept.

"I thought I'd never see you again," she said brokenly.

It was a long time before either one of them could speak again. "When I first saw you," Jacob finally said, "I thought you were Naomi."

"Why on earth would you think that?"

"They told me you were dead—it's in the camp records. That's why I was so shocked to see you." He tugged on the skirt of the blue tunic she was wearing. "And isn't this Naomi's?"

"Oh . . . yes."

"But how did you get it?"

"The church in Ephesus sent supplies and clothing for the prisoners; this tunic was one of the items. Naomi must have grown tired of it—after all, she had probably worn it two or three times." Rebecca laughed then, her joy spilling over with her tears. The brother she thought had been lost to her forever had returned.

Laughing and crying at the same time, Jacob turned to the Apostle and lifted him off the ground in a hug.

"You have arms like a vise," John said when Jacob finally released him. "I think you squeezed the life out of me. Of course, that wouldn't take much!" With John's raspy laugh echoing off the rocks, the three of them hugged each other again.

"Oh, Jacob. I have so much to tell you." Rebecca realized that her brother did not even know she'd had a baby. The overwhelming joy and relief she had felt at Jacob's unexpected arrival began to ebb, and her previous apprehension resurfaced. How would Jacob react to the news? "But first," she said quickly, "you have to tell us how you got here—why you came back."

"He came back to rescue us, I can tell you that," John said emphatically.

Jacob briefly recounted the amazing story of the admiral and the edict of liberation. "I guess that was the whole purpose of my being transferred to the *Jupiter*," he concluded. "So I would eventually encounter someone who could help end this nightmare."

John nodded as Jacob talked about discovering God's purpose. "I had the most astounding vision," he said, "sitting right there in the cave. It was my purpose for being here. Jesus showed me the things that are going to happen from now until He returns, then He told me to write it all down and take it to the churches."

John became animated, and he started to launch into an explanation of the revelation. Then he suddenly stopped. "Why am I rambling . . . I can tell you all about it later." Making a broad sweep with his arm, John gestured to the rocky hillside. "If the good Lord let me survive this, He'll let me live long enough to talk about it."

Jacob laughed again, then said, "I have a ship waiting in the harbor. If we hurry, we can sail before sunset. The more distance we put between us and Devil's Island by nightfall, the better . . ."

His voice trailed off as Marcellus came out of the cave holding the baby. Jacob's mouth fell open, and he looked from Marcellus to Rebecca and back. It was a moment before he could speak. "Yours?" he asked her.

"Yes, he's two months—"

"Did *he* do this to you?" Jacob's voice had an ominous edge as he took a step toward the medical officer.

"No!" Rebecca hurried to move between them. "Not Marcellus."

"Then who?" Jacob whirled to face Rebecca, his dark eyes unnerving in their intensity. "Who's the father?"

"Can't we talk about this later?" Rebecca thought her brother looked mad enough to kill, and it frightened her. If Jacob went after Damian . . . no! She wouldn't let him. If anything happened to Jacob now, she couldn't stand it; Rebecca had just gotten her brother back, and she wasn't losing him again.

"Later?" Jacob grabbed Rebecca and placed a huge hand on each of her arms, almost lifting her off the ground. His grip was firm, and his voice demanding. "You tell me who did this to you, and you tell me now!"

Rebecca began to shake. Jacob had never spoken a harsh word to her before. He had teased and tormented her like a typical older brother, but he had never been angry with her.

"Let her go!" John shouted. "Don't punish Rebecca just because you can't get your hands on the man who raped her."

At the word *raped*, Jacob lowered his hands and quickly stepped away. He closed his eyes and dropped his head, an anguished look wrenching his face.

Marcellus comforted the baby, who had started to cry.

Then Jacob looked up at Rebecca and repeated his question in a gentler voice. "Are you going to tell me who did this to you?"

"Not until you promise me that you won't go off and do something crazy, something that will only get you hurt."

"I'm not promising anything."

"Then I'm not telling." Rebecca turned and walked back to the cave.

When she went inside and sat down, she was still trembling. Jacob had made her think about things she had buried deep inside. Since Victor had been born, she almost never thought about the rape;

she was able to look at her son and see only his innocence, not the evil nature of his father. But now the memories of that horrible night flashed before her eyes, and Rebecca felt nauseated. Her shame, her hatred for Damian, and her desire to see him punished for the unspeakable thing he had done were far outweighed by her fear that Damian would destroy her brother or her son if Jacob tried to retaliate.

Marcellus followed Rebecca into the cave and placed the baby in the crib he'd pieced together from scraps. He sat silently beside her as they listened to John and Jacob shouting outside.

When she heard Jacob utter a piercing, primal scream, Rebecca knew that John had either told him, or that Jacob had guessed that it was Damian who had fathered her child.

"I'll kill him!" Jacob roared. "If it's the last thing I do, I'll find him and kill him."

"No, you won't!" John shouted back.

The two of them argued, with Jacob declaring that under the law of Moses he had the right to hunt Damian down and take justice into his own hands. "I'm the avenger of blood!" he yelled. "It's my duty."

John countered that vengeance belonged to the Lord, and *He* would mete out justice. "If you take up the sword, you'll die by the sword. That's what Jesus told us."

Rebecca tried not to listen, tried not to think. But she couldn't help thinking about it, and as she did, a new emotion rose and choked out her fear. Suddenly she was angry—angrier than she had ever been in her life—and she couldn't control it.

Fury propelled her to her feet, and she stormed outside to confront Jacob. "You're dead-set on seeking revenge," she yelled at him, "but did it ever occur to you that this wouldn't have happened to me at all if you'd been here?"

Rebecca raised both hands to Jacob's chest and shoved him as hard as she could. Caught off guard, he stumbled backward.

"You weren't here when I needed you. And why weren't you here

to protect me? Because you just had to get back at Damian. You're
the one who threw the rock and got yourself shipped out of here.
You're the one who left me all alone."

"Rebecca—"

"I'm not finished." She shoved him again, and when Jacob
grabbed her arms to stop her, she shook his hands off. Rebecca could
tell from his expression that she had struck a nerve, but she had not
finished giving vent to her anger.

"It's bad enough this baby will have to grow up without a
father," she said, "but I won't let him grow up without the rest of his
family, especially you. Do you hear me, Jacob? I've been through one
year of hell on earth without you here, and you're not going to leave
me to raise a child by myself. You're going to be there for me this
time, aren't you?"

Jacob looked stricken. He clamped and unclamped his jaw. "I'm
sorry I wasn't here for you," he said finally. "But I'm here now."

Rebecca used the back of her hand to wipe away a tear of frustration. She had probably wasted her breath; she knew Jacob might
still go after Damian if he had the opportunity. But at least she had
let her brother know how she felt.

"Yes, you're here now," John said. "And we're grateful."

Marcellus had reappeared during Rebecca's outburst, and he
spoke now. "I'll go on back to the camp, but I'll come to the dock
and see you off when you sail. You won't be needing me to take
Victor after all . . ." He briefly looked back at the cave and then at
Rebecca. "He's asleep in the crib."

"Come with us," John urged. "You don't have to wait for the
supply ship now."

Jacob flashed a startled look at the Apostle, and Marcellus protested
awkwardly. "No, that's all right. The supply ship will be here tomorrow or the next day."

"Nonsense. You'll come with us." John explained to Jacob that the
medical officer was now a believer. "His army stint is up, and Marcellus

was planning to take the baby to Peter in Ephesus and then deliver my letter to the churches."

"If it hadn't been for Marcellus," Rebecca said, "we would have died here. He's been like a father to me—" She stopped suddenly, a lump rising in her throat. "Father . . . Jacob, have you seen him? Do you have any news?"

Jacob's eyes grew dark with an unspoken pain, and Rebecca knew: her father was dead. One more grief to absorb. One more loss to endure.

"I'll tell you everything as soon as we sail," Jacob said. "It's getting late, and we should leave." He turned to Marcellus. "Come with us," he said. "You're part of the family now."

Marcellus nodded. "Thank you," he said. "I'd like that. I'm already packed and ready to go."

John linked one arm through Rebecca's and the other through Jacob's, then said, "Let's go home."

Home, Rebecca thought. She was going home, after all.

They went inside the cave and quickly retrieved the remaining copy of John's letter and the stool. John loved the rickety old folding chair and thought it would make a great souvenir.

Marcellus tore an old tunic and fashioned it into a sling that would keep Victor cradled against Rebecca's chest as they traveled down the mountain.

As they started to walk out of the cave, Jacob stopped and took a final look around.

"Those two rats—" he said to John. "The ones you named Damian and Domitian. Did you ever manage to kill them?"

"No," John said. A weary but triumphant smile split the old Apostle's craggy face. "But by the power of God, we overcame them. And in the end, that's the only thing that matters."

NOW AVAILABLE
Book Two in The Apocalypse Diaries

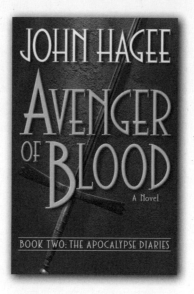

AVENGER OF BLOOD

The crowning of a new emperor in Rome means reprieve for John the Apostle and his young friends, Jacob and Rebecca. But when they return to Ephesus from their exile on Devil's Island, Jacob and Rebecca realize that the life they left behind has been shattered.

Both of their parents are dead. Their brother, Peter, has kept the shipping empire intact, but their older sister, Naomi, not only betrayed their father, she is now trying to seize control of his entire estate.

While Rebecca's fiancé, crushed by her return home with an illegitimate child, is keeping his distance, she attracts the attention of a young lawyer, an unbeliever drawn deeper into the family circle when Naomi's greed takes a vicious turn. Eventually Rebecca must choose between reconciliation with her childhood sweetheart, marriage outside the faith, or life of unmarried service to the church.

Jacob, consumed with bitterness because of the persecution of his family, is determined to bring an end to their suffering once and for all—by killing the man who has tormented them. Jacob's quest for revenge takes him far from Ephesus—and far from the purpose to which he once believed God had called him.

Avenger of Blood is the compelling story of a first-century Christian family whose lives have been torn apart by greed, betrayal, and revenge. Their triumphant story is a testament to the redeeming power of faith and love.

$19.99 • Hardcover, 352 pages • 0-7852-6789-1

ABOUT THE AUTHOR

DR. JOHN HAGEE, author of the bestsellers *The Battle for Jerusalem, From Daniel to Doomsday, Beginning of the End, His Glory Revealed,* and *Final Dawn Over Jerusalem,* is the founder and pastor of the 17,000-member Cornerstone Church in San Antonio, Texas. He is also the president of Global Evangelism Television, which broadcasts his daily and weekly television and radio programs throughout the U.S. and around the world. He and his wife, Diana, have five children and one grandchild.